ATTACK!

The enormous black shapes of the tanks were everywhere and right behind them were hordes of Germans, pouring in on the shell-dazed Australians. As Dick lurched to his feet, still coated in sand from the pit, a strange voice cried and a boot and the butt of a rifle came down past him. He brought his own rifle up quickly and the bayonet found flesh and creaked on bone. The German croaked and clawed at his groin. Dick pulled the trigger and his rifle sprang free. He fired into another shape on the edge of the pit. It toppled on him, bearing him down. It was already a corpse, gushing blood from the throat, but he fought, terror-stricken, to get free of it as though it were still alive, kicking and pushing it aside. He reached his feet again firing without aiming at each shape he saw.

Eric Lambert

The Twenty Thousand Thieves

CORGI BOOKS
A DIVISION OF TRANSWORLD PUBLISHERS LTD

THE TWENTY THOUSAND THIEVES

A CORGI BOOK 0 552 10191 5

Originally published in Great Britain
by Frederick Muller, Ltd.

PRINTING HISTORY

Frederick Muller edition published 1952
Corgi edition (abridged) published 1955
Corgi edition (abridged) reprinted 1955
Corgi edition (abridged) reprinted 1956
Corgi edition (abridged) reprinted 1956
Corgi edition (abridged) reprinted 1957
Corgi edition (abridged) reprinted 1958
Corgi edition (abridged) reprinted 1959
Corgi edition (abridged) reprinted 1960
Corgi edition (complete and unabridged) published 1963
Corgi edition (complete and unabridged) reprinted 1963
Corgi edition (complete and unabridged) reissued 1969
Corgi edition reprinted 1969
Corgi edition reissued 1976

This book is set in Plantin 9 pt.

Corgi Books are published by Transworld Publishers Ltd.,
Century House, 61–63 Uxbridge Rd., Ealing, London, W5 5SA

Made and printed in Great Britain by
Richard Clay (The Chaucer Press), Ltd., Bungay, Suffolk

What do they know of the world? Does living mean
Quite simply, Mother, to die very young?
Good for this, good for that. My good friends I am leaving—
Twenty years old—good for the armed forces.

LOUIS ARAGON

This is a novel about Australian soldiers in the second world war. There was no such battalion as the Second X; I have tried to make its members typical of many Australian infantrymen. Therefore the main characters depicted herein are composites of many men. To say that they have no relation to living persons nevertheless would be true—for the men on whom I chose to base them are dead.

BOOK ONE

THE PLAIN

1

ISMAILIA on the Suez Canal, January, nineteen hundred and forty-one. On one of the placid lakes lay an Australian troopship and above in the night sky was the hum of German bombers. The night was starless and the troopship was merely a lump in an expanse of black water. The Bofors guns opened up, their harsh cough hacking at the round core of the hum. The sky became suddenly alive with wicked little flashes. The hum kept steadily on.

On the ship, the troops lay face downwards to the decks, life-jackets around their necks, steel helmets on their heads. In a tiny cabin on C Deck four men lay, talking among themselves in low tones. The nature of their conversation was much the same throughout the ship, wherever soldiers lay in obedience to orders. They were saying, mostly with satisfaction, that this was their first taste of danger; they were arguing, humorously or excitedly, whether the bombers were after the ship or the town. The cabin where the four privates lay had only twelve months previously been a tourist class cabin holding two passengers; a succession of couples who swayed to the roll, were seasick, and often complained of the niggardly space. Now two temporary bunks had been added and these four men were considered fortunate—fortunate, that is, in relation to men some decks below them who lived and slept on tiers of dirty, foul canvas bunks, where fresh air never penetrated.

Of these four privileged soldiers one who lay directly beneath the porthole against the side of the ship talked less than the others. He alone did not sound excited, yet he was listening and remembering with quickened senses. He felt his mind absorbing the whole situation; the dark, the tense air of strangeness, the behaviour of his companions in new circumstances, the stillness of the ship, the savage bursts of gun-fire and the all-pervading hum of the bombers.

He rose to his feet and threw open the porthole. He was greeted with a wave of cool air coming out of the blackness and the sound of the bombers grown suddenly loud. There was a pause in the conversation but no comment at this violation of standing orders. Someone asked: "See anything, Dick?"

"Nothing. It's pitch dark." Then he added, "He's coming nearer."

The voice that answered the question was high-pitched, the voice of a very young man, and now it held an undertone of excitement. After this there came to their ears what was at first a vague rending of the air, as though someone were tearing a

11

piece of cloth. It grew louder until its nature was changed and it became the sharpest, loudest, most ominous sound that had ever smitten their ears. It ended abruptly in a deep, trembling concussion. Spray flew past the open porthole and the troopship shook uneasily from prow to stern.

"Missed!" cried the man at the porthole, and throughout the ship rose many sounds.

The hum of the bomber grew fainter and fainter, passed into nothingness. Soon after, the ship's siren sounded the all clear. The porthole was closed, the light turned on again, lifebelts taken off and stowed away. The cabin door was flung open to reveal Lucas, their platoon sergeant.

"Everyone all right here?" he asked.

His voice was uncouth and derisive. He was tall and black-haired. His eyes were amused, his nose and chin thrust forward wilfully. He came into the cabin and surveyed its occupants.

"He let a bomb go," he told them. "Just missed the ship."

"It was close," broke in the young man. "I felt the spray."

One of his companions threw back his head in mock despair. Lucas turned casually to the youngster.

"Did you open the porthole, Brett?"

Brett looked at the dark man vindictively. Inside him he felt the sharp antagonism that had passed between him and Lucas from the first; his resentment of Lucas's mockery and wit and fear of his personality.

"Yes, I did!"

"Report to the mess at seven thirty in the morning. Three days as a mess orderly might cure your habit of ignoring orders. Good night, fellers."

* * *

Dick Brett only served one meal as a mess orderly, however. Immediately after breakfast in the morning, the troops were lined up on deck and told to be ready to disembark within two hours. Lieutenant Crane, with Sergeant Lucas at his elbow, was speaking to Six Platoon. His manner was a mixture of familiarity, aggressiveness and condescension. To Dick Brett, Crane's unspoken attitude seemed to say: "I am Kenneth Crane, of the Cranes of Scobie, one of Australia's greatest and richest families. I am your superior in every conceivable way. There is a war on, however, and, unfamiliar as I am with you, I find it necessary to associate with you closely. I intend to be as pleasant about it as possible." Sometimes Crane found himself too blatantly talking down; then he adjusted himself by suddenly uttering soldier profanities, which sounded oddly vile on his lips. But he was manly and even likeable, most of the time, to the imaginative Dick Brett. He was large, fair and moved gracefully. He was a noted athlete. His features were marked by big yellow eyebrows, hard blue eyes and a mouth that formed words incisively and was apt to clamp shut.

"We're disembarking sometime today, chaps. Those planes dropped mines along the canal last night, which means all ships are immobilised for the time being. Every man will be ready to move within two hours. I want your quarters to be left clean. N.C.O.s will check. Dismiss the platoon, Sergeant."

Dick Brett lingered by the rail of the ship looking towards the distant shore. There was little to see but a mass of waving palms, out of which thrust a minaret and the flat roofs of houses. A hand across his back pushed him along the rail.

"Come on, Dick. Move along," said Sergeant Lucas.

"Keep your hands to yourself, Lucas!"

Sergeant Lucas laughed.

*   *   *

The troops sat around, backs resting against their piled gear, until late in the afternoon. They talked of where they were probably going and of how they would be taken there. They smoked, showed each other photos, or exchanged abuse uproariously. At length their officers appeared, brought them to their feet, told them to pick up their gear and be ready to move off. They filed up, out of the bowels of the ship, and down into barges at its side. The barges spilled them on to a jetty from which they moved over on to a road, to line along its edge. Patiently, they subsided once again beside their gear and waited for the next move. Many months had them accustomed to this kind of thing.

They still wore the heavy service uniforms issued in Australia. The afternoon was hot, dusty and dry. They undid the fronts of their tunics and spread them open. A few ragged Arabs appeared, to watch them from a distance, making occasional observations in quick-fire chatter. An Egyptian woman passed on the opposite side of the road, dressed entirely in black, moving lithely and gracefully. Above her yashmak, dark, liquid eyes surveyed the troops as they volubly admired her. Then she turned her head away and hurried on.

"She'll do me!"

"What's the Arabic for love, Mac?" someone called.

"That's not the word you want," Lucas told him. "Yeah," he added softly, looking after the woman, "she wasn't bad. I wonder if they're all like that?"

He continued to stare until she disappeared, his lips curved lustfully, eyes shining. His features looked cruel and predatory without their habitual mockery.

Tommy Collins ejected spit from his white little face.

"If I caught her up a dark lane I'd give her something to remember."

He put the stump of a cigarette back into his mouth and narrowed his eyes.

Tall, grizzled Andy Cain, with the angry mouth and the tired eyes, turned to regard Tommy.

"You'll end up in a dark lane with a knife in you if you go mucking round with their women, young feller."

Tommy joined his thumb and forefinger like a claw around the stump of his cigarette and dragged it from his thin lips.

"Ah, I'm not frightened of any Wog," he boasted.

Dick Brett watched him with a mixture of fascination and disgust. His mind went back to the day he had joined the army. He remembered a thin, pale, undersized youth, yellow-eyed from various debauches, who spoke in a high rattle of profanity, biting his epithets off viciously, eternally mouthing a sodden stump of cigarette. He had been next to Dick in the line at the recruiting depot. Filling in a form or replying to a question, his eyes were hard, wary and mobile as a ferret's. He had confided to Dick that he had just completed a month's gaol and celebrated his release the previous night at a brothel in Darlinghurst with a fat, fifty-year-old prostitute and several bottles of "plonk." With fierce vanity he had described the night on the wine-sodden sheets, the prostitute's drink-inflamed desires and his own pitiless prowess. When later, he discovered that he had not found a kindred soul in Dick he had become venomous and handy with unspeakable names. They had come to blows once already.

Dick looked up to meet the sardonic scrutiny of Lucas:

"We should have put young Dick here on to her. What do you reckon, Dick?"

"She's a human being, like us," said Dick. "And probably someone's wife as well."

Tommy Collins giggled.

"Perhaps," put in Andy Cain, "some mug's thinking the same things about a few of our wives at home."

"Worried, Andy?" asked Lucas softly.

"Some day," said Andy placidly, "I might have to job you."

Dick envied Andy's way of dealing with Lucas.

*　　　*　　　*

By dusk the last man was off the ship. In a long line they passed through the darkened streets of Ismailia with few to witness their passing.

They came to where the streets ran off into sand, to a railway line where a train awaited them. Their officers herded them aboard with sharp urgings. The carriages were long, grubby, strange-smelling, with hard wooden seats and dim blue lights in the ceilings that showed their interiors in a ghastly half-dark. Six Platoon lay tired and uneasy, wedged among their kit-bags,

14

packs, haversacks, webbing, bayonets and rifles. By the time the train moved off most of them had fallen into fitful sleep. In the strange blue darkness they appeared as heaps of limbs and lolling heads. The train rattled on through the heavy Egyptian night.

The Second X Infantry Battalion, of the Second Australian Imperial Force, had arrived in the Middle East.

2

NORTH and south ran the coastal plain of Palestine. Between the plain and the sea stood a line of sandhills, and the mountains of the Judean wilderness looked over the plain from the east. Parallel with the coast wound a thin white road and along this road, between the Arab city of Gaza and the Jewish city of Tel Aviv, workmen had built the camps of the Second Australian Imperial Force. The camps ran up shallow hills and along the valleys between the hills. Roads went in and out of a maze of tents which huddled about the administrative buildings of dark-stained timber. Orange groves nestled alongside the camps, hemmed in by candle pines which stood up like dark blades dividing the landscape. There were villages behind these groves: white square stone of the Jewish, hot drab mud of the Arab. And sunk among the grasses and the ruined groves along the coast were to be found the fractured pillars and cornices of Palestine's ancient masters; lonely places where sheep wandered and the sea wind whispered. The narrow white road became crammed with trucks and motor cycles pouring both ways endlessly. On the edges of the road platoons, companies, battalions of Australians in the famous slouch hat moved up and down on route marches or on their way to manœuvres farther inland.

Into such a scene the Second X Battalion was dropped in the early hours of a starless morning. It awoke at daylight in its crowded tents and began to inspect its surroundings.

*   *   *

The fifth day following the battalion's arrival was a Sunday. After church parade they were told by their officers that the rest of the day was their own. The officers added, however, that it was to be spent within the limits of the camp and that no leave would be given to visit the cities or neighbouring camps. They might as well have never spoken. After five days of being herded, heckled, lectured and marched; of guarding their tents from a few miserable Arabs; of various other experiences common to the armed forces—all grouped under the heading of "bastardry"—few of them were in the mood to spend these hours of freedom in the camp. By early afternoon the camp was almost deserted.

Dick Brett and Andy Cain walked together towards the main road where an endless stream of vehicles passed to and fro.

"Where are you making for, Dick?"

"I thought I'd have a look at Tel Aviv if it wasn't too far."

"About twenty miles, one of the Six Divvy blokes was telling me. Mind if I come with you?"

The youth was grateful for company on his adventure. The older man fell into step beside him, and a few hundred yards brought them to the main road. They walked down a little way to get clear of the small crowd of soldiers gesticulating to passing trucks at the road junction. A screech of brakes behind them made them jump for the safety of the ditch. An Australian head came out of the window of a truck, grinning at them.

"Tel Aviv?" asked Andy.

"I would be if I was going in the other direction, sport!"

There was a laugh from the truck and it moved on. They now knew in which direction Tel Aviv lay, at any rate. A few minutes later they were sitting in the back of a utility truck making forty miles to the hour. There was a soldier of the Sixth Division in the back of the "ute," who greeted them and took it upon himself to introduce them to Palestine and the fighting in Libya. Inclined to be condescending at first, he soon became friendly, then finally garrulous.

The road was muddy and crowded dangerously, the ute sped in and out between slower trucks and swept past Arabs in mule-drawn wagons or mounted on a donkey with the wife trudging behind.

"Be on that," their companion told them. "Dad rides, Mum walks behind. The donkey's worth more than the woman! If you want to make the old Wog wild, call him 'Yehudi bunduq' —'Jew bastard.' If you want to see the boys get wild, yell: 'Inter bint'—'You're a girl.' They'll lift up their clothes to prove you're wrong. Christ, you oughter smell their villages! The Jews are the same as Jews everywhere. Take you down right, left and centre!"

Neither of the newcomers appeared impressed with his remarks. Dick asked him then about the fighting in Libya, and they listened to him without comment as he described it; Andy in stolid interest, Dick excitedly, with shining eyes. As their new acquaintance proceeded with his narrative, Dick built up wild and terrible visions of battle.

They had done it on "next to nothing." He saw the one-eyed general sitting in Cairo poring over a map showing the long line of fortified towns that stretched from Mersa Matruh to Benghazi, with a large, well-fed garrison of Italians in each of them.

16

He had against it a division of Australians, a handful of tanks, decided what he might do, and one night crept up on Sidi Barrani. One after another, the coastal towns of Mussolini's brand-new empire fell to the handful of men in the big hats with their long bayonets and their lumbering tanks, cheerfully overwhelming the powerfully-armed enemy who outnumbered them fantastically. It was a savage, exultant vision.

"They've got the equipment, these Ities, but they're dingoes," said the man from the Sixth. "They'll throw everything at you from a distance—their arty's real good—but as soon as it comes to the hand-to-hand stuff up go the hands and out they come yelling for mercy."

The boy saw them, streaming out of their fortifications, herded in lines of thousands by solitary riflemen, determinedly bound for the haven of a prisoner-of-war cage while the black clouds of battle enveloped the desert about them. He was fiercely aware of being an Australian soldier and for the first time believed whole-heartedly in the legends of the terrible, laughing men in the slouch hats.

Andy's visions, if they could be described as such, were more practical and he was less inclined to accept the Sixth Division man's version of the campaign.

"Don't give me that stuff about a whole nation of cowards. What are they fighting for? That's what you've got to ask yourself."

"Musso!" chuckled their informant. "Il Doo-chee! He's their little tin god."

"Not for all of them, he isn't. He had to kill thousands of them to get where he is. I don't reckon they're dingoes—they just didn't want to fight for Musso and his bloody empire. If they were defending their own homes you might find them just as good as any of our own blokes. Perhaps we've got a few dingoes."

"The Aussie's the world's best soldier, that's what they all reckon." The veteran was resentful now.

"My bloody oath!" cried Dick.

"Would you want to fight for a bastard like Mussolini?" Andy asked him.

The truck slowed down at the entrance to a camp. The man from the Sixth jumped down and thanked the driver. To Andy he cried:

"Keep your head down, sport. Your turn'll come. Aussie for me. I've done me bit."

As the soldier raised an arm and waved, Dick noticed that his right hand was red and raw with newly-healed skin and that three fingers were missing.

Andy Cain fell into one of his frequent spells of contemplation and Dick was observing the country they passed through.

His romantic nature had always been obscurely stirred by what are called "Eastern scenes." Now he drank in what he saw and the actuality thrilled his heart. Sometimes they passed bare green stretches of low hills, deserted except for a few dreary sheep watched over by an Arab boy. Sometimes the red soil had been scratched up by a rickety wooden plough drawn behind a camel. Then they would speed through an Arab village, scattering donkeys, fowls, women and children who ran for the safety of the hot, malodorous walls of grey mud. The villages seemed filthy diseased things, beaten out of mud into rambling walls, archways and rough squares of dwellings. At the outskirts of the villages they sometimes passed the house of the effendi, the Arab landowner; a white, solid, immaculate place with an iron gate, high walls and colourful facings of mosaic. Groves of olives skirted the road, their branches twisting over the low stone walls.

The young man never forgot his first shock at the contrast between Arab town and Jewish.

Along the approaches to the Jewish village there were avenues of Australian gums; the buildings were neat white stone or brick. Brown-skinned merry children waved to them as they flew past. It was whiteness amid greenery. The Arab village was filth made out of filth.

Tel Aviv, as they came to its outskirts, seemed to be the Jewish village on a large scale; tree-lined streets, new white buildings. It was somewhat continental, but there was an over-crowded look about it too. The footpaths were crammed with people, the streets swarmed with vehicles. The uniforms of British and Australian soldiers were everywhere. The ute came to a standstill in a parking bay that overlooked the sea-front and the driver came round to speak to them:

"We'll be returning at two in the morning if you want a lift back with us, sport. Only be on time, we won't wait for you."

They thanked him and left to explore the city. They had not gone far when they met Sergeant Lucas. His smile was broad as he saw them, but not welcoming. It rather indicated that Lucas foresaw amusement.

"So! Privates Cain and Brett, I was wondering when I'd see you. The rest of Six Platoon seem to be here."

"Hallo, Frank," Andy greeted him. "Come to see the sights?"

"What sights?" asked the sergeant with overdone curiosity.

"We don't know. We've only just arrived."

Lucas waved his arm. "You can see the lot from where you stand," he informed them. "Blocks of flats, cafés, souvenir shops with fat Yids waiting to pounce on you. The brothels are down at Jaffa. Keep your eye on young Dick here or he'll be down there."

"How did you happen to know where the brothels are?" the boy asked him angrily.

18

Lucas ignored his retort. He went on his way, throwing over his shoulder:

"Be back by reveille, won't you, boys."

"Why do you always let him get you in?" Andy asked Dick.

Dick didn't answer. "I wonder if he'll put us in for being A.W.L.," he said at length.

"Not a chance! He's A.W.L. himself. Wake up, son. Come and have a drink somewhere."

Still smarting from his clash with Lucas, Dick accompanied him. They found a café on the sea-front where a Jewish waiter took their order for a bottle of the local beer. They sat and surveyed the long shore-line in front of them. The sea was calm, the air clear. Away to their left in the distance they could see the ancient port of Jaffa huddled untidily over the placid bay. Almost opposite them on the sand the rusted hulk of a small steamer heeled over high and dry. The waiter informed them that it had been there for some years now. It had arrived off Jaffa, packed with refugees from Europe, and had been refused permission to unload its passengers by the British authorities. The ship's master had promptly run it aground and men, women and children had struggled ashore with their bundles through the surf.

While they sat there the café filled up with soldiers in various stages of intoxication. Some of them were old hands, getting quietly drunk; others like Andy and Dick were enjoying their first visit. Some of their comrades from Six Platoon wandered in and out. Tommy Collins staggered in, drunk and foul tongued. " 'Ullo, 'ullo!" He flopped down at their table and leered happily. "Hey, Yehudi! Beer!" His face was as white as a sheet, his eyes looked clogged and debauched. "This joint'll do me. Been down Jaffa yet? Don't miss it . . . bottle of Alicante and a passionate young bitch—one thousand mils. Made her strip I did . . . started screaming when I ashked for the trimmings . . . up comes Madam . . . know what I do?" He dropped his head back and gave a shrill hoot of laughter. "I drag Madam on to the bed, too, and the young slut gets jealous, grabs me and starts yabbering . . . then Madam rounds on her. What a turn! What a turn! . . . Look!" He dragged out a gaudy bit of silk, roughly embroidered. "Fifty mils . . . Beat the Jew boy down. Send it to Mum . . . Good ole Mum. . . . She'll do me, this town." He swept his arm across the table, knocked his beer over and gained his feet. "Ah, what's the use of tellin' youse two coots? Where's me mate Dooley? Hey, Dooley!" He lurched out into the darkening afternoon.

"Hope that's the last of him," muttered Dick.

The older man ran a hand through his grizzled ginger hair and spoke in his slow, cynical way, almost as if he were pondering aloud:

"I know a part of Sydney where they breed Tommy Collinses. It might sound hackneyed, but it happens to be true sometimes about a man knowing no better."

Other men from Six Platoon came in and greeted them, and Tommy was forgotten. As if to even the balance it wasn't long before Andy's pet aversion came into the café. Percy Gribble was a neat, pompous little man with a toothbrush moustache. He was a former bank clerk. His khaki shorts and shirt were neatly ironed, his hat turned up as Routine Orders had directed. He had a camera case slung round his neck.

"Here's the bloody stripe-hound," muttered Andy. "Fancy him having the guts to go ack-willy."

"The little crawler might have got a pass," said Dick.

Percy hailed them with a friendliness not borne out by previous relations and also with an air of relief:

"Ah—another couple of ack-willies. How are you, boys?"

"Good-oh," they told him.

He seated himself and surveyed them urbanely.

"I've been photographing the town. Met a teller in the Ottoman Bank who used to work in the head office of my bank in London."

His use of the possessive "my" made Dick smile to himself. Andy scowled at him.

"What makes you think we haven't got a pass?" he asked.

A mild look of alarm passed over Gribble's face at the possibility of his being a lone wrong-doer.

"If I couldn't get one," he smirked, "I don't think you could. Anyway," he added confidingly, "it's O.K. Frank Lucas is in town too. I was staying in camp, but when I saw Frank sneaking out I thought if it's all right for him, it's all right for me. So in I came."

He rattled on, quite unconscious of the effect this last bit of information had on the other two.

"As a matter of fact," he told them, "Frank asked me to have a drink with him and we went into a high-class place, the San Remo, but they told us that it was only for sergeants and above. Well, I wasn't going to have any bloody Yid barring an Australian from getting a drink, so I just sat down and ordered a gin." He coloured indignantly at the recollection. "The bugger refused to serve me. Just because I was a private! I tell you this distinction's a bad thing—it'll ruin the army. Frank Lucas is a nice feller but, after all, he was nothing in civilian life. There's a delicate situation here in Palestine and we can't afford to have a soldier's prestige lowered in front of these bloody Wogs and Jews."

It had grown dark and a heavy blackout curtain covered the doorway. The café was crowded, noisy and lit brightly. Several Jewish girls had entered and were disposed among the soldiers at the tables. Dick, Andy and Percy Gribble were joined by more members of Six Platoon, until there was a small crowd around the table. The talk was uproarious as they compared experiences of the afternoon.

"The whole bloody population's out to take the soldiers down, I tell ya! When the war ends they'll proclaim a day of public mourning."

This was Chips Prentice speaking—huge, ruddy and sleek. Chips the famous footballer, the schoolboys' idol. His voice was powerful, richly veined with humour, and could raise laughter with the most banal remark. They hung on to his words and laughed delightedly.

The cackle of Dooley Franks, Tommy Collins's friend, was always the last to die down. He was a long, thin, rakish man in his twenties, with jet-black hair, and a grin and a voice that were impudence itself.

"A Sixth Divvy bloke put me up to the lurk," he told them. "If they've charged you too much, help yourself to something else and walk out with it. He reckoned the day of the air raid, when all the four-be-twos were in the air-raid shelters there was Aussies coming out of the shops everywhere with their pockets crammed with watches and things."

There was a renewed burst of laughter. Dooley was a renowned larrikin.

Somehow, two girls had joined them at the table and were being plied with drink, to the accompaniment of leers, rib-digging, and remarks with double meanings. They were young girls, but apathetic looking and given to continual shrugging; sipping their drink and drawing on cigarettes as though they were all that life had left them to enjoy. The one who sat between Dooley and Dick was slim and vaguely pretty. She soon became tired of Dooley's coarse hints and turned her back on him and spoke to Dick.

"You are very quiet, Aussie. Homesick? For your wife, perhaps?"

"I haven't got a wife," he told her shortly.

"Ah, your sweetheart then?"

"I haven't got a sweetheart."

"You are lonely then."

Her hand fell lightly on his knee. He looked at her. Her eyes were dark and seemed to hold an appeal.

"Perhaps I'm tired," he told her.

"Ah, it is this bad drink; you are not used to it. Come with me, yes? And I will make you strong black coffee."

She leaned towards him. Her hand closed over his, drew it up under her short skirt until his fingers were against bare flesh. He caressed it gently. He suddenly became aware that he was getting drunk. Looking across the table he saw Gribble smirk

21

at him knowingly and form words with his mouth that were inaudible in the shouting and laughter. The other prostitute looked over at the dark girl, nodded and winked at her. Gribble burst into a laugh.

Suddenly Dick was on his feet, seeing red, trying to hit Gribble across the table. Dooley, Chips and another man were pushing him back. "You bloody little squirt!" he was shouting at Percy. "Put your hands up!"

Gribble stood his ground, babbling indignantly to Andy. Dick threw Dooley aside and lurched. Then he felt very sick. The room and its sounds grew dim. He was vaguely aware of the girl's hand on his arm and her voice saying something; then he was out in the fresh air and Andy's quiet tones were urging: "Bring it up, son. Bring it up and you'll feel better."

He vomited steadily for a minute or two and did feel better.

"I'm all right," he gulped. He felt weak and ridiculous. "Leave me alone. I'll be back in a minute."

Andy left him. Dick knew he would not go back. After making a fool of himself he was generally unwilling to face those who had seen it. He was in some sort of a garden. Overhead the stars were brilliant. Unsteadily he made his way through an archway and out into the dark street. On the pavement a figure put out a hand to grasp him and a voice said:

"It was the bad drink. I will make you coffee. Come."

It was the girl from the café. She put an arm round him and guided him through the darkness.

"Just a moment," he said.

"When we are in. You speak then," she urged.

A few minutes brought them to a door, at which she fumbled with a key. She drew him in, shut the door and lit a small torch.

"The blackout!" she whispered. "I will arrange the curtains and then switch on the light."

"Listen!" He held her hard. It was time for Dick Brett to make some kind of gesture. He had swung drunken punches like a performing clown, been taken out to vomit, and then led off docilely by a prostitute. "I'd like some coffee all right, but I'm not spending money on you."

She drew closer, kissed him, and murmured:

"I do not want money from you. I have enough tonight. You are nice boy. You tried to hit that man because he said something bad about me. Yes?"

In truth, he could not remember exactly why he had tried to hit Gribble, but it was not on the girl's behalf, he knew that. All he could recall was his sudden sensation of feeling foolish, juvenile, and inept, and his flaring resentment. But this was an appealing picture: the chivalrous young soldier who would not see even a prostitute disparaged!

"Yes," he replied. "That's why."

22

She breathed harder, kissing him once more.

"Wait till I arrange the blackout," she whispered. She kissed him yet again. "You are nice, lonely boy." Then she was gone.

He could hear her moving about and the rustle of cloth. He stood in the dark, tingling, pleased with himself, all his confidence restored. The blacked-out city, the starry night, the woman in the dark room, the adventurer in the romantic situation.

Before he knew it she was back, pressing against him. With a sigh she drew him across the room, down on to cushions. His hands touched bare flesh, moved downwards. Exultantly he discovered that she was quite naked.

*   *   *

In the early hours of the morning he was sated and wanted to get away from her. Thoughts intruded of the long journey back to camp. She was only his second woman, and a new experience to him. He had imagined all prostitutes as haggard and unromantic creatures. This girl was sensuous and, in his possession, excitable. But now, his passion spent, her nakedness against his had started to become oppressive.

"I must get back," he said, sitting up and reaching for his clothes.

She switched on a bedside lamp, revealing a small, neat, comfortable room. She watched him approvingly as he dressed, smiling. He made a negligent display of his muscles. Then abruptly he became confused, and conscious of displaying himself to a stranger. To hide it he leant over and looked at a photograph of a man.

"My husband," she told him.

"Is he in Palestine?"

"He is dead."

"How long have you lived in Palestine?"

"Three years."

"And before?"

"In Czechoslovakia."

"Did you have to flee?"

"Yes. The Nazis killed my husband. He was a teacher."

He looked closer. It was a poor photo: a young man with a pale face and a high forehead.

"Did you love him?"

"Yes. How do you say? Better than life."

"More than life itself."

"More than life. But that is not true, no?"

"How not true?"

"I am still alive. I fled."

"What else could you do?"

23

"There were many who did not flee. Some died, some remain and hide. Me—I do not care."

"But you cared tonight when I tried to hit that man."

He said this easily now, almost convinced of his motive.

"A little. You are nice, lonely boy."

"Why lonely?"

"I watch you tonight. You do not feel—what is it?—same as those men. They are harder than you. You are uneasy, yes?"

"Perhaps."

He glanced at the photo and back at her.

"Why do you do this sort of thing? Why are you a——"

"Prostitute?" she said softly.

He reddened, stammered:

"I'm not insulting you."

"No—you nice boy. Come and kiss me."

He performed the act, trying not to shrink from her odorous nudity.

"I do not do this all the time. I work in factory, but wages are not enough. Sometimes I want a pretty dress, a coat, more food. You understand?"

"I understand."

"Besides this—I like to have a man. I am a warm woman."

He laughed at this.

"I must go now."

"You have not had the coffee."

"Can't be helped."

Now that it was time to go he felt awkward, sorry for her.

"I hope things get better for you."

"Wait," she said. "Which is your camp?"

"Julis."

"I am going to town of Rishon, not very far from there." She scribbled on a piece of paper. "You come and see me there. Good-bye."

She offered herself to be kissed, naturally and intimately. He felt superior and tender.

"You're a nice girl. It's a pity."

At the door he turned:

"How old are you?"

"Twenty-five. And you?"

"The same," he lied, and found his way into the night.

Outside, the stars still shone.

*   *   *

He picked up a truck on the outskirts of the city. Two sozzled voices welcomed him from the interior:

"Ar—ah! Hop aboard, sport!"

He complied and the truck lurched on. A bottle of wine was thrust under his nose.

"Have a swig, sport."

He took the bottle with the gesture of a hardened toper and helped himself to a mouthful.

"Thanks, sport." He handed the bottle back and idly he noted that he never called a man "sport" before.

Bibulously, a voice began to sing:

> *"A soldier told me before he died,*
> *I don't know whether the bastard lied,*
> *No matter how he tried and tried*
> *His wife could never be satisfied."*

"Lennie, yer bashtard! You stop singin' about wives, Lennie, or by Christ I'll job yer with thish bottle. The bitches!"

Lennie obliged:

> *"Hi! hi, Kathusalem, Kathusalem, Kathusalem,*
> *Hi! hi, Kathusalem,*
> *The harlot of Jerusalem!"*

They joined in and sang it through, swaying from side to side and passing the bottle at intervals.

"Wife trouble, mate?" asked Dick, in the manner of one who had his own problems with women.

"Hounded me for three years with a foggin' maintenance order. Put me in for wife-shtarving, the bashtards. Changed me name and joined up. Hope the bitch's shtill looking." He broke into raucous song:

> *"Oh, happy is yer life*
> *When yer haven't got a wife,*
> *And yer rolling, rolling, rolling, rolling home."*

Rolling home, rolling home . . . more like bumping home . . . not home, either. An old land under strange stars . . . strange people . . . pretty girl who didn't care. Dog with the women, this Brett . . . rolling home . . . rolling . . . roll . . . oll . . . ollll . . .

"Hey, wake up, sport! You wanted Julis, didn't yer?"

He found himself down on the road with the tail-light of the truck fading into the darkness.

3

COLONEL ORMOND FITZROY was addressing the Second X Battalion. The five companies, each one hundred and thirty strong, were drawn up in hollow square formation around their commander, who was attended by Mick Varney, the regimental sergeant-major. "Groggy Orme," as he was known to the men, was yellow-eyed from too much whisky the night before. He was inclined to speak petulantly and be less meticulous than usual about his accent:

"You are sadly mistaken if you imagine that being in a strange country and due to meet the enemy, perhaps in the near future, means that there will be any relaxation of discipline. I have built up an *esprit de corps* in this unit second to none in the A.I.F. and as long as I command it, it will remain so. I will not tolerate slovenliness, either in dress or bearing. I still insist that officers be saluted on appropriate occasions. We are entering the final and most important stage of our training. It is up to every man to make as efficient a soldier of himself as possible. You have a proud tradition to uphold; the eyes of your country are upon you. Wherever you came from and whatever your plans for after the war, forget them. Forget everything except that you are over here to do a big job. I know that some of the weaker minds among you are regretting that you ever joined up to fight for your country. It is too late now. You are in the army, you are in *my* battalion, and, by God, I will make you or break you. . . ."

Helped by his liver, he was wound up now and the troops, knowing him of old, resigned themselves to half an hour of it at least. The lineal descendant of one of the most famous figures in Australian history, the possessor of fabulous areas of grazing property, a member of a family whose name was a byword, he had taken command of a battalion that was prepared to stand somewhat in awe of him. A few months' experience of him and his ways had dispelled all this.

The clipped tones proceeded:

"Without detracting from the magnificent exploits of the Sixth Division, it should not be forgotten that they defeated an army that had no desire to fight. Sooner or later we will meet the German and will find him a much tougher proposition. . . ."

Captain Gilbertson, commander of B Company, became conscious of restiveness and muttering among the men behind him. He turned and sternly caught the eye of Lieutenant Crane. The lieutenant turned round to Six Platoon and whispered scornfully:

"Shut up!"

He faced his front again, quite unaware of the resentment he had caused behind him. Lieutenant Crane was often unaware of such things.

"The German nation has many advantages over us," proceeded the colonel. "It has been arming and training for war for a long period. It has a unity that we might well envy. Strikes are unknown and agitators are shot. While men are

26

dying overseas, people in Australia see fit to go on strike rather than produce the weapons of war. Some of our trade unions seem to be composed largely of traitors and saboteurs. . . ."

The muttering in Six Platoon now resolved plainly into the voice of Andy Cain:

"There aren't any bloody unions in Germany. They're all slaves."

"Quiet!" whispered Sergeant Lucas.

"Quiet, my foot! I'm not standing here and listening to him praising Hitler."

Then, to the consternation of B Company, Andy Cain walked slowly off the parade ground.

Not one member of Six Platoon heeded any more of the colonel's words. The speculation was too intense: what would Andy get for this? Had the colonel seen it?

They did not have to wait long. When they came back to their lines after the parade, Andy was sitting in his tent calmly awaiting the consequences. They crowded into the tent, voluble and sympathetic.

"What did you do it for?"

"Yes, why did you? No one takes any notice of old Orme."

"If you must know," Andy told them tiredly, "I did my block. I detest the man and I just couldn't stand there any longer and listen to that bullsh. He's a bloody Nazi!"

"It was only the grog working out," said Chips. "He's not a bad poor bastard."

"He's a Fascist," insisted Andy. "I was a fool to do what I did—no point in it. Still, I'm glad I did it."

They murmured their sympathy again.

"I don't see what there was to get so excited about," said Percy Gribble.

"You wouldn't!" said Andy.

"As a matter of fact," continued Percy, "I agree with him. These coal-miners and others ought to be pulled into gear. They're ruining the war effort."

"What war effort?" Dooley Franks asked him. "Do you call this turn-out a war effort?"

"Yes, I do call it a war effort, and this is a damned good unit, and Fitzroy's a good C.O."

"You'll get your stripes, Perce!"

"You make me sick!" exclaimed Dick.

The voice of Sergeant Lucas interrupted them.

"Outside, everybody! Break up this mothers' meeting."

Lucas detained Andy as he came out.

"Afraid it's a crime sheet for you, old timer. You're under open arrest."

"You surprise me," murmured Andy.

Lucas chuckled.

"You're a world-beater! Whatever possessed you to walk off a C.O.'s parade?"

"A principle, I suppose. I doubt if it's much use explaining to you."

The handsome sergeant grinned at him.

"I got rid of my principles some years ago. Look here, Andy, where will this sort of business get you? This war's going to drag on for years and years. Look after yourself; make a career of it."

"Is that what you're doing?"

"More or less."

"Why did you join up, Frank?"

"Experience—a free tour. Why did you?"

"It seemed the right thing to do."

"You must be unique. Do you know why most of this battalion joined up? Adventure; to get away from a wife, or the police. Some of them have been on the track or out of work for years, and the army means three meals a day and a bed to sleep in. But you—you're a patriot."

"I'm an anti-Fascist!"

"You take life too seriously, Andy."

"Do I? That's the worst of us half-baked socialists."

*   *   *

Six Platoon was dismissed at three o'clock that afternoon. It was still warm and sunny. Dick was making his way over the hill to a small Jewish settlement. At the summit he turned and stood surveying the scene below him. The plain made a wonderful pattern: a small white huddle of Jewish houses; a rambling grey Arab village; a dark square of orange grove; the raw red of a ploughed field; the zig-zag of a cactus-flanked lane; the white ribbon of a new road in curves and angles; and a cluster of army tents that looked like some foreign growth. The sun came through the clouds, falling over the peaceful land in broad blades of light.

The settlement was half a dozen houses on either side of a lane. The fronts of two of them had been turned into places of business: one into a café, the other into a curio shop.

It was Dick's intention to buy a curio of some sort to send home to his family. The shop was stacked with the typical mixture of jewellery and assorted trash; olive-wood boxes and bowls, filigree brooches, photographs, hideous silk scarves, phoney Arab daggers; all at prices giving the shopkeeper something like a hundred per cent profit.

He spent some time choosing a present, assisted by the young Jew in charge of the shop, finally deciding on an olive-wood bowl. During this time a Jewish girl had entered the shop.

"How much?" he asked the shopkeeper.

"Twelve hundred mils."

"Twelve hundred!"

He would have argued, but he felt it beneath his dignity as a soldier. He took out his wallet. A hand suddenly appeared over it, the hand of the Jewish girl. She stood in front of Dick and spoke rapidly to the man in Hebrew. Then she turned to Dick and said in good English:

"You must not pay that much money. It is only worth eight hundred mils."

She turned again to the young Jew and spoke more Hebrew to him. He smiled at her in a propitiatory way, spread his hands, and nodded.

"He will take eight hundred," she told Dick.

"Thank you very much!" he stammered, taken aback by the rapidity of the episode. He counted out the money and took the bowl. She accompanied him from the shop, after a parting shot at the lad.

In the road, she turned to him and said earnestly:

"It is not right that the shopkeeper should rob you like that. You did not mind my interference?"

"Not at all!"

In the same earnest manner she went on: "It is easy for many people to hate Jews. When they are like the man in the shop some people feel they have a right to hate them."

She was tall, broad-hipped and very brown-skinned. Her hair was jet-black, and smoothly set on the head. Her lips were large and vividly red, without lipstick. She wore a white blouse and a short, faded blue skirt.

"Australian shopkeepers are no better," he told her. "It's just that we find it harder to forgive a foreigner."

They were outside the café by this time. He was conscious of a desire to know this girl more intimately. Intrigued and flattered by the incident in the shop, he felt himself impelled by his self-esteem to carry this relationship further. In her large vital way she was attractive. He asked her if she would have a cup of coffee with him.

"I could not drink that coffee," she said in the same direct fashion. "It is rubbish. But perhaps you would like to come to my house and drink coffee with me—Turkish coffee?"

Delighted, he accepted the invitation. She told him her name was Naomi. She led him off the road, along a path through an orange grove. A short walk brought them to the top of a slope. She paused, indicating the scene below them. What he saw was like a small township, laid out to an orderly plan, surrounded on its edges by a farm and a sea of orange groves.

"You have never seen a Kibbutz before?" she asked.

"A Kibbutz?"

"A communal settlement. This is where I live."

29

"A communal settlement! Are you all Communists?"

"By no means!" She took his question as a joke. "There may be one or two Communists. Come. We will go to my house, and on the way I will explain to you."

She led him down the hill.

* * *

Andy Cain was escorted to the Battalion Orderly Room the next morning. Regimental Sergeant-Major Varney awaited them outside.

Such occasions were as the breath of life to Varney. Of a legendary stupidity, he knew Army Law and all the items of a battalion's routine down to the last shred. He was an encyclopædia of every useless, pettifogging, archaic detail of military correctness. A battalion parade, the drilling of a squad, the "criming" and sentencing of some unhappy soldier; the adherence to military precision until it became pure farce: these things brought joy to his dull mind. He was a living, infallible, sub-human mass of rules and regulations.

"Pris-nah n'escort . . . 'alt!"

He deprived Andy of his hat, as was the procedure with prisoners. He knocked at the door of the colonel's office and opened it.

"Pris-nah n'escort—queek . . . march!"

"Pris-nah n'escort . . . 'alt!"

Andy found himself facing Colonel Fitzroy.

The charges were read and Andy pleaded guilty.

The colonel studied the charge sheet at unnecessary length, finally raising his fine dark eyes to regard Andy coolly and malevolently. He smoothed his straight black moustache with his thumb, then suddenly slapped the charge-sheet with the back of his hand.

"This is utterly fantastic!"

Andy was silent. He wondered if Fitzroy knew his reason for leaving the parade. (A hundred to one he does, but he's too damn conceited to let on. Go on, sentence me, you posturing whisky-swilling swine!)

But it was not going to end as simply as that. The colonel was in the mood to expand on this outrage. If robot soldiery was the delight of Sergeant-Major Varney, the relish of his own words was necessary to the colonel.

He settled back in his chair to enjoy himself.

"The sheer impudence of this takes my breath away! Apparently you were neither sick nor drunk, and I take it you are not insane. Your action is indefensible! You offer your commanding officer a gratuitous insult by walking off his parade for no apparent reason. However, I am not looking at this in a personal light." (Not much, you aren't.) "It is the most unsoldierly

30

offence that has ever come under my notice. It's—it's—it's——"
Fitzroy felt for the right word, suddenly found it. "It's
anarchy!" he ended victoriously.

He was now thoroughly pleased with himself. He straightened
up and became businesslike:

"Well, have you anything to say?"

He half-closed his eyes and watched Andy shrewdly.

He knows! thought Andy. If I say nothing, that will give him
a victory over me, and that's what he's after. What a mind he's
got! What a power, he thought, for such a man to have. Suddenly he felt sick of the whole business. He wanted to escape
from this Orderly Room and this specimen of inherited privilege.
What was the use of butting your head against the brick wall of
his position and power? Such men always had the whip hand;
such men always would. Only a fool would make such a gesture
against the colonel as he had. Let him talk like a Nazi! Look
after your own principles and hang the rest! Let him have his
little triumph!

"No, sir. I have nothing to say."

He hardly heard the sentence of fourteen days' pack drill, or
the R.S.M.'s commands as he was marched out. They gave him
back his hat and he walked unseeingly down the road, confused,
hopeless and ashamed.

4

AFTER his first visit to the Kibbutz, Naomi sought Dick's company repeatedly. There was no conquest on his part and no
apparent infatuation on hers. It was plain that she liked him,
but no more, it seemed, than many of the young men around
the Kibbutz. He found himself puzzled as to why she had chosen
to befriend him, and his self-esteem required an answer. Eventually he took into account the good-hearted little prostitute in
Tel Aviv and he decided that he must be attractive to women,
not realising that any boy of twenty such as he, with his smooth
skin, a strong tall body, sensitive features, and that endearing
look of defencelessness, was attractive to some women. Naomi
was one of them.

If a few days passed without a visit from him she would ask
him why. He had begun to absorb her. She was moved more
and more by the desire to know everything about him. Behind
his moods of sullenness or braggartry she discerned that he was
unhappy, but whenever she tried to reach his inner thoughts he
would resist her.

One day she lost patience and became angry with him. She

had a gramophone and a large pile of records, to which he listened for hours on end. An accomplished musician herself, she soon perceived that he had very little knowledge of classical music. Nevertheless, she liked to convey the impression that he knew a great deal. Believing that this was one of his ways of smothering a sense of frustration, she never let him see that his pretence was clear to her. On this occasion she had just played him something rather rare, a fragment from Scarlatti, dated 1683. She went on to talk of Scarlatti's sister, who had been secretly married to a highly-placed ecclesiastic and of how Scarlatti had been in disfavour at the Vatican because of it. His answer showed her that Scarlatti was little more than a name to him. When he added some fancy of his own she asked him gently but maliciously:

"But which Scarlatti are you referring to?"

"Which?" he echoed blankly.

"Yes. Alessandro or Domenico?"

A little defiantly he took the plunge and said:

"The one who wrote this piece. Domenico."

"Domenico was not born till 1685," she told him.

"Well——" He stopped, went pale, and stared at her as he realised she had deliberately trapped him. He was terribly hurt. Instantly sorry, she came over and sat next to him, summoning all her earnestness. He sat avoiding her eyes, fiercely humiliated. For the first time he was conscious that she was twenty-eight and he only twenty. He suddenly realised that she saw deeper into him than he had imagined.

"You can always be yourself with me," she said, and left it at that. It did not seem necessary to say any more.

She went back to the gramophone and put on another record. He had not moved or spoken.

From that time on their friendship deepened. He began to tell her of his childhood and early youth in Australia. She was happy over getting to know him better, but she never told him why she had desired this. To her, at first, he had just been an Australian and Australians had aroused her curiosity. She had seen them in the township in their wide hats: big men, brown and free-moving, with keen, avid eyes, ready to laugh at anything. She did not tell him that his unhappiness was familiar to her. In the Germany from which she had fled she had known many young men like him. He belonged to a generation that had grown up between two world wars; many of their lives had been shattered in the poverty of the thirties. These years had left them aimless, bitter and uprooted. Now they were wanted—for war. That she felt so passionately about the young men was partly because of the brother the Nazis had killed. At odd times some mannerism of Dick's, some fleeting expression, would remind her of this dead brother. She felt a strange sort of consolation listening to Dick telling her about himself. But this remained a secret. She listened to him.

His childhood had been a typical middle-class one; humdrum, sheltered; with a snobbish, possessive mother who had stuffed him with illusions; a father who occasionally patted him absent-mindedly on the head. His father's life was taken up with his small factory, his car and playing the host to business acquaintances. In their living-room stood the red clock, which came to be the dominant symbol of his childhood. It stood about two feet high, made of rich-coloured wood, inlaid with ebony, silver and mother-of-pearl. Its face was of glowing white marble, and it stood on a massive base of red agate. His mother invented tales about it for his amusement, but never forgot to remind him that one day it would be his. To the boy it was a beautiful, fabulous thing. Whenever he was taken into another house he judged its occupants by the sort of clock they had on their mantelpiece.

The disintegration of this small, safe world began when he was ten. His father's pats became more absent-minded than ever and there was a permanent line between his brows. Dimly, the child gathered that something terrible and irresistible was happening in the world without. Then, from what the boy overheard his parents saying and from the little he guessed, he learnt that his father no longer had his small factory, that something had happened to him in common with a lot of others: he had "gone broke."

The family went steadily downhill to poverty. The red clock now presided in a dim, shabby room in the house they had moved to. His father went away to Queensland to work for someone else; his mother, to the boy's consternation, also went out to work for someone.

Dick was taken away from his private school and sent to a public school, to mix with a lot of children his mother had once forbidden him to play with. In that small, noisy society he learnt the beginnings of self-reliance. One day—he was thirteen at the time and in his third year at high school—he arrived home to find that the red clock was gone from the room. His mother had sold it.

Mrs. Brett had changed. To begin with, she had faced poverty with a well-bred shame, showing the world only the dignity and charm she believed to be the prerogative of her kind; but now she began to fight poverty with every means at her disposal, and neither dignity nor charm counted for much in this fight. She was determined that Dick should go to the university, and to this end she skimped, schemed, saved and sacrificed. Go to the university he did, but she had become so preoccupied with her task that she lost her awareness of him as a person. He lived in a void of loneliness. At the university he was proud, touchy and quarrelsome, haunted by their poverty. For a while he listened to a group who styled themselves the Decadents, who read Eliot and Auden and, rather than thunder against the lot of humanity, affected to bow their heads beneath it, humbly, tragically and nobly. They told him that his existence would be justified by getting drunk regularly, writing their kind of poetry and dying for hopeless causes. Hardly one of them, including Dick, failed to write something beautiful and obscure about the young English poets who died in Spain, quietly and dejectedly, with the death-wish in their hearts.

He was fundamentally too optimistic to stay with them for long. He began to realise that the world was more than the setting for his personal tragedy, and he began on new ideas. Convinced that fascism was evil, he became interested in socialism. A few months after the outbreak of war, he rendered his mother dumb with surprise and horror by joining the army. But in the end she faced the inevitable, as she had learned to these past few years.

"Why did you join the army?" Naomi asked him.

He pondered her question uneasily; then he went to speak.

"Tell me all your reasons," she broke in persuasively. "But don't say 'patriotism.' That's been said too often and meant nothing. Please don't say that."

"Very well, I won't. Not unless you call anti-fascism patriotism. . . . But, of course, there were other reasons—reasons I don't like to admit to myself. Oh, hell! I was very mixed up at the time. Things were terrible at the university. Neither my mother nor I was sure that I'd ever be able to complete my course. And even if I had got through where was a Bachelor of Arts going to find a job?"

"The war was an escape for you," Naomi concluded.

"Partly—but not entirely. I did really believe we had to fight the Fascists."

"The depression set so many of us adrift," said Naomi. "In Germany many of them drifted to Nazism. The more ignorant of them were such easy meat for Hitler. Just as boys like you were easy meat for this war."

"But we've got to oppose Hitler!"

"Were you told that before the war started?" she asked.

"No," he said. "We weren't. Not by our leaders, anyway."

"Of course not! That's why it has come to war. You were betrayed as surely as the young men of Germany were betrayed."

At this, she concluded the discussion and began to play some more music. She did not want to go on from there and tell him about herself and her brother. He had become very happy in her company and she did not want to spoil his happiness in any way. She was constantly aware that his visits must end sooner or later. No infantry unit stayed long in Palestine. Soon the Second X would, in its turn, disappear into the Western Desert.

During the few weeks before he left Naomi found herself living their moments together hungrily, as though he would never emerge again from the desert. Perhaps it was because of his resemblance to her brother Werner and the memory of the time he had left, never to come back. She would never forget Werner's pale, handsome face, with the vivid eyes smiling as she looked fearfully up at him. . . . "Yes, my dear," he was saying. "I am well aware two truck-loads of Nazis arrived here last night, and I know exactly what danger I'm in. I'm not only a Jew, but a Communist. . . . Stay indoors today." Then he was gone, and that had been the last time she saw him alive. She passed him some hours later, lying on the pavement, his head half shot away, his face streaked with blood and dirt. She had to walk past pretending she did not know him, for the Nazis were still watching from a window across the street and had just shot a little girl who had knelt down by her father's corpse which lay near that of Werner. And so she walked past him, her eyes staring ahead of her, her limbs moving as if she were a mechanical thing and trembling beneath her clothes, while her whole body and soul longed for the chance to kneel down beside him, to straighten the sprawling limbs, wipe the bloody face, make him look clean and dignified. But she had only murmured his name between her clenched lips: "Peace, Werner. Peace!" And she had not even known where they buried him.

5

THE camps along the thin white road seethed with the activity of departure. Twenty thousand men were soon to be on their way to the deserts of Egypt and Libya. Only six weeks after their arrival in Palestine they were getting ready to leave it.

One evening Dick came to the Kibbutz and told Naomi what she had been expecting: this was good-bye. "I can't stay long," he told her. "I shouldn't be out of camp."

She walked with him to the brow of the hill. There was the keen, cool tang of the orange groves in the air. Now that the time had come to say good-bye to her, he felt regret and a sense of something that had not been fulfilled. He had never been able to make up his mind whether she was in love with him or merely interested in him. She had learnt a great deal about him—but what did he know about her? He was surprised when he realised he knew so little. He seemed to have spent the whole time talking about himself. Somehow her superior wisdom, her mature charm, had made him rather shy of attempting anything more than a casual embrace.

"These have been a marvellous few weeks," he told her.

She nodded briefly at this remark, for she was busy with thoughts of her own:

"Will you be allowed to write?" she asked.

"Of course!"

"And you will?"

"As often as I can."

They stopped and looked at each other in the darkness. Above the white blouse her brown face and neck seemed dimly beautiful and mysterious. Her eyes were invisible except for pale gleams as she looked at him. His sadness at leaving her grew deep and hurtful and he knew that she had grown precious to him. When he gripped her shoulders and drew her to him she clasped him suddenly and fiercely. It was their first serious embrace and no word was said.

They commenced to walk. Silently they passed through the village where they had first met and reached the brow of the hill. Where normally the camps on the plain below would have been lost in a sea of blackness, they were tonight alive with the flickering of scattered lights and the dim glow that came from the shrouded headlamps of army trucks. It was an eerie, incredible sight. There was something fearful and urgent about these scurrying pinpoints of brightness, these sudden disembodied glowings, appearing, disappearing, flickering, rising and falling. And in the clear night air a conglomeration of sounds reached them that told their own story of excitement, of feverish activity; the drone of engines, the rattle of lanterns, laughing, shouting. . . . To the woman it was a tragedy, but to Dick it was for the moment something entirely different: another part of the "Great Adventure." While she pondered on how soon death would silence so many of these voices Dick was tingling with elation. This was It—they were off, "up the desert!" All other considerations were driven suddenly from his mind.

Naomi sensed his change of mood and the reason for it. She wanted to gather him into her arms, finding an excuse to comfort and protect him. . . . Then she pulled herself together half angrily and brushed her fingers furtively over her eyes. He did not need comfort at this moment and nothing could protect him from what he was going into. She was surprised to find herself fearful for his safety. From a chance acquaintance he had become someone that absorbed her. I'm not in love with him, she told herself, yet he means a lot to me. She found herself remembering how it had come about. What did it matter how it had come about? Would she never see this moody, sensitive young Australian again? She had a strange feeling that she would not. For some reason he seemed to symbolise all the tragedy of youth. Looking at the firm profile bent avidly towards those dancing lights, the eyes lit up at the thought of adventure, she wondered if he would ever realise how much better he had deserved than this.

He held her long and tenderly in farewell. "Good-bye!" he whispered, and plunged downhill.

Now that he was gone she did not hold back her tears but let them come softly down her cheeks.

After a while she turned and went back to the place she now called home.

*   *   *

The officers' mess of the Second X Battalion had been cleared of its furniture, the gaudy curtains taken from the windows. Only the flimsy wooden bar remained. A mess orderly in a white jacket was on duty behind it. The jacket had been the colonel's idea. It lent, in his opinion, the correct tone to the officers' mess. The colonel was standing his last few rounds of drinks to his brother officers.

The battalion was packed and ready to move. The stores were on their way to the railway station at El Majdal. The men sat in their tents beside their piled gear. There was nothing to do now but wait till three in the morning, when the battalion was due to march the five miles to El Majdal and entrain.

Most of the battalion's twenty-odd officers were assembled in the mess. Having issued them with their orders, the colonel had invited them all to have a drink with him.

The colonel was preparing to enjoy himself. He had planned this invitation some days before and thought hard over words suitable to the occasion. He had a habit of forming anticipatory images of how he would talk and act on certain occasions. This was one of the occasions and he considered it a solemn and important one. He needed no whisky tonight to improve his mood. He was in his best form: urbane, likeable and invincibly confident. His alert eyes beamed in his smooth, well-formed features as he surveyed the officers gathered round him.

Most of them were old pre-war acquaintances. Some of them, Crane for example, owned grazing properties as large as his own. Others, like Major Pomfret his second in command, shared the same business interests. The colonel's partiality was felt throughout the battalion. Back in Australia men had joined the battalion one day and become N.C.O.s the next; it would turn out that the suddenly-promoted man had been an employee of one or other of the colonel's grazing or business concerns. With their alert cynicism the rank and file of the battalion told them-

selves that promotion in the Second X was based on the extent
of one's pre-war usefulness to the colonel. Somebody had written
a piece of doggerel about it to the tune of a popular song. One
of its less insulting stanzas ran:

> *Have you worked for Colonel Fitzroy?*
> *Then you'll get promoted, old boy.*
> *You'll get your promotion*
> *This side of the ocean*
> *If you've worked for Colonel Fitzroy!*

The colonel had charged his glass with white wine on this
occasion, the whisky he usually drank not seeming entirely
appropriate for the toast he was about to give.

"Gentlemen," he began . . .

*   *   *

The battalion was in high spirits and making a tremendous
noise. There had been a beer ration of five bottles a man; the
beer fumes combined with their excitement at going "up the
desert" had left them hilarious since nightfall.

Descending the hill towards the camp, Dick stopped once
again to take the scene in. His elation had subsided and he was
in a better mood to contemplate the strangeness of the spectacle.
He had a momentary feeling of being nearer to the heavens than
the earth. The white stars blazed above him. The tents below
glowed faintly from the lanterns and rang with shouting and
singing. Yet out here, under the great sky, the affairs of their
occupants seemed puny and contemptible; the shouting no more
than a whisper in the cold immensity. He stood there in the
chill shining night and lost the last of his exhilaration. What he
was looking at seemed the beginnings of a tragedy, made only
the more ghastly by the distant sounds of carousal he could hear
the victims making.

His contemplation had become almost trance-like, and he had
to shake off the oppressive mood like something heavy from his
shoulders. He came swiftly down the slope and along the white
road as if he were pursued.

Entering the tent was like a plunge into another world. There
was hardly room for him to get in, it was so crowded with gear
and men. He stood blinking in the murky lantern light, and was
welcomed by a chorus of throaty shouts.

"Young Dick! Where've ya been, Dick? Here, mate, have a
drink."

He took the bottle with a laugh and a sense of joy and gratitude
at the welcome they had given him. It was only lately he had
wanted to be one of them. At the beginning, he had in his
nervousness behaved politely and aloofly, and they had grinned
and left him to himself or baited him for amusement like Lucas.

Lucas was here with them now, sitting in a corner with a bottle of beer and that sardonic grin on his dark face. As many of Six Platoon as was humanly possible seemed to have squeezed into the one tent. The air was heavy with the smell of liquor and blue with smoke.

"And what happened then, Tommy?"

Tommy Collins raised a bottle to his white face and gurgled deep.

"Well, then I fronts the other sheila and arsts her 'How much wahed ziggy-zigg?' 'Five hundred mils,' she says. Then the bludger arsts for his cut, and I hit the bastard. The other Wog gits out of the taxi, and I grabs the chromo and starts running. . . ."

They encouraged him with leers and shouts. Tommy Collins's exploits in brothels and drinking houses were one of their main sources of entertainment. While it was agreed that he was a degenerate little ruffian, he was funny when in the mood and that counted for much. To see Lucas amused meant more to Tommy than anything else; to call him Frank and hear him cackle at his stories. When deep in one of his drunken narratives he saw neither Lucas's contempt nor revulsion; Tommy was only anxious for his laughter, and revelled in it. And Lucas applauded and egged him on, entertained as a man might be at the antics of a stray cur.

Tommy's story petered out and he went outside to vomit. Very little was enough to make him drunk. Over in the other corner a chorus broke out:

> *"And when I die, don't bury me at all*
> *Just pickle my bones in alcohol."*

Their voices drew out the tune dolefully, filling it with false pathos.

"Here's to old Chips!"

"Poor bloody old Chips!"

Chips Prentice, the idol of the platoon, was gone to hospital with a minor dose of V.D. Such was his personality that V.D. had become almost glamorous now he had it. But he was missed, especially now; missed with his great, lithe body and his rich, bubbling voice that awoke smiles and commanded applause. Poor bloody old Chips!

Percy Gribble was expected to step into his shoes as section corporal and was doing his best to conceal his gratification by uttering louder and more frequent regrets than anyone else.

"Buck up, Dooley!" he cried, slapping a brooding Dooley Franks across the shoulders. Dooley jerked himself away and made an obscene recommendation.

"Fine mate you are," grumbled Tommy Collins, subdued now

39

after his vomiting. Dooley repeated his recommendation to Tommy.

The Nine Days' Wonder sat across Dooley's shoulders like the Old Man of the Sea, and nothing could shake him out of his fear. After patronising a brothel he had discovered that it was the same one where Chips had contracted his gonorrhœa. He had been laden with doubts and torments ever since. Soldiers believed, from lectures and printed orders, that gonorrhœa showed itself within nine days. Dooley had four days to go and the previous five had been typical of those of a man who had the Wonder: The first hesitant appearance on sick parade, with a complaint about "a burning sensation"; the medical officer's unsympathetic grin and his perfunctory reassurance. But once the Wonder has set in, no reassurance lasts very long. From then on the wretch becomes a pitiable nuisance, haunting the latrines or the Regimental Aid Post. He even develops the symptoms of V.D., or imagines he does, and goes running in a panic to the R.A.P., to be driven off with laughs or abuse from the orderlies. He feels himself unclean, despicable and socially leprous. There is nothing much to be done with him. After the nine days his torment generally drops from him like a cloak. Such a condition sat oddly on a man like Dooley. He was the last man they would have expected to see with the Wonder. It was incongruous to see Dooley, with his long clownish head, his great beaky nose, his larrikin's cackle and his shrewd preying on the "mugs" and the "galahs," obsessed with anxiety. Presently he got up and went outside and they let him go.

Andy Cain was the hero of the moment, having recently completed fourteen days' pack drill for walking off the colonel's parade. His reason for doing it was laughable to them, or beyond them, but he had tilted at authority: that was enough. He sat in the corner near Dick, taking no part in the singing or shouting, but accepting their adulation as he got quietly and steadily drunk on some of the local wine.

"Who went through on Groggy's parade?" someone asked.

"Andy!" they roared.

"You beaut!"

They toasted him and he toasted them back, tilting his bottle. He turned and winked recklessly at Dick.

"That's the style, sport. Drink it down! Drink and forget! When the world goes mad you go mad too, eh?" With his face suffused and his bottle held above his head he began to declaim hoarsely:

> " 'Would you care to break a window?' said the
>   Leader of the Push—
> 'I'll break the bloody house down!' said the
>   Bastard from the Bush."

40

They laughed and applauded him. But Dick looked sidelong at Andy and somehow felt sorry for him. In those hoarse tones had there been a note of anguish?

They commenced to sing, in unison this time:

> "*Oh my, I don't wanna die,*
> *I wanna go home.*"

*   *   *

The crowd had thinned out in the officers' mess, but the colonel, back to his whisky, still held court at the bar with Major Pomfret his second in command, his adjutant, Captain Hubert Stamp, Captain Gilbertson, B Company's commander, Lieutenant Crane and the medical officer, Captain Barrett.

"Yes, by God," the colonel was saying, "we've made quite a battalion of them. They'll acquit themselves well, I think." He felt mellow and gratified and wanted to say something that would please them. "Well!" he ended, "I hand-picked my officers and I have yet to regret a single choice I made."

The responses to this testimonial were subdued but various. Captain Stamp, in his early twenties; boyish, fresh-faced, with small arrogant lips, smiled briefly and murmured in his throat. The men of the battalion called him the Boy Bastard. Captain Barrett's bland cynical features remained as before, but he lowered his lids over his soft eyes for a few seconds. Captain Gilbertson, a slightly-built man in his late thirties, pale-complexioned, with fair crinkly hair, a long, pointed chin and rather anxious grey eyes, smiled gently and said: "Why, thank you, Orme!" He glanced sideways and grimaced briefly with his lips at Crane, who, however, was regarding the colonel intently. None of them there had ever seen Major Pomfret with any expression but that he was wearing at the moment. He was short, deep-chested, half-bald. But for the rest of his features being in keeping with their size and thickness you would have thought that his lips were pouting. He had a sweeping, broad forehead that hung like a cliff over round, stony eyes. It was a lowering, unattractive face, without spirit, betraying nothing. The men hated him for his toneless, aloof manner of address; his humourless devotion to duty. They called him the Animal.

Captain Barrett smiled softly, a little slyly and remarked:

"I believe you'd have hand-picked the men too if you'd been given the chance, Orme."

The colonel chose to accept the remark quite seriously, for he replied:

"I wish it had been possible. Believe me, we got some sorry-looking specimens when I first began to form this battalion." He turned to Pomfret. "Eh, John?"

Pomfret nodded. "Not the best material, some of them," he agreed.

41

"Wouldn't I know what some of them are like?" drawled Barrett. "I have to listen to the same tales every day of the week on sick parade. Some of these fellows have got malingering down to a fine art."

Crane laughed. "They wouldn't get much change from you, Basil!"

Captain Gilbertson interposed by saying to Barrett in a challenging tone:

"Just what percentage of the men who report sick would you say are malingering, Basil?"

Barrett shrugged indifferently: "Fifty per cent. The two main ills in this battalion are drunkenness and the failure to take ordinary decent care of their bodies. I had a case of tinea the other morning. Worst I've ever seen. I sent him straight off to hospital. He'd let it go until his toes were almost unrecognisable. Deliberately, I should say, knowing the man."

"Riff-raff!" muttered Crane.

"For a lot of them," continued Barrett, in the manner of one who had been asked for a judgment, "this war's the best thing that could have happened. A bit of hard discipline is damn good medicine."

The colonel downed the last of his whisky and told them briskly:

"Well, they've had that! And Basil's right. The other day on battalion parade, as I was looking them over, I thought: 'By God, we've done quite a job with you.'" He ganced at Barrett and added: "In spite of everything."

Gilbertson betrayed his feeling by asking, more satirically than he had intended:

"Aren't we to give the men any credit? After all, they have given us their best."

"It's not so much what they give," remarked Pomfret. "It's what you can drag out of them."

"I can't have that!" Gilbertson retorted impulsively.

He glanced around the others, acutely aware that all he had provoked was a polite lack of sympathy. He suddenly noticed the barman in his white coat standing on his own at the deserted end of the bar and the thought crossed his mind that perhaps the barman could overhear their conversation. The man's face was blank, averted; but for the first time Henry Gilbertson was aware of him as a human being. He was one of the human beings they were discussing. Henry Gilbertson felt a mild sense of shame. He had a desire for solitude. He was sure that this night of departure for the desert meant deeper things to him than it did to the others. He also remembered the half-written letter to his wife back in his tent. He finished his drink, said "I've a few things to do," and left the mess.

Outside in the darkness he could hear the sound of voices

singing at a distance. He began to walk along the road towards the officers' lines. A sense of being at odds with the world in general was nagging him. Damn it! This war was nothing but a gentlemanly adventure to his friends back there in the mess. To him it was something tremendous, urgent and just.

Henry Gilbertson's family was as wealthy as Fitzroy's or Crane's. Sixty years ago his grandparents had founded a newspaper; now Henry's father controlled one of Australia's great and influential dailies. Henry's grandmother still lived: to this day a shrewd, tolerant old woman of iron-clad principles and unbreakable will. Her insight, her constant liberality of thought had been one of the moving influences in Henry's life. It had been she who insisted on Henry becoming the paper's literary editor. To Henry's father a newspaper meant only circulation. It was to the magnificent old lady that Henry had always turned to thresh out his problems, to arrive at the meaning of many things. Together they had shared much of the bewilderment of the thirties; together contemplated its procession of betrayals. Henry was an anti-Fascist: this was his sole reason for being in the army. In this he considered he stood apart from his brother officers. Had not some of them regretted in his hearing that they weren't the allies of the Nazis against Russia? Where was he to find someone who felt the same about the war as he did?

Henry felt lonely and discouraged. He thought bitterly about his men, with whom he had striven to find common ground. To win their liking and respect had seemed essential, but his first efforts appeared only to surprise them. They had obviously not expected this sort of an officer. They were amused and suspicious for the most part. Some of them, in fact, seemed to regard him as a natural enemy. Their motives for joining the army were not always admirable, either—poor devils! Hard times, disillusion, boredom, adventure: these were some of the things that had driven them to become soldiers. They had come to the army almost as if it were a refuge from a life they wanted to flee. They were certainly more to be pitied than despised. There was no avoiding this fact, he told himself: to the men the officers were a separate and hostile class and he, Henry Gilbertson, was one of that class.

*   *   *

Dick and Andy left the fug of the tent together and sought the "rose-bowl" at the end of the B Company lines. The cold air smote their fume-laden heads, causing their feet to stumble and the stars to whirl. Singing softly between hiccoughs, Andy steadied himself against his friend as he relieved himself. A figure passed them in the darkness.

"Here it is, sport!" cried Andy.

"Good night, lads!" the figure hailed them.

43

"Who's that?" asked Andy.

"Gilbertson," Dick told him.

"Best bloody officer in this battalion. Good luck to you, Gilby!"

"Good luck, boys!" Henry's voice came back to them faintly out of the darkness.

"Bugger the officers," said Dick grumpily. "Bugger the lot of them. They're only here to drive us to the slaughter."

"Don't talk like that," said Andy, suddenly regaining sobriety. "You might be an officer yourself some day. This is going to be a terrible long war. Make a career of it. I tell you, it's the smart thing to make a good soldier of yourself."

"You should talk!" jibed Dick. "Walking off parades!"

"All right—you just watch me from now on." Andy stopped swaying. For a few seconds he was silent. When he spoke again his voice was intense. "I'm going to be the best bloody infantry-man that ever shouldered a rifle. Ah, I know! You think it's the drink talking."

The big man raised his arm and delivered a soft, trenchant vow to the stars:

"For once in my life I'm going to do something thoroughly."

*   *   *

At three o'clock in the morning the Second X Battalion moved swiftly and silently from its camp. For five miles the road rang with the tramp of boots. At the railway a troop-train awaited them.

It was a beautiful night. The moon came out late. It shone impartially on desert, city and sea. The Second X was only a small part of a vast exodus of men, weapons and supplies from the haven of the camps. That night many thousands of soldiers were herded into these darkened trains. Train-load after train-load crawled slowly across the face of the land.

BOOK TWO

THE FORTRESS

"GOOD morning, rats! And how are my self-supporting prisoners this morning?"

The voice was flippant, contemptuous and well modulated. It came from a large field radio that had once been the property of a fire-eating Italian general. It was the voice of Haw Haw the English traitor, talking from somewhere in Europe. It went on, to mock gently:

"And how's your air force? Oh, I forgot! You haven't got one, have you? Never mind, we'll send you some planes this morning. . . ."

The radio was installed in a niche that had been cut into the wall of a deep, spacious dug-out, the roof and walls of which were supported by rough lengths of timber. Besides the radio the dug-out contained a battered canvas stretcher, a large wooden box and, piled in one corner, several odds and ends of military gear. The men who listened to the voice of Haw Haw in the dug-out were Henry Gilbertson and about a dozen of the rank and file of his company. They listened silently and grimly, but were never far from smiling. When Haw Haw promised them "some planes" they looked at each other and grimaced. Though everything else he told them was lies, when he made this promise he kept it.

About ten minutes later they had emerged from the dug-out and were dispersing in several directions.

Six Platoon headquarters were situated in the side of a shallow wadi that meandered down a slight incline from the flat surface of the desert: another such dug-out as Henry Gilbertson's with a large pit immediately above it from which Crane could sweep the desert with his binoculars. A few yards ahead of Crane's headquarters was a web-like system of concreted weapon pits and narrow communication trenches—the work of the Italians.

It was an ordinary Libyan day, furnace-hot, with a glare that was like a knife across the eyes. Striking the stone-littered surface of the desert the light quivered vaporously. The sky was the colour of smoke. It was motionless. The sun was seen through it like a coin in a dim pool.

But there was life in that sky.

Six Platoon sat in their pits. They were not the men who, attired correctly and uniformly, had marched around the roads of Palestine or stalked the streets of Jerusalem and Tel Aviv in quest of adventures. Their shorts were bleached to a dirty yellow and their boots were worn to whiteness by the sand.

Gone was the slouch hat; in its place they wore the round steel helmet, painted yellow. Those who had discarded their shirts showed skins as brown as the wood in the butts of their rifles. Their eyes were keener, their faces leaner, their lips drawn finer.

For the umpteenth time, Dooley Franks wiped an oily rag over the Bren gun and covered it carefully with an empty sandbag, and for the thousandth time Tommy Collins, his "Number 2," checked the magazines. Sergeant Lucas glanced approvingly along his Italian Breda machine-gun. Corporal Percy Gribble fingered a boil on his neck. Andy Cain amused himself with a chameleon he kept on the end of a string. Dick Brett shovelled some fallen sand out of a pit. The whole platoon busied itself in a casual sort of fashion. Then, with one accord, they stopped and looked upwards.

There was a faint pulsing in the sky.

"Here the bastards come!" said Dooley.

The pulsing became a trembling, the trembling became a hum.

Then suddenly the noise of the dive-bombers burst out of the blue like a snarl.

"Here they are!" cried Dick, and pointed to the east.

They came out of the sun, black and evil-looking. Stukas. Their curiously-shaped wings were like those of hawks, poised to drop on their prey. There were two flights of them. One flight peeled off, dwindling in the direction of the invisible town.

The world became all noise. Around them the Bofors guns coughed out a torrent of explosions and the sky flowered with little white pom-poms of smoke. Farther back the heavy anti-aircraft brayed hideously upwards.

One by one the black shapes came earthwards, as if they hurtled down a gigantic slide. The shrieks of their downward passage pierced the sound of exploding bombs. The earth around the Australians vomited upwards in great black clouds.

The air became a fog of yellow dust and black smoke and through the frightful din came faintly the cries of men. Tortured ears rejected the concussions and grew dulled, hearing the bombing as muffled convulsions of the earth.

Then, as suddenly as it began, the raid ceased. The anti-aircraft fire dwindled to isolated bangs. The noise of the Stukas grew fainter and fainter in the distance. Human voices carried through the drifting smoke. One of the voices called, high-pitched and urgent:

"Stretcher-bearer!"

Forms came running through the haze.

"You all right, Dick?" Andy called.

"I'm all right," said a dazed Dick. But echoes of the bombing still thundered in his ears.

"They got a couple from Three Section."

Gradually the smoke was clearing.

Six Platoon came out of their pits to discover who were their two latest casualties. Dick clambered across the parapet and made towards the wadi where men were already gathered. Leaping across a trench, he noticed a figure huddled against its side. For a moment he thought it to be a corpse; but it was unmarked and a faint, regular trembling ran through it.

"Who's that?" he called.

The figure raised its head slowly. Percy Gribble's chalk-white face stared up at him dimly. The lips moved but said nothing. Dick turned and hurried away. He felt as though in seeing what he had, he was guilty of something shameful.

The two dead men had been placed on stretchers. Neither of them was well-known to Dick. One was a small grey man approaching middle age who had joined the battalion only a few days before it left Palestine. His remains formed an unnatural heap beneath a blanket through which the blood oozed. The other lay uncovered, his eyes looking up sightlessly to the sky. None of Six Platoon had known him very well either. He had been a big, fair, smiling young fellow, always pleasant, but shy. All they knew about him was that he had been a motor mechanic and had a young wife to whom he wrote every day. He was not marked, but his clothes hung from him in a thousand small tatters where the blast had ripped across his body.

Watched by the men of Six Platoon, the stretcher-bearers bore the dead men slowly down the wadi. Andy Cain gazed expressionlessly after them.

"That's that," he said.

The date was April, nineteen hundred and forty-one.

The place was Tobruk.

7

THE Second X Battalion's journey had taken them far from their camp in Palestine. The first stage ended at El Kantara on the Suez Canal. Here, late at night, they crossed the Canal and got aboard an Egyptian train. By morning they found themselves traversing the lush green maze of the Nile Valley.

The battalion was in an hilarious mood. Whenever the train stopped they put their heads out of windows and shouted at nearby Arabs or jumped down beside the train and gave vent to their feelings by chasing or tormenting the ragged men and boys who gathered round selling grapes and water-melons. As far as Dick could see, the land stretched flatly, an endless pattern of crops and plantations, interlaced with irrigation ditches. Once again, he was thrilled by the actuality of it: the date palms, the hot, dusty villages, the blind ox on the water wheel, the minaret of some distant mosque.

The next stage of their journey ended at Mersa Matruh, near the Egyptian border. They spent two weeks in this colourless flat town on the dazzling white sandstone shore. Under the glare of the sun this whiteness was painful to the eyes, making with the sea a contrast that was amazing and beautiful. The Mediterranean spread out, translucent green at first, then deepening to intense blue, limpid and laced with fragile shadows, lovely as a butterfly's wing.

In a bomb-blasted building along the sea-front, Henry Gilbertson established B Company Headquarters, and his three platoons dug in among the white sandhills nearby. He allowed his company to take it easy while they could. The shores became dotted with the naked, browned bodies of men, swimming and basking. One of the best and keenest swimmers of Six Platoon was Dick, who ventured farther and farther out into the harbour as the days went by. He burnt a deep brown and loved to feel the strength of his body as it glided through the water. A photo he sent home to his mother from Mersa Matruh showed a dark-skinned young fellow with a ragged moustache and a good deal more flesh and muscle than the one who had left Australia a few months earlier.

They were moonlit nights, and every night the Nazi bombers flew over and raided the town. In time the troops came to recognise the nagging snarl of their engines. On their third night in Mersa Matruh the heaviest of these raids occurred.

The town lay transformed in the moonlight, its harsh lines softened, the hot winds cooled. Bomb-torn, bullet-pocked buildings glowed pale and insubstantial.

Six Platoon had sat out late on the sandhills drinking the contents of several cases of stolen beer. Dooley and Tommy had appeared lugging them in a wheelbarrow just on dusk and divided up their contents, refusing to give any information beyond that the beer came from officers' stores. The platoon pounced on it gleefully and Dooley and Tommy swaggered under their praise. They were still carousing out in the moonlight when the bombers arrived overhead.

From the rim of a vast perimeter searchlight beams suddenly swung upwards like gigantic feelers, stiffly exploring the sky. The watchers on the sandhills began to argue over the number of planes.

"There's only three, I tell you."

"Six of 'em at least! Where do you get this three business?"

"Look! There's one caught in the lights!"

Sure enough, there at the top of one of the beams was a

long, slow-moving grey shape. Several other beams spun swiftly across the sky trapping the bomber in a criss-cross of light.

Now the anti-aircraft roared into life, savagely and resentfully, and the bomber seemed to be traversing a maze of bright, momentary eruptions as the shells burst around it.

"What shooting! They're nowhere near him," someone cried disgustedly.

The next moment the bomber began to glow amidships and lose height. The glow became a trailer of yellow flame and the stricken plane fled at an acute angle down the beam of the searchlight, then disappeared. There were a few seconds in which the whole world seemed to pause. Then in the distance was a roar and a great flash of orange light. Slowly it dimmed to a glow on the horizon.

Half a mile away a stick of bombs hit the earth with a series of gigantic thuds. On the first impact Percy Gribble's body dived down the sandhill and disappeared headlong into a communication trench, and above the sound of the bombs could be heard a ringing, scornful laugh from Andy Cain.

"She's right, Perce!" someone called. "They're bombing the other side of town."

"Come out and see the show, Perce!"

Gribble's head and shoulders reappeared. He smiled from drawn lips and said shakily:

"Better to be safe than sorry. I haven't got the hang of these bombs yet."

Suddenly the whole place glowed red as one of the raiders dropped a parachute flare. It floated earthwards slowly like a huge, burning star, illuminating the town so that it was seen lurid, fantastic and beautiful, like a glimpse into some tormented vision.

Then the bombs thundered down.

Walls disintegrated and their fragments flew. The ground rocked. A solid wall of screaming air flattened their bodies and stretched them prone on the ground, as high explosive tore buildings up like paper, tossing the rubble skywards.

The raid lasted half an hour all told. When they finally rose to their feet to look about them, the building that housed B Company Headquarters had disappeared. In its place stood a pile of rubble.

Out of the smoke and dust appeared a ragged, grimy Lucas.

"Stay where you are, Six Platoon, Company Headquarters was hit. There's nothing you can do."

"Any casualties?"

"Company sar major's dead. Gilby and I copped the blast."

Lucas came and sat down by them. He was dazed and weary but spoke with all his old mockery and aplomb. He held out a tattered sleeve.

"My last decent shirt!"

"Like a beer, Frank?"

Lucas glared his opinion of what seemed a miserable joke.

A bottle appeared under his nose. He sniffed it, took it and tried it with his lips.

"Christ!" he said reverently.

*   *   *

They buried the company sergeant major in the war cemetery of Mersa Matruh. The battalion's first fatality became one more white wooden cross among a hundred or so others: victims of bombing, strafing, or the garrison's own mines. There was a story about the minefields that lay around the deep defences of the town. An engineer officer and the only map on which the minefields were marked both went sky-high on a mine one day. So now a soldier was safe only when traversing well-known tracks in that dreary, flat, dust-clouded waste. They were dangerous, hastily-made mines, treacherous and unpredictable. The men who manned the gun-posts behind the minefields often watched three or four of them explode of their own accord.

Finally, late one afternoon, Dick ventured to swim right across the harbour. He could have had a calmer day, but there was not much time left now, for it was obvious that a movement was afoot for the battalion.

Two hundred yards out he was gliding up and down the slopes of a rhythmic swell. There was only slight danger, for he was a splendid swimmer and the Mediterranean was reputed to be without sharks. Nevertheless he felt a small venturesome tingle. To feel without fear always elated him.

Half a mile out he looked back. The sea-front had dwindled, blurred, become attractive and unfamiliar; the shattered buildings looked whole. Rising waves blotted out the sight of them all but the mosque, which seemed to be riding away from him on a crest.

Near the point he was making for he encountered a rocky islet about ten yards long and, watching his chance in between waves, clambered ashore on it. He stood looking back at the dim shore-line of the town, trying to pick out a few familiar points. Away to the west the shore deteriorated into dirty brown salt-bush flats. The large humps that dotted it he guessed to be camouflage nets covering twenty-five pounder guns. The whole shore, even from where he stood, seethed with a remote activity. Along an unseen road moved an endless belt of tiny black dots—vehicles. There must be about twenty thousand troops in this place, he thought. Something was on all right. But what? Fighting of some sort. Skirmishing, hit and run stuff out in the desert probably. Would it be against Hun or Italian, or both? Into this barren, remote place the destinies of war had crammed hordes of men, living like rabbits in dug-outs and pits, or like rats in the ruins of the town—waiting to be taken to some tumultuous feast of death and violence.

His attention was distracted from the shore-line by a strange-looking heap that lay on a sloping rock, stirring idly as the waves lapped it. He rose and went over to see what it was.

He found himself looking down at a hollowed, half-rotted corpse, without head, legs, or arms: a bony shell with sea-whitened tatters of flesh clinging here and there. The remnants of a tunic hung on the ribs. On the breast of this Dick made out a swastika and the insignia of the German Luftwaffe.

Some Nazi airman, shot down in the sea and washed up here on the shores of an enemy garrison. A sea-eaten, battered, anonymous thing. It was the first corpse he had ever seen and he was stirred deeply. He felt under some strange compulsion to imagine what this corpse had been in the days of its life. The discovery had infected his imagination. He became vividly aware of the picture it presented. Naked on a rock in the Mediterranean, he was seeing death for the first time in the shape of a hollowed-out corpse.

The wind seemed to blow through his turbulent thoughts. Here were the remains of a Nazi. Here was something that had once been a boy. What sort of world had it been born into? It was easy for him to imagine this. A crippled, humbled, defeated country. A confused, angry, poverty-shadowed world. A youth without certitude—one of the legion of the betrayed. Awaiting a miracle, for that seemed all that was left to hope for. . . . So Hitler. The fierce hysteria of the great rallies. Sieg Heil! Blood and Iron. The Master Race. Our Fuehrer. Sieg Heil! To-morrow the world is ours. Certitude at last. Something to believe in. Sieg Heil! Look, I am flying one of my Fuehrer's planes across the earth and below me is nothing but the evidence of our triumph. The dead lie in battalions, the living obey us. Soon it shall be like this over all the earth. . . .

Yes, it could have been something like that. Perhaps he had been thinking such thoughts the moment before he died. Sitting there creating a past for a corpse gave Dick a feeling of omniscience. It was when he began to multiply his vision that his imagination faltered. He could not see millions of men exactly the same. Men and their motives differed, but certain enormous facts caused them to act similarly in a mass. Suddenly he realised that he did not really know what fascism was. He only hated it because its results were frightful. The depth of his ignorance left him with a bitter, vague anger. What little assurance he had built for himself over the past few months tumbled away, leaving him lonely and afraid.

He began to search for something in himself that he could be certain of; something he could always hold up in the face of despair. What could it be? Courage! The courage to accept any and every future experience. He wanted to be quit of this rock at once, as though he could leave his thoughts along with it.

He rose, dived into the next wave, and struck out shorewards. Night was coming on. The waves were darkening. In their troughs it was as though night were already upon them. The shore was nearly invisible now but he swam on strongly. He felt hardened and defiant. He saw himself as a lonely atom caught between the immensity of sea and sky, advancing steadily into the oncoming night.

An atom of nothing but courage. . . .

*   *   *

When he reached the shore and clambered up a sandhill it was quite dark. Standing at the top of it was Lucas.

"How was Cyprus?" asked Lucas.

"Didn't quite reach it," said the new Dick.

"Would you mind covering your nakedness and reporting to me as soon as possible? Mr. Crane and I would like to consult you about a big move that the battalion is making tomorrow."

Turning to go, Lucas found his arm grabbed and held. He faced about again, calm and amused.

"So it's on at last, is it? Well, I've got something to say to you. If you want trouble, Lucas, I'm going to give it to you. I've been learning a few points from Dooley. Give me a go and I'll be as good a soldier as anyone in this company. But get this anyway—I've had you and your behaviour up till now. What's it to be?"

"What's it to be? O.K., Dick, me boy! I see you've grown into a man. Now get your pants on, mate, and come to Platoon Headquarters. Kenneth Crane, Esquire, desires some words with his platoon."

Lucas chuckled and walked away. Once again he had left Dick without a reply.

*   *   *

Between the Kenneth Crane who had addressed Six Platoon the morning after the troopship had been bombed and the man who spoke to them now as they sat on a sand dune around his headquarters there were certain differences. He no longer felt the need for condescension or familiarity, or if he did, he did not bother with them. They just didn't work. What also didn't work were his moments of harsh scorn, when his "riff-raff" perceived that the basis of his attitude to them was plain contempt. Towards the end of their training, Six Platoon had become almost a burden to him. The first flush of novelty had worn off his command; his platoon was neither servile, loyal, nor admiring. They were not half as cloddish or dull as he had believed. Some of them were very shrewd, some had wit. He often had the feeling they were laughing at him, as though they found his personality ridiculous. Yet he had overheard them talking tolerantly, even fondly, of that old woman Henry Gilbertson, who was getting more tedious every day with his chatterings about the "anti-fascist cause." Crane had been conscious for some time now of unhappiness and discontent. Being an officer of the Second X Battalion had somehow lost much of its savour. He contrasted his present frame of mind rather glumly with the earlier days of his lieutenancy. The men had admired him in those days; admired his strength, his body, his reputation as an athlete, the power of the name of Crane. It might have been said that in some ways they had feared him. His school-boyish, almost feudal visions of himself in the role of heroic young manhood (a role conceivable only for one of his own background) and his zealous henchmen—the men of Six Platoon—had seemed to possess some foundation at that time. Now such visions seemed ludicrous against their sly scepticism and there was an insidious sort of a feeling that his "henchmen" often found him tedious. There were signs of the latter now. They were there because it was compulsory to be there; they would look at him with a semblance of attention. But what would they be thinking? His leadership they accepted and mocked at behind his back. Yet he could not drive them. They considered they had rights that forbade that. What rights did they deserve really? These "rights!"—all they meant was that these men were to a certain extent immune from punishment for their ignorance and stupidity. He remembered it as the stupidity that allowed them as civilians to abandon tools and machines and say: "These will not be used again unless certain demands are met." How many times had he heard his father rail against this? . . . "This damned flabby humanitarian tolerance! This talk about 'rights' as an excuse to loaf. We're breeding a nation of socialist milk-sops!" As if the State were of less importance than their own miserable desire for a few more shillings in their pay or a hankering after a new washroom! Their consciousness as a class seemed scarcely tolerable. This ugly, amorphous, but necessary mass! Just as you needed dirt on which to build a marble palace, so you needed men like these to build a state; so you needed them in an army as a vast, mindless tide at the front of which men like himself could reach their full heroic stature. It struck him that perhaps their very necessity was their strength, and that sometimes they realised it and made use of it. Then, it followed, there should be greater powers of compulsion over them. For the first time he found himself disliking them emotionally. As he watched them settling down on the dune half-remembered words crossed his mind. Where had he heard them? ... "The dark beauty of violence. . . ."

Never before had he been so affected by these words or his dislike of the men he commanded.

*　　　*　　　*

"Quiet," said Lucas, then, as their murmuring continued: "Shut up!"

"Shut up yourself," drawled Dooley.

Andy Cain, at the front, turned and spoke to them:

"Gentlemen, if you please! Can't you perceive that our sergeant desires silence?"

There was a chorus of ironical laughs.

"Shut up!"

Lieutenant Crane's voice silenced them like the crack of a whip. The elation over tomorrow's move, which had caused their chatter, disappeared and into their silence came something tense. There was now too much silence. Then the atmosphere relaxed. One or two stirred, cleared their throats. Another coughed. But a collective thought was alive and clear among them: "This man is only temporary . . . the war won't last forever. . . ."

Lieutenant Crane began to speak:

"Tomorrow this unit moves closer to the enemy. . . ."

Half an hour later Six Platoon clambered back to their dug-outs in the dunes, and Lieutenant Crane went the other way towards Company Headquarters. He had told them nothing they did not already know, important as it was; had given admonitions heard a thousand times before. He had told them everything but the one thing they wanted to know: where they were going.

Having had his first headquarters blown down about his ears, Henry Gilbertson had moved into a nearby building that had survived the blast. When Crane entered he was sitting at a table studying a map by the light of a large petrol lamp. The room was otherwise bare.

"Well, Ken. Six Platoon all happy?"

"Happy enough. They're glad to be leaving this hole, anyway."

"They might be longing for it before they're much older."

Crane sighed a little tiredly. "A dose of action will do them good. The farther we've got from Palestine the more exasperating they've become."

Henry took his pipe from his mouth and studied the other a few silent seconds, then stated:

"You don't like your men as much as you used to."

"Whereas you like them more than you used to?"

"I suppose so. But this is how I see it. We're stuck with them and they with us. We've just got to get on together."

"Not at the risk of losing one's position with them."

"You can't hope to maintain your position with them if you don't yield here and there, Ken. We're all facing the greatest reality together—I mean death. They're getting less and less patient of any of the barriers and distinctions that prevailed at home. Even the attitude you adopted with them in camp has got to be relaxed. They're necessary for the job we've got to do, and they know it."

"The job we've got to do! What do they know about that, even? Did any of them join up with clear minds?"

"Did any of us have clear minds in 1940?"

"Men in our position know what to do when war breaks out, I hope."

"I'll let that pass. It's a little too pompous for me. What I'm trying to say is that I think the world's changing. When the war's over a lot of them will be wanting their price for winning it."

"Their price? Won't it be enough that their country's been saved?"

"Their country, Ken—or ours? I've overheard them asking that. Some of these fellows were short of a feed for years before they joined up. They'll be asking what was the use of saving the country if life can't give them better than that when they get home."

"Look, Henry—a lot of what you say is perfectly sincere, I know. But we can't compromise too far with the lower classes, in war or peace. If we do, they'll destroy us!"

Kenneth Crane had risen from the chair on which he had seated himself. He leant over the table towards Henry, his eyes alarmed, his voice tense with conviction. Henry took some time pondering this last outburst:

"If they destroy us, Ken, it will be because we deserve to be destroyed. Because we're no longer necessary."

This shook Crane, even coming from a notorious crank like Henry Gilbertson. Henry, shrewd enough to perceive that their argument had reached a minor sort of a crisis, decided to drop it:

"What a time to argue over class distinctions! Sorry, Ken." He slid a sheet of paper across to Kenneth Crane. "Let's talk about Dooley Franks. All I have here is this major's written account. What really happened?"

"Probably everything the major's written, if I know Franks. However, I've had a talk with Lucas and Gribble—Franks's section corporal."

"They were there?"

"Gribble was."

57

"What's the story?"

"To begin with, they were geligniting fish, which is against orders. This major appeared on the scene and told them to cease forthwith. Franks, it seems, told him to mind his own bloody business, that they were Australians and no concern of any stray officer of the British army."

Henry grinned: "Or words to that effect?"

"Yes. You can imagine the sort of embellishments that a man like Franks would provide. Well, the major demanded to know their names and numbers. Franks demanded to see the major's pay-book and identification first."

"Did he?" Henry hooted with laughter. "He was quite within his rights, you know. After they caught those two Huns masquerading as Poles the Divisional Commander laid it down that all ranks had to identify themselves on demand."

"Well, the major wouldn't. Franks promptly denounced him as a spy, pushed him into the sea and hit him in the face with a dead fish as he rose to the surface. The others pelted him with fish and stones. He had to swim a hundred yards along the shore to escape them. Is that the major's story?"

"More or less. He doesn't put it quite so humorously as you. Who else was there?"

"Cain, Perkins, Brett, Gribble, Collins. By the way, Gribble tells me he tried to restrain them, and took no part in the pelting. He asked me to make this clear, which I promised to do."

"Gribble? That's the man who still polishes his boots."

Crane took the remark as ridicule:

"He's got a sense of responsibility. A cut above most of the others, I'm glad to say."

Henry looked down at his own boots, which the sand had worn to the colour of blotting-paper, and grimaced.

"I wanted," said Crane, "to put in a word for him before you do whatever you decide."

"Ken—I'm going to do precisely nothing."

"Nothing! But—but this is a serious complaint from a major of the British army!"

"And I am a captain of the Australian army and tomorrow my company goes to Benghazi. What am I to do between now and tomorrow morning? Arrange to have six good men court-martialled and left behind? Franks is the best Bren gunner in this battalion. He handles a Bren as if it were a pistol. Just now that's more important to me than all the majors in the British army." He tapped the sheet of paper with airy contempt. "I never saw this. Due to the sar major's death and the total destruction of Company Headquarters—not to mention the fact of having been knocked cock-eyed myself—it was overlooked. Thank God Orme doesn't know about it! And don't you dare mention it to him!"

He rose, patted Kenneth Crane's shoulder, and said: "Come over to my doover and share the last of my whisky."

He put it down to Kenneth Crane's credit that he never brought the matter up again.

Henry turned his lamp low and they passed out into a clear, starry night, wherein a placid moon shone. The dunes where Six Platoon lived were far from placid, however. The voices of Tommy Collins and Dooley Franks were raised in hilarious abuse.

For some minutes the air was torrid with a creditable range of soldier obscenity. Then Dooley's voice took on a mocking falsetto:

"Private Collins!"

"Sir!"

"Kindly endeavour to restrain yourself, Private Collins. For the first time in your life here is a chance to do something, er—decent—for your country, Private Collins."

"Yes, sir!"

"That's me," said Kenneth Crane.

Henry grinned and held a detaining hand on the other's arm:

"Let's listen for a minute. We might hear something interesting."

". . . remember, Private Collins, you are riff-raff!"

"Yes, sir. Get fogged, sir!"

"Private Collins! Restrain yourself!"

The pantomime suddenly changed.

"Please, sir?" Tommy's voice took on a sub-human servility.

"Yes, Corporal Gribble?"

"Can I wash your socks, sir?"

"Certainly, Corporal!"

"Oh, sir! And can I wash your dirty underpants, too?"

"Yes, Corporal!"

"Oh, sir!" cried Tommy, raucously ecstatic.

Henry laughed quietly and asked:

"Is this authentic, Ken?"

"Certainly not!"

Andy Cain's voice broke in upon the performance, dry and malicious:

"Hey, you bastards! Please show a little more respect for your section leader."

"Wait till Chips comes back. He'll get section leader!" Half to itself, and as an afterthought, the voice added: "The little bastard!"

"Gentlemen!" chided Andy. "You have no right to refer to the corporal in such terms. He's only trying to save the Empire. And, remember, he's a banker."

"He's a bloody tycoon!" This was Dick. "Banks everywhere!" After a few seconds, he too added: "And he's a bastard!"

"There you are, Andy. Dick reckons he's a bastard too."

"Who, Brett? He wouldn't know."

"You want a fight, Cain?"

"Yes!"

The figures of Dick and Andy appeared on the moon-whitened dune, swaying hilariously in mock battle, crowing with shrill laughter. They rolled out of sight into a trench.

The two officers continued walking.

"They're drunk!" said Crane.

"I should imagine so. Where the devil do they get the grog?" Crane threw up his hands, half in humour, half in despair.

"God help them!"

Henry surveyed the stars.

"God help us all," he said.

*   *   *

At dawn the battalion moved out. Their transport converged on to the narrow tarred road, making a long procession: snub-nosed little trucks with enormous wheels that the troops called desert buggies; American utilities stripped of their canvas roofs; towering thirty-hundredweights; snarling motor cycles; all painted a drab yellow that the sun had turned to a near white.

The colonel stood beside his own truck which was drawn to the side of the road, and watched them go past. It was still half dark. In the east the sky was slowly being swamped with ruddy gold. It was chilly. The sound of the transport crawling along in low gear seemed curiously muted. The men who sat in the trucks huddled in greatcoats appeared in the dim morning as anonymous figures. They sat silently, swaying at times to the movement of the trucks. They seemed all the same. Just beyond the spot where the colonel stood there was a steep rise, and as each truck-load topped it he saw for an instant the dark shapes of many heads and shoulders; of profiles beneath the rims of steel helmets.

At this moment the colonel was seeing his battalion in a new and disturbing light. For some reason, the sight of the convoy creeping past in the early dawn had given him a perception of their enormous strength, and some foreknowledge of the destruction or defiance of which they would be capable. Under his command these men had been turned from a mass of raw civilians into a formidable machine. That he controlled the machine should have lent his thoughts at this moment the flush of triumphant pride. It was extraordinary but true that the thoughts of Colonel Fitzroy, whose birthright was to always be at the head of things, were neither confident nor proud. He was aware that the men had singled out his most evident weakness and labelled him Groggy Orme. He knew he was unpopular with them. That fact meant little to him. What dismayed him was the fact that some of them at least did not respect him. A few mornings ago he had been suffering with a hang-over after a night at a British mess nearby. A hang-over always left him at his worst: touchy, unable to concentrate, far too aware of himself and, because of it, thinking he detected mockery in every word or look directed at him. That morning he had been alert enough to perceive what was going on around him. There seemed to be some unspoken but persuasive intelligence at Battalion Headquarters that the colonel was "out of action" for the time being. He found that matters which came to him as part of the routine went to Pomfret by some silent conspiracy. In fact, he was left remarkably alone. When this struck him he began to think back and he came to the conclusion that it had always been so. On one of his "days" the battalion discarded him and went along without him. Immediately he made the discovery he tried to impose his presence everywhere at once; the orderly room hummed with men carrying out orders. But half an hour of it had run him down. Pomfret could not be shaken out of his machine-like efficiency and the high-pitched roar of the sergeant major rang phrenetically through his tortured nerves. He could not concentrate; decisions evaded him. Finally he gave up and left them to it. The same night he had passed by a parked truck and heard his own nickname spoken from the other side of it. "The Animal runs this battalion," a voice asserted. "Groggy stands around and plays the colonel, but the Animal runs the show. Groggy's a watchercallit—a figurehead." The colonel had walked away then. A figurehead!

Self-examination was not one of the colonel's habits. However, the powerful impression that his battalion had made upon him at this dawn departure, coming on top of these other somewhat vexing incidents, had forced him into it. He felt uneasy and depressed. This was the first time he had ever doubted his ability to be the commander of these men. Perhaps, he told himself, it was due to the totally new impression they had made on him. But he knew this was not the answer. His depression, his cold sense of being inadequate, had its roots in several things: in the discovery that the whole battalion, from Pomfret down, accepted and despised his weakness with the whisky bottle; the echo in his mind of that voice coming out of the darkness like the judgment of the ranks: "Groggy's a figurehead;" the plaguey insistence in his thoughts of a question: how would he have got on but for Pomfret, that glum, soulless model of efficiency?

The last vehicle of the column came past. A provost corporal on a motor bike swung his machine alongside the colonel's utility and saluted:

"All correct, sir!"

The colonel returned the salute. He walked over to his truck, got in beside the driver and ordered him to start up.

The provost rode off, rapidly overtaking the column. As he came abreast of one of Six Platoon's trucks Dooley's head poked out of the back and cried:

"Greasy copper!"

Tommy's head now appeared next to Dooley's:

"Provost bastard! Hope yer get killed!"

The provost smiled a little grimly, a little knowingly, at the familiar demonstration of hate, and sped past.

As the morning passed the sun climbed higher, blazing down on the surface of the desert, from which rose strange waverings of vapour to delude and harass the eyes.

8

ON January the twenty-second, 1941, an Australian digger hung his hat from the flagstaff of the Italian garrison of Tobruk. In a day and a quarter the Sixth Division had overrun the greatest fortress in Mussolini's Cyrenaica, taking prisoner twenty-five thousand of his soldiers. By early February the division had conquered the rest of Cyrenaica and occupied Benghazi. A few weeks later they were relieved by the Ninth Division. In a nameless spot in the desert south of Benghazi, the Second X took over from a battalion of the Sixth.

Henry Gilbertson led his company in to their new positions and was greeted by a rearguard of a lieutenant and six men. While the lieutenant conferred with Henry the six men of the rearguard showed the platoons the dug-outs they were to occupy and the weapon pits they were to man.

It was a pitch-dark night. The rearguard were kept answering questions well into the night: what the water supply was like; what sort of rations were they getting; where was the enemy; what were the "furphies;" what "lurks" there were, if any, in such a God-forsaken spot. The rearguard seemed rather surprised to find that B Company knew all about Bren guns, hand grenades, minefields, Vickers guns, Boys rifles, two-pounders, tommy-guns and mortars. One of them explained to Six Platoon:

"We thought you would be the same as the Ninth Divvy mob that took over from the Second N along the ridge there the other night. Cripes!" he recalled incredulously, "they knew

62

how to fire a rifle and that was all. One of the Second N jokers was telling me how he was showing a Ninth Divvy bloke how to prime a grenade in the pitch dark by the feel of his fingers —putting in dets. and shaking like a jelly! It's a bloody crime, that's what it is, sending blokes up here who haven't even been properly trained, let alone equipped. They reckon there are Huns round El Agheila, too."

The Sixth Division man shook his head in a mixture of sympathy and indignation. It was mostly lost on B Company, for the Second X was an efficient battalion. Nevertheless, as one that had been more or less thrown together, the Ninth Division as a whole was far from fully trained or well equipped. When the rearguard departed the next day they left B Company a number of captured Italian machine-guns and mortars. The desert buggies that carried them away disappeared in a cloud of dust—the last the Second X saw of the men who had over-run Mussolini's North African empire. These veterans were not to guess that the rather pitiful division they left behind would be the first men to deal the Nazi armies a reverse on land.

They soon discovered the whereabouts of the enemy. Rommel's Afrika Corps was now in the desert, with its huge tanks, motorised divisions and fanatical Nazi Youth. Mauled by the far stronger armour of the Nazis, the flimsy British tanks withdrew. The Afrika Corps kept advancing. Seven weeks after the capture of Cyrenaica the Ninth Division was fleeing helter-skelter for Tobruk with Rommel in close pursuit.

Vehicles shouldered each other crazily on the crammed roadway. To keep fleeing was the only thought. Some of the battered transport broke down and was abandoned. Some of the division was overtaken and made prisoner. In Nazi prison camps Australians came to talk of the "Breakfast Battalion." Its commander, perhaps under the delusion that he was still engaged in leisurely manœuvring with his militia company somewhere back in Australia, ordered the battalion to "stop for breakfast." His officers demurred, pointing out that Nazi scout cars were only a few miles away. The colonel repeated serenely that "the battalion would stop for breakfast." Those of his companies who could manage it disobeyed and kept on fleeing. The colonel and about a hundred of his men stopped for breakfast. For the next four years they partook of that meal in Nazi prison camps : a long time to stop for breakfast.

The tide had turned against the impudent force that occupied Cyrenaica. Rommel recaptured Benghazi. Six days after, the Ninth Division and the remnants of a British armoured division reached Tobruk. The Benghazi Derby was over. In Tobruk they turned to stand before Rommel and all that he had to hurl against them.

That was the day before Good Friday. But the troops came to call it Black Friday.

*   *   *

Major Pomfret was down with dysentery. The Second X's Tobruk headquarters was a large underground cavern, lined with timber, split into compartments and led into by a long narrow ramp. Down here, behind a hessian curtain, Pomfret lay and struggled with his illness. He would not leave the battalion. Captain Barrett visited him constantly to check his condition. Alone, oppressed on all sides by stale-smelling earth, he worried and tried to keep his thoughts clear.

Within a few hours now the battalion, he was convinced, would face its first severe test. In the great arc of trench system that was called the Tobruk perimeter the Second X and its sister battalions crouched and awaited the onslaught of Rommel's Nazis. Pomfret knew the battalion only in the mass. Of its military capabilities he knew more than even Fitzroy. In Pomfret's mind the whole unalterable mechanism was laid out neatly. As he saw a map of the area that the battalion was defending he absorbed the details swiftly and clearly, without hesitation. The calculation of supplies and ammunition, the number of bodies needed to defend a given point, the disposition of Vickers guns, anti-tank guns and mortars—such things were no more than the normal exercise of his mind. That two new factors now existed—lives lost and bodies maimed—did not upset the rhythm of his calculations: he merely made allowances for them. He neither trusted nor encouraged his imagination.

Lying here, he only heard in odd snatches how the battalion was faring. He ached to see and talk with Fitzroy. Furthermore, he was obsessed by an old fear. It was prompted by the thought of Fitzroy being without him. Facts, details, calculations were things that Orme liked to ignore; he struck a pose, gambled, adventured and enjoyed himself at it. If the gamble came off it lent to Orme's actions the appearance of audacious brilliance. Pomfret never resented this, for Fitzroy's manner was suited to a reputation for brilliance. Long ago, Pomfret had become convinced of one thing: that with his help Fitzroy could accomplish anything.

Pomfret did not believe in the war. He considered it a mistake. He admired Hitler and thought it deplorable that they were fighting Hitler instead of the Russians. His loyalty was to Fitzroy. His belief lay in the Fitzroy empire of wheat, cattle, wool, steel, shipping, sugar and newsprint. Every detail of Ormond Fitzroy's stake in the fortunes of his family was known and defended by Pomfret. To him, Fitzroy's arrogance and pride were as natural as his wealth.

Now and again above his head, Pomfret heard muffled explosions and knew that a battle impended like a storm.

*   *   *

The cold-blooded logic of the defence plan left Colonel Fitzroy marvelling. The Nazis would attack first with tanks which were to be let through. Infantry would then deal with infantry. The little two-pounder anti-tank guns were not to engage the Nazi tanks unless certain of a hit with their first round. With their 75-millimetre cannon, the Mark IIIs and IVs were capable of placing themselves beyond the range of the two-pounder and still destroying it with their own guns. Rommel's forces were already well east of Tobruk and the division was cut off. Their only course was to hold Tobruk.

Reports from the companies began to pour in on Battalion Headquarters. Tanks massing here, patrol activity there, B Company area being heavily shelled. The adjutant set his staff smoothly to work, and secretly the colonel admired the way he did it. Sulky young beggar but knew his job!

Fitzroy's depression left him as suddenly as it had arrived. Full of relief at the chance to prove to himself that he was equal to the task, he became a demon of energy—a slightly bewildering demon. Unknown to Fitzroy, the youthful Adjutant occasionally went in desperation to Pomfret for advice. Fitzroy could not bear to be doing nothing; he was too afraid of that chilly sense of failure.

Already the brigadier had mentioned him in despatches because of the battalion's patrol activity. Like blind feelers Fitzroy had sent out reconnaissance patrols. Twice these patrols had clashed with Nazi patrols and mostly by chance returned unscathed and victorious, with prisoners. One of the prisoners had proved informative: the brigadier had been delighted. The third patrol sent out disappeared without trace.

The colonel did not let up, either on himself or Battalion Headquarters. He was face to face with a new sort of reality, a harsh, unyielding reality which neither pose nor clever words could elude. There was no elaborate social structure here—nothing to get behind, no way of concealing causes and effects. A single decision could mean the annihilation of the men crouched out there on the perimeter watching the Nazi armour milling around them in the dust. Once or twice he had a swift and horrible vision of this mass of Nazis and their huge tanks pouring over and crushing the Australians in their dusty yellow clothes.

Henry Gilbertson looked through his binoculars, sweeping the stretch of desert that comprised B Company's front, wondering bitterly why the anti-tank trenches ceased on his left

65

flank. The ground was thick with the eruptions of Nazi shells, the air smoke-laden and full of the shrill sound of shrapnel. It was amazing how quickly the ears became used to the unnatural din of shell-fire.

"No infantry yet," he muttered. "Those cursed tanks are prodding for the weak spots."

A shell exploded deafeningly and hideously almost directly above him. The earth around him trembled and the noise of falling sand followed.

*　　　*　　　*

In the concrete-lined strong-posts of the former Italian garrison Six Platoon crouched and looked out through a framework of concertina wire at the Nazi tanks. Great black monsters, some of them lumbered casually across their vision, others approached close with astonishing speed, their tracks throwing up clouds of dust as they turned and circled in an endeavour to draw the anti-tank fire. Their turrets were like brutish squat heads, their guns like long snouts; guns far outranging the small two-pounders of the Australian anti-tank crews.

The shell-fire eased and finally died. The Mark IVs began to come in closer, weaving and swerving, flaunting themselves before the anti-tank crews. Still the crews lay tensely behind their tiny guns, grim and unprovoked. Had any one of them fired at this stage the position would have been pin-pointed immediately and pounded by the Nazi cannon. Along the whole front where the attack was mounting the Australians crouched and held their fire.

The comparative silence that followed the cessation of the shell-fire was uncanny. It seemed to Dick that he was watching on a glaring screen the antics of strange metallic monsters at play. There was no fear in him as he watched at this moment, only curiosity and a sort of elation. He felt part detached, standing outside of himself and admiring his astonishing lack of fear.

"Look at this bastard," said Andy at his side.

One of the Mark IVs detached itself and crept in closer than any of its fellows, looming black only a couple of hundred yards in front of the wire. Leisurely it swung sideways. In the instant that its vulnerable flank was exposed a two-pounder fired waspishly. The tank jolted, came to a halt. Another shell tore into its side. Smoke began to pour from its turret.

"You beauts!" yelled Dick.

All along the line men echoed his savage cry.

The hatch in the tank's turret flew open and a black figure clambered out and fell to the ground. Andy and Dick took aim together, both firing as the figure rose. It stumbled, went to its knees, rose again. Then, on their right, Dooley's Bren rattled briefly. The German spun round, collapsed and lay still.

Other tanks had come in close and lay disabled or smoking as the two-pounders found the vulnerable stretch of armour between the tracks. Across the desert one of the German tank men was running for cover. A Six Platoon man rose upright in his trench, taking aim with his rifle at the scurrying figure. There was a short burst of fire from out front, and the Australian went backwards spurting redly, his neck almost severed.

"Who was that?" asked Tommy Collins.

"Wally Perkins," said Dooley.

"Christ!" said Tommy softly. "Poor old Wally."

The tanks retreated, sending an occasional shell or spasmodic bursts of machine-gun fire over the Australian defences. The Brens replied.

"Hold your fire!" shouted Crane. "Wait for their infantry!"

Quiet prevailed again for a brief while.

"Listen!" said Andy.

Dick strained his ears but at first heard nothing. Then very faintly came the sound of lorry engines.

"Their infantry's coming up," said Andy.

On the skyline a black figure appeared for an instant, then disappeared. It happened again. The skyline seemed to be wavering with movement.

The tanks and field-guns farther back began again, laying down a screaming barrage of metal. With an all-obliterating bang the parapet of the trench above Dick's head disappeared. His ears began to clang strangely. When the shock of the explosion cleared from his head the shelling had almost ceased. Instead there was the harsh rattle of machine-guns.

"Here they come," Andy was saying.

"Fire as you like!" yelled Crane. "Let the bastards have it!"

The desert beyond the wire was now alive with Nazi infantry darting for cover behind the camel-thorn hummocks. Their Spandaus engaged the Brens in a fierce, clattering duel. Leaning on the shattered parapet, Dick brought a crouching figure into his rifle sights. In the instant before he pressed the trigger he was aware of his calm, of a strange cruel relish for what he was about to do. Then he pressed the trigger. The German jerked backwards and lay still. He had killed a man. It was as easy as that.

All through the afternoon of that Good Friday, along several miles of the Tobruk perimeter, the Second X and its sister battalions exchanged fire with Rommel's Nazis. At nightfall, the Germans withdrew along the front of the Second X. The stars came and looked down on a peaceful desert littered with corpses and a few tanks. It seemed that they blinked sadly, as though pondering the necessity for such scenes.

The Australians came forth, buried their dead, and sent their wounded away on stretchers. But they did not rest. They waited alertly throughout the night. The events of the day left them with no illusions. They had been nothing—merely a preparatory skirmishing for what was to follow. Very soon now Rommel would cease probing and attack.

*   *   *

It was Easter Saturday.

"Look at that crawling little dingo," Andy told Dick. "He hasn't put his head above ground or fired a shot yet."

Dick glanced over at Percy Gribble.

Percy sat quietly a short distance away, bent solicitously over the bandages on his legs which were covered in what were called desert sores. It was early, and as yet the day was almost without incident. Just on dawn a tank had nosed over the horizon, stood there for some time while its crew observed the land, and disappeared. A Spandau crew which had dug in overnight opened up soon after, and was promptly wiped out by a mortar bomb. Now, for a time, all was quiet.

The honours of the previous day had gone to the anti-tank crews. From their strong-posts the infantrymen had called to them: "Good on you, mates!" And the gunners had smiled and waved back, but observed to each other:

"They'll be cursing us before the day's through."

Said Dooley: "In Sydney today they'll be lining up for the start of the Doncaster."

Tommy mused: "I wonder if there are any Wog sheilas back in Tobruk."

"Women in Tobruk!" sighed Dooley. "You make me tired."

Over at Platoon Headquarters, Crane asked his sergeant how the men were shaping.

"Cheeky as ever, sir," Lucas told him.

"Too bad about Perkins," said Crane.

He felt quite indifferent about Perkins. With the opening of the German attack, all doubts and fears, all his nagging disquiet, had left him. The sense of power and superiority returned to him. His orders had produced the death of a score or so of the enemy out front. Once again he loomed magnificent in his own imagination. He had wielded the power of life and death. Red visions of victorious slaughter filled his mind, giving him deep pleasure. Constantly those words had come back to him. Where the devil *had* he heard them? "The dark beauty of violence . . ."

"If the tanks come in," he said, "they are to be let through. The infantry are our pigeon."

Lucas nodded. There was no change in him. Here was the same cynical, competent Lucas; here were the mocking eyes, the indifference. His shirt was sleeveless on the right side. There was a welt on his shoulder where a bullet had grazed it. His eyes were red and weary. Sweat and sand had caked on a three-day beard. But it was the same Lucas.

"Ammunition's got to be conserved," Crane proceeded. "We may as well face it. We're surrounded here and probably the only way we'll get anything in—rations, ammunition or reinforcements—is by sea. You'd better get all section leaders here at once."

Lucas left Platoon Headquarters and ran crouching along the communication trench. He came upon Dooley and Tommy taking their ease with a cigarette just where the trench joined the wadi.

"Tell all section leaders to come to Platoon Headquarters at once," Lucas ordered Dooley.

"Tell 'em yourself," said Dooley.

"That's an order, Dooley," Lucas said.

"And I'm disobeying it, Frank," replied Dooley, and took another draw on his cigarette. "Tell 'em yourself."

"I'll attend to you later," said Lucas, and hurried on.

"Oh, yeah?" drawled Dooley.

A few seconds later Percy Gribble came past them.

"Why, hullo, Perce!" exclaimed Dooley. "I didn't know you was here."

"Well," chuckled Tommy. "If it ain't our section leader! I thought you were back in Tobruk advising the general."

"Where you been hiding, Perce?"

Percy regarded them wretchedly and bitterly. "There are still A.M.R. & O's up here," he told them. "You'll go on an A.4 if you're not careful."

Their immoderate laughter followed him along the trench. His face as he left them was a mask of anguish.

Dick and Andy dozed lightly against the side of their weapon pit. A rattle of fire and the howl of ricocheting bullets brought them both on their knees, alert, rifles in their hands.

"It's on again," observed Andy. His cynical calm was something that aroused Dick's envy.

*　　　*　　　*

All day that Easter Saturday the Nazi tanks probed the battalion's front, their infantry scurried behind the tanks making short advances towards the concertina wire. In the distance on their right flank, B Company saw about twenty Nazis reach the wire. They were mown down under a solid wall of fire. Half a dozen figures were left hanging over the wire like discarded dolls.

69

Still the Mark IVs could not draw the anti-tank fire. The Nazi infantry advanced to the wire, but never pressed home their attack. Another man from Six Platoon was killed; two more were wounded.

So continued the thrust and parry all that day and the next. On Sunday night the Nazis attacked in force.

* * *

After the first Nazi thrusts Fitzroy visited his companies and praised whoever he encountered. He was especially attentive to B Company which had suffered the heaviest casualties. Here the colonel found a changed Henry Gilbertson. There were no doubts or misgivings about Henry now that his company was in action. He took it for granted that his company could do anything demanded of them. The men who had puzzled him and sometimes earned his pity he now admired. He was happy and confident. To Fitzroy he said:

"You need have no fears about these fellows, Orme. They know what a Nazi is now and they'll kill all they see."

The colonel came upon Dooley and Tommy in the wadi cleaning their Bren. Halting, he stood and asked them:

"And how's the Bren standing up to it, chaps?"

They stared at him. He was the last man they expected to speak to them, but to be addressed so affably left them speechless for a few seconds. Dooley's agile wits were the first to recover. Recalling some former words of Crane, he carefully excluded all mockery from his voice and replied:

"An excellent weapon, sir."

"Excellent!" echoed Tommy.

The colonel had recently adopted British officers' slang; his next question was in that vein:

"And how many bleeding Huns have you bagged with it?"

Tommy and Dooley consulted each other impassively with their eyes. Dooley shrugged modestly.

"About fifty so far, sir."

"Fifty! Damn fine show! Well, good hunting!"

And the colonel went on his way.

"Fifty!" giggled Tommy. "Yer bloody liar!"

Dooley did not reply. Instead, he gazed at the colonel's receding back and remarked:

"That bastard's mad. He oughter be in the Boy Scouts."

* * *

It was Easter Sunday night. Once again the Nazis had withdrawn out of sight. Nowhere had they pierced the Australian defences.

The night was gentle and bright. Across the parapet Dick looked out over the stretch of desert where he had seen Nazis

70

scrambling for three whole days. Their corpses were vague lumps on the stony ground. Under the starlight they had lost their meaning. So far the slaughter had seemed mainly an impersonal thing fought at a range of a few hundred yards. You could not discern the features of the man you killed. You pressed the trigger and a figure fell, like a puppet that had lost its strings. It was amazing how soon you ceased to be moved at the sight of a corpse. He felt glad for his encounter with the corpse at Mersa Matruh, for he believed that his thoughts on that day had prepared him for this and what else there was to come.

Andy slept on the floor of the trench. One of his boots lay out of the shadow, glowing in the moonlight. Dick wanted to sleep like Andy but he knew that he could not. If he retired into that shadow and closed his eyes thoughts would come racing across his mind. So there he leaned on the parapet reliving again and again the last three days.

The moonlight had transformed this strip of desert and the scattered corpses. It was incredible to remember it as the scene of these violent happenings. Surely this was a cold, white, dead land where nothing ever happened; a place that drew the spirit away from reality and left it no longer sure of anything.

It was a scene made for melancholy, a scene in which to contemplate remotely the tragedy of mankind. It caused you to think of certain tremendous facts. Dick was overwhelmed by a wonder of the circumstances that had brought him from his home half-way across the world to a nameless bit of desert which they were defending savagely from a horde of Nazis—torn away from all that was safe and familiar.

Simply, terrifyingly, the thought of death came to him. He could die as easily as Perkins had died. He would not even understand why he had died. Proud young body, lost and rotting in this dead land. His heart turned over icily; deeply, wordlessly, he emitted a sound. He was terribly afraid.

That sound broke the spell of his contemplation. He leant over tensely, listening.

Andy stirred. He sat up and his grizzled head emerged from the shadow. He grunted.

"We aren't on guard yet, are we?"

After a few seconds Dick told him:

"No."

"Then get some sleep."

More silence.

Andy dropped his eyes from his friend. At length he arose and joined Dick at the parapet. Without speaking they gazed out over the battlefield. Dick had not yet looked at the other. Although he reclined wearily he did not seem to be at rest.

It was Andy who broke the silence:

71

"You remember when that mob of Huns came over the sky-line this afternoon with those tanks sweeping down in front? I thought we were all done for." He paused. "Christ, I was scared!"

Finally, Dick looked at him. The calm profile told him nothing. He did not know why Andy had wakened and spoken like this. But he was afraid of what Andy might have guessed.

Away on their flank there was a brief racket of gun-fire. It spluttered into silence, but now the night air seemed to be charged with menace. Farther down the trench a voice spoke.

A few minutes afterwards the barrage began.

As they cowered deep in their trenches it seemed only a matter of time before they would be shattered. It did not seem possible that as much as a square inch of ground would be spared by the storm of thunderous metal that now fell upon them. The still, white desert that Andy and Dick had looked across only a few minutes ago now heaved in fountains of dust and smoke; shuddered, roared and screamed a thousand times in a second. On either side of the trench the earth was convulsed. It leaped and trembled, threw them flat, deafened and mindless. Sand poured in on them from the ruined parapet.

Farther along there had been a direct hit. Shrilly, a man called: "Christ! Oh, Christ!"

Another voice appealed for a stretcher-bearer. The wounded man howled unspeakably. Again the voice pleaded:

"For God's sake! His inside's pouring out!"

Shrilling metal that sang to a hideous background of detonations:

Crump! Zeeeee! Crump! Zeeeee!

Zeeeeeeeeeeeeeee!!!

Flashes that lanced at the seething smoke.

Dimly the cries of men.

Crash! Crash! Crump! Zeeeeeeee!

The sounds were thinning. It became possible to count them. With a last rumble the bombardment ceased.

The sudden quiet was wondrous. Plainly, a voice was heard whimpering like a child. Then the night air began to hum and rattle. It was the sound of approaching tanks. Soon they loomed up a hundred yards away, black and gigantic, lurching and clanking, gathering speed as they bore down. This time there was no doubt about their purpose.

They came straight through the wire like a great dark wave. The roar of their engines was all round; then they were on the infantry. The side of one of them loomed up near Dick and Andy. They cried hoarsely to each other and grovelled in the bottom of their pit. The world was blotted out as the tank passed above, half-burying them in sand.

The enormous black shapes were everywhere and right behind

72

them were hordes of Nazis, pouring in on the shell-dazed Australians. Moonlight glinted on a sea of bobbing helmets. As Dick lurched to his feet a strange voice cried and a boot and the butt of a rifle came down past him. He brought his own rifle up quickly and the bayonet found flesh and creaked on bone. The Nazi croaked and clawed at his groin. Dick pulled the trigger and his rifle sprang free. He fired into another shape on the edge of the pit. It toppled on him, bearing him down. It was already a corpse, gushing blood from the throat, but he fought, terror-stricken, to get free of it as though it were still alive, kicking and pushing it aside. He reached his feet again firing without aiming at each shape he saw. Andy was out of the ruined trench, his rifle at his hip, three dead Nazis around him. Still they were coming through the shattered wire. They lurched, doubled, screamed and fell as the Bren guns poured a hail of bullets into them. Andy slammed another clip into his magazine as a Nazi came at him his gun spurting. Andy sprang aside and met him in the face with the butt of his rifle. Dooley, still in his pit, hugged his Bren gun and exchanged bursts with a Spandau fifty yards away. Crane stood firing his pistol calmly into the mass of enemy. Out of the corner of his eye Dick saw Lucas empty a burst from his tommy-gun into a Nazi crouched to throw a grenade. Then, without knowing it, he had a grenade in his own hand, pulled out the pin and hurled it into an approaching knot of the enemy. Three fell, another staggered on blindly, hand to a bloody face. Dick ran forward and bayoneted him in the belly; it felt as soft as butter. Something hit his foot hard, flinging it upward, out of control. When he got up again only the top of his right boot remained and his foot tingled dully.

The Nazis were thinning out. Andy was on his belly wriggling towards the Spandau. His hand came up as he threw a grenade. It burst in front of the gun and after the explosion a Nazi ran towards them crying hoarsely, his hands above his head. Andy rose deliberately to his feet and shot him through the stomach. Another Nazi began to run. Dooley arose in his trench, Bren at hip, and fired a burst into him. Tommy loomed behind Dooley and fired into the head of a wounded Nazi writhing near the gun. Lucas ran across in front of them, stood on the edge of a trench and fired downwards into it. The Nazis still on their feet wavered, turned and commenced to run. Whooping, the Australians clambered out after them.

"Back to your posts!" yelled Crane.

"Back!" cried Lucas waving his arm frantically towards their pits.

A hundred yards to their flank a Spandau began to fire and tracers cut brilliant lines in the air. Away to their left the battle still raged. Out of the smoke to their rear came more Australians with a lieutenant leading them.

"What platoon's this?"

"Six."

"Where's Seven?"

"Over there."

They ran off towards Seven Platoon's position. The lieutenant called over his shoulder before they disappeared: "Seven Platoon's been overrun. Most of them dead!"

"Let's go and help 'em," said Tommy.

"Stay where you are, everybody!" rapped out Lucas. "Back to your own pits. Clear them and prepare for the next attack."

At Platoon Headquarters Percy Gribble tremblingly guarded seven Nazi prisoners. Dick and Andy hauled the dead Nazis from their pit and shovelled out the sand that the tank had pressed in on it. Crane checked their casualties hurriedly: three dead, seven wounded. Four of the wounded were walking wounded, the other three lay on stretchers near Company Headquarters.

A bullet had grazed Andy's temple singeing a furrow of hair. The bullet that had torn Dick's boot off had not entered the flesh, but his foot was painful to walk on. He hobbled over to their pit and sank down beside Andy. A delicious sleepiness crept over him. He shook his head and forced his eyes open. Slowly the lids closed, against his will.

"Do you realise," Andy was saying, "that there's a fleet of tanks behind us on their way to the town?"

"Yes," said Dick dully. "What about it?"

"What about it!" exclaimed Andy. "I just hope they don't come back this way—that's all."

"Don't care if they do."

Dick opened his eyes. Had he said those words or merely thought them?

The voice of Sergeant Lucas brought him awake:

"There's movement out front. I want a three-man patrol."

"I'll go," said Andy, rising.

"Me, too," said Dick, also rising.

"Don't be a bloody fool," Lucas told him. "You'll cut your foot to pieces." He grinned at Andy. "How is this young bastard?"

"He's out on his feet," replied Andy.

"Get down to Company Headquarters and see if you can get another boot."

Dick hobbled off. At Company Headquarters he found Henry Gilbertson.

"Hullo, young Brett! You too?"

"No, sir. Just got my boot shot off. I was sent to see if I could get a new one."

Henry sighed. "Boot shot off! Worse things have happened tonight. Come down here."

He led Dick down into a spacious dug-out, and pulled a pair of boots from a heap of gear in a corner.

"Right or left?"

"Right, sir."

He watched Dick as he tried the boot on.

"Fit?"

"Good enough, sir."

"Had it?"

"Just about."

"Better get back before the shit starts to fly again."

"Thanks."

As Dick went to go, Henry touched his shoulder briefly and said:

"Those Huns outnumbered us five to one. You fellers are the salt of the earth. I'm proud to be with you. Believe me."

Dick was too surprised and confused to answer, but as he limped back he found his tiredness leaving him. He felt proud too.

Two hours later the Nazis attacked again. Met with a torrent of machine-gun fire, most of them died on the wire. The survivors turned and ran, and the Second X went after them. Before dawn came a few more tanks were seen to speed through gaps in the defences.

The sun came up redly, climbed the sky and, as it grew brighter, pitilessly revealed the thickly scattered corpses of the Nazis. At dawn the Australians stood-to but there were no further attacks. Away to the left flank of the Second X could be heard the sound of machine-gun fire. But there was not a live Nazi in sight, except for those being herded back to the prisoner-of-war cage.

*   *   *

The reports that reached Colonel Fitzroy over the field telephone that night all indicated victory. The Nazis had everywhere been repulsed. His elation generated a fierce energy. Pomfret knew he was seeing him at his best, and was glad.

In the early hours of Monday morning thirty odd German tanks were far inside the perimeter and making for the town. The telephone hummed with reports of their progress. Just before first light the colonel and his staff left the underground headquarters and manned emergency trenches on a mound immediately above. Standing together in a pit Fitzroy and Pomfret scanned the paling horizon. Nearby on their left flank a troop of twenty-five pounder guns was waiting to engage the tanks over open sights.

Dawn found several tanks feeling their way along the skyline. As the land lay revealed they moved into formation and swung towards the Second X positions. More of the ugly dark shapes came over the skyline. In all the morning the only sound to be heard was that of the tanks.

They seemed to come on incredibly slowly. They looked monstrous, deliberate, irresistible. The whole world seemed to be tensed for the clash that was to come. The engines had swelled to a steady roar. For the first time in his life the colonel thought about death.

He glanced at Pomfret, but Pomfret's features said nothing. They were just as they had always been. A sense of unreality, a strange resignation came over the colonel.

"Any moment now," said Pomfret with calm callousness, as though the man beside him had asked a question aloud.

Hardly had he spoken when the guns let go.

"There they are," Andy told Dick. "They're trying to get out again."

A few hundred yards away on their left Nazi tanks were making back for the perimeter and their own lines beyond. Two of them stopped and poured smoke as two-pounder shells struck them. One of them turned and its cannon flashed as it engaged the crew of the anti-tank gun. With a scream of steel it scored a direct hit on the two-pounder. Camouflage blown away, its shield shattered, a little gun lay smoking, its barrel tipped up in the air, a dead Australian slumped next to it. Over the skyline came two British tanks with guns crashing. The Mark IVs made swiftly for gaps in the wire. One was halted by a shell from a British tank; the others disappeared and the Australians stood up in their pits and jeered them outwards.

Andy chuckled. "I wonder how they felt when no infantry or artillery followed them in? All on their lonesome, with two-pounders everywhere and twenty-fives firing over open sights!"

Comparative quiet came over the battlefield. Dick looked out over the desert with its littered corpses, shattered wire and wrecked tanks. They no longer meant anything to him. His mouth hung half open, his bloodshot eyes throbbed dully, his limbs seemed clamped into immobility. Stupid with exhaustion, he watched the Mark IVs disappear. Inwardly he moaned for sleep like a child. Sleep . . . beautiful, blank, dreamless sleep. . . . Oh, to be mindless and feel nothing!

*   *   *

A few days later the radios were hailing the victory of Tobruk. The announcers told of the tanks destroyed, the enemy killed or captured. For the first time on land the Nazis had been defeated, they told the world. Their impersonal voices could say little about the men who had won the victory.

The voices could not describe them as they washed the dust

from their beards and shaved, or as they rebuilt the trenches crushed by shell-fire or Nazi tanks; as they tenderly cleaned and oiled their weapons; as they took a mouthful from a water-bottle or munched their bully and biscuits. They were not there to see a figure, as it watched out over the desert in the phantasmal glare, turn suddenly sideways then away again, as if he had half expected to find his dead mate still standing there. Only the soldiers knew the pain of their bitter, yearning images: of a wife or a girl; of things like children, gardens, dogs, pubs, beaches in the sun.

From Europe the radio voice of Haw Haw taunted them: "Come out, rats! Come out with your hands up!"

But the name given them in contempt they accepted and kept. They became proud of it:

The Rats of Tobruk.

9

A BOOT came down past his face and then the butt of a rifle. He brought his own rifle upwards and the bayonet found flesh and grated on bone. . . . The Nazi screamed . . . he pulled the trigger but the bayonet was stuck . . . he could not let go the rifle either . . . he began to run, the rifle frozen to his hands, dragging a screaming Nazi with him . . . away they careered over to No Man's Land. . . .

"Hey, Dick, wake up!"

Panting, he was suddenly awake and free of the nightmare. Reality came back to him dully. He was lying in the sand on the bottom of the trench, Andy's face above him. Moonlight came down whitely.

"You were doing an awful lot of twisting and groaning."

There was an anxious little edge to Andy's voice. His eyes were intent.

Dick rose, shedding the greatcoat that had covered him. He leaned against the side of the trench and said:

"I'm all right now."

His voice was small and weary. Andy turned away. He looked out through the crazy pattern of wire, across the narrow strip of minefield, the flat, cold desert spotted with camel thorn. Farther along he could hear Dooley and Tommy talking together. He pondered for some minutes.

"Forget it," he said at last, and did not look around.

"What should I forget?" There was affront in Dick's voice.

"The whole rotten business. When they shell you or bomb you,

77

you have thoughts you're ashamed of. When you have to kill someone you think you'll never get rid of the memory. But it's either you or him. That's one of the laws of life. That's why I say forget it. You can be proud of yourself—you're a good soldier. Forget the rest. It wasn't your making."

"I gave myself almost exactly the same advice. But you can't control your dreams."

"The trouble with you," Andy told him, "is you've yet to learn the futility of protest."

Dick almost sneered at him. "And what about you? I've seen you do some protesting."

Andy answered without resentment. "You know, you're the only bloke in this platoon who still digs at me about walking off Groggy's parade."

"I'm sorry, Andy."

"That's all right. That was the most futile thing I ever did." Andy turned now and smiled at him, and in his smile was pity and affection. "You're a bit ashamed—that's all—because I know your state of mind."

Do you know all of it, Andy? Last night we did a patrol, you and I and seven others, lying in a hollow while twenty-odd unsuspecting Italians were digging not fifteen yards away. Do you know how I felt as I lay there waiting for the signal from Lucas to begin slaughtering them? The minutes dripped, Andy, like slow drops out of a tap. . . . We were waiting ever so quietly and patiently to kill them. They were laughing softly as they worked. How clear and musical was the clink of their shovels in the night air! Then we were on our feet spraying their laughter with death. What about the one who ran at me shouting hoarsely words I did not understand? There was something almost comical about his face as I shot him. How he rolled his eyes and finally turned them into his head. How quickly the glaze came over them! Why, they glazed as I watched them. I had the feeling that I was condemned for ever to stand and watch the blurring features of the man I had murdered.

A Very light soared across No Man's Land and slowly came earthwards, the desert glowing strangely beneath the brilliance. It fell, burnt out, and there was only the moonlight once more. A machine-gun rattled briefly in the distance.

*   *   *

"A nice convenient wound in the arse," said Tommy. "That's what I want."

"Pity someone don't shoot your dick off," Dooley retorted with an evil grin.

"A nick in the arse," affirmed Tommy. "Just enough to get a man out of this dirty hole."

"You don't want much!"

"Good old Tel Aviv!" Tommy's eyes became distantly lascivious. "Alicante and a Wog slut!"

"All you ever think of is your guts and what swings on it."

"What else should a man think of?"

"I dunno—ask Crane. He'll give you an ear-bash about doing something for your country."

"My country!" Tommy's voice was scathing. "What's my country done for me?"

"Gave you free board once or twice, didn't it? And the dole."

Tommy spat out of his thin little mouth.

"I'm gonna get out of the bloody infantry. Palestine's the shot. Base bludger, me! Into Tel Aviv every day. A man can get away with almost anything over here. Back home he'd be up on about six charges. They can leave me over in Palestine as long as they like." He giggled. "I'll fight like bloody hell for the King in Tel Aviv."

"You're a bad bastard!" said Dooley affectionately.

*   *   *

The night was very dark. Lieutenant Crane looked at the luminous dial of his watch. Three minutes to nine. From near at hand came the click of a rifle bolt and the sound of boots on stones. Five slow-moving figures came dimly into view. They approached without word and halted, standing around their Platoon Commander. It was Two Section, led by Percy Gribble: Andy, Dick, Tommy and Dooley.

"All set, sir."

Faces were gradually resolving themselves palely in the darkness. The moon had not yet risen. The air was chill. They shivered a little under their thin shirts. Crane spoke to the circle of faces:

"This is an offensive patrol. We want a prisoner. Understand?"

They nodded silently.

"They're up to something out there and we've got to find out what it is. We're not out to attack any strong-posts. We'll be looking for a working party. If anyone gets separated he knows how to get home. Find the Pole star and keep it slightly to your left. Everybody happy?"

"Happy as pigs in mud," snarled Dooley.

Crane ignored him. Inside he tingled excitedly and pleasurably. Dick stared at him, sensing the man's abnormal love of the violent and the adventurous. He'll get the lot of us killed one of these days, he thought. He felt dulled to the whole thing. His imagination no longer worked. He was accepting each hour with the stolidity of an animal.

He could see a glint of teeth as Andy flashed a glance at the

79

silent and palpitating Gribble beside him. Percy's hand gripped the rifle so tensely that it had grown hot and wet.

Crane consulted his watch again. Nine. He took out his compass, setting the luminous arrow on a bearing of two hundred and five degrees.

"Single file," he said, and led them off.

They picked their way between a maze of weapon pits and zig-zagging communication trenches; through the gap in the concertina wire where stood a sentry who bade them softly, "Good luck." They stopped for a minute at the edge of the minefield where a board with a black triangle on it was hung, while Crane found the track through the bewildering criss-cross of stakes and apron-wire. They filed through, looking cautiously to either side where loud and hideous destruction lay a few inches below the dust. Crane paused to check his bearing and they plunged stealthily into the blackness of No Man's Land.

Night for a time had conquered all. Stars, ineffectual and pale, seemed to peer for a lost moon. It seemed at times to Dick that the desert only lived for the return of the moon; the white, unreadable disc that brought the bombers and covered the desert with a remote tranquillity, bathing the most hideous of its objects in a false and peaceful shroud.

No moon cast delusions this night and the air had sweetened the hot breath of the dust. In the disquieting lull that had fallen over the perimeter, corpses had been discovered and buried and the air was no longer vile with their putridity.

Wordlessly they penetrated the night for a thousand paces. Andy, who was counting them, tapped Crane's shoulder when the thousandth had been taken. Crane motioned them to earth and they lay there for some time with their heads to the ground, listening. Night and silence enfolded them. What am I doing here? thought Dick. He sensed the darkness about him, surveyed the wan stars, dug his fingers into the lifeless dust. He felt abandoned and empty, infinitely tiny. What am I doing here in this spot, stretched out like a lizard? His predicament almost dragged out of him a dry, bitter chuckle. He despised himself. His doings were ridiculous, without dignity, absurd use of a human being. The earth ought to shake, he thought. It ought to throw us off like a cloud of dust. It should get rid of us, once and for all.

Prone on the ground, their vigil had yielded them nothing. Rising to his feet, Crane led them onward. He quickened his pace now. The night was getting on and their task was still unaccomplished. They had only gone a few hundred yards when Crane stopped as though he had run into a wall. He went to earth. The rest of them sank also, a fraction of a second behind him.

Crane's abrupt disappearance into the ground meant only one thing, and they hugged the earth tensely now, their senses wide awake and vibrant. For a minute there was only the beating of the heart and that mysterious inward whirring that follows a sudden alerting of the senses. Then after a few seconds of stillness, they heard the faint clink of steel tools.

The patrol edged forward on their stomachs between the low camel-thorn bushes. Now a voice mingled occasionally with the sound of tools. A number of men were working with picks and shovels. A voice spoke in German, so clearly that Dick imagined for a moment that it came from directly above him. Still they could see nothing. Then Crane detected just in front of him a dark pyramid: a dozen rifles neatly piled. A boot swished in the sand close by and he froze. A Nazi sentry strolled past, his rifle held at the port. He turned about a few feet from Crane's head and receded into the darkness. Crane turned his eyes back over his shoulder looking for Percy Gribble, who should have been immediately behind him. But it was Andy who moved up softly next to him. They spoke in whispers, their heads hugging the sand together.

"Where's Gribble?"

"About a hundred yards back. I made him stay there as soon as I heard those Huns."

"What the devil for?"

"He's packing them badly. He's quite useless."

Crane did not hesitate. "I'll deal with this sentry. You stop them from getting to their rifles. Franks can cover us; Collins and Brett will have to try for the prisoner. Too dark to try for more than one. They'll just bolt. Got it?"

"Got it."

Andy's form wriggled off stealthily. Crane waited. After two or three minutes Andy was back.

"All set."

Crane drew his revolver, rose in the sentry's path, and shot him through the chest. Andy sprang up to kneel beside the piled rifles. He shot a dark form blundering towards him. The Nazis discarded their tools, exclaiming in the darkness, darting wildly about as the figures of the Australians appeared in their midst. Dick and Tommy wrapped themselves around the nearest Nazi to them, bearing him down. They could hear the agonised labouring of his breath as they held him. Tommy hit him in the mouth. "Surrender or I'll kill yer!"

The rest of the Nazis fled. It was done.

Crane sprang elatedly towards the prisoner and inspected him briefly.

"An officer. Good show! Now let's get out of this."

Tommy and Dick dragged the prisoner to his feet, helping him with a kick. So they fled, dragging their captive with them through the darkness. After a minute or two they were joined by a silent, cringing Gribble.

Dooley and Tommy were searching the prisoner as they moved with him. Dooley took his compass, Tommy a fountain pen. He protested with a wrench of the shoulders, but was reminded of his predicament by another jab in the back.

Crane led them home with his head singing. The thought of his success was near to ecstasy with him. They had almost to run to keep up with him as he strode ahead. The triumphant, the splendid Kenneth Crane; monarch of the dark kingdom of violence.

Dick hurried behind him, but he was thinking only of sleep. The spectacle of Tommy and Dooley looting the prisoner, gleefully driving him onwards, aroused no commentary within him on the behaviour of human beings. The whole night's doings were degrading. Who cared about that? He alone in all the world. Damn him for a sensitive fool! "Forget it," Andy had said. Soon he would be asleep.

Now they were at their own wire being challenged. Now they were through it. Crane, Dooley and Tommy remained with the Nazi, the others broke away and went to their holes in the earth.

Crane led the way to Company Headquarters. There they found Ted Olley, the company sergeant major, alone. He told them that Henry Gilbertson was out "talking to the men." Carefully, Crane adjusted the hessian blackout and turned up the hurricane lamp in the dug-out. He looked around from his task to find Tommy relieving the Nazi of his epaulettes, and Dooley about to take a watch from the man's wrist. The Nazi was sneering as he watched them. He was only a boy—an Oberleutnant. Fair hair, icy blue eyes, a slit of a mouth. A face full of vanity and contempt, without mercy. His eyes showed controlled hatred as they watched Dooley and Tommy. He stood erect and still, the thin lips broken by a sneer.

A hot feeling of shame swept over Crane. What would this enemy officer be thinking of him for allowing this?

"Give those things to me," he commanded.

"Why?" asked Dooley, eyeing him insolently.

"Because I ordered you to."

"These are mine," protested Dooley. "I saw them first."

"You're a soldier," said Crane between his teeth as he sought to control his rage, "not a looter."

"They're ours!" cried Tommy.

"If you don't hand those things over I shall order the sar major to place you both under arrest."

"Better give 'em up, boys," urged Ted Olley unhappily.

"Since when has it been wrong to rat a bloody Hun?" demanded Dooley.

"For the last time!" shouted Crane. "Hand them over."

He was desperate now, almost beside himself. He felt that the Nazi's sneer was partly over the challenge to his authority by

82

the two soldiers. They looked at him in wonder. They had never seen him so violent or enraged.

For a few moments Crane and the two men looked at each other in silence as the question of their obedience hung in the balance. Then, with as much defiance and indignation as they could convey in the motion, Dooley and Tommy handed their trophies over. Although they burned with a sense of injustice, they already had a good collection of loot and there would be, after all, other nights.

Crane almost smiled as he took the things from them. He drew his revolver and covered the Nazi.

"Now you can go," he told Dooley and Tommy.

"Sar major, go and find Captain Gilbertson, will you?"

Alone with the young Nazi officer, Crane handed him back his wrist watch and the epaulettes.

"I apologise for my men's behaviour. You speak English?"

"Yes."

Crane stiffened his shoulders. "You are my prisoner," he said formally. "You will be treated as your rank deserves."

The Nazi looked at him without replying. The expression of the Nazi's eyes had died to a cold glitter. His face was a mask of pride and tragedy. He stood very erect.

Unconsciously, Crane pulled himself a little more erect, too. He feels it, he thought. He's humiliated at being taken prisoner . . . just as I would be. Immediately, another thought came to him: He's like me. He'd rather die than be humbled before lesser men.

The gaze that he now fixed on the Nazi was one of admiration and understanding. Here, thought Crane, was a man of a superior mould like himself, a man nurtured in the cult of violence, now impotent and confined. It was a tragedy that he, Kenneth Crane, had brought about. But that was war. Tonight had been a battle of two giants which he had won. Victor and vanquished both despising mercy, the usage appropriate to superior beings would be observed. For spiritually, thought Crane, he and the Nazi were brothers. What a moment of heady ravishment this was for Crane! Captor and captive, neither offering nor expecting mercy, faced each other as enemies; yet between them lay an unspoken sympathy, as between two brave men, heroes and leaders among men. And yet enmity had been necessary to produce this splendid moment! And suddenly those words came back to him again, more mystically lovely than ever: "The dark beauty of violence . . ."

*   *   *

Percy Gribble came in several yards behind the patrol. Undetected, he crept off, along the trench to an unused pit. Here, he subsided, burying his head in his arms. After a while his shoulders began to jerk at regular intervals. He was crying.

*   *   *

"The bastard!" fumed Dooley as they came out of the company dug-out. "The dirty, rotten animal! Sticking up for a foggin' Nazi!"

"Dry yer eyes," Tommy told him. He was tired. He felt no sense of outrage; he was grateful for such loot as he had and not having to fight for the right to keep it. "You got a compass."

"I hate the bastard!"

"Private Franks!" scoffed Tommy.

"Ar, shut up!"

*   *   *

The next day was like many that had gone before. Monotony had settled over the perimeter, relieved only at night-time by the clash of patrols far out in No Man's Land. By day the desert lay mute and trance-like in the merciless glare of the sun. The soldiers slept in the dim dug-outs or sat yarning on the shady sides of weapon pits. The sand was alive with little black fleas and among the sandbags lived rats that scuttled across men's bodies when they lay asleep. Weapons were cleaned and oiled, water swigged from water-bottles, bully and biscuits munched joylessly. Occasionally, Lucas or Crane scanned the shimmering surface of the desert with binoculars for signs of life. But nothing stirred; only the deluding waves of vapour.

Lucas in his shady hole was visited by Andy Cain.

"Good day, Andy. Sit down, mate."

"I want to talk about Percy."

"I was coming along to see Percy."

"You'd better leave him alone a bit longer."

"Poor little bastard!"

"Fog him—he's no worse off than the rest of us."

In the dimness, Lucas's face looked up at Andy and grinned.

"You hate his guts, don't you?" he asked.

"I despise him," said Andy, quite unperturbed. "He's a snob and a crawler and a bloody little standover. How can you hate half a man? No, I don't hate him," he went on. "It must be a terrible thing for a man to get like Percy. He shouldn't be up here—why don't they send him back?"

"Crane won't hear of it. I did suggest it, but Crane's got no sympathy for him. He says he can stay up here until he gets knocked or finds a bit of guts."

"Percy was Crane's white-headed boy. I suppose Crane hates Percy for being such a disappointment. Crane can't bear to be in the wrong."

Lucas laughed slyly. "You're his white-headed boy now. He

reckons you're a hell of a good soldier. Percy's got to toss in his stripes and you're to be section corporal."

To hide his gratification, Andy said surlily:

"So I should be. I've been leading the section since the first time Percy heard a bomb fall."

"Well, as from now you *are* section leader. Watch your step and you'll go a long way." He gave Andy another sly, mocking look. "I reckon when I first knew you, you'd have taken it as an insult if you'd been offered promotion. I'm almost disappointed in you."

Andy laughed without mirth. "I understand myself pretty well by this time. I was always disappointing someone or other. You know, my father was a clergyman—gave me a good education and a strict Christian upbringing. Know what I did at twenty-one? Became an atheist; wrote anti-religious articles for the Rationalists. Nearly killed the old feller!"

"You're a cranky bugger!" said Lucas. "I bet you gave your wife a wild spin."

"I suppose I did. I've had more jobs than I've got fingers and toes. We busted up just before I enlisted."

Suddenly Andy was silent, staring at the ground with grave, remote eyes.

Lucas gave this information the deference of silence. "Well," he said at length, "you've got the worst section in the platoon, what with Dooley, the one-man rebellion, and that little animal Tommy."

"I don't know. Haven't you noticed how everyone in this place tends to become the same? Like a steam hammer, this perimeter. Everything's flattened out alike. Even the minds all think alike after a time: 'Will I get knocked? Mail, smokes, sheilas, beer. And how can I get out of the army?'"

*   *   *

Out of the gloom a string of men approached the gap in B Company's wire.

"Who goes there?" the sentry challenged, without sounding over-concerned about a response.

"The girl guides," said Tommy's voice.

"Who do you foggin' think?" asked Dooley.

"Oh, it's you Six Platoon coots. Was that you doing the shooting out there?"

"Us—and some Huns," Dick told him.

"Do 'em over?"

"Casualties were inflicted," intoned Dooley.

"Good evening, Corporal Cain," the sentry mocked.

"Get fogged," Andy told him.

They filed through the wire, Andy at their head. They moved slackly, wearily. They seemed as though life would never again surprise or perturb them. Their desperation, their knowledge of death were consummate; but also they knew how utterly barren and repulsive life could be. Courage was no longer something to be proud of. The routine of their warfare had settled on them with a hideous monotony. The abuse came out of them without rancour and the jokes fell dead from their lips.

"You jokers must have influence," went on the sentry. "This is your third patrol this week. How d'you do it?"

"We insisted!" snarled Andy.

"Get out of my foggin' way, Hawkins," Tommy told the sentry.

Farther inside the wire, Henry Gilbertson loomed up and met them.

"That you, Andy?"

"Yes, sir."

"Anything startling?"

"No. Ran into an enemy patrol at seven hundred and forty paces on the one-thirty-seven bearing. Killed three. Rest escaped. Here are the papers we got off the bodies."

"Fighting patrol?"

"Well, they fought us."

"Armed to the teeth they were," said Dooley.

Henry addressed them briskly:

"Good night's work. I've had the sar major keep a hot meal for you at company. Run along and eat and then get some sleep."

"You beaut!" Tommy told him.

"Sleep!" remarked Dooley. "If you hadn't mentioned it I'd have never thought of it." He yawned.

They went to their holes, put their rifles and tommy-guns away and filed down the wadi to Company Headquarters with their mess tins. They had no other thoughts than for their stomachs, already quivering for the stewed bully and tinned vegetables.

"Bloody good bloke, Gilby," Dick told them.

"Best officer in this bloody unit," Dooley replied in glum assurance.

"They reckon Groggy's on it again," observed Tommy.

"How could he be? He drinks whisky like water. There wouldn't be enough," Dooley objected.

"I don't mean paralytic," Tommy explained. "But I heard that he's getting his whack."

"Who told you?"

"That sig who was up yestiddy."

"Whisky in this place!" cried Dick with hatred. "Pity they didn't send a bit up here."

"They do," said Andy. "For officers. Crane's got a bottle."

"That the patrol?" came Ted Olley's voice.

"No, it's the Ladies' Aid Society."

86

"Well, there's some stew here for you, girls."

"We know."

They were abreast of the sergeant major now and they could discern him smiling.

"There's a reinforcement, too," he told them.

"One whole reinforcement!"

A voice greeted them from out of the gloom—a deep, rich, jubilant voice:

"How are ya, mates?"

They started, turned, and stood quite still—speechless.

"Did you hear that?"

"It can't be!"

"It is!"

"Well, I'll be fogged! It's him!"

"Chips! You old bastard! How did you get here?"

"I swam," said Chips.

*   *   *

Dooley was Crane's runner for the day. He lay dozing against the shady side of the wadi near Crane's headquarters when he was aroused by a flat, quiet voice:

"Where's Lieutenant Crane?" asked Major Pomfret.

"Just down there at Platoon Headquarters."

Dooley jerked a thumb and closed his eyes again.

"What's your name?"

"Franks." Dooley reopened one of his eyes.

"Franks what?"

"Franks nothing."

"Get up and stand to attention."

Dooley opened the other eye to stare. He grinned and rose slowly to his feet, standing slackly.

"Straighten up."

Dooley moved his shoulders a fraction of an inch.

"Now." The voice was still without expression, the eyes dull and dispassionate. "What's your name?"

"Private Franks."

Dooley's features darkened; his eyes were narrowed and his mouth pursed. There was hate and resentment in the look he gave the major.

"You've still left out a word."

"My name is Private Franks—full stop!"

Goaded to a fury, he almost spat the words. He had clenched his fist and started forward.

Pomfret's eyes never even flickered. His face betrayed not an atom of emotion. He turned about and left Dooley standing there.

A few minutes later Crane came striding up the wadi with a thunderous expression.

"Franks!"

"Sir!"

"You're under arrest. Come with me."

"Ah—ha!" sighed Dooley.

*   *   *

"Dooley's in strife again," said Dick.

"What's he done this time?" asked Andy.

"Had a run-in with the Animal."

"What happened?"

"Oh, it seems the Animal wanted a 'sir' and a salute and Dooley wouldn't oblige."

"Is he on a crime-sheet?"

"I believe so. Isn't it fantastic! Here we are, like rats in the ground, living from hour to hour, never knowing whose turn it is to die next, and Dooley's to be paraded and charged for not saluting the Animal!"

"More fool him."

"What do you mean?"

"He should have saluted and called him 'sir.' It doesn't cost anything. Give him six salutes and a Hail Mary thrown in. Why make an issue of it? It's silly."

"Silly, is it?" Dick was agitated now. "I suppose they're not silly, with all their palaver! I can remember when you'd have gone on an A.4 rather than sling him a salute."

"We live and learn," Andy said.

"Yes—we certainly do," remarked Dick bitterly, and walked away from him.

"Dick!" called Andy.

But Dick did not answer him.

*   *   *

Henry Gilbertson was speaking over the field telephone to Pomfret.

"About Franks, John."

"Yes," said Major Pomfret's voice.

"I'd like to scrub the A.4 and bawl him out myself."

"Wouldn't do, Henry. Respect for rank must be maintained, particularly in the line."

"Is this discipline, John?"

"He was insolent to me."

"Don't you think they expect a little—er, informality in the line? After all, they know very well they may be dead tomorrow."

"I fail to see what bearing that has on it."

"Put yourself in their place. Imagine their feelings."

"I am not interested in their feelings. The charge is to be proceeded with. Action's no excuse for insolence."

"Right!" snapped Henry.

He slammed the phone down and turned to Ted Olley.

"I can't get him out of it."

"If ever a man was aptly named, it's him," said Olley, nodding at the phone.

Henry sighed. "Let's have Franks in and get it over with."

He felt unhappy and ashamed when Ted Olley marched Dooley into the dug-out. He felt almost as though he were betraying one of his own men. Dooley stood impassively, looking a little bored.

"Once again, Dooley."

"Yessir."

Henry opened Dooley's pay-book, the pages of which showed liberal sprinklings of the red ink with which fines and convictions were entered.

"What a pay-book!" he sighed.

Dooley grinned.

"Like a pak-a-poo ticket," he agreed.

Henry studied some of the entries.

"A.W.L. Improperly dressed. A.W.L. Failure to obey a lawful command. I got you out of that blue at Mersa Matruh, but you'll have to go up this time. It'll probably be field punishment."

"That'll be a change," drawled Dooley. "I don't care what you bastards do to me."

Stung to the raw, Henry cried miserably:

"Don't associate me with them! I'll do my best for you blokes whenever I can. But this is the 2 I.C. All I can do is remand you to the C.O."

"Well, remand me! See if I care. It's worth doing field punishment to get out of this bloody hole."

"Here," cautioned the sergeant major.

"That's enough, Dooley," said Henry, looking the essence of unhappiness. "Look," he continued earnestly. "Up here, I'm just one of you, or try to be. As far as I'm concerned you can call me Gilby, as long as it's remembered that I'm the company commander . . . But you can't buck the army. You know that," he ended somewhat inconsequentially.

"Yessir," said Dooley casually. Then he looked a little ashamed himself. "I've got no snout on you, sir. None of us have. As a matter of fact we're all your way."

At once, to hide his pleasure and confusion Henry slapped the pay-book and cried:

"March him out!"

Six Platoon hailed Dooley on his return, gathered round him and demanded a report of the proceedings. Dooley gave them one, distorted only when he mentioned the expressions of mutual regard between the company commander and himself. Dooley's version portrayed Henry as almost in tears and begging forgive-

89

ness. "Like a bloody old wet hen!" he ended, shouting with derision.

Chips chuckled.

"Mum Gilbertson," he remarked.

From that time on Henry was always Mum to B Company.

*   *   *

Tommy Collins lay in Two Section's strong-post and decided that if he didn't get out of Tobruk soon he would go mad. It hadn't been too bad when the Easter battles were on. You'd had no time to think then and it gave you a chance to prove you had guts—which was important to Tommy, for he valued personal courage highly. But now, with only an occasional skirmish, a man had time to get bored—and remember.

Up till now the army had meant freedom for Tommy. For the first time in his life he had got drunk, accosted women, started fights, without keeping one eye over his shoulder for a policeman. Somehow the war seemed to have licensed drunkenness and the pursuit of women : as long as you wore a uniform no one seemed surprised at what you did. His week-end leaves in Sydney, his excursions to Jaffa and Tel Aviv had been wild and free, and for the first time he felt himself to be living fully. Women and drink were plentiful and cheap; always on hand was the answer to a sudden lust. Yes, back among the flesh-pots Tommy had been grateful for the uniform which made him liked and tolerated.

For the hundredth time he cursed the bravado that had made him join the infantry. His mate Dooley was back in Tobruk doing field punishment, so now there was not even the consolation of their clowning. Tommy brooded and had visions—painful, hungry visions.

Streets and pubs, plates of food and the rooms of brothels! The plump, acquiescent bodies of prostitutes in the Jaffa dives! The dark-red Palestine wine, the weak beer, the drunken rides home in the backs of trucks. And now this! Desert and wire, fat black flies, dry burning days, cold remote nights, long, lonely patrols, shelling, bombing and strafing, bully-beef and hard dry biscuits—utter barrenness and the constant menace of death.

Tommy sat and cursed life savagely.

Then a shadow fell across him. He looked up to see Chips Prentice and at once he brightened.

"Hello, Chips me boy! How's Three Section?"

"Off your arse, Tommy."

"What for?"

"Patrol."

"Aw, be fogged!"

"Dinkum. Where's Dick Brett?"

"Back in the wadi."

"Two blokes from each section to report to Crane at once."

"You're pullin' me leg!"

"This is dinkum, I tell you. Lucas is back at Company with the jeebies and I'm acting platoon sergeant. Crane and I and six men are going out in Bren-carriers after a couple of strong-posts the Jerries set up a few nights ago. Fifty rounds per man. You'll get grenades at platoon. We rendezvous with the carriers at the bottom of the wadi at sixteen hundred."

"Where's Andy?"

"He's crook too. Now I'll go and tell Dick."

Chips was gone. Tommy sat down again and cursed. Then he sprang up and shouted towards the wadi.

"Who's gonner look after this place?"

"Gribble!" came back Chips's voice.

"Gawd help us!" cried Tommy, and spat viciously.

"So help me, Christ, I'll get out of this hole one way or another."

*　　　*　　　*

The two drivers stood up in their Bren-carriers and awaited Crane's patrol. One was a dark, thick-bodied, handsome fellow, Potts by name. However, the whole battalion knew him as Go Through, due to his having been absent without leave more times than any other six soldiers together. The other was a young man in his early twenties, half aboriginal; tall, thin, graceful and swift of movement, with a broad face and big dark eyes. His name was Hughie Drover.

"Fancy being up here all the time," observed Go Through, looking about him.

"Bloody lizard couldn't live here," agreed Hughie.

"Mick Varney was trying to tell me that there's hares and gazelles out in the desert," went on Go Through. "Reckons some of 'em were found dead, killed by the shell-fire."

"Someone's been pulling old Mick's leg again," Hughie reflected. "You've only got to tell him you heard an officer say it and he'll believe anything."

This amused Go Through. It wasn't only funny, it was accurate. He smiled, not so much with the mouth as with his wide neat teeth.

A string of men came in sight down the wadi.

"Here's our fighting patrol," announced Go Through.

"What platoon is it?" Hughie asked, shading his eyes. He was bare-headed. He had long ago forgotten where he had left his steel helmet. Whenever he could, he went bare-foot.

"Kenneth Crane and his merry men."

"That bastard!"

"How are yer, Chips?"

"You, you bastard!" exclaimed Chips amiably to Go Through.

"What a mob to take out into No Man's Land!" jeered Hughie with a sudden, face-possessing grin.

Mutual derisive expressions of regret at the identity of drivers and those about-to-be-driven were bandied back and forth, and Crane stood ungreeted and unnoticed. Scowling, he called them to order after a few minutes of this and commanded the riflemen to mount the carriers. The carriers swung round, lurched in a sudden boiling of dust, nosed over the shallow banks of the wadi and sped across level desert towards the concertina wire.

Standing up in the carriers, Six Platoon obtained the widest view yet of the perimeter they were holding. On either side of them were concrete-lined strong-posts like their own, huddling behind erratic whorls of concertina wire and a maze of minefields.

"So this is the Red Line," said someone.

"You ought to know," Go Through told him. He jerked his thumb behind him. "The Blue Line's back there. They're still digging like mad. And minefields! The Ginger Beers have laid so many mines they've lost trace of some of 'em and they're going up on their own bloody mines!"

The carriers sped through the gap and out into No Man's Land, rattling and jerking over hard, flat stones and then diving and swaying among the camel-thorn hummocks. They spread out to twenty yards apart, stopping at intervals for Crane to take a compass bearing and survey the heat-blurred skyline with his glasses.

Suddenly he bent, indicating a line to his front with a rigid arm. The carriers lurched forward. They had hardly begun to move again when a shell zipped by and burst blackly about fifty yards behind them. They crouched lower as stones and metal rattled against the sides of the carriers. Another shell sped over, nearer this time, for the rattling against the carriers was harder and heavier. Bullets sang softly in the air above them, then shrilly and cruelly as the Nazi machine-gunners found range.

"We're gonna cop it!" yelled Go Through.

The clatter of the machine-gun now came plainly from their left flank. Crane's carrier lurched suddenly into dead ground and he waved Hughie to follow him in. As Hughie swung the carrier round the front of it seemed to disappear in a great, clanging burst of smoke. The carrier stopped dead, her front stove in by a shell. What was left of Hughie was lifted out of the seat and lay across the armouring behind, head and limbs lolling at either end of a twitching, glistening, red pulp.

To the other occupants of the carrier it prompted no thought. Their eyes recognised it and their bodies abandoned the carrier with its mangled, hot flesh, scrambling from a similar fate into the safety of dead ground.

Now the wheeze of the mortar-bomb was added to the shell-fire about them. For a few lunatic minutes they crouched and their bodies shook to explosions and became fogged in dust and smoke. Then it slackened and finally ceased.

They spat out sand and looked anxiously about them. Crane now spoke directly to Go Through:

"You and I and Two men will go up to where this bit of dead ground ends. Bring the carrier above ground just enough to engage them with your Bren. Prentice, you take the rest and work round the other side. As soon as you hear the carrier open fire, rush them."

Chips, Dick, Tommy, and two men from Three Section lay tensely against the slope as the carrier moved off. The sound of its engine became faint. Then the Bren rattled.

"Over the top!" cried Chips and ran crouching into the open. They scrambled to their feet and made, bent over, for the sound of the machine-gun. Tommy was firing his Bren from the hip. The Nazis were visible now, a hunched mass around their gun. Their arms windmilled and stick-bombs came out at the Australians. The two men from Three Section fell dead. A grenade thrown by Chips found the Nazi gun and hid it in a cloud of dust for a few moments. Another stick-bomb came over, this time at Dick. It lifted him away from the ground bodily, blinding him. He staggered about, hands to eyes, exclaiming deeply. He teetered on the edge of a shell-crater into which Tommy pushed him. As Tommy swung the Bren back on to the Nazis, their machine-gun poured a burst into his body. He slid down after Dick, into the crater.

With a grenade in each hand Chips went on alone, tossing them as he went. He spattered the gun-crew with bursts from his tommy-gun, coolly and mercilessly, until the magazine emptied. He threw his last grenade in among the mortar crew, crying:

"Split this up among you!"

Crane and the others, running across towards him, heard it plainly. There was one live Nazi and Chips brained him with his steel helmet. When his comrades reached him he was in sole possession of the Nazi strong-post.

*   *   *

Dick opened his eyes to see the night sky. He looked straight upward at stars that were small and dull. It was deathly cold. He moved his eyes, but the fiery pain that filled them caused him to close them once again. He reopened them slowly. Thought stirred in him obscurely and now he looked for an accustomed thing—like the parapet of the strong-post, the shape of Dooley's Bren, the watching head of Andy or Tommy. But there was none of them: only a jagged ledge of earth above him, whitened by moonlight. He let his eyes travel, and facing him he saw Tommy Collins.

He tried to call Tommy's name but only a groan came out of him. He tried again, and this time spoke the name.

But Tommy didn't answer, didn't move. He lay against the side of the crater, arms flung outward, one leg bent, his face staring upward steadfastly. Rather than shine on that face, the moonlight seemed to have been absorbed into it, for the face was dully tinted blue. Its mouth was black and bitter, the lips stretched wide, the teeth between them clenched. The eyes seemed all white. They had no depth, no light—no life.

He knew then that Tommy was dead. For alive, Tommy had only been contemptible, but now he was terrible. The body, held for ever in its final desperate posture; the eyes with the blind white stare; the mouth frozen in its last cry of agony.

He tried to rise, to turn his head away from the sight of Tommy. Again the sharp pain filled his eyes. His head throbbed and spun; then he felt as though he were floating.

In his delirium he was with Tommy, but Tommy was alive again. He was beating Tommy with his fists because he was sick of the things Tommy said. Tommy was on the ground; his thin, wry mouth was sucking in air. "All right, I've had it," he was saying . . . "I'm sorry, Tommy. Let me help you up." But Tommy looked up with the eyes of an enemy, eyes that didn't understand. There, the two pairs of eyes were held for an eternity . . . not understanding . . . Then Andy was there and he helped Tommy up. But now Tommy wasn't hurt—he was drunk. "Alicante," he laughed, and reeled off waving a bottle . . . "They breed 'em!" said Andy . . . "Sydney." Suddenly, Tommy looked back, and his face was mild, childish and tragic . . . "Sydney" . . . Dick was going along in a tram, looking for where Tommy lived. He had to tell someone about Tommy. Rows of houses looking like concertinas huddled between factories . . . somewhere among those furtive black warrens was where Tommy lived . . . The tram was roaring . . .

It was the sound of engines he could hear. He went to cry out but checked himself. The instinct to survive brought him fully alert, telling him to listen. Now he lay in cold reality, ears striving to identify the engines. Nazi or British?

The engines stopped. He heard voices.

Nazi or British?

They were very near. He could detect the sound of boots on the loose stones. The sound came nearer, then faded to his flank.

There was a sharp, sickening smell in the crater. Something sluggish and glistening twisted from Tommy's body and ended near Dick's boot. It was Tommy's entrails. Slowly, they seemed to come a little closer.

The voices were forgotten. He had to get away from this thing that had crept out of a dead body and was seeking contact with his own. He jerked and whimpered as he tried to escape. His body was rigid and painful. He suddenly thought he was paralysed and at the same moment the thing he was trying to escape came another inch towards him. His ultimate resistance gave; he cried out aloud and fell back unconscious.

Movement. Soothing, swaying movement. Boots softly hitting sand. Subdued voices. One standing out. Chips!

". . . must have been somewhere round there, but I thought Tommy was with me all the time. Poor little bastard!"

"Chips!" he tried to call.

The movement stopped. The stretcher descended slowly to earth. The stretcher-bearers moved around to the side of the stretcher. Chips's great frame bent over him.

"Chips," he said again.

"How are you, Dick?" The deep rich voice was softened and tender. "Did you think your Uncle Chips had forgotten you?"

The atmosphere of safety, the strong, protecting voice of good old Chips! The feeling of coming home after a long voyage.

When they got him back to the Regimental Aid Post Captain Barrett said he was suffering from shock and slightly feverish. The M.O. told Chips that Dick would be all right within a few days, and he would keep him under observation at the R.A.P. He administered morphia and put the patient into a dug-out.

That done, the M.O. stood breathing the cool night air. He felt very grateful for it. The day had been quite a busy one for him. C Company had been heavily shelled and seventeen wounded that morning. Barely had he got those away to the rear than the casualties of Crane's patrol had been brought in: young Brett lying drugged in a dug-out and just across the way five dead men, all ready for burial in the morning.

10

Six Platoon Headquarters was a cleft in the side of the wadi, reinforced with stones and covered by an old tent-fly. Immediately above it, in a commanding position, was a weapon pit manned when necessary by Crane, Lucas, and Crane's runner. By now, strong communication trenches, reinforced with sandbags, connected Platoon H.Q. and the concrete posts of the old Italian garrison which the sections manned.

Seeing it again after a week at the R.A.P., it all seemed strange to Dick, the events connected with it remote.

Back at Battalion H.Q. life had been slower and far more pleasant. The colonel had discovered a small cave in a bit of dead ground, had the pioneer platoon enlarge it. Fashion a ramp down to its depths out of the displaced earth, and here he had established himself. Officers, N.C.O.s and men attached to Battalion H.Q. had dug themselves in with varying degrees of comfort along the sides of the hollow ground. They gave Dick a stretcher and a spot under a solitary fig tree. There were the remains of a stone wall there also and between this and two pieces of angle-iron he stretched a German groundsheet and lay dozing under its shade for most of the day. He lay and thought of very little. He relished the peace and the ease and listened to the occasional harsh rustle of the fig tree, coming out of his lair only at meal times.

Battalion H.Q. was a small community with Varney, the regimental sergeant major, as the inevitable butt of its humour. Varney had striven steadfastly to maintain the routine of the camp. His passion for army forms, correctness of the approach, precision in all things, was not affected by the battalion's new surroundings. And he had the support of Major Pomfret. The H.Q. men hated them both; but not impartially, for Varney was laughable whereas Pomfret was "a plain animal," as they put it. They derided Varney, mocked him, defied him openly or covertly. On one occasion, a number of them had gone off without leave to a dump half a mile away for material to rein-force their doovers, as they called their dwelling-places. Noticing their absence, Varney had asked their whereabouts, only to be met with grins and vague replies: "They're not far off." Frus-trated in his attempts to discover the missing men he suddenly roared: "Call the roll!" Then followed an hilarious parade of all other ranks at Battalion H.Q. Dusty, grubby, scrubby-faced men in tattered shorts, shirts and battered tin hats; boots worn white by the sand; some without shirts or socks. A tatter-demalion, unshaven crowd of grinning men, overwhelmed by the ludicrous spectacle of a roll-call in this God-forsaken spot! The wanderers were paraded and solemnly reprimanded. And long after, for no apparent reason, a man at Battalion H.Q. would suddenly shout out: "Call the roll!" and raise a storm of laughter.

The hygiene squad had dug a deep pit and above it built a handsome latrine with a special hessianed-off section to protect the officers from the vulgar gaze as they defaecated. The day after it was completed a bomb had destroyed it during a Stuka raid. On a second occasion it went up, according to legend, when a stray shell hit it; although several knowledgeable men had whispered something about a grenade being dropped down it. Despairing, the hygiene men built their next latrine above the bomb crater—with no hessian.

Dick saw the colonel only once, talking volubly, Pomfret walking in silence at his side, nodding now and then. Fitzroy still sported his British forage cap and had added to his wardrobe a pair of "sneakers"—suède boots with heavy crêpe rubber soles, and a pair of dark glasses. He was a regular caller on the officers of a British artillery unit nearby.

During his rest, Dick received a summons from the adjutant. Perhaps three years older than Dick, he sat at an improvised desk and distantly and superciliously asked Dick whether he would like a job in the Intelligence Section. Dick told him, "Thank you, no."

"There are a couple of stripes in it, Brett."

Dick repeated his refusal.

"You lack ambition," remarked the adjutant, and dismissed him.

Dick turned to leave the dug-out.

"Brett!"

"Yes, sir." He faced about again.

"Haven't you forgotten something?"

For a moment Dick was nonplussed. Then he gave a salute. He left, feeling humiliated and cursing under his breath.

Outside, he ran into Go Through.

"You in strife?" asked Go Through.

"No! The Boy Bastard tried to kid me into the 'I' Section. That's all."

"How are yer, colt?" enquired Go Through softly.

"Me? I'm all right."

"Like a trip?"

"Where to? Alex?"

"Into Tobruk. See the sights. Have a swim. Me and Lieutenant Temple's got a special job to do. Come back tomorrer. Like to come? No one'll miss yer."

"What'll Temple say?"

"OO? Arch? He won't say nothin'! He's one of the boys. Don't like Crane and that mob."

"Good! I'll come."

Lieutenant Temple, of the carrier platoon, awaited them at the wheel of a small desert buggy; a large young fellow, sunburnt almost black, with a vivid ginger moustache of fascinating proportions and a close-shaven head.

"I'm bringin' a mate, Arch," Go Through announced.

"Who is he?"

"Dick Brett from B Company. He was in that stoush with Hughie the other day."

"Glad to know you, Dick." Lieutenant Temple put forth a hand. "So you were with Hughie?"

"I was in his carrier."

"Bloody nice lad, Hughie," remarked Temple looking straight

97

in front of him. "Go Through!" he suddenly roared. "How much foggin' longer has a man got to wait for you?"

"Don't panic, Arch," advised Go Through, who had his nose in a box of tools. He hoisted them into the back of the truck and began a struggle with the decrepit tailboard.

"Go Through's the slowest bastard in the A.I.F.," Temple told Dick. "He wastes half of my life."

"Dry yer bloody eyes," rejoined Go Through, getting in beside them. "He's on me back all the time," he confided to Dick. The truck started with a vicious jerk and Go Through sat down suddenly and painfully. "You bastard!"

Lieutenant Temple appeared highly pleased.

The wheels of trucks had churned the dust on the track they took till it was a fine powder. It rose in a choking yellow cloud and billowed about them so that their surroundings were blotted out. They seemed to be lost in a thick golden fog through which the sun was felt but not seen. It swirled about them, settled over them, penetrating to their scalps, inside their ears, and into their boots where it was mingled with sweat and lay like a scab. They wore gas goggles to protect their eyes and these had to be wiped constantly as a misty scum came over them and the eyes began to sting with sweat beneath them. The truck kept on its course merely by following the ruts left by many vehicles, in which it staggered, swayed, heaved and lashed about furiously, as though it were trying to leap out of them. A maze of stakes and apron wire loomed up suddenly on either side.

"Minefields," Temple told Dick above the roar and clatter of the desert buggy. "Couple of fellers wandered in there the other night. One got killed, the other had his foot blown off. There are enough minefields around here to blow up the whole of the Afrika Corps."

"That's the way to win this war," put in Go Through. "Blow all the bloody Huns up at once on the one big minefield. That's what yer need! One dirty big minefield!"

Temple's moustache quivered in laughter.

"Go Through's always thinking up bright ideas for ending the war at one fell swoop."

Half seriously, Go Through fell to defending his military theories:

"Yair, and I got better ideas than some of the galahs that give us our orders. Some of them ain't fit to run a brothel—mentioning no names," he added with a dark glance sideways.

Temple's moustache actually waggled. His teeth came through it in a grin as he watched the track ahead of them.

"Well, why don't you work your way up to the top and show us how the army should be run?" He turned to Dick. "I offered him a couple of stripes and he told me to bung them—the rude thing!"

"A couple of stripes!" Go Through's voice seemed to curdle with scorn. "Listen to the bastard!" Destructively, mercilessly, he proceeded to analyse the rank of corporal. "A corporal's the scum of the army. He's a poor bloody in-between that no one loves. The officers and sergeants are on his back and he's on the men's backs. The corporal has to pass on the bull that the officers and sergeants hand out and take the kicks from the men when he does it. He cops the abuse from the men because he ain't separated from them like the officers and sergeants. He has to sleep and eat with the blokes they make him stand over. All for a couple of bob a day extra! Not this feller!"

Dick discovered that he was enjoying himself. For the first time since they had brought him in from the perimeter, he felt that life was his business, and still to be lived. His ego rose gratefully to the surface and joined the present situation.

"No one's down on our corporals in Six Platoon," he protested. "We've got to have 'em and we've got good blokes."

"Well, I'll admit," conceded Go Through, "that it's probably different in the rifle companies. If a corporal makes a coot of himself there he generally don't last long." (Dick suddenly thought of Percy, now a private once again.) "But, in general . . ." Go Through concluded vaguely, his argument suddenly gone tame.

It was Temple who rescued his argument from its anti-climax.

"A corporal can be the worst rank in the army," he said. "I had a miserable bloody life when I was one. You've got a good bunch of N.C.O.s in B Company," he told Dick. "That Chips Prentice is a soldier and a half. Just quietly, he's up for a decoration."

Dick found no cause for surprise at this. Chips with a decoration seemed natural. Chips was made for such honours. Chips the Magnificent! Chips the unconquerable!

The track swung round a wide half circle and now Dick saw that on its left a long line of concertina wire ran, looking as if it had been frozen stiff in the middle of some terrible convulsion. The powdered sand of the track gave way to a hard flat surface strewn with stones and pocked with shell craters. A hundred yards to their right the whole country had been converted into minefields. That landscape looked unreal, something dashed across the wavering screen of the air. The maze of iron stakes and apron wire was like a mass of lines scribbled in sepia, more tangible because of their darkness; ominous, forbidding and remote. Human feet didn't belong there. Time meant nothing to the place. It gave no quarter. Its answer was death.

Behind the concertina wire Dick saw sandbagged weapon pits, strong-posts and zig-zagging communication trenches. They all looked brand-new to him. The sandbags had not yet been bleached dirty white by the sun or tattered by bullet and shrapnel. Several men stood up and watched the truck as it went past. The truck passed close by one of the posts. A stocky fellow with a shirt that hung open from the waist, a steel helmet stuck right back on his head and a fuzzy ginger beard, stood with his hands on his hips and called a greeting to them. There was something urchin-like, defiant and humorous about him as he stood there and spat. The sort of man who would enjoy himself somehow, anywhere. Another stood up in the pit. He had no shirt and wore an Italian pith helmet. He was dark, aquiline, long in the leg and round-shouldered. As his teeth smiled in a face burnt chocolate brown, he looked knowing, patient and sly. There was a Berretta strapped to his waist. In fact, the whole armament of this particular post seemed to be by courtesy of the enemy. There was a German Spandau mounted next to him and nearby a heavy Breda.

The desert buggy clattered by. Fifty yards farther along a soldier hailed them, and the Australians knew at once, by his build and dress, that he was an Englishman. With contempt they took in his stockings, pulled right up and turned over just below the knees, the wide, skirt-like shorts, the black boots and puttees. He even had his respirator slung round his shoulders. He was very short, but wide and stocky, with thick legs and a flat, amiable face. He was a corporal.

Temple brought the truck to a stop alongside him. "Good day, Tommy."

The Tommy saluted him, and Temple, who had discarded his helmet, merely nodded.

"Could you give me a lift as far as t' rawd, sir?" the Tommy asked in a northern accent.

"Hop aboard, choom," chuckled Go Through.

With a slightly bewildered expression the Tommy climbed up and squatted behind them. The truck lurched forward.

"Want the main road?" asked Temple.

"Yes, please, sir. Ah've got to show ration trook way in to ower pawst."

"You belong to that machine-gun mob?" asked Go Through with a quickened interest.

"Aye, thut's oos. Northumberland Fusiliers. We're giving supportin' fire to the Second Y." Suddenly, the Tommy's face broke into a smile and his body as well as his personality seemed to relax, as though finally convinced he was among friends. "Only," he added brightly, "we call owersels the Australian Fusiliers now."

Go Through guffawed. "Good on yers! You'll do me, Tommy! The Australian Fusiliers!"

"Like being with Aussies, do you?" asked Dick.

"We're good pals," confided the Tommy. "We couldn't catch

100

on to their ways at first. We never knew when they were serious and when they weren't. And they used to act so daft! And then, the way they cheek their officers and N.C.O.s soomtimes!"

Temple began to grin. "Yes, it's terrible! We get no respect from them. None whatever! They treat me something awful."

"You poor old bastard!" cried Go Through. He patted Temple's shoulder. "Never mind, Arch, I'll be real nice to yer from now on."

The Tommy's grin was different now: half incredulous, half delighted at something that was to him fantastic. The Australians and the way they went on were still a little legendary.

He hopped off and thanked them when they reached what was obviously the main road. Dick could see telegraph poles and a pipe-line. There was a fair amount of traffic passing to and fro: desert buggies, utes, thirty hundredweights, two-tonners, motor bikes and an armoured car or two.

Temple pointed back the way they had come. "They're Blue Line posts we passed. Blue Line runs roughly parallel with the perimeter—the Red Line. That's two lines of defence the Huns have got to get through before they reach Tobruk. Two lines of infantry with Vickers support, minefields galore, plenty of artillery, a fair number of anti-tank ditches, stone cairns . . . We're a hard nut to crack, when you come to think of it."

"How many men garrisoning this place, do you reckon?"

"About twenty thousand, I hear. Besides us they've got Pommy artillery and mug gunners, armoured cars and 'I' tanks and a few Indians. And ack-ack galore. Those Stukas and Henschels get a pretty hot time over the town. This road leads right into town."

Temple started the truck up again and turned into the road. He pointed out to the left to a couple of dark snub-nosed shapes. "Mark IIIs knocked out in the Easter battle. We'll be passing the prisoner-of-war cage soon. It's just near the junction of this and the Bardia Road. Like to stop and have a look at the prisoners?"

Dick smirked. For the first time with these men he felt a little superior. He was from a rifle platoon. He had killed Nazis and Italians. He had been through it; knew what it meant to be shelled till you shook, overrun by tanks, run blindly into machine-gun fire, be blown over by a stick-bomb.

"I've seen plenty of Huns, thanks," he said.

"Yes," Temple replied, "but not caged up. You ought to see the looks on some of them."

"I'll go and have a look," said Dick decisively. A vain edge of his mind saw an opportunity to show off, look bored at the Nazis, tell Temple and Go Through a few things.

"Righteo!" exclaimed Temple, and the next minute swerved the truck. A heavy three-toner flew by, yellow mudguards rattling madly, canvas flapping, men in the back hanging on for dear life. "Mad bastards!" he yelled.

"You should talk!" sneered Go Through, well acquainted with Temple's recklessness at the wheel. "See those jokers sitting on their quoits over there?" he asked Dick. "They're some of the 'bush artillery.' They've got Itie guns, and they've put great long lanyards on 'em. They load 'em, take cover, pull the lanyard and hope for the best. Gawd knows where the shells go. They've got no instruments on 'em and half the jokers working 'em were cooks and batmen and that. Gawd, it's funny to watch 'em. 'Two telegraph poles to the right,' someone'll yell. 'Hoist 'er up a foot, Bill! All set! Take cover!' Bang! There's a foggin' great cloud of dust and the old gun jumps like a kangaroo! The mad bastards'll blow themselves to buggery one of these days for a moral."

Dick went into quiet laughter. There was something rich and warm about Go Through's profanity. The very tones of his voice as he described something brought you a vision that was vulgar and uproarious.

"What road's this?" he asked.

"This is the El Adem Road, colt." Go Through pointed to another road coming in from the right. "That's the Bardia Road. The prisoner-of-war cage is over on our left."

Temple swerved off the road on to a track. The cage was already visible: posts about ten feet high with six strands of barbed wire and a sentry on each corner. Temple brought the truck to a standstill and they climbed out and approached the wire.

"Nearly all Ities," said Go Through.

These Italians were easily distinguishable from the Nazis, apart from their greater numbers. Everything about them was brighter. Even their personalities, it occurred to Dick. Some of them, catching the eyes of the Australians who gazed at them, even smiled in a friendly way, as though there were a joke between them. Other more practical souls among them stood around in vaguely hopeful attitudes with mess tins in their hands. With their dark, vivid faces, their rapid chatter, their greenish uniforms peppered with gaudy badges, the whole chuckling, vociferous crowd of them seemed to convey the bright insouciance of a flock of parrots. What an anachronism they were, these light-hearted, cynical conscripts, milling to their surrender across the stretches of a bitter, empty desert while Britisher and Nazi fought for the main fortress of what Mussolini had proclaimed his empire. One thing was apparent—they couldn't care less about Mussolini and his empire. Nor did mere contempt help you to understand them. Perhaps it was good for your own morale to tell yourself they surrendered in their tens of thousands because the very mention of the word

"Australiano" struck fear into their hearts. You could believe it in the frenzy of battle and it was the kind of arrogant illusion that Crane encouraged. Dick could remember that once or twice when the fancy had taken them the Italians had resisted as strongly as the Nazis. And standing there watching them, undismayed prisoners, obviously not considering themselves enemies, Dick discovered a final adjective for them—shrewd! That's what they were. They knew there was nothing in Libya for them, those gay and simple men. Their hearts were back in Italy. Not all fascists here!

"Bad lookin' lot of bastards," Go Through was saying. His eyes were indicating the Nazis. They sat or stood in a small close knot, well away from the Italians, whom they ignored. Their faces were either blank or brooding. Big men most of them; no laughter in their eyes, no fullness or compassion in their mouths. Hardened, hewn, those faces were, with cruel clefts. Hitler appeared to have accomplished a more thorough crime than Mussolini. Born of one war, one could imagine their minds, beaten, warped—a horde of brutes all ready for the next.

"C'mon," said Go Through. "I've seen me eyeful."

As the truck swung back on to the road and made for Tobruk, certain words of Henry Gilbertson's came back to Dick: ". . . a gigantic plot against democracy and the common man whose spearhead is Nazi Germany . . . but it's the real war all right now—the anti-fascist war! . . ."

And as the truck sped on he let his face take the rush of the wind and felt suddenly glad to be where he was.

"There she is!" proclaimed Go Through. "Tobruk! Come to beautiful Tobruk!"

"Queen city of the Mediterranean!" intoned Temple. "Bask on its beaches among the wreckage and the dead fish! Witness the thrilling spectacle of the daily Stuka parade! Walk in the shade of its rubble-strewn streets! Regular tours to the perimeter to see the celebrated fireworks display! Spend your next holiday in beautiful Tobruk! Book now and avoid disappointment!"

The road had taken a wide bend and again met the water pipe-line which had crossed and re-crossed it. They were close to the waterfront now, and for the first time in many weeks Dick saw the sparkle of the Mediterranean. There was a haze over the distance, as though the horizon had drawn in close. The rich blue sea moved gently, but across it the sheen of sunlight flashed like knife-blades. Two ships lay close in, half sunken. They did not look like ships whose sailing days were over, but rather as though they wallowed at rest and would soon rise and thrust their way out to sea again. The far shore of the harbour stretched into the haze. Opposite them stood the little

103

town, neat, white and forlorn-looking. The buildings, like white boxes, were far less marked than Dick had imagined. But here and there was a ragged wall, a broken edge, or a torn corner —like slices of bread that had been gnawed at. And in the shadows between them, sometimes spilling on to the footpaths, a pile of rubble. And there on the waterfront was an untidy wharf, and up against it, veiled by camouflage nets and seething with men, lay a small ship, being unloaded. The men worked like ants, to and fro in crooked files between trucks and the tiny ship, their bare shoulders burdened under cases or their arms drawn taut by ammunition boxes.

"They don't waste any time unloading a ship," Temple commented to Dick. "The sailors like to get out before the Stukas come. The waterfront's an unhealthy place during a raid and that, of course, makes the unloading parties go like navvies."

When Dick had taken in the scene Temple started the truck again. He took it up past the waterfront, swinging into a narrow street and pulling up where a great mountain of rubble made an unintended dead end. Above, not far distant, rose the tower of a church. A tree leaning awry across the sidewalk half hid a doorway that was curtained by a blanket. A form in nothing but shorts thrust it aside and glared at them:

"Yers take yer time, don't yers?"

Go Through climbed down, ignoring the reproach. "Are we in time for a cup of tea? That's the main thing."

The glarer showed that his hospitality was unimpaired by growling: "I suppose we can squeeze one out for yer." He addressed Dick. "Want a cup of tea, sport?"

"His name's Dick," said Temple. "This is Happy, Dick."

" 'Ow are yer, Dick?"

"The miserablest poor bastard that ever drew breath," contributed Go Through, indicating Happy.

Happy poured malevolence out of his eyes, and retorted: "Yair? Well, there's more fogging Bren carriers to be fixed out the back there than yer could poke a stick at! Yer gonna have yer finger out for the next day or two, I'm telling yer, yer fat bastard!"

Temple winked at Dick. "Mates!"

Go Through slapped Happy's shoulder. "How are yer, Hap, old feller?"

"Up ter," replied Happy. He winked woodenly at Dick. "Come in, Dick."

The walls of the room they entered were painted lime green. There were two ornate, rickety iron cots and between them a large wooden case strewn with a variety of commodities: cigarettes, shaving gear, mess tins, a bayonet, a pad and envelopes, an Italian pistol, the photo of a woman in a gilt frame, a tin of bully-beef, a large piece of whitish metal cut in the shape of

104

a rat. There was a ladder leading to a manhole in the ceiling, through which came light. The walls had been scribbled and drawn on so thickly that lines of writing sloped into each other in a maze, and the contours of drawings tangled and interlocked. Scores of Australians had written their rank, name and number and the town they came from—laconic testaments to their passage; the only personal evidence of their part in a chapter of history. Some of them might be dead, or lying wounded in a base hospital, or even back in the town the name of which was written: Private Fred McGinnis, VX——, Orbost, Vic; QX——, Private G. W. Wilson, Charters Towers; SX——, Private H. Spencer, Mt. Gambier. Best beer in Aussie. Above the doorway someone had scrawled: Corporals and below. There was a pencil drawing of a nude woman with thick emphasis at the breasts and crutch. There was a Primus stove in the centre of the room and on it a blackened tin. From the depths of the case Happy fished out three tin mugs, handing them to his visitors. To Dick he remarked:

"The joker who owns this has sypho. D'yer mind?"

"Not in the least," Dick told him.

They sat on the jangling cots and drank the tea that Happy poured for them. Pausing in the middle of what was a passable imitation of a faucet Go Through observed to Temple:

"Makes a good brew of tea, the old coot."

"That's about his sole use," Temple responded.

Happy's reply had not reached his lips before a field telephone in the corner of the room squeaked a summons. "Excuse me, gents. 'Ullo! Yer don't say! Thanks for lettin' me know. . . . It's on," he told his visitors. "Air raid red." He went to the blanket, drew it aside and bawled: "Air raid red!"

Faintly, a voice answered him from the distance. Before the blanket dropped back and muffled it they heard the sound of engines and a distant popping of gun-fire.

Happy groped beneath the bed and dragged out a steel helmet and his boots. He put the helmet on the top of his head and drew on the boots.

Temple got off the bed and began to mount the ladder.

"Let's come up and see the fun."

Dick and Go Through followed him. Looking down, Dick searched for Happy to see if he followed also. But Happy had disappeared.

Up on the flat roof the glare of the sun assailed them and for a few seconds they could see nothing. The haze had gone from the sky. It was now clear and infinite. High up in the east was a formation of black dots. They came tranquilly through a blue background, patterned with bursts of white smoke, like a floral curtain. Only the heavy guns sought them as yet. They were too high for the Bofors. Then they seemed to poise and come earthward at an angle. Their sound became frantic and strident. Every Bofors in Tobruk hammered metal skyward.

The Stukas streamed down through the screen of bursting shells. The whole morning whistled, rattled and thundered. One of the Stukas was hit. It writhed to its doom, twisting and turning as though to rid itself of the smoke pouring from its tail. It fell into the sea with a huge boom and a gigantic mountain of spray.

The first stick of bombs hit the earth: Baroom! Baroom! Baroom!

Miles to the east, something burnt in ponderously rolling clouds of black smoke.

"Look at this bastard, will yer?"

Go Through pointed. A plane was coming in swift and low on their left. Directly in front of it a Bofors still pumped shells at it. Something black and jagged flew off the plane's rear and seemed to whirl lazily in the sky. The Stuka began to smoke. But still it came on and still the Bofors spat at it. They saw the bombs leave its underside, skimming earthwards, straight at the Bofors.

Baroom!

On the roof they instinctively went flat. They looked up. The Nazi was now visible in detail; its markings shone dully. The tail-plane hung in tatters. Somewhere close a Bren opened up on it. More and more smoke came out of it. Then it disappeared behind the far rooftops of the town. They held their breaths, waiting. Then came what their tensed ears expected: a gigantic thump. Black smoke spurted skywards. Out of the smoke and dust around the Bofors a dancing figure, bare to the waist, tossed its knees up and shook hands with itself. The bomb had missed the gun and its crew.

Back along the waterfront a line of white umbrellas of spray slowly subsided, cutting right across the bows of the little ship. But she was intact. On her stern someone was operating a Lewis gun.

But the hideous orchestration of the battle was diminishing. One by one the red-hot barrels were becoming silent. As the raiders made to sea it flared up once or twice in spiteful spasms. Within a few minutes the planes were gone and their sound faded into nothing.

An incredible silence came over the town. Once more it wavered and sparkled in the glare of the sun. And above them, fashioned by the sky winds, arched the long whorling of sombre smoke, like a gigantic wreath over Tobruk.

*   *   *

When Dick reached Battalion Headquarters the next morning he was waylaid by R.S.M. Varney.

"Private Brett, the M.O. has been asking for you since yester-day afternoon. Where were you?"

Dick stared at the dark, cloddish face. This pest, this simple-ton! What a perfect instrument for someone like the Animal. (I'm not going to bother to lie to him.)

"I went into Tobruk."

The merest trace of satisfaction crossed the R.S.M.s features. "A.W.L.!"

"That's right—A.W.L."

Varney pondered dully and pleasurably, savouring in some obscure fashion the opportunity to apply the book of rules. As a peasant told his beads, Varney rehearsed the Army Law. He sighed heavily.

"I have more trouble with B Company men than any others. I suppose that's what comes of having a company commander who doesn't command you half his time."

Dick was taken devilishly with glee. Obviously Mad Mick was echoing the Animal. But——

"Sar Major," he replied formally, drawing himself to atten-tion and putting as much self-righteousness as he could into his tones, "You have no right to talk to an O.R. in that manner about a brave, efficient officer. I'm not sure I shouldn't report to him what you have said."

Varney's fat brows and cheeks swelled until his small eyes glared out of clefts. His jaw grew puffed and ruddy.

"You . . ." he growled in his oaf's voice "report to the M.O."

That was the way to deal with Varney's type! Quote the book of rules back at them. Frighten them with their own devils.

He found Captain Barrett in the R.A.P. It was hard to per-ceive whether the captain was cynical, bored or sick. Perhaps he was all three. He was a short, plump man, half bald. The plumpness ran to his features making them nondescript. He wore a ragged, silky moustache; his eyes were pale and hopeless. His methods of examination and diagnosis were simple. They were based on the premise that anyone who reported sick was either malingering or enlarging on his suffering. Neither pos-sibility angered or revolted him : he was only wearied by the necessity for exposing the patient's deception. Back in Palestine, he had called a man who had come to him frequently with stomach trouble, a malingerer, and he had threatened to put the man on a crime sheet if he came complaining again. Some hours later the man had been rushed to hospital with ruptured stomach ulcers and his life barely saved. The story, when be-came current in the Second X, earned the M.O. the title of Butcher Barrett. He was disturbed neither by the incident nor the title. The man had been unfortunate in that he had suffered from the sins of many another malingerer. How to pick out

107

the occasional genuine case among the many sham illnesses? When Henry Gilbertson once suggested a thorough examination, Barrett had replied that an M.O.'s job was not to discover illness, but to make it next to impossible for a man to evade duty on medical grounds.

Barrett was just preparing to examine a man as Dick entered: a fellow with sickish yellow skin and dull eyes.

"You again, Cummings?"

"Yes, Doctor, me again."

"'Sir,' if you don't mind, Cummings. There are no doctors in the Army."

"You're telling me!" said Cummings bitterly.

"That'll do, Cummings. Is your back still troubling you?"

"Yes, sir."

The M.O. allowed his eyes to shift upwards. "Your back! Where does it hurt you, Cummings?"

"Same place as last time."

"And where was that?"

Cummings indicated. "Here."

"Oh, yes. Give him some more of those tablets, Corporal."

"Look sir." Cummings's voice trembled. "Those tablets are no good. I still can't sleep for the pain. Every time I raise a pick it hurts like hell. There must be something wrong with my kidneys."

"Your kidneys are a long way from where you showed me, Cummings. Keep taking these tablets. And don't be afraid of swinging the pick, Cummings. Next, please."

The man went out past Dick looking distracted, muttering to himself. Next to prison, thought Dick, and R.A.P. must be the most humiliating place in the army. No wonder a man would sooner say nothing and endure pain than experience its degradation too often. Barrett fulfilled his purpose, as he discerned it, admirably. A man in the sick line felt shoddy, dishonest, depraved. Better wait till you had to be carried away.

"Private Brett, sir," announced the medical corporal, recognising Dick.

"Enjoying your little holiday, Brett?"

"Yes, thank you, sir."

"Too bad it must end."

"I'll be glad to get back."

The M.O. grimaced gently at such stupidity. He wrote something across the sick report; then looked up at Dick still standing there. "You may go."

Dick went, thinking furiously about Barrett.

Poisonous little bastard!

Yes, thought Dick, trudging up the wadi to Platoon Headquarters, I feel as if I've been away for six months. As one or

108

two familiar landmarks came into sight, he felt almost a shock of anticipation. Good God—homecoming!

A small calibre shell burst raucously down the wadi and he jerked flat against the stony ground. A hundred yards away! —what was the matter with him? Yes—he was home all right.

Just outside Platoon Headquarters he came on Lucas, Chips and Andy lying on their backs in the narrow strip of shade along the edge of the wadi. They caught sight of him almost together and cried greetings. He grinned, and felt as though he were doing it childishly, enjoying their welcome. They questioned him lazily, offhandedly, and he answered them similarly, sensing they weren't much interested in his replies. The perimeter, or more particularly this strong-post, was their world. He let a few minutes go by before asking the question he wanted to, and the one they expected of him:

"How have things been up here?"

There was a silence, after which Lucas said: "Livened up. We got shelled to buggery an hour ago."

"Oh—anyone hurt?"

"Clem Dawson got his."

"Clem." Dick tried to remember the man. For an instant Dawson's features flashed brilliantly across his mind and then he found it difficult to recall them even vaguely. Or even much about him. He was dead. That was that. One more for the day's situation report.

"Poor old Clem," he said at last.

"Yair," said Chips.

"I went through to see the town yesterday." He spoke steadily, casually, identifying himself strongly with the three N.C.O.s.

He told them about the town and the raid.

"Dooley's back," Lucas told him.

"Yes! What did he get?"

"A fortnight's field punishment."

"What did he say about Tommy?"

"Nothing."

"Think I'll go and have a yarn with him. Consider me reported in," he added to Lucas.

"Right-oh, Corporal!"

"Eh!"

Lucas grinned. "That's right—I forgot to mention it. Andy's taking Clem's section and you're taking over Number Two."

"Me!"

"Yes, you."

"Right!" said Dick calmly.

He walked away.

He found Dooley in the strong-post, bent solicitously over the Bren.

"Good day, Dooley."

Dooley looked up and smiled at him.

"Good day, Dick! Keep your head down, mate. I got sniped at earlier."

"How did the F.P. go?"

"Aw, it was pretty crook the first week. A provost I got into a blue with in Tel Aviv was barkin' the orders. Christ! Did that bastard bore it up me? He was a real dead coot. But the second week I got a pretty decent sort of joker. He used to take me out of sight and sit down and yarn with me. I asked him what he was doing in the provosts and he told me. He used to be a bombardier. He was knockin' round with a sister from the A.G.H. Anyhow, he gets pissed one night, pinches a ute from the transport lines, takes the sheila into Tel Aviv, gets her full too, and drives her back to the hospital in the early hours of the morning. Well, he's got her in the back of the ute, when the Registrar lamps them and flashes a torch and wants to know who had the truck out and who's in the back of it. The bombardier tells the sort to run. She hauls up and goes for her life and the bombardier jobs the major so he can't find out who the woman is. Well, they give him his choice of a dishonourable discharge or joinin' the provosts. So he joins the provosts."

"What a choice!"

"I'd have taken the discharge. The dishonourable part wouldn't have bothered me." He looked up swiftly and added: "You was with Tommy."

"Yair."

Dooley paused, then said:

"How're you feelin', Dick?"

"Extra good, Dooley. Did you hear we're losing Andy? Going to take over Clem's section."

"And who're we getting?"

"A real bastard!"

"Who, but?"

"Me."

Dooley bent over the gun again, smiling.

"You'll be all right, mate," he said.

From back down the wadi a voice yelled ecstastically:

"MAIL!"

*   *   *

To Henry Gilbertson from his grandmother:

. . . Yes, as you thought, the atmosphere here has changed. There is a consciousness abroad that we are committed to a long, hard war. There is a lot less bewilderment. A lot of our friends who used to wonder what Chamberlain—and the rest of the British Tories—were up to now know, and are a little shamefaced that they did not perceive the efforts to manœuvre the Empire into alliance with Hitler. We should not despise them,

Henry; we were not much better ourselves, with all our liberal-minded attitude. We have lived too far from the common run of humanity, you and I, Henry. It is they who decide the ultimate battle of any epoch. Once again they have won. They called for war against Germany. Churchill answered them. Curtin did out here. Your father is busy slandering him in his editorials. The literary section misses you: it is not what you made it. It is no longer seen by the young Leftists as the one corner of the daily press where their souls can shine at all. They are a little suspicious of it. Miller is clever, but a dilettante. . . .

To Dooley Franks from his father:

. . . a bottle of whisky, put it in a hollowed-out loaf of bread and sent it off to you. Things are livening up at work owing to war orders and there's a lot of overtime going. It's the first time in ten years the old pay envelope's got into double figures. Now don't think I'm going to start off again about what a mug you were to join up so soon, son. Perhaps the way things have turned out you did the right thing, even if you didn't know you were doing it at the time. Curtin was saying on the radio the other night . . .

To Andy Cain from his wife:

. . . no, Andy, I can't quite believe you've changed so suddenly, and even if you have, well, you always do things too late. It will have to wait till you come back, Andy, till I see you. Oh, Andy, you know you've always done things on a sudden impulse, without worrying about me or the consequences. I really did believe things could be better between us after you got out of that job. You said you were going to think of only you and me from then on, and the next thing I know you've joined up. I don't know, something carries you away and you never stick to it anyway. What is he after? I used to ask myself, what does he want? Either you don't know or you are afraid to take what you want. Once you told me it was only me you wanted . . .

To Dick Brett from his father:

. . . to do my own small part in the war effort. I am a Government inspector, Dick! My duty is to examine goods made by private firms under Government war contracts. Yes—you've guessed it: my old line, boots. Boots for our boys . . .

From his mother:

. . . and you will be careful, won't you, dear? Bombs and bullets are no respecters of persons. I was talking to a soldier in at the canteen the other day and he told me that the artillery was far more dangerous than the infantry. I forget what his reasons were. I am sending you a pocket volume of Rupert Brooke. Since he was a young poet who wrote in the last war, I thought you might like to have it. I am starting to build up a little fund for when you come out of the army . . .

To Kenneth Crane from his brother:

. . . won't be long before I'm over there giving you bloody footsloggers some supporting fire. I don't regret having gone into the artillery. We've got a grand bunch of blokes in the officers' mess. Our signals officer is none other than old Tubby Evans! He's grown a huge moustache; what he calls an "artillery moustache." The only snag among all the officers is the M.O.—a bloody Jew, a typical bloody Jew. One good thing Hitler did was to wipe them out. Being in Palestine, you probably know it better than I do.

Things are going well on Scobie. Julietta is due to foal again, but I am not sending the foal with the others for the yearling sales. I'm definitely going to keep it and race it myself.

Jones and Finey, two of our oldest hands, sneaked off and joined up last week. Of course, I sympathise with them but we can't all go off and fight. The dad warned the rest of them that any others who joined up without his permission could look elsewhere for jobs after the war. When I think of all the shirkers who won't join and who could! We'll know what to do with them when it's all over. Wool prices . . .

To Chips Prentice from one of several girls:

. . . I haven't forgotten our last night, Chips. Not a thing. I remember everything you did—everything. It was wonderful, Chips darling. And I'm going to save myself for you. No man's going to touch me till you get back . . .

"Gawd!" ejaculated Chips.
"Good letter, Chips?"
A gurgle. "It's a ripper!"
"Can I have the sporting page?"
"They're all sporting pages."

There were no letters for Lucas. He got very little mail. He had no regular mate. He was affable enough, but he stood alone. There was a fence around the essential Lucas. You could laugh with him, work with him, but you could never approach his thoughts. You could never read his mood. He was always the same.

He stood and watched the platoon read their mail. They sat or lay, faces anchored to the fluttering white sheets. Every now and then, though, a head would jerk up with an exclamation of pleasure, scorn, or surprise: "Listen to this, will you? . . ." Or perhaps no words at all: just sounds they made in their

absorption. Their minds were far away from this place. . . .
They were in bathing trunks, a towel around their shoulders,
going down the hill to the beach on a sparkling summer day.
The hot asphalt was burning the bare feet but the light wind
brought the clean tang of the sea. It was a hazed, enamel sea
and the serried sparkling of its surface shuffled in the sun. The
Norfolk pines were like a frieze of dark lace at its nearer edge . . .
They were in a bush pub, in the cool dim bar with its worn
brass and the fly-soiled pictures of long-dead racehorses, looking down the main street. Heat assaulted the rich red surface of
the street and quivered upwards again. It was a broad, aimless
street, seventy yards wide at least, with the verandahs of shops
only partly visible behind the pepper trees and flowering gums.
The day was caught in the toils of lethargy and the beer was
sharp, tantalising and deliciously cool, and the bar redolent of
hops and damp wood . . . They were in a small boat along the
Whitsunday Passage, not far out from the creamy beach and the
slim, grey, feathery palms. The water was so clear you could see
down into the green depths of a sea-grotto, like a cellar in the
sea's floor, a floor so beautifully and harmoniously coloured that
to gaze at it too long was to be lost to everything else. You could
just see the great, fleshy, lugubrious mouth of the groper . . .
They were out on the black-soil plains, where the pasture was
the greenest of all greens and the ground like black porridge,
and if you braked the truck too suddenly it "turned round and
looked at you." The plains where the great, sleek, half-wild
cattle lumbered up and stood watching you steadfastly . . . They
were under the torrid, low sky in the cane-fields of the north,
razing the massed, curved blades of the cane. The naked, brown,
glistening backs subordinated to the rhythm of the knives.
Swish, whack. . . . They were in the clattering streets of their
cities, with the flashing neons, the plump, desirable girls, the
inveigling cinemas and smoke-hazed clamorous pubs. . . . Col-
lectively their minds spanned a continent and their hearts grew
fierce with the desires that rose from their visions.

The town of Tobruk, thought Lucas, the besieged town of
Tobruk, in the deserts of Libya. Post 96 on its perimeter—
that's where we are. For an hour it was no longer real to those
men.

Memories came to Lucas, but not poignantly or overwhelm-
ingly. A commercial traveller's was a good life. There was a car,
you knew everybody, you were always moving, always meeting
new faces, observing with secret amusement the things you saw.
Always a new town, a new bar, another woman, one more pal.
But never get too deep, too involved. No emotion, no con-
cessions. Behind the bonhomie was the motive, the one motive
that all men shared: to extract something from you. Behind

113

the softness of the women the desire to entrap you, enfold you and possess you in the eyes of the world. Remember that and you could get a lot of fun out of life. Your hypocrisy grew an overlay of charm. It led men to trust you and deal with you and women to lay themselves out for you. Never trust a man, keep it up to a woman, but never for too long. . . .

To Andy Cain from a stranger:

Dear Mr. Cain,

I like to mind my own business, live and let live I say but when a man is away fighting for his country and his wife is carrying on behind his back as everybody knows its someone's duty to let him know, and it isn't just gossip it's what I saw which I won't give details of except to say he's there nearly every night and stays all night as the milkman sees him leaving early in the morning and kissing her good-bye and her still in her night-dress. His name is Butler and he's a leftenant in the permanent Army which is all I know. I hope I have done the right thing. Signed, a Friend.

Crane, as he read his elder brother's letter, reminded himself that he had been the first to see fighting in the war, and felt proud and gloating. It seemed to make up for the long-stored memory of the unease that he used to feel in his brother's presence; the suspicion of secret laughter. Now he brought forth the memory of the humiliations of his boyhood and triumphantly flung against them the fact that he was in action in Tobruk while his brother cooled his heels back in Australia. He was possessed by a half-formed hope that somehow his brother Hugh would be kept there for the duration.

His keenest memory was of the afternoon that he had been reading on the verandah of the famous, two-storied homestead of Scobie. At the time, he had been twelve years of age. The book he had been reading was called "The Boys' Book of Great Heroes." He was in the middle of the chapter that told of Richard the Lion-Heart and the Crusaders. Suddenly he had sprung up, exalted, his mind clamorous with great visions. He had become an invincible leader of multitudes. He left the verandah and, in his agitation, he felt himself to be striding across a field that was covered in enemy dead. He was looking for his army, to lead it onward to the next battle. They would beg for respite, but he would gaze down on them with a tremendous scorn and his glance alone would be enough to drive them forward. He came upon the two aboriginal boys, Coomer and Pilli. Half an hour later his brother had seen him, armed with a long sapling, leading Coomer and Pilli, who carried small spears, across a paddock, shouting orders back over his shoulder at the boys, reviling them for their cowardice and for lagging behind; beating savagely at the bushes that were his enemies, while the two black boys danced, laughing, around them, occasionally thrusting a spear into the leaves. A tremendous battle, won by his bravery alone! He had never forgotten his brother's mockery. Hugh had been a sly cynic, even at the age of twenty. He had not dared turn round as his brother derided him, for he was aware of the suppressed giggles of Coomer and Pili. He realised they had been laughing at him all along. He was no longer the conquering hero, but a lonely, overwrought, humiliated little boy; but he stood there stubbornly, still holding his sapling, his hatred enclosing him like a cloud. Later, he had caught Pilli behind a shed and beaten him till Pilli could not raise himself from the ground.

The hope that his brother would be kept in Australia became for a moment all-powerful. He saw himself returning after the war in tremendous dignity, with decorations on his chest. He was suddenly taken with the ferocity of his desire to win a decoration. He thought with hatred of Chips Prentice who had already got one.

"What's up, Andy?" asked Chips. "You look crook."

"I've had some bad news."

"Serious, mate?"

"Serious enough, Roger the Lodger."

"The bastard! A man's over here . . ."

Chips's words dwindled off and he spoke his sympathy out of his eyes. He wandered off and left Andy alone with his thoughts. He sought Lucas and said:

"Poor old Andy. He's been rogered."

Lucas shrugged. "He's not alone by any means."

"A great consolation that is!"

Andy had an image of his wife—so clear, lovely and poignant that his anguish became almost physical. The man he had become looked back with hatred on the man he had been for losing her. If she took him for a fool it was because he had been one. She was right. He had been a whirlpool of schemes, theories and ideals, plunging suddenly along a new road without fear or reflection—and never going far along any road. Always the urge to dominate something . . . always ending up sick of it all—unsatisfied, bitter, as though his spirit had some unappeasable hunger.

How vividly he saw himself now. That which had sent him to the war had put him on the last road of all. There was no turning back. Only death or a wound could call a halt. For once, too, he wanted to see what was at the end of the road. He wanted to be thoroughly and completely good at something.

Here he was, where there was no answer to something that

115

had happened half a world away—except to go on the way he was going. The answer to his past lay in Tobruk. He began to have a strange gratitude for being there. He had a sudden wolfish desire to be involved in fighting again—to be Andy Cain, the good soldier, killing quickly and thoroughly. That and nothing else. With a great convulsion of the will, he tried to overthrow the thought of his wife.

* * *

At dusk on April 30th, shell-fire began to pound the front of the Second X. They crouched in their posts as the earth about them shuddered and roared. Hardened now, they waited patiently for the attack that would follow. Percy Gribble held his fingers over his eyes, pressing till the fingers showed white against his face. When he uncovered his eyes they darted about ceaselessly as though they would fly out of their sockets. Over the telephone Henry Gilbertson reported calmly to the colonel. Once again a numbness had come over Dick's mind; it was a dark cave, and in its depths were fear and horror. In odd flashes of thought, Andy wished for death. Only Chips seemed unchanged.

"Cut it out, ya mad bastards!" he cried. "Before you hurt someone!"

The twilight became filled with drifting dust. As the shells grew fewer the posts were spattered by long-range machine-gun fire. Wickedly, the bullets swished and plopped into the sandbags or howled frenziedly past. The wounded lay against the side of the trenches and felt the warm blood soak their dressings.

"Here they come!"

The darkness of the earth was extended into the fading sky by the shapes of tanks. They deployed sluggishly in the gathering dusk and their engines were like the hoarse gurgles of swine. A two-pounder flashed into action and one of the tanks jerked and stopped, but immediately two others turned their guns on the flash of the two-pounder, flaying it until it lay in fragments, its crew mangled around it. The tanks came forward shelling and machine-gunning. At intervals Nazi infantry detached themselves from the tanks and went to ground, from where they poured rifle and machine-gun fire at the Australian positions.

As the darkness fell some of the tanks lay wrecked in the minefields, others that survived broke through the wire and speeding between the weapon-pits made for the rear of the Red Line. Behind them, the Second X heard the explosions of mines mingling with the sounds of the Nazi tank-guns.

The darkness became webbed brilliantly with the lines of tracers. The surface of the earth thundered and trembled and

116

the air above it was torn and rent by the hordes of rushing missiles. And at odd times, piercing the din, could be heard the cries of men.

The Nazi infantry arose and ran for the wire as if borne on the waves of hoarse sounds from their throats. Machine-guns swung to and fro across them. They flung up their arms; screamed; clutched at their stomachs; jerked, stumbled, writhed, fell. Their shadows wavered, gestured, staggered. They were figures on a stage lit by the flashes of shells. The Australian counter-barrage had now begun to fall among them. They hesitated, retreated, only to be overrun or impelled forward again by those behind them.

The attack raged in spasms throughout the night. Dawn came in with the rattle of machine-guns.

In the still, merciless grey of the first light the posts stood-to and scanned their front. As the sun came burning upward out of the darkness a wind seemed to spring from its heart. But, though the machine-guns never ceased, no Nazi appeared. The eyes of Six Platoon throbbed as they gazed.

"Why don't they come?" whispered Percy. He repeated, more loudly: "Why don't they come?"

"They'll come soon enough," said Dooley.

Percy stared outwards and though his voice made no sound his lips still said, "Why don't they come?" in a peevish, accusing tone, as though the Nazis were doing something wrong.

A tank rumbled on their right and flame rushed out of the barrel of its gun. A two-pounder replied, and the shell made a spurt of dust near the Nazi tank. As the light grew stronger, so did the wind, and eddies of dust began to fling themselves in their faces.

Suddenly Andy pointed. "Look!"

They could now see the strong-post on their right where the ground began to slope upwards, and the ascending pattern of trench was clear to their eyes. It was filled with Nazis. The corpses of a dozen Australians had been flung out of the trenches on to the ground above. Then a great wall of smoke and dust began to hide the sight from their eyes. A mortar from the captured position began to lob bombs on Six Platoon's posts.

Henry Gilbertson was speaking on the telephone: "Freddie Three's now occupied by enemy. Freddie One is pinned down by fire from its front and the right flank."

Pomfret's calm voice came back over the wire: "Freddie One must hold on as long as possible."

Henry gave the call signal for Six Platoon and Crane's voice answered: "Freddie One."

"This is Freddie. You are to hold on. How are you situated?"

"Two dead, seven wounded. We can hold on. Can you direct artillery on to Freddie Three?"

"Yes. Hold on. I've an idea things are going to get worse."

Percy Gribble had begun to argue quietly to himself.

The survivors of the overrun post on Six Platoon's right had fallen back to reserve trenches two hundred yards behind. All the morning they carried on a duel with machine-guns and mortars against the Nazis in the post from which they had been driven. The gentle rise of the ground exposed the Nazis in their newly-won position to the fire of Six Platoon's Brens. From the weapon-pit above Platoon Headquarters, Lucas hammered at them with the Breda. Support from the artillery had temporarily silenced the Nazi mortars by noon.

As the commander of Two Section, a new pride and exhilaration eventually came over Dick. He was confident, hard-voiced, reckless. From somewhere far above he was watching a grim, red-eyed man commanding a strong-post, calm and admirable on the edge of death. What if I die? he thought. Everyone dies. There were worse ways to die. There were worse ways to be remembered than as a brave man. "He was a good soldier and game as Ned Kelly." He seemed to hear someone saying it. But don't let me be blinded or disfigured. Merciful fates—not that! For one tiny instant, a dim, terrified being with a piercing hunger to live, arose in the dark mass of his thoughts. He submerged it savagely, with a panicky lurch of the stomach.

Percy Gribble was firing steadily with his rifle; a pasty, muttering automaton. All colour and expression seemed to have left his face. It was a smudge, even to the lips. His eyes seemed to have been driven back into their sockets; they were like wisps of black silk. He had soiled his clothes in an earlier spasm of terror. His legs were stained and the stench came sickeningly in between the sharp gusts of explosives.

It was their worst fight yet, their most terrible and violent, and, with the exception of Crane, Lucas and Chips, despair had begun to claw at their minds. Dooley now fired longer bursts with the Bren, exposing his head for minutes on end, mouthing desperately and viciously behind his gun: "Cop this, you Hun bastard! You woman-killer! You Nazi bastard!"

Something spun him round like a leaf in the wind. He fell flat, his shirt fluttering at the shoulder. He lay breathing like a bellows, cursing filthily. Dick dropped his rifle and leaning down examined the shoulder. It was furrowed, with two great flaps of seared flesh, welling blood. He took Dooley's field-dressing out of his shirt and fixed it tightly over the wound, bringing the ends of the bandage under Dooley's armpits.

"They didn't get the bone," panted Dick. "How do you feel?"

118

"Fog 'em!—I'm all right. Wait till the blood stops and I'll be at 'em again."

"You'd better take my rifle. You'll never manage the Bren now."

Dick sprang to the Bren. With the Nazi position ringed in the back-sight he fired a short burst and was oblivious to the Spandau fire about his ears. He changed the magazine, took sight again and traversing the gun, fired a long, raking burst. He was rewarded with an indistinct lurch and the sudden up-flinging of an arm. Dooley was back beside him now, firing the rifle slowly and awkwardly. During all these minutes, Percy had not even turned to look at them.

Replacing the hand-set of the phone, Henry Gilbertson turned to Ted Olley and said: "They've got Hill 209."

The C.S.M. looked gloomy. The position on their right, now occupied by Nazis, was the base of the shallow hill. The whole hill now belonged to them. The only piece of commanding ground in the place.

"Christ!" he said quietly.

"At least fifty tanks got through between sunset and dawn last night. I wonder how many the minefields stopped?"

"All of 'em, I hope," said the C.S.M. and looked a little brighter.

Outside, under heavy shell-fire, stretcher-bearers were bringing wounded down the wadi.

Six solid hours of shell-fire had failed to dislodge Six Platoon from its position. In the mid-afternoon three tanks bore down on them. The surviving anti-tank gun covering Post 96 engaged them recklessly, halting one. The other two were blanketed by shell-fire from the British artillery and finally driven back. Once more the reverberating curtain of a barrage fell on Six Platoon. As it lifted, more Nazi infantry came behind it. Their flanks, enfiladed by Lucas's Breda, wilted, staggered and fell, but others of them reached Three Section's post, killed Chips's Bren gunner with a stick-bomb and made along the communication trench to the weapon-pit, shouting triumphantly. Chips met them head on, mowing down the first with his tommy-gun. Then he let fly with a grenade, flattening against the side of the trench as it exploded mightily in the narrow space. The two Nazis still on their feet took one look at the mangled remains of their fellows, and surrendered to him. He drove them before him to Platoon Headquarters, in a series of ducking, darting bursts along the trench. Now they were prisoners, the Nazis were terrified of being hit. Chips brought them cowering up against the safer side of the wadi and Crane's runner came out and covered them. Chips ran back to his section post.

"Next time they'll overrun us," thought Crane. He sprang to

the hand-set, but the phone was dead. He tried it again and again. Nothing. The signaller had been wounded hours ago and taken away. He called for the runner and brought Lucas down from the weapon-pit to cover the Nazis.

Crane thrust the signaller's haversack into his runner's hands. "Here—follow that line down and mend the break."

Without a word, the runner took it and began to follow the thin cable. It ran down the wadi and then into open ground seared by shell-fire. They watched him crawl along examining the wire, Lucas and Crane from the wadi, Chips from Three Section's post nearby. As he reached open ground, they held their breaths. He went along on his stomach running the line through his fingers. Shells burst about the tiny figure, obscuring it completely. A runner sped in from Henry Gilbertson.

"Your phone's dead. The boss wants a situation report."

He panted. He had lost his shirt; his chest was grazed and scored and covered in dust. "Christ! It's vicious out there!"

Crane sent him off with a message for Henry Gilbertson, the two Nazis scampering before him.

A hundred yards out in the open Crane's runner had found the break in the line. He lay on his side next to it, fingers fumbling. Then, just before more smoke obscured him, he waved. Lucas ran into the platoon dug-out and tested the phone. He came out again and waved to the distant runner, who started to crawl back. Thirty yards from the end of the wadi he rose and commenced to run. A shell burst in front of him and his figure sank like a wraith in the cloud of the explosion. When it cleared he was seen lying on his back, jerking.

Down the wadi stalked the huge form of Chips Prentice. He made at a crouching run for the wounded man. He bent over, hoisted the other on his shoulder and began to trudge back. The shell-fire speeded up frenziedly and it seemed the ground spurted upwards blackly everywhere but where he stepped with his burden.

Lucas ran out to help him, but he had no sooner reached the open than he fell, rolled over, half rose, then began to crawl, dragging a shattered thigh. A few seconds later Chips reached him, bent over, and with an arm around Lucas's waist dragged him along as well. When he reached the end of the wadi, he dropped Lucas, and sinking to his knees, lowered the wounded runner to the ground. His chest heaved, his face was grey, yet he smiled. Together he and Crane brought the two wounded men the rest of the way.

In the late afternoon, the Nazis on Six Platoon's right came out of the captured position to attack the Australians in the reserve trenches two hundred yards behind. Beneath the shell-fire Six Platoon still managed to harass the Nazis' flank. The attack wilted. The Nazis fled back.

Half an hour later a tank came up and crept half-way towards the reserve trenches. Three Nazis dropped from it. Only one was armed; the other two carried some bulky apparatus on their backs. They crawled forward. The next moment the Australian trenches were enveloped in a wall of flame and a great wave of smoke. From the trenches a figure appeared on the edge of the parapet, then another wall of flame struck it and it was gone. Percy began to laugh, quietly, mirthlessly, with a horrible air of reason and concentration. Six Platoon howled its hate. Dick was sobbing, crying out he knew not what. Dooley, exhausted in the bottom of the pit, hung on to Dick's foot, in case he should try to clamber out.

Henry Gilbertson listened to something over the phone. Then he replaced the hand-set and turned to Ted Olley with a stricken face.

"They just used flame-throwers on Seventeen Platoon."

His runner rose quietly from the corner, picked up a rifle and made to leave the dug-out. At the entrance, Henry grabbed him and held him, looking startled and horrified. Just outside sat Chips's two captured Nazis.

"No, you don't," breathed Henry. "We don't shoot our prisoners."

The runner dropped the rifle. He suddenly seemed to have lost all his strength. He spoke quietly:

"My brother's in Seventeen Platoon."

"I know," said Henry, and avoided his eyes.

At dusk, Crane phoned Henry and made his situation report. It was a grim report that affected even Crane:

"Five dead, eleven wounded. Five hundred rounds of rifle, two thousand of belt ammunition. Strength: one officer, four N.C.O.s, twenty other ranks."

Six Platoon was hemmed in on three sides. Their path of retreat lay through a slender belt of minefield, on which the Nazi tanks had, so far, mostly come to grief. Those that evaded the mines had been knocked out by British tanks. Crane knew how near to capture or annihilation his platoon was. If Nazi sappers could penetrate the minefield and the remaining Australian anti-tank guns be eliminated, Post 96 would fall to the Nazis, and the remains of his platoon either scorched to death as those on its right flank, marched off as prisoners, or more likely shot in cold blood.

He did not mind dying. He had made up his mind that if the situation became hopeless he would do something mad and magnificent that would win him a posthumous V.C. He already saw his widow at the investiture, the reverent stories in the newspapers, even a memorial; a boat named after him. The visions were like a remote fever in his brain.

Appalled by his company's losses, but still confident and implacable, Henry made his report to Battalion Headquarters. It was the adjutant who took the report, then the colonel came on the line: "Well done, Freddie! Hold on! Johnnie's bringing up a perambulator tonight! Hold on!"

Hold on! The words had echoed around Battalion Headquarters all that day. It was the colonel's answer to everything; the expression of his seething inner panic, his vast sense of helplessness.

When the remnants of Seventeen Platoon went back to the reserve trenches Pomfret had perceived several things: that the reserve trenches could not be held, and were not worth holding, because the minefields and machine-gun posts behind were the strongest in all the perimeter and would delay the Nazis indefinitely; also that Six Platoon could render the position untenable in a matter of an hour or two. The survivors of Seventeen Platoon should therefore be withdrawn and sent over to join Six Platoon. Their presence in the reserve trenches would be merely a useless sacrifice. To Six Platoon they would be invaluable.

The first time the colonel had instructed them to hold on Pomfret had pointed these things out to his red-eyed, keyed-up commander. The colonel brushed these ideas aside:

"We're not giving an inch of ground we don't have to, John. They stay."

"It's not a matter of giving ground, Orme—Six Platoon can enfilade the post—the Nazis can't keep it if we hammer them before nightfall. If we leave them there overnight they could keep it."

"I can't agree."

"Listen, Orme. These Seventeen Platoon men could not hold it anyway. They're dazed from shell-fire, outnumbered, running out of ammunition. I don't think they can do it."

The colonel threw up his chin and told him harshly:

"This is the Second X, John, the battalion I've made. They can do anything."

The last message from Seventeen Platoon before their phone-line went dead then came through. Pomfret took up the hand-set and asked humbly:

"Let me order them out, Orme."

Fitzroy took the hand-set from him. He squared his shoulders arrogantly and barked into the phone:

"Hold on!"

Pomfret turned away. The expression on his face startled the adjutant. It blazed with anger.

Half an hour later B Company phoned through. It was the adjutant who took the call. He turned a horrified face to the colonel:

"They used flame-throwers on Seventeen Platoon. No sign of life."

The colonel sat down on a box and hid his face in his hands.

"Johnnie's bringing up a perambulator" was good news for Henry Gilbertson. Joyfully he told the C.S.M.:

"Thank God! C Company's counter-attacking tonight."

C Company crept through the minefield gap and counter-attacked just on nightfall. The battle raged a few hundred yards away on Six Platoon's right, but they saw little of it. Slumped in the bottom of their pits, they heard only its sounds; the crashing and the screaming that their ears now accepted as a common manifestation, just as in a lunatic asylum madness becomes the normal thing.

But at dawn, the helmets in the position on Six Platoon's right were still those of Nazis. The ground about was scattered with Australian corpses. The counter-attack had failed.

Then artillery blanketed the Nazis in their newly-won position. Before the eyes of the Australians there grew a black forest of smoke.

Then came a sand-storm, and it blew for two days.

11

IT is August of that same year. Tobruk, and its miles of trench, are quiet for the moment in the glowing dusk. The floor of the wadi is level and spacious; this is a well-known spot. It is several miles behind the Red Line, and they call it Happy Valley. Some say it should be Bomb-Happy Valley, for it escapes the attention of neither dive-bombers nor Nazi guns. Perhaps, originally, it was Bomb-Happy Valley. Who knows for certain? So many tales have been told around it already, for, like all places where men, live, die and work together, it has its legends.

Down the wadi comes a file of men. They march slowly, out of step, and mostly in silence. The dull clink of their weapons is clear in the evening air. At first their faces look all the same, burnt deep, with several days of beard, their eyes red-rimmed with the whites gleaming, cheeks hollowed, lips straight and grave. Their shirts and shorts are stiff like canvas with mingled dust and sweat, and streaked again with the sweat of that day. Their legs are bare and burnt almost black; their boots are worn pure white. Some who still have them wear their tunics, for the air will soon be deathly cold; and their headgear is, as before, motley: a steel helmet, a crumpled slouch hat and an Italian pith helmet. Their packs, haversacks and ammunition pouches have become as white as their boots, and their weapons gleam dully in the spots where they have worn, for they have had five months of use.

They are a strange spectacle. They were once ordinary men, but now they do not belong among ordinary men; in a city they would seem like a vision. Their sameness is not only that of their dark brown faces, their silence, their fatigue, for they have shared together, for many months, the most abysmal, the most terrible of human emotions; each has in turn, and in his own way, been a hero, a panting coward, an entity with a mind crying its anguish at death. And while each has shown to his fellows most of his deepest self, each hugs to himself, grimly and pitiably, what is left. No one of them will ever be quite the same again.

As he reaches a turn in the wadi, Henry Gilbertson stops, turns round and says: "B Company—halt!"

They gather in close, for it has become very dark.

An hour or two later the moon has risen, shining straight down the wadi. The depths of slit trenches and the shadows of men are deepest black. Many of B Company are already asleep, but the glow of a cigarette and the murmur of voices, bursting occasionally into a laugh or an oath, show that not all of them have succumbed to their tiredness.

Dick and his mate Dooley are sitting propped up against the side of the wadi. Dooley is smoking. Whenever cigarettes are handed out, Dooley gets Dick's ration, for Dick doesn't smoke. Nearby, Andy is stretched out in a blanket, apparently asleep, for he neither speaks nor moves.

The ration truck has been up with a hot and surprisingly palatable stew. They have all eaten heavily and those that smoke have enjoyed the cigarettes that the truck also brought with it. This small luxury has subdued and contented them; they have lain down conscious of the week of idleness that lies ahead of them. . . . B Company is out of the line for "A Rest."

It is ten minutes since either Dick or Dooley has spoken. Dooley puts his hand to his cigarette, draws deeply and pleasurably, takes it from his mouth and says:

"How'd a few beers go, eh?"

"All right, mate."

Surprising how easily the word "mate" comes to Dick's lips these days. He is very lean now. He seems older; the lines have hardened on his face. His eyes are dimmer than they were and no longer seem to ask questions; but his manner shows that this

124

is not because those questions are answered. He is a good section corporal.

"I wonder," muses Dooley, "if there was anything in that furphy?"

"What furphy?"

"About the division being relieved within a month."

Dick gives a cynical recital of the rumours that the driver of the ration truck brought with him: "There's a roster for leave to Cairo and Alex.; we're going to fight our way out at the end of a month; there are two shiploads of beer in the harbour; Groggy's gone insane. Take your pick."

"I'll take the last one," says Dooley, "it's the most likely."

They sit in silence for a while.

"If it'd get me out of this joint, I'd put on a mad act meself," resumes Dooley.

"You'd do nothing of the kind," retorts Dick, and looks up as a shadow falls near them.

"You two coots still awake?" asks Sergeant Chips Prentice, who has replaced the severely wounded Lucas.

"No, we're snoring," rasps Dooley.

Chips, the first man in the battalion to win the Distinguished Conduct Medal, sits down near them.

"Any news, Chips?" asks Dick.

"I've just been talking to Crane. He's got plans."

"He would, the bastard!" bursts out Dooley bitterly.

"He's not a happy man, our little Ken," chuckles Chips.

"He never was."

"He's crooked as hell on old Mum," says Dick.

"Mum's worth a dozen of him," asserts Dooley.

"And you know why I reckon he's crooked," Chips goes on, in a confidential way, "Mum's Military Cross. I tell you, the coot's nothing but an overgrown boy scout. He's busting himself to get a decoration, and Mum gets one instead."

"And so he should've!"

"My bloody oath!"

"Probably," sneers Dooley, "he'll get disinherited if he don't come home with a D.S.O. or somethin'. The Squire of Scobie!" He spits.

"Ever seen his wife?" asks Chips. "I saw her with him in camp back home one day. Calls for him in a dirty big Packard Christ! She's a slasher!"

"Bet she's playing around while the Squire's away," grins Dooley. "All them society sheilas have morals like cats."

"I'd play with her," says Chips yearningly.

"Thank Gawd I'm not married," exclaims Dooley. "There's blokes getting rogered right and left already."

They all pause, half turn and glance towards the silent figure of Andy Cain. But Andy neither moves nor makes a sound.

His back is turned, otherwise they would see that his eyes are wide open, bitter and remote.

"What's Crane got in mind for us?" Dick asks Chips.

Chips lifts his head to the strange Northern stars. Heartbrokenly, dramatically, he ejaculates:

"Lectures on camouflage!"

They sit there speechless, marvelling at the comic enormity of such a thing.

* * *

It was after midnight now, but Dick had not slept. The moon had gone. He lay chilled in his blankets, trying to arrest the thoughts that raced across his brain like insects in a confined space. Tonight he could not rise above them and find tranquillity. He could not, in his imagination, stand apart at a vast height, and see himself lying sleepless here in the dark of a broad wadi. He tried to picture Tobruk and found that he couldn't. Often, before, he had seen below him the little white town, the desert rising in flat stony shelves to the upland, wrinkled with wadis like the face of a very old man; laced with roads and tracks and bordered by endless miles of wire, like webs; patterned with trench systems.

He was trying to see himself as he was now, peering as if in the dark to discover what would emerge from the months that were just past—some message. But he saw nothing except his outward form, a thin, burnt infantry corporal, beginning to look hard bitten.

It was early morning before he fell asleep.

* * *

The survivors of Six Platoon lay around the wadi in little knots, warming themselves in the early sun. Dick, Dooley, Chips and Andy were joined by a hesitant Percy Gribble, who gave the company a timid grin and sat down by Dooley. Dooley had long ago ceased to harass Percy, for Percy was no longer a thorn in his side. He had become instead an object of unspoken compassion, and Dooley treated him with gruff kindness. Six Platoon looked on Percy's terror as something to make allowances for. Now that they had all suffered abject terror, the sudden blind, instinctive desire for flight that sometimes possesses all men under fire, and each knew how close he had come to being like Percy, there was no contempt for him, no aversion. He had become a subdued little man. Even Andy tolerated him.

Chips, lying on the broad of his back, was squinting at a news-sheet that Henry Gilbertson had sent over and was reading aloud from it:

"Another big raid on London. Twenty German bombers shot down."

126

"There won't be any London by the time this war's over," someone remarked.

"There won't be any Berlin either," said Chips.

He spoke in a toneless, hard voice and they all looked at him, for this was the nearest they had ever seen him to anger.

Pete Barrow rolled over and turned a youthful, earnest face to Chips. He spoke so seldom that they listened to him attentively. He was the Bren gunner in Andy's section:

"What good would it do if we wiped a few of their cities off the map? It's the battlefield where we'll have to beat them."

Andy came out of his glum brooding to sneer, and ask him, harshly:

"Well, London's a battlefield now, isn't it?"

"Then that makes women and kids soldiers," retorted Pete, looking stubborn and offended.

"That's right," said Andy. Bitterly, he observed: "Nice little civilisation we've got, haven't we?"

"Civilisation's what we're trying to save," Dick told him. They looked at each other belligerently, not for the first time lately.

Chips's boom shattered the sudden tensity of feeling among them: "Who's robbing this coach? Do you want to hear the news or not?"

"Carry on, mate," Dooley told him. "Professor Brett will deliver notes on the news at the end of the session."

"Where was I?" resumed Chips. "Yes! The Russians have recaptured the villages of . . . of . . . they've recaptured three villages."

"Good on yer, Joe!"

"I'm glad I'm not fighting there," said Peter, looking awe-struck. "Three minutes after a man's dead he's frozen as stiff as a board."

"They don't have to die," amended Chips. "Their fingers drop off while they're still alive."

"I wonder if the Russians take any prisoners, with the Fritzes shooting the women and children?"

"I wouldn't, be-Jesus!"

"Uncle Joe'll win!" Dooley proclaimed.

"What do ya reckon, Andy?" asked Chips. "You were a politician, weren't you—or something? How about the Reds?"

"They'll win," said Andy indifferently, and went back to his thoughts.

"When's the British Army going to land in France? That's what I want to know."

"The day before the war ends," said Andy, looking up again.

"When's the war going to end?"

"Yair. When are we going to get out of this hole?"

"Never! We're the Forgotten Men, I tell yer."

"Who gives a fog what happens to Tobruk? Let's all go home to Mum!"

So the chorus of discontent went on for some minutes, half humorous, half bitter, proclaiming distrust in the higher command, contempt for officers and disbelief in everything officers told them, as well as a deep scepticism as to why they were here at all. It dissolved, as always into a wry and yearning silence.

At length someone said:

"What are you going to do after the war, Chips?"

"Marry a millionaire's daughter and become a respectable bludger."

They all laughed and the pessimism of a few moments ago changed swiftly to a series of hilarious resolutions.

"I'm going to buy the local baths, fill 'em with beer, then dive in and drink me way out."

"What are you going to do, Dooley?"

"Start a revolution! Hang all screws and provosts, put Groggy and Crane and the Animal and the Boy Bastard behind bars and make 'em dig latrines for the rest of their lives."

They yelled and rocked in spasms of delight. One by one, they offered Dooley terrible elaborations of his plans.

Lifted out of his reticence, Pete laughed and cried: "Mad lot of coots!" Half ashamed, he then resumed his earnest schoolboyish expression and wistfully said:

"I'm going to breed a herd of beautiful cows. Round as barrels and loaded down with milk. Listen, I've got a cow at home, a real champion she is, and when I get out of the army I'm going to take her to Aberfeldie Alexander."

"Who?"

"Aberfeldie Alexander." Under a fusillade of grins, Pete was blushing fiercely. "He's a famous stud bull."

"Like Chips," someone said.

"By cripes!" roared Chips with a magnificent imitation of rage. "Who said—"

"Any sick?" asked a new voice.

The C.S.M. stood there with a paper form in his hand.

"Any sick?" he repeated. "The truck's waiting."

"Sick of the army!"

"How's your shoulder, Dooley?" asked the C.S.M.

"All right—much to my regret." The shallow flesh wound had only earned him three weeks in the beach hospital.

"I'd better have these looked at," said Pete, rising to his feet and indicating his legs, covered with sores.

He went off down the wadi with Ted Olley. Without a word Percy rose and accompanied them.

"Aberfeldie Alexander!" gurgled Chips and was overcome once more.

"Where's the Squire off to?" enquired Dooley. With casual, hostile eyes, he followed the manly form of Crane stalking along the farther bank of the wadi.

"Where yer going, Squire?" he yelled suddenly, and dropped his head, looking steadfastly at the ground. The others looked everywhere but at the distant figure of Crane, which paused an instant, scrutinised them and resumed marching.

The next moment there was a great hollow roar, a loud crackling on the stones about them, and a gigantic shadow fled over their suddenly flattened bodies. The Nazi plane skimmed down the wadi, guns chattering. Dooley turned on his side and regarded the plane which was already a dwindling speck above the horizon.

"Happy Valley," he said bitterly, despondently.

A minute later the C.S.M. walked slowly into Company Headquarters. He sat down on a water tin, pursed his lips and shook his head.

"Who did they get?" asked Henry.

"Young Pete Barrow. Blew the top of his head off."

Henry let out a deep breath and grimaced.

The C.S.M. sat without moving, staring apparently at nothing.

"I wonder what'll happen to that cow. . . ."

Percy threw himself down at the first warning of the strafing plane. He huddled against the earth, half out of his mind with fear. The thought of his back exposed to the chattering bullets made him claw desperately at the sand, where he lay tensed and shuddering. In a few seconds it was over. Now he felt weak and cold. He lay there for a while, in order to control his features and feel some strength flow back into his limbs. Then he climbed up on to his knees and saw next to him the shattered head of young Pete Barrow.

The next few hours were the bitterest of Percy Gribble's life. While the C.S.M. recovered the identification tags from Pete's body and went to find a stretcher to remove it, Percy stood and looked at it. For the first time in months he was calm. He had the sensuous exhaustion of someone who had reached the end of a struggle.

Many times before, the desire to escape had possessed Percy, taken him up like wings, and left him trembling where he was. But now he had reached the happy and reasonable conclusion that he must either escape or go mad. For months he had lived with the shame of his terror, the contempt of his mates, then their pity and finally their kindness. There had been then humiliation of relinquishing his corporal's stripes; of the knowledge that he who used to consider himself in most ways superior to the rest of Six Platoon, had failed to master his fear as they had. But now none of these things mattered.

The C.S.M. came back with a stretcher and a blanket over his shoulder. He put them down, looked keenly at Percy and said in a diffident way:

"Could you give me a hand with Pete, Percy?"

Percy nodded, and took the legs of the corpse. Together they lifted it on to the stretcher. The head lolled, and the C.S.M. averted his eyes from the trail that it left in the sand. Then he covered it with the blanket and stepped between the shafts at one end of the stretcher.

"Are you right, Percy?"

Percy nodded again, and they lifted the stretcher up and bore it towards the truck that had come to bring the sick back to the regimental aid post, waiting now for Percy the coward and the corpse of the boy who had wanted to breed beautiful cows. The driver dropped the tailboard and watched the stretcher as they slid it into the truck.

"Who is it?" the driver asked.

"Young Barrow," replied Ted Olley.

"He was only a kid," said the driver resentfully.

"Yes," said the C.S.M. "Hop in, Percy."

Percy obeyed, and the C.S.M. handed him a sheaf of paper. "Give these to the M.O., will you?"

The truck lurched off, and the C.S.M. turned and walked back to Company Headquarters.

Once or twice, as the truck lurched heavily, Pete's body jumped as though it still had the power of life. Percy watched it indifferently. His thoughts were a long way away.

How unreal the circumstances that had brought him finally to Tobruk, to a piece of trench that was alive with terrible memories. That it had all sprung originally from a choice of his own only deepened his bitter self-pity. How different much of the past seemed now—how false! Percy considered the irony of his predicament. He needn't have been here at all; he had not been compelled to join up. There had been a lot to remain home for. A wife, a ten-year-old boy, a small car, a house not yet paid off. Suburban respectability had suited Percy. The bank—that had been the basis of his security: his position in the bank. It seemed a thing of terrible irony that it had been the bank where had begun the chain of events that brought him to Tobruk—to this tragic pass. Percy felt as though he were a victim of some subtle trick, and the bank was the villain. For, one day soon after war broke out, the Board had called the entire male staff together to be addressed by one of the directors, General Sir Timothy Betts, retired. Sir Timothy had looked both portentous and benign. He had desired to tell them that when they joined up, the difference between their present rate of pay and their army pay would be met by the Bank. There! What did they think of that! The Bank would do Its Bit For The Boys! This was it. Sir Timothy's manner made it clear that he spoke on the assumption that all the staff under fifty—those that could be spared, anyway—were on the point of joining up. It was obvious that he looked on them as brave and patriotic Australians, eager to go and fight. Up to this moment, it had never occurred to Percy to join up. Sir Timothy had not neglected to point out that the forces needed officers, and that bank clerks would almost automatically become officers. Well, some had. Those that joined the Pay Corps had. But Percy had been charmed by the assumption of such a distinguished soldier as Sir Timothy that he, Percy, was without question a brave and patriotic man. With the same instinct that had made him such a faithful servant of the Bank, Percy—that brave man— had joined a fighting unit, the Second X Battalion. In this calm and wise mood that had now come over him, Percy realised that he had joined up also because he had not thought to do otherwise. The Bank had spoken.

This was what the Bank had done to him, Percy Gribble; this was the strange result of Sir Timothy's speech. For the first time in his life, Percy's mind revolted. It became swollen with hatred and protest. As the truck bore him over the stony wastes of Tobruk he sat, bitterly cursing Sir Timothy, the Bank and the war.

Having attended to the corpse of Pete Barrow, Captain Barrett went back to the R.A.P. tent where Percy awaited him.

"Well, Gribble?"

Percy faced him and said simply: "My nerves have gone, sir."

Without a word, the M.O. leaned over and put a finger on Percy's pulse. With his eyes on his watch, he remarked:

"You aren't the first to tell me that."

"So I'm told," replied Percy composedly. "I know that there have been one or two others, including officers."

"Do you know that only one of them ever got out of Tobruk?" There was an odd little note of relish in the M.O.'s voice.

"I only know," replied Percy, "that for five months I've suffered the tortures of the damned. During the Salient Battle, by going half mad, I managed to make myself carry on—at least to stand up in the trench and control my limbs a little. I even killed a couple of Germans. This morning we were strafed and a man lying next to me was killed. Private Barrow. Something went in me. I know I can't go on now. I suppose I'm what you'd call a coward. I can't help it. I'm quite happy about

131

it. I've had to be honest with myself. I may as well be honest with you."

The M.O. was silent. Others had come to him, as Percy had, some cringing, some whining, some bluffing. In his sly, polite manner, the M.O. had set traps for them, ignored their pleadings, or threatened them with a charge of malingering. With a faint surprise, he had become aware of a subtle streak of sadism in himself, for he had actually begun to enjoy a function that had formerly bored him. Percy had spoilt his fun. The sad-eyed little man who now confronted him was not begging or bluffing. He looked his would-be tormentor straight in the eye and told the truth about himself. The M.O. realised that he had listened to a man baring his soul. He felt slightly revolted; he did not want to hear any more, yet he looked up at Percy with something like admiration. Percy, who so often had pretended dignity, now possessed it in such a measure as to shock a man like Barrett. In the depths of his shame he had found something he had never had before.

The M.O. took up his pen and began to write. As he watched him, Percy knew that his career as a fighting soldier was ended.

Back in Happy Valley it is night once again. Suddenly the sleeping figures of B Company are awakened by the sounds of distant battle. The horizon flickers and grumbles. Machine-guns chatter endlessly. Some of them sit upright with a jerk, then remember that the battle does not concern them, that they are out for "A Rest." They listen, turn over and try to sleep again.

And someone remarks:

"Some poor devil's copping it."

BOOK THREE

UNREST ON THE PLAIN

12

REVEILLE flowed softly through dreams and deep sleep. The first notes trembled, as though the bugler shivered. In the distance another reveille sounded for a sister battalion. Men in the tents sat up coughing and cursing; lit cigarettes. The air in the tents was heavy and foul. As the flaps were thrown back a chill came in that bit to their marrow. They groped for jerseys, tunics and greatcoats.

From the top of the company lines the C.S.M.'s voice called: "All out, B Company!"

A few shrouded and crouching forms emerged from the tents into a dismal, frozen darkness. They stood outside the tents blowing, coughing, rubbing their hands, or speaking in grunts. In ones and twos they began to trudge slowly up the rise to the company parade ground. From the Company Headquarters tent Crane's voice bellowed impatiently:

"Hurry up, B Company!"

By the time B Company's three platoons had fallen-in the darkness had lightened to a grey drizzle. All through the maze of tents that the Second X occupied, voices were crying out orders, encouragement and abuse. The camp was awakening.

Crane, acting commander of B Company, awaited them attired in shorts, sandshoes and a jersey, his face flushed with energy.

Huddled in their thickest clothes and stamping their boots, B Company looked at him with loathing and longed for the return of Henry Gilbertson from the training battalion. Crane had taken temporary command of B Company in the manner of a man who had gained at last a right that had been long denied. He spoke to them with such arrogance and plagued every waking minute with such a whirlwind zeal that many who had so often derisively stated that he was mad began soberly to think they may have been right.

Glumly they answered their names as the roll was called. The last man reported himself present. They all knew what was coming next.

"Off with those greatcoats!" he cried.

At the same time he pulled his jersey over his head and bared a deep, magnificent chest. From the ranks came a rumble of desperate profanity. Crane flexed his arms and skipped again, nervous as a dog on a leash. A voice called out, half snarl, half sneer:

"What a beautiful torso!"

The ranks rang with laughter. It stung Crane to the raw.

Almost beside himself at the sudden ridicule he roared: "Quiet!" Again: "Quiet!"

The mirth subsided, and the C.S.M. glanced at Crane uneasily. Crane's rage lent a deep suffusion to his face and caused his body to shudder slightly.

"Who said that?"

Gasps and murmurs rose from B Company. Surely not even Crane was going to take this any further! The question was repeated:

"Who said that?"

There was a long silence. Then an angular figure stepped out from the ranks, slumped inside a greatcoat that hung on it baggily. Out of the collar rose the long, clownish head, narrow eyes and beaky nose of Dooley.

"I did," said Dooley, and he grinned.

Crane, standing at attention, did not look at him.

"Report to the company orderly room after breakfast." As Dooley rejoined the ranks Crane babbled venomously: "Take off that greatcoat!"

Then it began. Physical training. Almost every morning since their return to Palestine and their arrival at their new camp, Hill Fifty-seven. To the accompaniment of the stentorian sing-song of Crane:

"Running on the spot—ready—commence!—halt! Arms bend! Heels ra-a-a-aise! Knees bend! Steady! Arms str-r-retch!"

Fifteen minutes of it in the ghastly frozen dawn. Such lunacy never happened under good old Mum!

It ended with more running on the spot, after which they were dismissed. They stumbled back to their tents, coughing and spluttering, reviling Crane.

"I hate the bastard!" growled Dooley. "I hate his dirty, aristo-cratic guts!"

"Do you reckon he'll put Dooley on a charge, Chips?" some-one asked.

"He's mad enough to do anything," said Chips.

A weak sun had begun to struggle over the low hills, dully revealing the churned black mud and a thousand footprints, each full of water.

Into the wash-houses men were swarming, towels flung over their shoulders. With hard icy water, they tried to make a lather, and rubbed blunt blades over stinging faces. The faces emerged bleeding and raw. They sang, shouted, skylarked. The wash-house was a riot of noise. It was a week now since destroyers had brought them out of Tobruk, and truck convoys had dropped them back in Palestine in a new camp, a mile away from their old one. The battalion had been flooded with reinforcements from the training battalion. Rosters for leave had been posted:

five days to Jerusalem, four days to Haifa and Tel Aviv, a week to Cairo. Tomorrow the first of them were due to leave.

"Here yer are, colt."

The stocky frame and the black curly head of Go Through swung away from a tap and abandoned it to Dick.

"Go Through! How are you, you old villain?"

"Not bad, colt. How's yerself?"

"Great! What's this I hear about you getting blown up?"

In a slow, casual voice, as he vigorously rubbed his arms, Go Through replied:

"Yair! Me and Arch Temple was out in the salient, coupla days before we come out of Tobruk. Left-hand track run over a stray mine and arse-over we went."

"And neither of you hurt?"

"No, colt!" Go Through looked meekly into Dick's eyes and softly, confidentially said: "They couldn't kill the old Go Through."

"No, I don't suppose they could. What would the Second X do without you?"

"Yair, that's right," agreed Go Through with a reasonable air. "Look at the revenue the army gets out of fining me."

"You'll end up in Jerusalem," said a desolate voice.

It was Happy, glumly fingering a half-frozen face. His eyes glared out with the same unhappy resentment as the first time Dick saw him. "'Ow are yer, Dick?"

"Jerusalem!" Go Through broke in. "I'd even break out of there."

Happy nodded his head up and down vigorously several times as though disgust had choked his speech off.

"Listen to him!" he finally spluttered. "Blokes who've been in Jerusalem boob reckon that it's ten times worse than Pentridge, Boggo Road and Long Bay put together. The screws there'd as soon bash you up as light a cigarette——"

"They're nearly all ex-coppers!" someone broke in vindictively. "What'd you expect?"

"And criminals!" added another.

"Sadists!"

"Mongrels!"

"Scum of the earth!" Happy summed up.

The whole wash-house joined in a torrent of hatred against military gaolers. Some of them were telling their neighbours of meeting fellows who had done time in Jerusalem Gaol, of the tales they told and the marks these men could show on their bodies.

"Here's the leading candidate for Jerusalem," Dick said to the wash-house as Dooley came in.

He told them about the early morning parade. Dooley took their mirth without a change of expression.

137

"Hullo!" he greeted Go Through dryly. "You still in camp? Thought you would have gone through long ago."

"Waitin' for pay day," Go Through explained.

"How many fines you had?" asked Dooley with an air of professional curiosity.

"Oh, about twenty!"

The men around them were grinning broadly as they listened.

"Reckon I might get me leave cancelled for slingin' shit at Crane," mused Dooley. He shrugged. "I'll probably have to go through meself again."

He said it as though going A.W.L. was as casual a thing as shaving, which he was now doing.

"Might shoot through to Haifa," he mumbled through the lather. He looked sideways, suggestively, at Go Through.

Go Through pulled a singlet over his head. He pursed his lips, opening his eyes until they were wide and thoughtful.

"I'm putting in a couple of nights at the 'swy'," he said, "to try and build up me bank. Why don't you have a go, too?"

"A man ought!"

"Be in it!" urged Go Through.

"All right. See yer down the swy school tonight."

"Good-oh!" cried Go Through.

He gathered up his toilet gear and left.

Dooley and Dick walked back from the ablution benches with one of Six Platoon's reinforcements. He was a man well above middle height, slightly stooped and with a frail look about him. His cheeks were high-boned and freckled. His hair was colourless but his eyes were a dusty blue, small and constantly changed his sober expression with a sudden flare of merriment. His name was Sullivan and he was known as Slim.

"He'll leave me off the leave roster right enough," Dooley was saying to Sullivan. "He and I are old enemies."

"Why don't you make it difficult for him to wipe your leave?" Sullivan asked him.

"How do you mean?"

Dooley stared at him.

"Apologise to him. Say you yelled out what you did in a friendly spirit."

"Apologise to that animal!"

"Make sure there's a witness when you do it. Then if he wipes your leave it's victimisation. You'll have some sort of case."

Sullivan spoke on, unperturbed by Dooley's affronted glare.

"Are you trying to tell me," said Dooley in outraged tones, "to apologise to Crane?"

Sullivan nodded gravely.

Dooley looked dangerously at the tall man.

"I wouldn't crawl to that bastard if you paid me a thousand quid!"

138

"I'm not advising you to crawl to him. I just advised you to show him up."

Dick laughed offensively at Sullivan.

"You won't say that when you know Crane a bit better," he told Sullivan.

"Listen, Slim," said Dooley, angry and serious, "if you want a quiet life in this platoon, don't go crawling to Crane."

Sullivan turned aside as they came to his tent. He looked at Dooley and smiled gravely as his eyes lit up for a moment.

"I've never crawled to anyone, Dooley!"

He gave them a good-tempered wave of the hand.

*   *   *

Men became profane at the mere mention of training battalions. They were set in dreary, dusty camps on hills around the city of Gaza. Through them had to pass reinforcements freshly arrived from Australia and members of the battalions coming back from hospitals or military gaols. Henry Gilbertson had been sent to take command of the Second X's training battalion. To many officers, being sent to a training battalion was either a disgrace or a misfortune. In particular, officers who had seen action resented leaving their companies and being relegated to a camp that groaned in the lifeless clutches of training routine. Also, the training camps were far away from Tel Aviv and other places of pleasure. Men were generally willing to do anything to get out of a training battalion and up to a regular unit.

The moment the colonel mentioned that he was considering whom to send to the training battalion, Henry more than half expected that he himself was already in mind, although the colonel made a great show of indecision. Henry knew very well there were a number of timid and worthless officers who should have been back at the training camps, or preferably right out of the infantry. Most of these, however, had the advantage of being the colonel's peace-time friends and were now his loyal flatterers, and they would no doubt be spared a spell at the training battalion.

The morning Henry farewelled Crane and handed over command of B Company he stood in the entrance of the tent for a moment and looked back. Crane had already forgotten him. He sat purposefully at Henry's desk, his face bent over a situation report, aglow with conceit and gratification.

"Damn his hide!" thought Henry. "This is what he's been waiting for. These fellows are in for a time now!"

He walked away, hot with contempt, and bitter with a sense of loss. He had grown very fond of these men.

Returning members of the battalion were grouped together in the one platoon, and were known as "ex-men." They were nearly always troublesome. Fretting to get back to the battalion, contemptuous of reinforcement, officers who often knew less about infantry training than they did themselves, they were the envy and admiration of the reinforcements longing to be members of a unit.

One day the ex-men's platoon and two platoons of "reos," as the ex-men called the reinforcements, were being drilled by a reinforcement officer called Hollis, a man in his early twenties with an adolescent voice who tried to hide his nervousness beneath a mixture of bullyragging and unbearable disdain. The ex-men laughed at him, flouted him and used all the acquired cunning of the hardened campaigners to outwit him. He hated the ex-men and singled them out for abuse.

The atmosphere on this particular morning was tense with mutual hatred. The reos who had had months of him were choking with resentment and the ex-men obeyed his orders sluggishly, with a weary contempt.

The louder he screamed at them the worse their drill became. He marched, wheeled, halted, open-order marched, gave them small arms drill, stood them at ease, called them hysterically to attention. They made the movements as though they were drugged.

At last, white and trembling, he gave up and faced them, his temper almost gone. For a minute he glared at them. Then he burst out:

"You look like a pack of bloody convicts. Your drill's a bloody disgrace!"

Through the three platoons swept a wave of suppressed muttering. Then the lanky figure of Sullivan stepped smartly to his left front as the drill book required and said equably:

"And so are you."

Then he stepped back into the ranks.

"What did you say?" stammered Hollis thinly, his eyes looking a little alarmed.

Sullivan repeated his precise movement.

"I said: 'And so are you.'"

Hollis was suddenly calm and subdued.

"Report to the orderly room," he said.

He broke off the three platoons and followed Sullivan.

He swept into the orderly room with Sullivan and said to the orderly room sergeant sitting there:

"Staff! Get out an A.4. I'm charging this man."

Just then Henry entered from his office next door.

"What's the trouble?"

"Insolence! Insubordination!" Hollis answered. Then he added: "Conduct to the prejudice."

He related the episode to Henry.

Henry sighed.

140

"Yes! Get out an A.4, staff."

"Get out two," requested Sullivan. "One for me."

They gaped at him.

"I wish to charge Lieutenant Hollis," explained Sullivan gravely. "He told us we looked like a pack of convicts. Behaviour unbecoming to an officer. I forget which section of Army Law it comes under."

"There is such a charge," said Henry, looking startled and perturbed.

"You charge me!" squeaked Hollis.

"A private may charge any officer," replied Sullivan with the same grave, easy air.

One side of Henry's face became distorted as he fought a smile.

"I'm sure Lieutenant Hollis regrets any slur he may have cast on you fellows," he said. "We're all inclined to be jumpy down here. Sullivan, if I can persuade Lieutenant Hollis to forget the matter will you do the same?"

"Gladly, sir. I regret any slur I may have cast on Lieutenant Hollis."

"You may go, Sullivan," said Henry.

Henry took Hollis into his office and shut the door. The sergeant heard nothing of what transpired therein, but ten minutes later Hollis stalked out looking very mortified and Henry, chuckling, said to the sergeant:

"We won't be needing those A.4s, staff."

As he closed the door of his office again, Henry hooted once with laughter.

The sergeant related the whole thing in his mess at lunch. The mess orderly sped over to the men's mess and passed it on. The mess rang with shouts of triumph.

There was bottled beer at the canteen that night and Sullivan was toasted in the lines. As for Sullivan, although he patiently pointed out that the incident was merely an example of how important it was to know the men's rights, even in the army, few heeded him, and nearly everyone got drunk.

However, one or two remembered what he had said.

*   *   *

"Bah—TAL—ION!" roared Regimental Sergeant-Major Varney.

There was a poised silence. The ranks of the Second X stiffened and stood without a quiver.

"Ah—ten—SHUN!"

With one great hollow clicking of boots, the Second X came to attention.

The R.S.M. about turned. He marched towards the colonel as though his joints were bound with wire. In a flurry of heels he halted, paused a minute, then swept his arm up in a salute that unwound like a spring and left his fingers quivering a fraction of an inch from the brim of his hat.

The colonel returned his salute and took over the parade. The battalion had been warned there was to be an inspection. Boots had been polished, rifles cleaned and oiled, webbing adjusted to a nicety. The colonel walked along the ranks, his eyes going up and down each man, from the puggaree on his hat to the toes of his boots. His eyes were sharply critical, his expression as stony as if he were inspecting cattle. Up and down, up down, went the appraising eyes.

When the inspection ended, the colonel ordered the companies to form a hollow square. Then he stood them at ease and began to talk to the Second X. He looked a natty, finely-groomed figure as he stood with a stick held in his armpit, and addressed them:

"This battalion is now at full strength again. The gaps left in our ranks after the long and arduous siege of Tobruk have been filled by reinforcements who have yet to see action. They may be asking themselves: 'What sort of a battalion have we come to?' Let me answer their question. They have come to the best battalion and I intend to keep it the best. I will not tolerate any looseness of dress or bearing. Lack of respect for officers I shall punish as severely as I am able. Unsoldierly habits will not be tolerated. Do not imagine for a moment that there will be any relaxation of discipline because you have just come out of a long campaign. There is further action ahead of us. The German has by no means shot his bolt. We must keep on our toes . . ."

So it went on. The new men listened to him with a certain interest, but the old hands stood and stared straight ahead of them, hearing but not heeding.

After the parade, the battalion split up into companies again, which in turn split up into platoons.

Lieutenant Manning, a new officer, took Seventeen Platoon on a short route march. He was trying hard to get acquainted and ingratiate himself with the men. He had been a sergeant in the Second Y and after gaining his commission had been sent over to the Second X. He knew that there were only six survivors from the Tobruk campaign in Seventeen Platoon. He had been told how the platoon had been overrun, had retreated, been ordered by the colonel to stay where it was, allowing it to be surrounded instead of saving itself, and the remnants burnt to death by flame-throwers.

After fifty minutes' marching he called a halt. The men broke off and lay along the grassy verge of the road. The sun was beginning to raise steam from the damp, grey walls of an Arab village just along the road. It sparkled vigorously along the tops of the orange groves, and on the road which shone like oilcloth.

The lieutenant was listening to the men talking in order to find some means of breaking into their conversation. He wanted to talk to them badly. He felt cut adrift as an officer, and out of his depth. The six Tobruk survivors lay near him. They always stuck together, and looked a close-lipped, hard-bitten lot. They were discussing something in low, scornful voices:

"Standing up there and telling the reos what a great bloke he is! The boys will tell them a few things."

"It's a pity he couldn't have been knocked!"

"What! Then we'd have had the Animal for a C.O."

"Well, what of it? The Animal's at least a good soldier."

"Yair, I hate the bastard, but he's an A.1 soldier. All Groggy can do is soak whisky and make speeches."

"A man ought to put in for a transfer to the Second Y."

One of them looked up and said to Manning:

"What sort of a mob's the Second Y, sir?"

"Damned good mob. But you wouldn't be any happier there judging by the way you're running the colonel down."

"Run him down!" someone spat.

"You heard, did you?" another asked.

"Don't worry," smiled Manning. "It won't go any further. But what's the use of these hate sessions? What's he done to deserve it? He can't be as bad as you make out."

A man looked at him, his eyes sorrowful and said simply but wisely:

"You weren't with us in Tobruk!"

*   *   *

B Company stood in a long, straggling line outside the company cook-house. Behind two great steaming dixies mess orderlies ladled stew into the square mess tins held out by each man as he came past. Standing near a smoking camp oven watching the line stood Baxter, the company cook.

He was an unlovely specimen. His hair was clipped short but stuck out everywhere as though it had never seen brush or comb. His skin looked pallid and unhealthy, like that of a newly-plucked fowl and every pore of it was a little black dot, for his face exuded dirt. His eyes were red, debauched and venomous. He was famous for his waspish temper and his abuse. He spent most of his nights drinking beer, of which he seemed to have an endless supply, and often when a sentry woke him at five or six in the morning, it was just after he had fallen into a drunken sleep, and he would curse and revile the sentry filthily. He stole a lot of the company's rations, which he sold to the Arabs in the nearby village. Generally he brought drink with the proceeds, but occasionally he found an Arab woman willing to yield her body for an armful of food. Through this he had twice been to hospital with venereal disease. However, after almost being knifed by a jealous Arab, he was keeping out of the village for a while. He carried always in his mouth a spit-soaked stub of cigarette. His apron was so thick with long-worn dirt that it shone like a mackintosh.

The troops hated him and condemned his cooking. He would fly into rages at any complaint. Once, in a drunken fit of spite, he had urinated into a boiler full of stew he was preparing. Many men swore he boiled up his dirty aprons with their stew. He had only held his job this long because his off-sider was an honest and conscientious cook who tried to make up for Baxter's short-comings, and because officers rarely took much notice of the men's complaints about food.

Captain Barrett would shrug indifferently and say: "They'd complain about the food no matter how good it was. They get the privilege of complaining to the orderly officer and abuse the privilege. They complain about nothing!"

Baxter watched them morosely as they filed past, chatting, laughing and exchanging friendly abuse.

The stew smelt heavy and greasy. It was greyish, with big, pale blobs of vegetable floating in it.

A man slapped his dixie down and hitched his trousers:

"What's this? Camel?"

"No," scowled Baxter. "Jackal."

"Can I have the Pope's nose?" someone enquired.

There was a howl of laughter.

"When're you going to have a wash, Baxter?" another asked casually.

"When I get back home," replied Baxter, unmoved.

"You'll never get home—the Wogs'll cut your throat."

"You know," someone else observed with a great show of seriousness, "I reckon if a man was to sprinkle a bit of mush-room spawn on Baxter's face, he'd get a fine crop of mushrooms the next morning."

Baxter's little eyes contemplated their laughter sullenly.

Some refused the stew, saying they would fill up with bread and tea. The mess-tent did not hold more than half the com-pany, and the rest of them squatted on their haunches, on the cold muddy ground outside. There was still plenty of stew left in the big dixies.

"Any more for any more?" cried a mess orderly.

"Is it any good?"

"Sure!" the mess orderly called provocatively.

"Then stick it up your jacksy. A good thing never hurt you." And they all laughed at the ageless joke.

"Mess—sit fast!" yelled the voice of the Battalion Orderly Sergeant.

"Sit easy!" said the Orderly Officer. It was Lieutenant Temple.

"Any complaints?"

"This bloody stew!" chorused a score of voices.

"What's wrong with it?"

"Someone dropped a dead dog in it," suggested Dooley.

Temple held a tin full of it up to his face:

"It looks all right to me."

"Try a bit," urged Sullivan and handed him a fork.

Reluctantly, the lieutenant did so. He rolled a piece of hot fat around his mouth and swallowed it with difficulty.

"Not the best," he acknowledged. "I'll pass the complaint on."

They cheered his announcement ironically.

With a grin, Temple and the sergeant left the mess-tent.

"Going to the swy," was all Dooley told his tent-mates, and, hurrying through the battalion lines, plunged into an olive grove on the outskirts of the camp. Here, in a clear space where the earth had been trodden shiny and flat, a game of two-up was conducted nightly.

"Hullo!" Go Through greeted him. "It's rainin' heads."

"Well, what are we waiting for?"

"He'll spin out in a minute. He's done four straight."

"And he's tailed them!" declared a voice.

The man who ran the two-up in the Second X was Tony Horne, a great, slouching, grey-faced man in his forties with a long hooked nose. His eyes were yellow and merciless. They seemed to be made of fine, golden lines that ran in to a pin-point of a pupil and they could look at a man interminably with a piercing, unwinking stare. He seemed to hover, and miss nothing. They called him the Vulture. He was reputed to be enormously rich and made no bones about the fact that he had joined the army to make money from gambling.

"I want a spinner," he rasped.

"Right!" said Dooley, and took the "kip." He threw a crumpled pound note into the ring and lined the three shining pennies along the kip.

"I want a quid in the centre!" called Tony Horne. "I want a quid in the guts!"

A five hundred mil note was tossed in.

"I want five hundred in the guts!"

Another note sailed in.

"Set in the centre! Get set on the side!"

Money was being laid swiftly around the ring.

"I'll back his head!" announced Go Through.

"Right-oh, sport! A quid?"

"You're set!" said Go Through.

"Is everyone set?"

"Come in, spinner!"

Dooley walked to the centre of the ring. He held the kip straight out in front of him, then suddenly, with a stylish flick of the wrist, sent the pennies spinning skywards. All eyes followed their upward flight and necks craned over as they hit the ground.

Tony Horne inspected them.

"Heads it is! I want two quid in the guts! Gentlemen, I require two fiddleys in the old comic guts!"

Dooley spun heads seven times straight, leaving his winnings in as a bet each time. On the eighth spin he left only his original stake in a spin-out. He gave five pounds to Tony Horne, as was customary with big winners, and left the ring with a hundred-odd pounds.

On the outskirts of the crowd he was joined by Go Through, who said with rich glee:

"You little beaut! I backed yer each time. I'm winning eighty."

"Enough to go through on, d'yer reckon?" grinned Dooley, all the more determinedly casual because of his success.

"Yair! With this and our pay we'll buy Jerusalem."

"Why wait for pay day?" asked Dooley with a restless movement. His lips tightened, his eyes were flickering avidly, as though his mind were running away ahead of his body. "Why wait?" he repeated. "Let's go tonight."

"Not me!" said Go Through. "It's only two days to pay day and I've got a poultice in that pay-book of mine."

"All right!" said Dooley. He looked absent-minded, strangely disturbed.

"See yer tomorrow!" he cried, and walked away, not with his usual slouch, but almost at a run.

He reached his tent and sat down, hands on knees, staring straight ahead, strangely transformed, as though he were slightly feverish. His eyes gleamed and changed like the surface of a gathering wave. His mind reeled with lurid, tangled, enticing visions: steaming rich food, glowing magic drink and the waiting white bellies of women.

*   *   *

In Tobruk Dick had almost forgotten Naomi, but now he began to think of her again. A lot of what had formerly passed between them now seemed remote and contemptible. He recalled a feeling of security, of being half-mothered in her presence because he had told her about the tragedies of his boyhood and she had understood; a sense of friendship; a kiss. Now, these meant nothing. His thoughts and feelings about her now were reckless and direct.

He looked forward to seeing Naomi again because she was a woman, a very desirable one. He laughed at himself because he had not already taken her body. She was older than he, more mature. She would have expected it. She must have laughed at him secretly for respecting her!

He recalled the swelling, broad form in the faded blue skirt, and around it he built a vision of future delight.

Meanwhile, he was becoming a first-class N.C.O. and Crane had said he would be a sergeant soon.

Back among the civilised amenities of the officers' mess, the colonel regained his former confidence. He drank prodigiously, gathered his friends around him and told them what splendid officers they were and modestly bore their praise in return. He had received the D.S.O. for the battalion's heroic defence of the Tobruk perimeter during the Battle of the Salient, the battle in which he had sent Seventeen Platoon needlessly to its death. The day on which he first wore the ribbon the officers had toasted the colonel in the mess, and he had made a restrained and manly speech, saying how he wore the ribbon on behalf of the battalion, and to remember "those splendid chaps" who had fallen in the siege of Tobruk.

"Especially Seventeen Platoon!" thought Henry. And he walked away, sickened and aghast at the irony of it.

Major Pomfret still carried out his duties in the background; soulless, efficient and patient. When Temple mentioned that the men were complaining over the food he replied:

"The M.O. tells me it's eatable. What do they expect? There's a war on!"

The last saying had appealed to Crane, who remembered it. One morning as he made the company do its physical training he urged them angrily to better efforts, shouting: "There's a war on!"

It seemed such a ludicrous thing to shout out to a lot of battle-weary men jumping about like clowns in the dreary dawn that the entire company burst into howls of laughter.

13

LUCAS's thigh wound had been a terrible one, but not as bad as was at first feared. A piece of shrapnel had torn into his muscle and partly shattered the bone. For four months he had lain in a military hospital in Palestine with the thigh in plaster-of-paris. Gradually, the suppuration and blood from the wound soaked through the plaster and left a large yellowish stain with a red edge. It resembled a map, Lucas used to think as he gazed at it moodily.

It began to stink unspeakably. A thick, fœtid smell of moist rottenness pressed up his nostrils and made his stomach lurch. After a while he became used to it and at times caught himself savouring the smell of the dying flesh like an animal.

The man in the bed on his left, who had a lung wound, complained about the stench in a thin, evil voice. He was a Seventh Division man who had been shot in Syria by a Vichy Frenchman. He had lain propped up on the pillows for six months, his pyjamas sagging on a sharp, emaciated frame. His face, like white shiny wax, was drawn tight in a desperate stare of suffering. He would turn to Lucas and, his eyes rolling like two dark marbles, wheeze petulantly:

"Oh, my God, you stink!"

Lucas would look across at him without pity and grin.

The bed on Lucas's right was occupied by a twenty-year-old boy with both his legs blown off. He lay quietly without complaining, his eyes turned upwards with a soft, fearful, questioning look. He hæmorrhaged frequently and the nurses would rush up blood transfusions and injections to deaden the pain. He only spoke when there was something wrong, and then his mouth would open and shut soundlessly like a fish's, and Lucas would lean across and ask:

"Want the nurse, son?"

The curly head would nod ever so slightly and when the nurse came the boy would speak to her in an old, tired voice.

During the night the boy would be convulsed with pain. He would screech frenziedly and utter a high doleful shriek like a dog. There would be groans and mutters as his cries woke the rest of the ward.

The nurse would come running and give him an injection. Gradually his cries would lessen and subside into childish little whimpers. Then he would groan once deeply and fall unconscious.

They pumped the blood into him and as fast as it went into his body it oozed out through the shattered stumps.

One night, without a sound, he flooded his bed with blood and died. His face in the morning was like a piece of white marble.

Suffering had made the man with the lung wound evil-minded and petty. He gasped, whimpered, snarled, and his eyes rolled in self-pity. Lucas lost patience with him and grew weary to death of the wheezing, querulous voice.

"Where's that nurse?" the man would ask. "I want something. A man could be dying for all they care. Call the bloody woman. I'm in pain!"

In the end pneumonia supervened and they put screens around his bed for him to die as privately as possible. And after the body was taken away Lucas could feel only relief.

A week or two before the plaster was cut away, Lucas was allowed out of bed to learn to walk again. As he stood for the first time in four months, with a nurse holding his arm, he felt strangely tall and didn't know where to put his feet. He found it hard even to stand on his own. His feet and legs felt weak and small, while the rest of his body felt top-heavy and enormous. He took a few hesitant, assisted steps and then sagged. The plaster on his thigh felt as heavy as iron. Then he was put back to bed.

He went through this ordeal for several days, until his limbs regained strength and confidence. Within a week he could hobble round on his own.

When the plaster was cut off there lay revealed a great purple valley in his thigh. The surgeon said the bone was as good as ever and the wound had healed marvellously.

The savage moodiness that had possessed him for the last four months began to drop away. As his body strengthened, so did his desires, his cynical interest in life itself. He began to appraise the bodies of the nurses as they moved swiftly up and down the length of the ward in their grey linen dresses. He sickened of the plain over-cooked hospital food and began to wonder where he could get something to drink. He slept for only a short time at night, waking alert and vital in the small hours, his frame disturbed by deep yearning.

He would get up, don his dressing-gown, and go out to the little office at the end of the ward where the night sister sat. After this had happened several times he became friendly with her and she would make a hot drink for him, and they would talk. One night, with a swift avid movement, he grasped and kissed her. She responded but would allow him to do nothing more. He merely held her wrist and fumbled with her, but she freed herself and unconvincingly reminded him she was his superior officer. She was a young woman and it amused him to watch her on these occasions, troubled by his attraction for her, and fearful that they might be seen. Once he had to pull himself together, trembling with desire and mockingly surprised at himself, for he had almost lost his head and tried to force her submission. After that, he contented himself with holding and kissing her and whispering violent phrases in her ears. She promised herself to him if they could get leave together.

Then she was relieved by another night sister, a buxom, cold-blooded creature of forty whom he instantly rejected.

"A man-eater!" he thought, and sought fresh amusement.

He learnt that the hospital was only a mile away from the old camp of the Second X, and that by taking the path through an orange grove next to the hospital he would reach the hill that overlooked the camp. When he learnt this he recalled that one of the shops near the Jewish settlement sold wine.

The very next afternoon he was making his way through the orange grove towards this shop.

It was the first fine day for a week. A white warm sun shone in a watery sky. The landscape had a pale washed-out appearance. The rain had softened the black soil until it was like jelly, but an hour or two of sun had hardened its surface, leaving it with a pale grey crust that cracked into long, crooked fissures whose edges curled up like sheets of cardboard. The orange grove smelt dank and oppressive. He felt it around him like a heavy green curtain.

At the top of the slope the path ran into a sunken, muddy track that wandered between great, green walls of cactus. Obviously it led into an Arab village, he thought.

A few seconds later an Arab peasant came trudging on spindly grey shanks along the lane. He greeted Lucas jovially, in the manner of the fellaheen:

"Syeeda, George!"

"Syeeda," responded Lucas.

"Baksheesh, George?" the Arab went on, tipping his head to one side, and looking at Lucas with a sort of wary impudence.

"Ana maskeen," said Lucas grinning.

The Arab beat his chest:

"*Ana* maskeen!"

"Yehudi bunduq!" scoffed Lucas.

"La!" growled the Arab resentfully. "La!"

He turned away, looked back once over his shoulder with hard, narrow eyes and then went on his way.

It was obvious to Lucas after a while that he had lost his way. However, he shrugged and kept on. It was a pleasant day for walking. In a few minutes he got to the top of another rise and found himself on the outskirts of the communal settlement. He paused for a minute to take in the peaceful and orderly pattern of the settlement, then began to descend. Half-way down he ran into a dozen big Friesian cows in charge of a Jewish girl. She was sturdy and dark-brown, with sandals on her feet, a pair of shorts that pinched her buttocks, a white blouse and white handkerchief tied around her hair. She smiled at Lucas, calling out something in Hebrew that was liquid and song-like. He called back at her, but she only laughed and shook her head. After the dull, painful months in the hospital bed she was like a flashing vision. He stared after her hungrily, stirred deeply.

Presently a youth hailed him and spoke English in a friendly way.

"Can I get something to drink here?" asked Lucas.

"Yes!" the youth assured him. "Coffee? We do not have tea."

"No! Something out of a bottle."

150

"Jakob!" called a female voice and asked a question in German.

Jakob called something back and from behind a shed came Naomi.

"Good day," she said to Lucas.

Lucas looked at the burnt, boyish features, the broad, ripe body and had the same feeling as a few moments previously.

"I was asking this young fellow if I could get a drink of something."

"Out of a bottle," added the youth, grinning.

Naomi said something to him sharply. He shrugged sulkily and slouched away.

She turned again to Lucas and said doubtfully:

"We have Rishon wine. . . ."

"Sounds good! Where can I buy some?"

"We do not sell it here," she replied. "I can offer you some."

He looked at her, eyes lively, teeth half revealed in a grin:

"That's kind of you!"

He managed to put the shadows of several meanings into the words.

Naomi inclined her head gravely to one side.

"You will come, then?"

She made towards a small wooden hut of dark timber. Seeing him limp, she made herself walk slowly.

"You have been wounded?" she asked.

"Yes. In Tobruk."

"Is it right for me to ask your regiment?"

"No, I don't think so. But I don't mind telling you, since I'm not with them. It's the Second X Battalion."

"Ah!" she said softly.

He looked at her sharply:

"You know it?"

"I have heard of it from someone. You are still in hospital?"

"Yes. I've been away from my unit for four months."

"Then you would know nothing?"

"Only the same as you would from your newspapers. That the Australians have come out of Tobruk."

She nodded silently.

She opened the door and motioned him into the hut. It was one room, simply furnished. In the far corner was a divan bed covered in a bright rug, near it a square wooden cabinet, a low table and three stools in the centre of the room. The walls were of unvarnished wood with a number of small prints hanging along them.

From the cabinet she brought a bottle of dark red wine and two tumblers.

Lucas watched her as she poured the wine. When she bent over, one side of her blouse hung loosely and he could see a swelling golden breast. A shaft of sun coming in the window lit up a little quivering pool of lighter gold between her breasts. The blue skirt tightened around her thighs like a skin. She brushed a hair away from her temple and so drew his attention to her ears, which were small, dark and perfect. The neck that arose from her plump shoulders was thick, smooth and round, and the skin on it had a polished look.

He veiled his eyes quickly as she glanced up and offered him a glass of wine.

She squatted cross-legged on the floor.

"We like to have Australians here," she told him. "They do not act like some of the English. They are more friendly."

He nodded, still with his eyes half-veiled. He sipped the wine, which was heavy and sweet.

"Do you like the wine?" she asked.

"Yes," he said absently.

"A lot of Australians do not," she went on. "It is too rich for them."

He nodded, only half hearing what she said. When she turned away for a minute he looked at her again.

His eyes were fierce with yearning.

On his first visit to the settlement Lucas stayed only a short while, for he did not want to be missed from the hospital, which he had left without permission.

Several mornings later he came again, and, as before, Naomi invited him into her hut. This time he did not bother to hide his desire from her. He gazed at her steadily with an expression of arrogant appraisal and hunger. She looked away, disturbed and then resentful.

When she began to find his hot stare unbearable she looked up, and at that moment, as their eyes met, Lucas leant over and grasped her. He kissed her lips and then smiled pleasurably. At first, she did not resist. After he kissed her she gazed at him. She saw in his face nothing but gay cruelty and tried to push him away. He held her mercilessly hard and putting a hand inside her blouse fondled her large soft breasts. Shocked as she was by his expression, something tender and fierce in her surged in answer to his embrace. She felt his hot, smiling lips over her face, his hand on her body. Involuntarily, she clung to him now, her desire as fierce as his own. He lowered her to the bed. As she felt his fingers about her body she was flooded with a great sense of passion and release.

*   *   *

After Lucas had been wounded, Andy Cain had become wretched and isolated. There was no one else in the platoon whose company he cared for now.

152

For many weeks his mind had been racked with memories of his wife. He had not been able to wrench her completely from his thoughts, despite the face of calm that he was able to show to the outside world. Then one night he realised that losing her meant that he was rid of the final link with his old life, with all his former failures.

He became oblivious to everything but being a perfect soldier. His features were unsmiling. He was more coldbloodedly reckless than ever. He seemed indifferent to the pain and fear of others as well as his own.

One night, just before the battalion had come out of Tobruk, some of the platoon had ambushed a Nazi patrol out in No Man's Land, capturing two Nazis.

"We need only one prisoner," Andy had said, and bringing up his tommy-gun shot one of the Nazis dead.

They were still in danger and a long way from their post and there had been no time to argue with him then. But what he had seen in Dick's face had told him that the last shreds of their friendship were gone.

When the battalion settled down again back in Palestine he was promoted sergeant of one of the other platoons in B Company. He applied for leave to Cairo and getting it, went off on his own.

*   *   *

Dick came to Naomi's hut at dusk one evening. He saw her outside and when he was about ten yards away called to her. She turned, and at first did not recognise him.

"Who is it?" she asked in German.

"Naomi," he called to her again.

She took a step forward and stopped, peering.

"Dick?"

"Yes! It's me."

He tried to sound casual, but failed. He ran up to her and stood facing her. Meeting her at last had made him strangely apprehensive.

She let out a deep breath.

"You are safe then?"

"Yes. Quite safe!"

She spoke in a low calm voice:

"You did not write."

"I did—once."

There was another silence between them. This is absurd, he thought. It was not the vision he had been building up. Suddenly he felt fiercely possessive. He took her in his arms. She lay passively against him while he kissed her. Then she threw her head back and laughed, but in the dark he saw the gleam of tears in her eyes. She swallowed, took his face in her hands and kissed him in a forlorn, hungry way.

"I thought you were dead!"

As they went into the hut he said to her:

"I have got five days' leave to Jerusalem. I want you to come with me."

She did not speak, but by the way she leant submissively against him he was confident she would come with him.

That night he shared her bed in the hut and the next day they caught the bus for Jerusalem.

In a grey drizzle the bus climbed up between villages and olive groves, on the narrow roads that wound along the sides of gaunt old mountains. Although it was mid-afternoon, when the bus reached Jerusalem it was half-dark.

It was bitterly cold. The gutters sang with water. Buildings huddled together in a showery mist. Heads down, the people they passed went soberly on their way.

They took a taxi and Naomi directed it to a large stone block of apartments. She went into an office near the front entrance and Dick waited in the vestibule. Presently she came out with a key.

"I have got a room," she told him, and putting her finger through the ring, spun it around.

Together they went up.

The room was on the third floor. It was large and chilly. The walls were painted green with a black frieze of some Hebraic design. There was a big, low bed, a wardrobe, a chair, a small table in the centre. The floor was of cold, scrubbed tiles with a rush mat by the bed.

When she had unpacked from a small bag the few things she had brought, Naomi lay back on the bed. Dick had taken off his greatcoat and stood peering out the window. But there was little to see at this time: only a vague wilderness of roofs with here and there a dome or a minaret looming through the murk.

Naomi lay watching him through half-closed eyes. He had changed, she thought. The softness of youth was gone from his features; they were tanned, roughened and a little gaunt. He was thinner. But he had changed inwardly too. This time he had come to her confident and possessive, showing her at once that she must change her attitude. Now, if she comforted him, it must be as his mistress, and if she dared ridicule him, it must be as an equal. These few months of the war had burnt up something in him. His youthful braggartry was gone. His conscience and his unhappiness were still there, but hidden beneath an exterior grown manful and adamant.

She watched him tenderly and proudly. The fierceness of his love-making had left her elated as never before. His body, vibrant with a long-stored hunger, had seemed to draw on untapped wells of passion in her own. That morning she had

154

awakened languorous and happy; happier than she had been for many years. Looking in the mirror, it had seemed to her that her eyes and cheeks had begun to glow. All day she had been conscious of her body as something tender and passionate, something belonging wholly to him.

Negligently she raised her knees until her skirt fell back, and revealed her sturdy brown thighs. She ran her fingers along a thigh, then spoke to him:

"Are you hungry? There is a café downstairs."

As he turned to look at her she saw his face soften. It wore the look that she knew of old.

He did not answer, but gazed at her ardently. A kind of reckless joy came over her. Without taking her eyes from him she took off her blouse and bared her breasts, rumpling the skin of one in her fingers. Still he said nothing. His lips began to smile. Elatedly, she wriggled softly from her dress, and spoke to him in German, in a low, deep voice.

"What does that mean?"

"It is from a song. It means I belong to you."

He looked at her delightedly.

"You're a fine figure of a woman. To think I used to admire the willowy type!"

"And now?" she mocked.

He came over, sat down on the bed, and feigned indifference.

"In answer to your question, I am a little hungry. Let's go down to this café."

She laughed.

"Will you wait while I change my dress?"

"I hope so! Here, let me help you."

He took the dress she had taken out and lowered it over her head. Looking up at him, she cried:

"Why, you act as if you were my husband!"

The café Naomi had spoken of was in a basement. It was large, and scattered with stone pillars. Next to each pillar was a table. There was a small bar over in the far corner, and just near the entrance a young man glumly rippled the keys of a piano.

Nearly every table was occupied. Australians were in the majority, mostly with women. Several of his own battalion hailed Dick as he came past seeking a table. He returned their greetings self-consciously, for at the same time they leered intelligently at Naomi. Most of the women they had with them were flashily-dressed prostitutes or girls who earned a commission from the café for each drink their escorts bought. A waiter in a white apron brought their order and asked an outrageous price, which he reduced after several rapid and scornful remarks from Naomi.

155

She lifted her glass and her eyes smiled at Dick above the rim.

They drank a silent toast.

Her eyes gazed across the room for a minute, then she laughed.

"What's the joke?" he asked.

"That Australian over there," she told him. "He thinks I am a prostitute. He's making signs to me."

Dick flushed fiercely, and muttered:

"Damn him!"

"Dick! You are jealous?" she asked playfully.

He began to feel unreasonably annoyed. He disguised his state of mind by saying self-righteously:

"When I see the way some Australians behave in the cities I'm ashamed of them. Every woman's a prostitute to them."

She became serious and reproached him:

"It is not your friends you should be ashamed of. Nothing else is offered them but drink and bad women. They are lonely, Dick, and a long way from home, from their women. In a war we lose all our roots, all the things we have built our lives on. We are afraid of death, we drift, we seek consolation anywhere. The worst in us is let loose."

"Yes, you're right." He pulled himself together, smiled and took her hand:

"They're not all as lucky as me!"

She smiled at him warmly as she finished her drink.

"All the same," he went on, "I have seen some disgusting things."

"Such things happen with all armies of occupation," she told him.

He beckoned to the waiter and ordered two more drinks.

This time he drank with zest.

"You're wonderful!" he told her.

After another lot of drinks they ordered a meal. Dick watched the food avidly as it was placed before him. He was taken with a delicious sense of enjoyment, and talked gaily as he ate. He began to make plans for the morrow:

"I want to see the Church of the Sepulchre. It means nothing to me in a religious sense, but it's worth seeing, anyway, I suppose. And of course the Dome of the Rock, the Garden of Gethsemane, and——"

"Well, well," a bantering voice interrupted. "What have we here?"

It was Lucas, standing beside their table and looking incredibly amused.

"Hullo, Frank!" he cried in surprise.

"Hallo, Dick," Lucas smiled mockingly at Naomi. "Hullo!" he said to her.

Naomi smiled at him.

"Frank, this is Naomi——"

"Naomi and I are old friends, Dick."

"He came to the Kibbutz one day from the hospital," Naomi broke in swiftly.

"Yes, that's right," agreed Lucas, delightedly.

"You are on leave from the hospital?" Naomi asked with a sudden spiteful glance at Lucas.

"Only until tonight," he replied, and with a cruel grin at Naomi added significantly: "Unfortunately!"

Then he turned to Dick and asked:

"Having a good time, Dick?"

Proud that Lucas had seen him with a beautiful woman, a woman Lucas had met too, Dick stood up, smirked and said hospitably:

"Just arrived, Frank. Draw up a chair and I'll give you all the battalion news. How's your leg?"

"No thanks, Dick. I've got to go. Andy was down to see me at the hospital a few days ago and told me all the news. And the leg's nearly healed. I'll be back with you soon, mate."

"But aren't you going to have just one drink?" cried Dick, disappointed.

"Trouble is, there's a hospital bus waiting for me outside. I only came in to round up a couple of strays."

"Well," said Dick, reluctantly. "See you later."

"Yes!" He winked at Dick and grinned again, as though he were highly diverted. "Have a good time!"

To Naomi he said:

"You too!"

"Well, dammit!" Dick exclaimed. "He might have stayed and talked a minute. I've not seen him since Tobruk."

He felt a little piqued.

The life seemed to go out of their evening after that. Seeing Lucas had stirred things in his memory that he had managed to hide from himself. Once more the war loomed as a gigantic backdrop to his life, in front of which he and his plans were contemptible. Naomi had spells of glum silence and her gaiety came on and off her features like a mask. In the end they gave up all pretence. Suddenly they both felt tired.

They climbed the stairs to their room in silence. Dick was thinking of Andy. Andy had been down to see Lucas but told no one else about it. Changed as he was he might have told the rest of the platoon that Lucas was all right! He imparted nothing these days—neither help, advice, nor information; but to tell no one about his visit to Lucas seemed unutterably harsh to Dick. It revealed Andy as someone who had become self-centred to the point of madness.

157

His thoughts went back to Lucas. Again he had that feeling of pique. Seeing Dick again had meant nothing to Lucas, only a sort of amusement at meeting Dick in the company of a woman he had also met. Nothing went deep with Lucas; life was a mockery to him. Of course, that was the basis of Andy's friendship with him. Andy was becoming similar to Lucas in his own miserable fashion.

Oh, hang Lucas!

War was a disease, and while it ran its course the only treatment was to forget when you could. He was just beginning a week of forgetting. The wine downstairs had tasted good, and here he was sharing a bed with a woman he was sure he loved.

As the door of their room closed behind them he seized Naomi roughly and kissed her. She returned his kiss a little sadly and walked over to sit on the edge of the bed. She looked down at the floor, her eyes thoughtful and troubled. Then she raised them and looked at him.

"I think it is best to tell you something," she began. "Perhaps I don't need to. But if he tells you it will be worse, and I do not trust him. He would tell you just as a joke, if he wanted to—if he knew about us."

He looked at her stupidly.

"If who knew us?"

"Your friend—Lucas."

"What's it to do with Lucas?"

"Nothing, really. But you see, I have slept with him."

"With Lucas?"

He repeated it, wondering at the detached way in which he spoke the words. It sounded like some nasty joke he didn't want to comprehend.

"Yes. He came to the Kibbutz regularly for a little while."

A wave of angry grief swept over him. He stood and stared at her without speaking. She in her turn sat and gazed back at him steadily, looking patient and sad. In his humiliation and rage he sought for words that would cut her, break through her composure.

Finally he grinned and said conversationally:

"Tell me about the others. Perhaps I'm acquainted with some of them too."

She accepted the insult meekly.

"I was afraid you would be hurt," she told him. "There are no others to tell you about. He came to the Kibbutz by chance and made love to me when I was lonely and depressed."

"Poor little woman!" he sneered. "Pining away while I enjoyed myself in Tobruk!"

He loathed himself for saying these words. They sounded unutterably shoddy.

"I thought of you a lot while you were away. I hoped to get

158

your letters. Finally, I convinced myself you were dead. I was sorry you did not make love to me before you went. I should have made you. But you were too unhappy, too full of yourself. I tried to help you. I really felt there was something between us because of that. Lucas was nothing to me. I dislike him. But I have a body. It is not a nun's. I owed you nothing. I thought you had been killed or had forgotten me."

"Forgotten!" he echoed bitterly. "Most of the time you have to forget."

He had seated himself on the bed beside her. All the anger had gone out of him now. He felt calm and wise and a little sorry for himself.

She took his hand and asked gently:

"It was very bad in Tobruk?"

"It's better not talked of. I'm sorry I was so rotten to you just now. I had no claim on you. I was just surprised."

He thought for a minute, then laughed:

"Still, if Lucas were still in Jerusalem I'd like to punch his nose!"

He stood up, feeling restless and no longer tired. He had a sudden yearning for a lot of drinks and male company.

"I think I'll go down to the café for a while and have a few drinks."

He went down on his own. He had not asked her to come because he did not want her with him.

The café was now crowded, clamorous and hazed blue with the smoke of cigarettes. The Australian army seemed to have claimed it for its own. The pianist was now one of a four-piece band. Half a dozen couples danced to its music in the middle of the floor. Over in a corner sat Dooley and Go Through with two women. They were gloriously drunk.

They caught sight of him and beckoned him over:

"'Ow are yer, colt! Come'n 'ave a drink. Hey, George, bring another chair and one more glass."

They must have been tipping the waiter well, for he abandoned another table to comply with the order.

"This is Dick, girls," announced Dooley, waving a hand at the two women.

Dick sat down, smiling.

"And when did you two shoot through?"

"'Sh'afternoon," Dooley told him. "We're staying till the oscar runs out, ain't we, Go Through?"

"You mean," said Dick, "until the provosts picks you up."

"Provosts!" Dooley waved again. "We've got that fixed, ain't we, Go Through? Mob of 'em came in half an hour ago inspecting leave passes. A great greasy provost fronts us and asks for ours. We was just about to drop him and make a run

159

for it, when—guess what? Guess who comes up and squares things for us? Go on, guess!"

"Jesus Christ," suggested Dick.

"No—Tony Horne. The old Vulture!"

"Thash right," Go Through answered Dick solemnly. "The Vulture. Got the coppers squared he has, colt. The old Vulture knows how to spread the dough where it'll do the most good."

"Stick to this joint," Dooley advised, "and if yer get into a blue of any sort, yell for the Vulture. He just about owns the joint. There he is, over by the bar."

Dick turned and caught sight of Tony Horne's grey features through the haze.

"Low bastards, them provosts," said Go Through. "See Tootsie here?" He indicated a plump, perspiring woman at his side in a tight black dress. "She's on the game, aren't yer, Tootsie? She was workin' for Madam Marie in Tel Aviv. Do yer know what the provosts do there? They come round the brothels to clear 'em out every night and cop a free one from the girls. A couple of 'em even live with the girls. And if the girls squeal the provosts threaten to have the place declared out of bounds to troops. Got to be pretty low to blackmail a crow, ain't yer? . . . Sorry, Tootsie! A lady on the game, I mean."

"Got to be low to be a provost," growled Dooley. "We won't be showing our noses anywhere but here, then we'll be safe."

"But where are you sleeping?" Dick asked them.

"We're stayin' with the girls, colt, just up the road a bit. Breakfast in bed, all mod. cons."

Go Through leered at his woman and pinched her thigh. She laughed, and a pair of formidable breasts shook beneath the dress.

"Well, good luck to you!" cried Dick, and finished his drink off. "Have one with me."

"Just one, colt. Then we're going. Hey, George!"

After the drink they made unsteadily for the door, assisted by their two women.

Tony Horne knew Dick from their Tobruk days. He was one of the stretcher-bearers who had carried Dick in from the perimeter the night Tommy Collins had died. When he saw Dick sitting there on his own he beckoned him over to his table. Picking up his drink, Dick joined him.

"How are you, young Dick?"

"Hello, Tony. Is this place Second X Headquarters? I've met half the battalion here."

"It's my headquarters anyway. Have a drink."

"I've got one here."

"I mean a decent drink." Tony turned and addressed the waiter behind the bar. "Here, Moshe, throw over a clean glass.

No, don't come round—chuck it. Thanks, Moshe! Here, try this. Vodka, the very best."

The vodka spread fiery fingers over Dick's chest. He looked at Tony Horne. In a subtle manner Tony seemed to have changed from the man who ran the two-up at the battalion. His features had taken on a benign look, his harsh mouth had slackened and drooped at the corners. Even his angular shoulders seemed to have subsided in the chair. His bushy brows fell sleepily over his eyes and dimmed their piercing stare. Only by one or two faint signs did Dick realise that Tony was sodden with drink.

The atmosphere had become oppressive. The whole place swam in the blue haze, the air they breathed was thick and stale. Above the hubbub of voices rose the wail of a saxophone, with the heavy throb of a drum in the background. Near the piano a girl stood singing. Her eyes looked out above the crowd fixedly, without expression, her voice was plaintive and monotonous as she mouthed the words:

> *"Smile a while*
> *Until we meet again."*

As he watched her, Tony's eyes became dim and despondent.

" 'Until we meet again!' What the hell's he got to sing that for? These blokes know that half of them'll never meet their wives and mothers again! Silly bloody songs like that only rub it in. Something gay." He shouted across the room to the pianist. "Hey, Mordecai, cut it out!"

The pianist looked up enquiringly and smiled as his eyes met Tony's.

"Cut it out! That song's no bloody good! Play something gay! Something gay!"

The pianist gave a placating, bewildered smile, and the saxophone player swung his instrument towards Tony and looked at him with eyes widened by the effort of his playing. The singer neither turned her head nor altered her expression. She just kept on singing.

Tony's lips went thin and tight.

"Cut it out! That song's no good! Give the boys something gay!"

Just then the singer ended a verse. The pianist looked over helplessly to a man who sat at a cash register behind the bar. The man nodded slightly. Mordecai dipped his head and began to beat out a new tune. The singer, without altering her stare, took it up half-way through the second verse.

Tony subsided back into his brooding.

> *"Life will be bliss*
> *We'll live on a kiss.*

" 'Live on a kiss,' " he mumbled forlornly. "Yair, that's just about what you blokes'll get when you go back. Kisses to keep alive on. A pat on the back and then a lot of kicks in the arse. Just like the last time."

It seemed to Dick that Tony had reached the stage of drunkenness at which all songs had a melancholy import. But Tony was now looking at him.

"I was about your age when I was on Gallipoli," he said. "Hey, Moshe! Are those mates of mine still in the room there? Only one of them? C'mon, Dick. Grab your drink and follow me. We'll go and have some peace and quiet."

Tony rose and buttoned up his tunic which had been hanging open. As he did so, Dick saw something that a fold of the cloth had formerly hidden. Three service ribbons of the first world war.

What Dooley and Go Through had told him about Tony's influence did not seem to be mere drunken talk. As Tony went behind the bar Moshe stood aside respectfully and the man at the cash register pulled back a curtain to let them pass into the back region. Half-way along a passage Tony opened a door and showed Dick into a small, dim room furnished with a table and chairs. Sitting there with a drink in his hand was one of Six Platoon's reinforcements—Sullivan.

"Hello, Slim!" Dick greeted him.

Smiling, Sullivan returned his greeting and told him to sit down.

Tony subsided into a chair with a little grunt and looked with a sort of evil benevolence at the other two.

There was a knock at the door.

"Come in!" said Tony.

Moshe entered.

"You require more drink, Mr. Horne?"

"Yes, Moshe. Bring another couple of bottles."

Moshe withdrew.

"You're somebody around here, Tony," remarked Dick.

Tony grimaced confidentially:

"Dough talks anywhere!"

He waggled a forefinger:

"Remember that, Dick. Money talks anywhere."

"I will. Slim's in my section, Tony. Did you know?"

"Slim's in your section, is he? Listen, kid, I've known Slim——how long I known you, Slim?"

"About fifteen years, Tony."

"That's about right. Many's the time he's come to Tony Horne for a bit of help. Haven't you, Slim?"

"That's true, Tony."

"You know bloody well it's true. Any time you want help, come to Tony. If he likes you he'll help you, eh, Slim?"

"That's right, Tony."

"You know bloody well it's right."

"How did you get leave?" Dick asked Sullivan.

"I didn't. I'm A.W.L. I arranged with Chips to report me as present. I'm getting a lift back at midnight."

"Yes," proceeded Tony, who appeared not to have heard any of this, "Slim and I are old mates. Back in the depression years, eh, Slim? When you were organiser for the Unemployed Workers. Eh, Slim?"

"That's right, Tony. We always knew where to come if we needed a fiver in a hurry."

"Bloody oath you did! And who tipped you off the day the New Guard tried to bash you up? Eh?"

Instead of answering him this time Sullivan gave him a friendly but knowing smile.

"You ask him," Tony told Dick dolefully.

"And who," asked Sullivan gently, "made a pile of dough by running swy games among the relief workers?"

"We've been through that before," said Tony with more animation. "Some blokes would rather gamble their last tray than buy a pie with it. So Tony runs the swy. You know what I've always said, Slim." He turned to Dick, "Any man that works for the capitalists is a mug. Always been a great supporter of the Cause, haven't I, Slim?"

"That's right, Tony."

"Bloody oath it's right. Worked for the capitalists once. Fought for 'em."

Tony pinched the left breast of his tunic between thumb and finger displayed his three ribbons to Dick.

"Know how old I was when I was on Gallipoli? Eighteen. Only wear these ribbons on leave. Told 'em I was thirty-nine when I joined."

"And who are you fighting for now?" Dick asked with a wink at Sullivan.

Tony slapped his hand down hard on the table and roared:

"Tony! I'm working for Tony and no other bastard!" He leaned over, staring at Dick. "Know why I joined the army this time? Make dough. The digger's the world's best gambler. That's why I joined the army. . . . You know what you are, Dick? You're one of the mugs."

"Is a man who fights for his country a mug, Tony?"

"What made you think you were fighting for your country? Listen, do you know why we were sent over here at first? I'll tell you. To keep the Arabs and Jews quiet here and help the Turks attack Russia. It's just sheer luck we came to be fighting the Huns. That right, Slim?"

"Not just luck, Tony. The people wanted an anti-fascist war,

163

they kicked Chamberlain and Menzies out, and now they've got it."

"That's right," said Dick. "The phoney war ended the day Germany attacked Russia."

"But—why—did—you—join—up?" asked Tony, slowly and doggedly.

"Partly because I was restless, partly to fight for my country." Tony hit the table again.

"Hear that, Slim? Fight for your country! I was just like you in 1914, boy. Wanted to fight for my country. Girls admiring your uniform. Old fellers in pubs patting you on the back and calling you 'Digger.' You know what they sent us to Gallipoli for? Because Britain promised the Czar to get a hunk of Turkey for him. Know what they used to call the Turk in the other war? 'The unspeakable Turk' " Tony grimaced repulsively. "Now what is he?—'Our gallant ally!' G-rrr!"

Tony emptied his glass. He looked at Dick, closed an eye and raised a finger. He brought a wallet from the left-hand pocket of his tunic and began to search in it.

"Know what country the shells were made in that the Turk plastered us with at Gallipoli? I'll show you something from a newspaper."

"You don't still carry that cutting around with you!" exclaimed Sullivan.

"Bloody oath I do! I'll carry it around till the day I die."

Tony at last drew from his wallet a small, yellowed newspaper cutting with tattered edges.

"This is what a bloke said in the House of Commons. Read it."

He gave the cutting to Dick. Above it someone had written the date in ink: March 11th, 1926. It was only about half a dozen lines:

> *A British firm had been supplying the Turkish artillery with shells which were fired into the Australian, New Zealand and British troops as they were scrambling up Anzac Cove and Cape Helles. Did it matter to the directors of these armament firms, so long as they did business and expanded the defence expenditure of Turkey, that their weapons smashed up into a bloody pulp all the morning glory that was the flower of Anzac? ...*

Tony took his cutting back and restored it carefully to his wallet. He stared at Dick without speaking.

There was a knock at the door and Moshe came in with a bottle, left it on the table and went out again. Tony had not stopped looking at Dick.

"And when we came back," he said quietly, "we got the dole."

164

Suddenly he stood up, became almost formal. In spite of all the vodka he had drunk he was quite steady. His eyes looked out with something like the old vulturine stare.

"Dick," he said, and held out his hand; "it's been a pleasure to talk to you."

"You've done most of the talking, Tony."

"If you want anything, come and see me. I'm spending all my leave here. And now I'm going to bed. Good night, Dick. 'Night, Slim."

And without a stagger or a hiccough, Tony was gone.

"So that's the Vulture!" observed Dick.

"That's him," said Sullivan, grinning. "A one-man revolution with an eye mainly to the welfare of Tony Horne."

"And rather generous, Slim."

"Yes, a very generous bloke in some ways."

"He's quite a thinker too. I mean that cutting he showed me and the things he said."

"Tony's no fool. A strange mixture. When I was organiser for the unemployed I could touch Tony for funds regularly. One day he walked in on me, slapped down twenty quid and walked out again. We staged a demonstration, used some of that money to pay for signs and things, and when the police broke us up with batons, he laughed at us. Said we were mugs."

"Oh, so you're a mug too, to Tony?"

"Oh, yes, I'm a mug."

Sullivan parted the hair just above his ear to reveal a scar.

"That's a souvenir I got from the police."

Dick rose.

"I'm dog-tired. I think I'll call it a day."

"I'll come to the street with you," offered Sullivan, "I need some fresh air."

As they went along the passage Dick said to him:

"You know, things like that cutting Tony showed me—I wonder how many people saw that and thought about it, and wondered about a change."

"Change is always there," said Sullivan. "Change of some sort."

Suddenly they were out again in the café, where they were met by a wall of sound; the blare of the music, shuffling feet, drunken shouts, the shrill laughter of women. It was nightmarish, unbearable. Hurriedly, they made for the door.

Outside it was still drizzly and cold.

The strains of the music penetrated forlornly into the deserted street. It was like a dirge. The saxophone sobbed and wailed, but behind it the drum beat persistently, like a steady throbbing of anger.

When Dick reached the room Naomi was in bed asleep. He stood watching her for a while, smiling to himself. The scene of a short time ago seemed ridiculous and far away. He was not so sure now that he was in love with her.

Outside the walls of the old city, the city of New Jerusalem had sprung up in recent years. Their room was in a large stone apartment house in the New City.

The morning was sparkling and clear and from the window Dick found the Old City spread out beneath him. The eastern walls of buildings shone wetly to the sun, like drops in an old man's beard. In the shadows the walls brooded, dead-grey, embittered by time. Above the massed square shoulders of the city the Dome of the Rock rose, round and magnificent, molten white in the morning sun.

The sparkling beauty of the day filled his mind with a sense of promise and release. He turned eagerly, urging Naomi to get out of bed. In answer, she put out a plump brown arm and drew him to her. She kicked off the bedclothes and displayed herself lazily. She never seemed to tire of his admiration of her. He smiled back fondly but fleetingly, his mind possessed by the gleaming vision of the window, elatedly determined to enjoy fully the vague intoxication of such scenes. Smiling at his impatience, she rose and dressed and led him downstairs to the café for breakfast.

The only other occupant was Tony Horne. He answered Dick's greeting curtly. From Tony's expression, the session of the night before might never have been. Though red-lidded, his eyes had the same intent stare, his face the same bitter lines as the man who ran the two-up back at camp. There were the inevitable glass and bottle in front of him.

"That your breakfast, Tony?" Dick asked him.

Tony nodded.

"No steak and eggs?" Dick asked, searching for the note of the night before.

One of the harsh furrows near Tony's mouth flickered.

"Hair of the dog," he said.

Dick gave it up and applied his mind to breakfast.

Half an hour later, they had passed through the Jaffa gate and were traversing the narrow, odorous streets of old Jerusalem, pushing their way between gentle little donkeys and long-robbed Arabs, ignoring the wandering sherbet-sellers, the fruit, the pottery, the trinkets, the cake, the coffee vendors, whose voices called to them from the dark alcoves that lined the narrow ways.

Naomi took him first to the Church of the Holy Sepulchre. The ugly little place seemed to huddle, as if in fear of the walls that towered on either side. Inside was thick-smelling, coffee-coloured darkness, hung with islands of candles and misty brass. As to the guide who showed them through, it was Dick's cynical thought that the man's recitation must have been repugnant to a true believer. He told them a conglomeration of facts about the place in the slick, emotionless tones of a uniformed spruiker outside a cinema. They lit small candles and entered the sepulchre itself, and stood there in the yellow light while the guide told them of many things that the worn white stone might have been, but never what it actually was. To Dick the place seemed unwholesome. He escaped as soon as he could. At the door an effeminate young monk was soliciting money.

Next she showed him the Wailing Wall nearby. A solitary old bearded Jew stood bowed against it, now and again touching the stone with his forehead. His lips moved, but they could not hear what he said. When he turned away, his eyes saw past them. He came by Dick, bent, old, but full of an ageless dignity, like an embodiment of his race.

On their way back past the Church of the Holy Sepulchre, they encountered Dooley and Go Through. Suddenly shy, Naomi preferred to walk ahead a little, while Dick stayed and talked to them.

"I thought you were sticking to the café," he greeted them.

"We was, colt," Go Through explained, "but you can't come to Jerusalem without seeing the sights, can yer?"

"A man would look a gig," added Dooley, "writing home and telling 'em all he saw of Jerusalem was a drinking place!"

"Here come those two sky pilots again," muttered Go Through out of the corner of his mouth.

Approaching them were Padre Hobbs, the Second X's Protestant chaplain and Father Bourke, the Brigade Roman Catholic chaplain. All smiles, they bore down on the Second X men.

"They're trying to round up a party to go over to Bethlehem," Dooley warned Dick.

"It's Corporal Brett," boomed Father Bourke's rich, faintly Irish, voice. "No use asking him, I suppose."

"He's down as a Protestant," said Hobbs, "but he's more protest than anything else, I think."

He smiled thinly at his joke, a frail, mouse-like man with shrewd light eyes whose mouth was never without a cold, empty pipe.

"Well, he's fond of scenery, isn't he? He might come for that reason."

"No, thanks!" said Dick hastily.

"Oh!" Father Bourke continued. "So you know what we're up to doing, the Padre and I?"

He blew out his big red face, then spread it with a boisterous smile.

"Yes," Dick told them, not too amiably. "I have a lady with

167

me." Well aware of the Father's anti-semitism, he added with mild malice, "A Jewish lady."

The Father glanced up the street where Naomi waited, short-skirted and bare-legged as usual. His grim "Humph!" conveyed a sharp sense of his opinion about the sort of Jewess who would accompany an Australian soldier.

"Dooley!" Father Bourke grinned waggishly. "Whatever's to become of ye? You're a disgrace to your flock."

Dooley grinned back at him.

"I've told you before, Father, I'm a renegade. You won't get anywhere with me."

"And I wonder where you learnt such a big word," put in Hobbs, with a hint of petulance.

Dooley scowled at him.

"From my old man," he replied.

"Ah! There's a couple of C Company lads!" exclaimed Bourke suddenly, and he and Hobbs left them.

"That Hobbs give me the gripes," growled Go Through.

Dick farewelled them:

"Be good, boys!"

"And you be careful," Dooley told him, his eyes on Naomi. "Remember Chips!"

Dick turned away, fierce and offended. It would be quite useless to try and convince them that Naomi was not a prostitute.

"Where to now?" he asked as he rejoined her.

"Mount Scopus," she replied, and at the firm pressure of her fingers on his arm he turned to look at her.

Her eyes were glowing and possessive.

He looked away. Something formless seemed to be gnawing at his mind: a sense of being incomplete, of being hampered and held; a sudden vast restlessness.

"What's to see at Mount Scopus?" he asked.

A taxi brought them back to the café just on nightfall. He was glum, and cold. All the exhilaration of the morning was gone. They talked spasmodically. He ate his food indifferently, plagued by half-born thoughts. To make better company of himself, he drank a great deal.

They went up to their room early. He looked from the window over the darkened mass of the city and his thoughts became calmer, a little clearer:

I always want an answer to everything, my mind plagues me. What is it we seek? Certitude? Peace? What the hell am I after? What do these other fellows want out of life? Lucas thinks life's a mockery and mocks it back; you can never dig down to his feelings. He'd serve any and every cause well, because he's concerned about Lucas alone. No violent loves or hates. No loyalties. Lucas is wrong. . . . Think of how

168

*Andy has become. Andy had violent loves and violent hates,
not none of them seemed to be organised. He changed direction too often. Indecision. Not enough faith in himself.
Nothing done. A lost battle. Now it is Andy alone, Andy
bitter, Andy hateful, Andy selfish to the core, Andy the good
soldier.* Andy is wrong. . . . *What about Chips? Chips the
beautiful gay animal. Tender as a child, terrible as a panther.
Everything is thoughtless joy. Strong as a lion. Fights like a
threshing machine. Game as Ned Kelly. Fear's only a word
to him. A man among men. Impossible to copy. His life's
like a sea of rich velvet. But nothing deep. All instinct. Go
with the tide. Always the next wave.* Chips is wrong. . . .
*Henry Gilbertson is a fine fellow. Thinks deeply. Generous.
An idealist. Cultured. Courageous. Millionaire family.
Powerful section. The same social level as Fitzroy. But very
different. Power is Fitzroy's personal property. It blows up
his ego. He misuses it. Henry wants to use his power dif-
ferently. He's only one. His power was fed on injustice.
Henry is a freak. Fitzroy and Crane are typical. Henry will
crash.* Henry is wrong. . . . *What did Tony Horne say?*
"Money talks anywhere. A pat on the back when you go and
a kick in the arse when you come back. . . . You're one of the
mugs. . . ." *Tony. Honest most of the time. A bird of prey.
Even on those with whom his sympathies belong. A rebel
of a sort, but sneers at an honest rebel. Mugs. A cynic, Tony.*
Tony's wrong, too. . . . *Dooley. I like Dooley. Much nearer
home. A rebel. An adventurer. Worked at everything. In
the bush. In the factories. A boss-hater. Believes in the
Unions. Hates Fitzroy and Crane. A born rebel. Renegade
Catholic. He'll always take advantage of a mug. The typical
Australian? Tall, burnt, lanky, eagle-beaked. Dooley hates
authority. Sometimes he even resents me. What would you
call Dooley? Larrikin? Militant? Anarchist? Hard, generous,
comical. Good mate. Thousands of Dooleys. Unconquerable.
But hard to combine with sometimes. Dooley has a destructive streak. The oppressed need discipline as much as the
oppressors.* Dooley is wrong.

*I've never thought about these men so clearly before.
Change. Things happen, you react. Perhaps imperceptibly,
you are affected. More things happen. Then, suddenly, you're
different. It's been building up.*

Good-bye to the tragic young poet.

*Good-bye to the unhappy young soldier with the brazen
front and the mourning heart.*

Good-bye to the braggart.

New times. New men.

Everything's changing.

Including me.

169

14

EARLY in December, 1941, the brigadier sent for Colonel Fitz-roy and asked him to explain certain instances of mass indis-cipline in his battalion. The colonel put it down to the sudden entry of Japan and America into the war. After Pearl Harbour, he explained, men had begun to worry about things at home. They were wondering how far south the Japs would advance. There had been persistent rumours about large numbers of the Middle East force being sent back to Australia at once, and any talk of going home always seemed to make them restless. The colonel neglected to mention that he and many of his officers were partly responsible for any such restlessness, be-cause of their time-honoured habit of telling the troops they were being betrayed at home by incompetence and apathy. For the colonel and his cronies the war had become a monstrous and perturbing thing. The A.I.F. was no longer the *élite*, adventurous force they liked to imagine it. It was only a small part of a vast anti-fascist world front. Back in Australia the army was growing to an unheard-of size. The people had united. It was unpopular to vilify the war effort.

Enthusiastically, Henry Gilbertson was in the habit of point-ing such things out. This eventually goaded the colonel into calling Henry a Communist. To the colonel's astonishment Henry chuckled as if he had been complimented.

The brigadier accepted the colonel's explanation, adding a lecture on morale. His self-esteem writhing, the colonel re-turned to the Second X savage and vengeful and threw them into a week of unremitting drill and infantry training. At night the tents were loud with the muttering of tired and tormented men.

B Company, notoriously the most mutinous of the com-panies, had been in the forefront of the trouble. One morn-ing, instead of turning out on Crane's parade for physical training, they had quietly gone off to the ablution benches. To Crane, this was sheer mutiny. Hot with anger, he started off for Battalion H.Q. with the intention of having the whole com-pany placed under arrest. Then, forcibly calming himself, he thought the matter out and realised that such an occurrence was a reflection on his ability as a commander and he would be wiser to handle the thing himself. Accordingly, he sent for the C.S.M. and the platoon sergeants.

"They just said nothing and went off down the wash-houses, sir," he was told. "When we called them out on parade they ignored us."

"They hate this P.T., sir," Chips told him.

"Do they!" snapped Crane. "There'll be a night parade to-night. See how they like that."

The night parade was fixed for seven. When the time arrived, only the N.C.O.s remained in the company lines. The rest of the company had disappeared.

This was too much to keep secret now. Already the battalion buzzed with the news: B Company had "jacked-up!" Crane called the N.C.O.s together and shouted at them accusingly for half an hour. He called them useless, spineless, cowardly. They were quite unable to control their men. They listened to him in silence. When he had ended they still had nothing to say. He dismissed them. They left feeling wronged and bitter. Their sympathies were all with the company. They knew that the fault was Crane's. The men were fed up with his absurd zeal, his physical training, his contemptuous bullying tones. The whole company hated him.

No charge sheets were made out. The colonel had a long conference with Crane, and sent the company out to the desert near Beer Sheba for a week. They came back grim, dirty and subdued. For many nights thereafter the sole talk in the company lines was of their hatred of Crane.

The colonel discussed these occurrences with Major Pomfret, who gave certain advice. The colonel took it.

There followed happy results to the B Company jack-up. There was no more P.T. in the foggy dawn and, best of all, Henry Gilbertson was recalled from the training battalion to resume command of B Company. Crane took over Six Platoon once more, harsh and glowering at his reverse.

When the company had been ordered out to Beer Sheba many of Six Platoon had been in favour of a further refusal to budge. There had been argument, swaying back and forth; tempers had flared; some had been for a total jack-up. Finally, at the height of the dissension, Sullivan had intervened. Speaking rather diffidently as became a reo he told them that the two previous jack-ups would have stirred up enough attention to have their grievances considered.

"There'll have to be some sort of a punishment," he said. "Groggy can't ignore two jack-ups, whatever the reason, but he knows that men don't jack-up for nothing. He's certain to enquire into things. Now our C.S.M.'s all for us. We'll ask him to be sure to tell Mick Varney the complete story. Mad Mick'll tell Groggy. Let's do this field punishment and see what happens next."

Dick supported him, others followed and finally the whole platoon agreed on it. Dick was elected spokesman for the platoon and passed their decision to the other platoons.

When a cheerful Henry Gilbertson took over B Company

again, he decided to act as though the company had never blackened its record with two successive jack-ups.

"Good old Mum," they said.

Dick had been very proud of his leading role and his election as spokesman for the platoon.

Sullivan grinned.

"Limited action for limited gains," was his comment.

The night after Henry came back Dooley and Go Through returned from their illegal wanderings drunk, hilarious and defiant. They hesitated when they reached the battalion lines, debating whether they should report in immediately or wait until morning. It was well after lights out.

"Let's have a good night's sleep first," urged Go Through.

"Thash the idea," agreed Dooley. "But before we go bed— one important thing."

"Wass that, sport"

"Must say good night to the officers."

"Christ!" breathed Go Through. "Fancy me forgetting that."

"Good night to Mum," said Dooley, weaving and swaying between the guy-ropes of tents. "Mum's back they reckon."

"Must say good night to me old mate, Arch," Go Through assured himself, following intently behind Dooley.

It was very dark and they meandered back and forth a lot looking for the officers' lines. They found them eventually and stood swaying and leaning on each other at the end of the lines.

Their beery, raucous tones hit the still night air in between bursts of laughter.

"Good night, Mum! This is yer mate Dooley; good night, Mum!"

"Good night to yer, Arch! This is the old Go Through come back to yer. 'Ave yer missed me, Arch? Good night, you old bastard!"

"Can you hear me, Mr. Crane?" cried Dooley. "Is the Squire of Scobie there? Is Fuehrer Crane there? Good night and get fogged!"

Crane could hear him indeed. Half the battalion could. He emerged from his tent, found a sentry whom he sent for the guard, and went looking for Dooley and Go Through in the darkness.

"Are you awake, Groggy?" yelled Dooley. "I'm saying good night, yer whisky-bashing old coot!"

"And how about the Animal?" asked Go Through. "Are you awake, Animal? What are yer doing with the Boy Bastard? Naughty, naughty!"

Staggering round in the darkness as they laughed, Dooley

and Go Through lost each other. As Crane's wrathful figure loomed up in front of him, Dooley took it for Go Through's.

"Where'd you get to, yer old bastard?" he asked, and put out both arms.

As soon as Dooley's hands touched him Crane threw them off and stepped aside. His foot found only space and he went headlong into a slit trench.

"Guard!" he yelled. "Guard! You're under close arrest, Franks!"

Dooley peered into the slit trench and made out the enraged features of his platoon commander.

"You, you bastard!" he said, and staggered off, calling for Go Through.

*   *   *

Dooley and Go Through were both under close arrest in the guard tent. Besides being charged with A.W.L. and abusive language to officers, Dooley was charged by Crane with assault. Dooley heard the first two charges in bored silence but angrily challenged the assault, maintaining that Crane had stumbled and fallen into the slit trench.

"You were too drunk to know what you were doing," snapped Crane.

"I can only remand you to the C.O., Dooley," said Henry. "You'll get detention this time."

"I didn't hit Lieutenant Crane," said Dooley indignantly.

Henry ordered him to be marched out. He was inclined to believe Dooley innocent of any deliberate attack on Crane. He half resolved to ask Crane to withdraw the charge against Dooley, but a look at Crane changed his mind. Relations between Crane and himself had become a little strained. Crane would reject any such suggestion and enjoy doing so. It was not worth while asking him. Instead, Henry went to see the colonel and told him what an excellent soldier Dooley had been in Tobruk. Temple was there too, putting in a kind word for Go Through.

Dooley told the men guarding him and Go Through of Crane's charge, and the news was sent on to B Company.

"He's a goner," said Chips. "It's Crane's word against his, and Groggy's got to take Crane's."

In ones and twos they stole down to the guard tent to see Dooley, doubly afflicted with a hang-over and the injustice of Crane's charge.

"I never hit him," he swore stubbornly. "He stumbled and fell. Pity I didn't hit him."

The colonel gave Go Through twenty-eight days' detention and sent Dooley on to a District Court Martial. A week later Battalion Routine Orders informed them that Dooley had been

sentenced to ninety days in military prison. The word ran
through the battalion that, but for Crane, Dooley would have
received only the same sentence as Go Through. Even Crane
was struck by the hatred that he saw at times on the features
of his men.

15

GUARDED by two provosts, Dooley was taken to prison in a
utility truck with heavy wire doors at the back: the army
Black Maria. One provost sat next to him, the other opposite.
They were big men, especially chosen for such jobs. They both
carried revolvers. Their gaiters, belts and shoulder-straps were
pure white, the brass buckles polished till they shone like gold.

One of them lit a cigarette and offered Dooley one. Gruffly,
he refused.

"You'd better take it, mate," the provost advised. "It'll be
your last smoke for three months."

He held the packet in front of Dooley and, grumbling his
thanks, Dooley took a cigarette which the provost lit him.

The provost took a few puffs and began a conversation:

"It's a bad place we're taking you to, mate."

Dooley only half-heard him. He seemed able to concentrate
on one thought alone. Crane. Crane's evidence which had got
him this ninety days' sentence.

"You've got my sympathy," the provost went on, "although
you probably haven't earned it. Most men that end up in boob
deserve to be there."

Dooley was silent, staring out through the wire. He had forgotten that provosts were his natural enemies; he was indifferent
to what awaited him in prison. He was aware of one thing
alone. This was Crane's doing.

The other provost sitting opposite Dooley proceeded to give
advice:

"Don't go in with a chip on your shoulder, that's all. Just
forget your pride and make up your mind to do everything
they tell you. Some of the screws like you to crawl to them.
Well, crawl. Whatever they do to you, just take it. There's
nothing else you can do. In boob you've got no rights."

The provost at Dooley's side blew out a cloud of smoke.

"They're a bad mob, those screws," he said sympathetically,
"but they're necessary. They make military boob so bloody
terrible that no one ever wants to go back again. They've got
to, otherwise half the army would be getting itself in boob
to have a bludge or keep out of the line."

174

Crane was a liar, thought Dooley. It had been an officer's word against a private's, and they always took the officer's in such cases. It was the army law. When it came to one man's word against another's the one with the lower rank was the liar.

"You blokes hate provosts," went on the man at Dooley's side, "but wait till you get a taste of them screws. They sent a young fellow off his nut a few weeks ago."

Not even the benefit of the doubt, thought Dooley. "An undesirable," the major presiding had called him. Dooley recalled a recruiting poster back home: "Join the Fight for Freedom."

He laughed inside himself bitterly and savagely. His hatred rose to a climax, and behind his eyes he felt the blood throb murderously. Passionately he swore to himself that he would never pick up a rifle again or fire another shot. Let the Nazis win the war. They couldn't be any worse than Crane and Pomfret and Fitzroy.

Now he became fully aware of the provost talking to him. Dooley looked at the man contemptuously, and in a thick, harsh voice said:

"Save your words, copper. And get this straight: I never hit that officer."

The two provosts grinned, looked at each other and winked.

The gaol was three stories of stone inside twelve-foot walls. It looked as if it had once been a school or a hospital. The utility stopped outside a pair of massive iron gates, one of which swung open for them. Here the provosts handed Dooley over to two military gaolers along with a sheaf of papers. They took him up a flight of steps to a door marked: "Commandant," and knocked.

A thin, polite voice bade them come in.

When they entered, Dooley found himself facing a major sitting behind a desk. He was a plump, powerfully-made man with small, handsome features. He had straight black hair plastered down on his head like a skull-cap. On either side of his upper lip ran a thin line of moustache like a knife blade.

The major studied Dooley's papers at length. Finally, he leaned back and raising his eyes to Dooley, said:

"Striking an officer, eh?"

"I didn't strike him," said Dooley.

The major smiled.

"I'm disappointed," he remarked pleasantly. "I picked you as one who would say: 'Yes, and I'm glad I did it.'"

"I didn't strike——"

The major's hand came down on the desk with a crack.

"Prisoners can't speak unless given permission. Keep your mouth shut!"

Then he smiled again.

"Would you like to hit me?" he enquired. "I assure you, before you get out of here you will. We have special treatments for soldiers who strike their officers. Haven't we, Staff Sergeant?"

This was the first of several encounters with Major Portman, the gaol commandant.

From the major's office Dooley was escorted to another room where the two guards searched his pockets and took their contents. They did not find much: a handkerchief, part of a letter, some odd coins, and a wallet.

"Not much money, soldier," one of them said to Dooley. "You'll get these back when you come out." He grinned and showed big, dirty teeth. "If you're a good prisoner."

The other man was searching Dooley's wallet. He ran his eyes over a letter that was in it and then pulled out a photo.

"Who's this old harlot?" he asked.

"You dirty animal," said Dooley contemptuously. "That's my mother."

Immediately, the two of them sprang on him. He fought them fiendishly, all his pent-up hatred and resentment in the blows that he dealt them. But they soon overpowered him. A knee thumped into his stomach and the room swam in front of him. He fell to the floor retching. A boot struck his ribs and a pang of sickening agony shot through his body.

The man with the dirty teeth knelt on Dooley's chest and took a handful of his hair.

"The first thing a prisoner learns is never to answer back," he said in conversational tones. "He says: 'Permission to speak, sir?'—and if he gets permission he speaks. Now get up and stand to attention."

They hauled Dooley to his feet and he stood there swaying and panting. Gradually, his vision cleared and he got his breath back. Venomously he spat at them:

"Dirty foggin' screws!"

The man with the dirty teeth went over to a cupboard, opened it and took out two webbing belts. He looked at his friend and grinned.

"Down below?" he asked softly.

"Yair. Down below. Get going, soldier."

They thrust Dooley out into a passage and took him down two flights of stairs to a small, bare room. They locked the door. Dooley clenched his fists and stood facing them.

The man with the dirty teeth took off his hat and laid it in a corner. His thuggish features glowed with pleasure. His companion was pale and thin-mouthed, with a severe, clerical expression. He wore metal-rimmed glasses which he took off and cleaned.

"You a Jew?" he asked Dooley.

Dooley did not reply.

"I hate Jews," said the man with glasses. "They crucified Christ. I'd like you to be a Jew."

"Perhaps he's a Commo," suggested the man with dirty teeth.

"All Jews are Commos," his companion said gravely.

He replaced his glasses and swung a vicious blow with the belt at Dooley's left hand. The heavy metal of the buckle cut into Dooley's fingers like a knife. With a cry of pain he clasped his other hand over them, and at the same time the man with the dirty teeth swung his belt around Dooley's neck. His throat felt as if it had been seared with flame. Silently, mercilessly, the two guards proceeded to flail him with the belts. He put his head in his arms to protect it and ran about the room trying to dodge the swinging belts. The blows rained down on his arms and body; sharp, agonising blows that drew spurts of blood or left livid contusions.

They beat him like this for five minutes. Then he was taken out and put in a cell on his own. The cell contained nothing but a blanket. Later he was brought a slice of dry bread and a tin mug of water. He tried to swallow the water but found it almost impossible. His throat was swollen and blue. His fingers were cut, bruised and covered in dried blood. His body was one great throb of pain.

There were about a hundred and fifty prisoners in this particular gaol. Some of them were hardened wrong-doers, men with criminal pasts; others were like Dooley. There were deserters, men who had stolen army stores or been caught selling arms to the Arabs, men who had struck officers or N.C.O.s. They all had one thing in common: hatred of the men they called the screws.

Dooley was left in his solitary cell for three days. On the fourth morning he was escorted out into a spacious yard, and for the first time beheld the faces of his fellow prisoners. They belonged to men of various ages between twenty and fifty, and all bore in some way or other the stamp of the prison. Some of them were mean and vicious, with the look of the criminal; some were furtive and cringing; and others, like Dooley, tight-lipped, defiant.

Throughout the day this yard rang with the shouts of the screws. The prisoners were broken up into squads with a screw in charge of each. Wherever the prisoners were taken, whatever they did, it had to be at the run. To walk was an offence. Throughout the day, bodies of prisoners jogged up and down the yard. Sometimes they were loaded with packs that were filled with stones and drilled for hour upon hour.

It was also an offence for prisoners to talk to each other. If a prisoner wished to address a screw, he had first to say: "Permission to speak, sir?" Nevertheless, at odd moments men managed to drop a word or two out of the corners of their mouths.

The screws had methods all their own for the punishment of those caught talking or lapsing into a walk—a beating up such as Dooley had got, and three days' "solitary," or running up and down, up and down, with a laden pack, until the man dropped from exhaustion.

Each screw inflicted his own particular torments and indignities on the prisoners; each had his own way of satisfying his hunger for the sight of suffering. The screw with the glasses, who had helped beat Dooley up on his first day was known among the prisoners as the Shark, and it was in this man's squad that Dooley found himself. One of the Shark's favourite amusements was to make a prisoner dig a hole about a foot square and two feet deep, fill it with water and mix the soil in until it became a miniature quagmire. Then the prisoner, still in his boots, was made to stand in the hole and mark time to the strident "Left, right, left!" of the Shark. Most prisoners accepted these "punishments" silently as preferable to being beaten up and put into solitary.

There was a big young fellow in Dooley's squad called Moffatt, who had struck an officer. He had features that were still simple and likeable but stamped with a look of stubborn endurance. He had perfected the trick of speaking without opening his lips. There were the scars of a recent beating on his face. He had the admiration of all the prisoners because he had refused to get down on his knees to the Shark and had still been refusing after an hour's beating. The Shark was often taken by the whim to have somebody kneel to him. Daily, behind Moffatt's closed lips his voice would mumble a resolve:

"Some day I'm going to kill the Shark."

When the Shark turned his back, Moffatt's eyes would look at him, afire with hatred.

The first time the Shark told him to kneel, Dooley stood gazing at him for some seconds. As he fought the impulse to hit the cold, fanatical face his body twitched from the effort. Then he sneered, shrugged and kneeled.

What there was of the prisoners' food was coarse and nauseating: in the morning a blob of cold, lumpy oatmeal, a hard-boiled egg and a slice of dry bread, for the midday and evening meals generally a mess tin of greasy, grey stew. Never any tea. A screw supervised the serving of each meal. As each prisoner received his food he had to stand to attention in front of the screw, hold up his tin of food, and shout:

"One meal all correct, sir!"

Never a mug of tea. Never a cigarette. Sometimes a man would groan:

"Christ—if I only had a smoke!"

Little by little Dooley learnt about the screws, who they were and where they had come from. During the night, lying on the hard boards of a six-man cell, he thought deeply of the screws, exhausted as he was. He was stirred by a strange curiosity about them. Perhaps this curiosity was born the first time he reminded himself that these men were Australians and had been living in the same country as himself for many years—some of them in the same city of Melbourne. Although he shared the instinctive scorn of the ordinary Australian for a policeman and, because of it, the scorn of the soldier for provosts and screws, Dooley had never thought at all about the reason for their existence before, or how such men came to be. One thing he came to believe with all his heart and soul—that they were far worse than any of the men they guarded.

He learnt that the Shark had once been in the political police in Victoria. He was a "religious maniac" the other prisoners told Dooley. Several of the screws were former policemen or prison warders. The man with the dirty teeth had been dismissed from the Police Force for taking bribes. He had been a detective in the Vice Squad. Another had first entered the gaol as a prisoner, sentenced to ninety days for selling army stores to the Arabs, and when his sentence was completed had been drafted back to the gaol as a screw at his own request. Moffatt told Dooley that this man had a long civilian record as pickpocket, dope-peddler and police informer. Of Major Portman, Moffat only knew that he had once been a police detective and was a sadist.

Dooley learnt how Moffatt, because of his defiance, his verbal scorn of the screws, his bullock-like endurance, had been singled out daily for thrashing or degradation. He told Dooley how Major Portman had once sent for him.

"He was sitting there," said Moffatt, "all grinning and polite. 'Moffatt,' he says, 'prisoners aren't allowed any mail but I'm going to make an exception in your case.' He picks up a letter from the desk. It was from my wife. He opens it and starts to read it. I knew he had no right to open and read a man's mail—not even Blamey has; but I said nothing because I thought he might read it out to me. A man should have known better than to expect anything decent from that animal. He reads the letter through while I stand there—six pages. Then he looks at me again—still with that smarmy, polite grin on his face. 'Your wife is well, Moffatt. She's having the time of her life. Probably caught a load off someone by this time.' I did my block, just like he wanted me to. I went mad and tried to get at him." Moffatt grinned vengefully. "Christ, I called him some

179

names! Then he had me dragged away. Four jokers held me while the Shark bashed me."

There was the same ending to all Moffatt's narratives. Confidently, solemnly, he would say:

"One day I'm going to kill the Shark."

Sometimes the clear, young man's eyes of Moffatt seemed to enclose deep, unnatural fires.

In the mornings the figure of Major Portman was to be seen at one end of the yard watching the men as they were put through their daily ordeal. Always his face wore the merest supercilious dent of a smile. To the prisoners he was like the spirit of the place, with his thick brute's body, his white fop's face.

Dooley's bitter tale of Crane's wrong-doing left no impression on the others. How he came to be there did not seem very important to them beside the terrible fact of being there. But night after night, shivering under his blanket, he lay awake through the long, painful hours and fed his mind on his hatred of Crane, hugging it to him like some precious consolation.

It was a black, pervading thing that steeled his self-respect and gave his endurance a purpose.

16

THE character of an infantry battalion changes. Men are wounded and sent home, others are killed; officers, N.C.O.s come and go. Reinforcements arrive, sometimes in a trickle, at other times in streams. But some men seem to remain and bear charmed lives. Remain to be laughed about, to coin sayings that become the property of the battalion and, sooner or later, of soldiers in general. They are always there, to put into a rich, scornful phrase the feelings of rebellious men. They are the property of the battalion. Everyone knows them. Even the officers feel at times the strength of popular opinion about such men and are forced into leniency they don't desire to show. Two such men were Go Through and Tony Horne.

Go Through had been A.W.L. more times than he could recall. He had a cheerful and natural disregard for the dignity of officers and N.C.O.s that, somewhat miraculously, had never brought him the trouble that it had Dooley. When Go Through passed the colonel, he did not salute, but called:

"Good day, Colonel!"

He did the same with Major Pomfret, and the major had the wit to perceive that Go Through was incorrigible and did not crown his unpopularity by taking any action about it.

Tony, though only a private, was a power in the battalion for other reasons. Half the battalion owed him money. He was generous when the inclination took him, pitiless when he decided to be otherwise. For men less astute than himself he had a deep contempt. He trusted nobody. He addressed officers with thinly-veiled hostility. Tony expressed his scorn of authority loud and often, but he sneered at B Company's mass defiance as futile and told Dick they were all mugs.

Tony expressed himself in bitter words about Dooley's imprisonment. Daily he broadcast his hatred of Crane, deriding that famous name and all who bore it. Go Through invented a name for Crane that the whole battalion immediately took up: Framer Crane. At night in the battalion lines voices yelled it: "Framer Crane!"

A fund was started on Dooley's behalf, of which Sullivan was elected treasurer. Sullivan had been Dick's nomination. Even Tony Horne was stirred to enthusiasm by the idea. He opened the fund with a donation of twenty Palestine pounds. Men out of whom he had wrung small debts, shook their heads, smiled and said:

"There's no doubt about the old Vulture!"

Unrest ran through the battalion. It revealed itself when a man went A.W.L. or abused an officer. Rumours sped through the lines of other units that were on the point of being shipped back to Australia. Inventing rumours became an occupation. Some had elements of fact, others were utterly fantastic. At the bottom, however, they were all an expression of confusion and frustration. The war had long ceased to be an adventure. It had become grim and gigantic. First Hitler had attacked Russia, now Japan had set the Pacific afire and her armies were flooding southward. The camps had finally sorted themselves out. Now it was fascist against anti-fascist facing each other in a death struggle. In this peaceful spot among the orange groves and candle pines they felt remote and forgotten. Seven hundred men became daily more intolerant of the petty and vexatious routine of the camp. On battalion parade, in front of the strutting, bawling spectacle of Regimental Sergeant-Major Varney, they were more convinced than ever that they were watching something sub-normal and farcical. The colonel's speeches did not seem to belong among reasonable men. Their hatred of the unpopular officers grew wider and deeper. Vindictive tales ran through the lines about the colonel, Major Pomfret, Captain Stamp, Captain Barrett and Crane. Barriers of mistrust even grew up between the men and officers like Henry Gilbertson and Lieutenant Temple. For the first time in a long while, Henry had that despairing sense of a hardness in them that he could not penetrate.

At B Company, Baxter's cooking became worse than ever.

181

Spontaneously, B Company seemed to agree that the time had come for some sort of demonstration. At least half of the company favoured another jack-up.

Matters came to a head in a different fashion, however. It happened when B Company's turn came round as duty company. Six Platoon was duty Platoon. Crane was Battalion Orderly Officer and Chips Prentice Battalion Orderly Sergeant. That night Baxter served up more of his detested stew.

Chips came into the mess-tent, called the men to "sit fast," then Crane appeared and told them to "sit easy."

"Any complaints?" he asked.

With one voice the company answered:

"This bloody stew again!"

Crane treated this with an impatient grimace. The B Company food had been complained about so often, and Captain Barrett so often rejected all complaints as false, that Orderly Officers treated them as a chronic annoyance.

Crane gave no further recognition of their complaint, but after a perfunctory glance around the mess, turned to leave.

"What about this stew?" voices insisted.

The resentful muttering continued. A man with a tin full of stew in his hand, his eyes angry and resolute pushed his way up to Crane.

"What about this stew? It's not fit for a dog and we want something done about it."

Crane favoured the tin of stew with a long look.

"The M.O.," he replied, "has said repeatedly that the stew is quite wholesome."

"The M.O.," the man told him, "doesn't have to eat it."

He was a short, tubby fellow with round, earnest features, Peter Dimmock by name.

"You can't be hungry," Crane said. "If I were hungry, I'd eat it."

"I'll bet you a fiver," the man shouted, "that you wouldn't eat this tin of stew."

"I've no desire to take a fiver from you," replied Crane contemptuously.

"Money up or shut up!" said a voice.

"Silence!" roared Crane and was answered by another babel of protest.

"Bring the M.O. in," said Sullivan who had risen and approached Crane. "See if he can stomach it."

"The M.O. is not in camp," said Crane.

"Wouldn't be much good if he was," retorted Sullivan.

"Silence!" roared Crane again, with equal lack of response.

The mess was in an uproar. Under cover of the general noise, anonymous voices were now hurling abuse at Crane.

"I'd like to ram it down your throat, tin and all!"

"Framer!" sneered several voices.

"Get that little bastard, Baxter," someone yelled and several men slipped out of the mess.

The situation was now beyond Crane's control. With an "Excuse me, sir," Chips held up both hands and cheerfully roared:

"Hold it!"

There was immediate silence. It was Chips who had spoken and what Chips said had glamour and potency among them.

Chips lowered his hands and said, smiling:

"Mr. Crane doesn't cook the food, boys. As Orderly Officer he can only pass on your complaints."

With the eye that Crane couldn't see, Chips winked. He had seen the men slip out to get Baxter. "There's nothing to stop you having a friendly word with Corporal Baxter. He'll listen to reason!"

The anger went out of their faces. The whole mess grinned at Chips, who composed his features and turned deferentially to Crane. Crane drew himself to attention and said harshly:

"If there's any more disturbance in this mess I'll call out the guard."

Then he swung round and left, with Chips behind him. At the entrance to the mess-tent Chips turned and winked swiftly again at B Company and hurried after his officer.

A few seconds later half a dozen men thrust a struggling Baxter through the flaps of the back entrance. He was greeted with a mixture of jeers and growls.

"What do you mugs want?" he demanded, hands on hips in a truculent fashion. He was as deplorable a sight as ever: tangled hair, dirty face, filthy, glazed apron. His eyes flitted quickly round the circle of hostile faces.

Peter Dimmock now thrust the tin under Baxter's nose and said:

"Here. Eat this!"

"Go to hell," snarled Baxter.

"Why won't you eat it?" demanded Dimmock.

"I'm not hungry."

"Make him eat it!" shouted someone, and every voice took it up.

Dimmock thrust out the tin until it touched Baxter's nose.

"Eat it!"

"Eat it yourself!"

"Then have it this way!"

The next moment Dimmock had emptied the whole tin of stew over Baxter's head.

There was a deafening cry of approval from B Company. Baxter clawed stew from his hair and eyes, swearing filthily. He staggered from the tent pursued by howls of laughter.

183

Dimmock, normally a modest and unnoticed man, had become the hero of the moment.

At breakfast the next day, Baxter staged a jack-up of his own. He told the mess orderlies of the day that he would not cook for the company.

"O.K., Baxter!" they told him and cooked all three meals that day while Baxter sat sulking in his tent, drinking beer. They were the best meals the company had eaten for some time. At the evening mess the hat was passed round and yielded the mess orderlies about four pounds each. Such was their delight they promptly volunteered as mess orderlies for an indefinite period and undertook to cook the company's meals providing the hat was passed around once a week. They also promised to watch the ration store closely and keep Baxter away from it. Thoroughly frightened at this, Baxter, under cover of a stream of profanity, resumed his duties.

His stew took a decided turn for the better.

Andy Cain spent a lot of his spare time poring over infantry training manuals. A comparative newcomer to the sergeants' mess, he was nevertheless recognised already as an authority on a lot of things. His reputation was that of a lonely, single-minded man, someone whose whole heart belonged to soldiering and nothing else. Along with Chips and several other sergeants, he was tipped for a commission. Sergeant-Major Varney was a reliable indicator when it came to the granting of commissions. If his manner towards a sergeant or warrant-officer became distant and deferential it was invariably a sign that that man was due soon to go to the officers' training unit. To Varney officers were a mystically superior race. There was a possessive quality in the respect he gave them, in the perfect salutes he performed countless times a day. Officers were Varney's personal gods.

Chips was the battalion's idol, and ever since Tobruk men had been saying that Chips should be an officer. This was not so much their desire, for they were afraid that as an officer Chips would be compelled to curb his exuberant good nature, his endless capacity for jesting, and place himself at a distance from them. It was rather that the Second X had resolved a class-conscious attitude: it seemed a grim injustice that men like Crane and Stamp should come straight into the army with commissions while someone like Chips—a man worth six of either—had come in as a private and was still only a sergeant. When finally it became known that Chips was due to go to the next officers' training unit, the battalion was both gratified and regretful.

Within a few days of this news, Andy received a message to report to the colonel. He was quite confident that he was to be told the same thing as Chips. He made his way towards Battalion Headquarters, grimly satisfied. Something in his life had at last come to fruition, something he had stuck to and pursued to the end. He had justified his existence to himself.

At the Orderly Room he reported to Varney and Varney's manner, rigidly formal, was all the confirmation he needed. A minute later he was facing Colonel Fitzroy.

"At ease, Sergeant."

Sitting at his desk, the colonel addressed Andy politely. There was nothing in his manner to indicate that he might have been recalling the previous occasion on which Andy had stood before him, for walking off parade. The colonel's manner was that of the ideal C.O.—courteous, detached, authoritative.

He ran his eye over some papers on his desk, then looked up, and leaning back, spoke to Andy:

"You probably have some inkling why I have sent for you, Sergeant. This battalion is to provide five N.C.O.s to go to officers' training unit. Yours is one of the five names finally sorted out. Your record in Tobruk was outstanding, and since the unit has been back in Palestine you have been a highly efficient N.C.O. Captain Gilbertson has spoken very flatteringly of you. Men like you are the strength of an infantry battalion. We need you. Sometimes it is my duty to decide whether a man will do better as an officer or an N.C.O. Often I am obliged, reluctantly, to conclude that, good as an N.C.O. is, he just does not possess that little extra something that makes the officer."

Andy had a few moments of suspense and dismay. The colonel was looking at him enigmatically and gave no sign of continuing with what he had to say. The same old game, thought Andy with bitter resentment. The relish of his power. He stood quite still, keeping his passionate thoughts from his features.

The colonel now allowed his expression to show a slight perplexity. He compressed his lips and tapped a few times on his desk. Then he leant forward with a decisive motion, and resumed:

"Naturally, we examine a man's record thoroughly when he is being considered for a commission."

Here it comes!—thought Andy. He's going to knock me back, after all! He felt a flood of savage frustration.

"There's only one black mark against you. I refer, of course, to the occasion you broke ranks and left a C.O.'s parade, an action you failed to explain at the time——"

In an agony of anxiety Andy made to speak, but not soon enough to interrupt the colonel's flow of words.

"However," continued the colonel, suddenly becoming cheerful, "that's past history, and since I did not stop any of your pay there's no red mark in your pay-book."

(It's all right! He's not knocking me back. He just wanted his pound of flesh.)

"I think," announced the colonel, with an air that was now plainly generous, "you can safely assume you will be one of the fortunate five."

In this moment of vindication Andy almost liked the colonel. Grinning, the colonel added:

"I doubt, after this news, whether you will be committing any more unexplainable breaches of discipline, eh! to make me change my mind?"

Andy smiled pallidly. He felt weak after the recent suspense. "No, Sir."

The colonel underwent another change of manner; it was now relaxed, one of taking the other man into his confidence.

"Speaking of discipline—there has been a noticeable deterioration in the unit lately, even instances of wholesale defiance. Most of it seems to emanate from B Company. There are trouble-makers in this battalion, Cain. Most of my men are decent chaps who bear hardships cheerfully. But there's always the whisperer, the man who turns their petty grievances into unpleasant incidents. Sometimes he does it because he's come to hate the army and sometimes for his own damned amusement. Well, we've caught one or two such men. There are seven men from the Second X serving gaol sentences. It's often difficult to catch the trouble-maker, however. He's clever and underhand and keeps in the background. Out of some mistaken sense of loyalty his comrades won't betray him."

Andy was silent, although he knew that the colonel's theory of secret plotters was ridiculous. This was no time for contradiction. There were a few like Tony Horne who stirred up trouble and kept out of it themselves. What did the colonel expect him to do about it?

"What we need in this battalion," went on the colonel in his best manner, man-to-man, "is a little bit of detective work."

(Detective work! Is he going to ask me to suggest a spy?) Not till this moment had Andy quite realised the colonel's hopeless ignorance of what went on in his battalion. Detective work!

The colonel's manner became more man-to-man than ever.

"What impresses me most about the report I have on you is your refusal to put up with any nonsense from the men. You strike me as someone who would place loyalty to the battalion above loyalty to some malcontent who doesn't deserve it. Soon, I hope, you will be one of my officers. Even greater loyalty will be demanded of you. Being an officer, Cain, demands certain superior characteristics. We, the officers, are the leaders.

186

We win battles. Our success as officers is measured by what we can make the herd do. We are not here to be liked. We are here to be obeyed."

The interview was over. He was outside again, walking away from Headquarters immersed in the turmoil of his thoughts. The colonel's speech was fantastic: based on some vision of a battalion seething with intrigue. It was eloquent of the colonel's self-deluding ideas. Nevertheless, there were men bound to be in the thick of it in the event of any further trouble. The nearest approach to a plotter was Tony Horne. There was Go Through, busily spreading mountains of propaganda against Crane. There was Peter Dimmock, who had emptied a tin full of stew over Baxter's head and now inspected Baxter's cooking severely and passed on his verdict to the mess line at each meal. There was that reo, Sullivan, who appeared very handy with advice at certain times and was reputed to be a Communist. And there was Dick Brett. Dick, his one-time friend. Dick had been one of the leaders in the jack-up. Dick was very vocal over any grievances of his section. He had come out of himself and was very much "one of the boys" in Six Platoon. Dick's was the first name of those occurring to him that aroused any feeling in Andy. The others no longer meant anything to him; other men and their problems had become remote. Because of many things, Dick seemed a little less so.

Why, an inner voice asked him, did he have the feeling that he was cutting the very last link with his one-time mates? He recalled the expression on the colonel's face a few minutes ago, and could not escape the feeling that its unspoken message had been: "I'm making an officer of you and that means you're one of my men now. Once you showed your contempt of me before the whole battalion—now I hold your ambition in the palm of my hand. You've come to heel, Cain, and I'm being generous with you!" The old Andy Cain would have turned round, walked back to Battalion Headquarters and told Fitzroy to shove his commission.

He half turned, and another voice arrested him, mocking and bitter, reminding him mercilessly of a man who had gone to the war wallowing in the sense of his own failures: of a man who had lost the woman he loved. Only a short time ago, on his way to see the colonel, he had been grimly triumphant because he thought he had at last accomplished something, seen it through to the bitter end. Now, because it had become one step farther away, he was preparing to abandon it. This was his last chance to complete something, to be something, to succeed at something. Did it matter very much now what it was he succeeded at, or what he might destroy in order to do so, he who was now all alone?

Lieutenant Andrew Cain. . . .

17

It was only five days to Christmas. The land lay huddled and drab under a leaden sky. At a distance, the orange groves looked black. From morning till night the roads were wetly scummed. It rained heavily and long and in the Australian camps the black earth turned into a treacherous, clinging mess. The Australians went hunched in their greatcoats, with their wide hats pulled as low as they would come. For the first time in forty years, Jerusalem lay blanketed in snow.

The Second X were unresponsive to the approach of Christmas Day. They expected some parcels from the Comforts Fund, they learned gratefully that there was to be an issue of bottled beer; and with many of them at this time, their thoughts turned a little more often, a little more poignantly, towards their homeland. But that was all. Miserably they performed their duties, cursing the tedium of their comfortless camp. They invented "lurks"—ways of evading duties. A man told off for kitchen fatigue would swear he was already on picket and when told for picket would swear just as earnestly he was on kitchen fatigue.

B Company saw more changes in its ranks. Chips and Andy left for officers' training unit and Lucas was recalled from the training battalion in time to go with them. Dick became sergeant of Six Platoon.

He knew enough about himself now to realise that there had been a time when he would have been conceited at reaching the rank of sergeant. Now he had a calm pride but, more than this, he felt a little sorry. Being a sergeant meant he would no longer eat or share a tent with the men he had come to call his mates. There would be a lot of things he could no longer share with them; there would be things they would not confide in him. This mateship was the most precious thing in their lives, born out of fearing death together, scorning it together, laughing at and hating the same things. It was born of a thousand incidents, a thousand habits and jests that had grown among them. From now on it would not be quite the same. He would even give them orders that would rouse their resentment he used to share with them. Well, better for them to have an old mate as platoon sergeant. They liked him and respected him. He knew how to handle them and get them to do things. He would try and be like Chips whenever he was in doubt. You couldn't ask for a better model than Chips as a platoon sergeant.

When his promotion was officially posted he was required to report to Varney, who personally escorted him into the sergeants' mess. Varney rapped out observations on the way in rapid, clipped phrases, but just a little less formally, a little less dreadfully, to show Dick that he had risen in the sergeant major's social scale. Varney was a regular army man. Dick wondered whether Varney ever had any private thoughts, any life beyond his military duties. He was so much a type that Dick could not imagine him as ever being any different from what he was now. That Varney had grown from infancy to his present stage seemed preposterous.

"S.D. uniform for the evening mess," Varney was saying. "No gaiters. No webbing belt. If you do come off duty, for instance, with belt and enter mess, unbuckle; especially at the bar—otherwise you shout drinks all round. Army custom. Only fair to warn you."

Back in the past, thought Dick, Varney's mind had been displaced by a military textbook.

The sergeants' mess of the Second X was favoured with a wooden hut. Half a dozen messing tables had been placed end to end and covered in calico. There was a chair and a place set for each member of the mess. In a corner was a flimsy plywood bar.

"Drink with me, Sergeant."

Varney ordered two beers from the orderly attending to the bar and handed Dick a glass.

"Cheers!" he snapped.

It was the most human expression Dick had ever heard him utter.

Other sergeants drifted in gradually and Varney made a point of introducing Dick to any who came to the bar. Dick didn't know any of them well. He felt a little lost, and it was hard to accustom himself to the new terms on which he stood with Varney. Even this much intimacy with Varney was excruciating. He was relieved when B Company's sergeant major, Ted Olley, entered the mess and came over, smiling. He shook Dick's hand and said:

"Congratulations, Sergeant. Welcome to the mess. You have to buy me a drink, you know."

He was a wiry, weatherbeaten little man in his forties.

"I'll do that gladly, Sar Major," Dick told him.

"Call me Ted. We've just time for one. Mick's just given the cook the tip. Come and sit next to me. Don't sit down until Mick does, and don't even look at your food till he starts on his. Likes his little bit of palaver, does Mick."

He winked.

When the meal finally began, mess orderlies brought out soup on china plates. A hand set a plate in front of Dick and a mournful voice said:

" 'Ow are yer, Dick?"

It was Happy.

"Hallo, Happy!"

"Never thought you'd end up in the snake pit. Come down in the world, ain't yer?"

Dick did not know whether Happy was joking or in earnest. Happy's resentful features never altered. He made a joke in the same doleful tones as he said something unfriendly.

A sergeant down at the end of the table was annoyed at Happy's slowness:

"How about a little bit of service? The soup'll be cold before it gets to us. Hustle it up."

"Yer'll get it over yer head if you try and hustle me, sport," retorted Happy, and shambled off kitchenwards.

Tony Horne sat on a box in the entrance of his tent glowering at a cheerless vista of guy ropes, water-filled slit trenches and sticky, black mud. The lanky figure of Sullivan came trudging through the morass towards him. Three inches of mud on the soles of his boots made Sullivan look taller than ever and caused him to wobble dangerously as he walked. He wore fatigue clothes. The legs of his trousers were caked with mud and his face was clotted with dry, black splashes.

"Good day, Tony."

"The old Slim! Where've you been?"

"I got landed for a mucky job down at the Q.M.'s store."

"That'll teach you to keep out of sight."

"You never do any fatigues, I take it?"

Tony lit a cigarette. Sullivan sat down, reached for a nearby bayonet and commenced to prise mud from his boots.

"Never done a fatigue since the day I joined," said Tony laconically.

Sullivan grinned at him, took the cigarette packet from the stretcher and helped himself to a smoke.

"They no doubt use your exceptional ability in other directions."

"I'm a stretcher-bearer," Tony smirked. "I minister to the sick and suffering. Non-combatant, protected under the Geneva Convention."

"Pity help the sick and suffering," observed Sullivan.

"Dr. Horne—that's me."

"Bludgers I have met!"

"How's things at B Company?" asked Tony equably.

"Same old bastardry. I've come to see you about something."

Tony's eyes emerged from under his brows in a hard stare.

"How much this time?"

"It's something more important than dough."

"There's nothing more important than dough."

In reply Sullivan handed Tony a letter. "Your sister wrote to

190

me. Hasn't heard from you for months, she reckons. Thought you might like to read the news."

Tony, looking a little shamefaced, took the letter and gruffly said, "Thanks."

Sullivan grinned and drew on his cigarette. "Mum Gilbertson's coming across to play poker with the boys tonight. They thought you might like to be in it."

"I'll be in it. What sort of game does Mum play?"

"Terrible! It's like taking toffee off a kid."

"They tell me Peter Dimmock's shot through."

"Yair. Three days ago." Sullivan looked up at his old friend. "And you lent him the dough to shoot through."

Tony smirked. "Couldn't let him go through on just a couple of quid, could I?"

"I bet," said Sullivan, "you put the idea into his head, too."

Tony's answer was a large grin, and Sullivan answered him with another.

"Heard about Crane's tent?" he asked.

Tony's innocent stare was purposely overdone. "What about Crane's tent?"

"Someone cut the guy ropes the other night. Bit of a shambles."

"Serve the bastard right! Who did it?"

"I dunno, but I wouldn't mind betting you put 'em up to it, you bastard."

Tony sighed. "I get the blame for everything!"

"Some day," remarked Sullivan, "some poor bastard's going to cop it because of you egging them on."

"B Company doesn't need much egging on!"

"You're telling me! The whole battalion's fed-up, savage as meat axes. And why shouldn't they be? If Groggy doesn't take a pull at himself, they'll go into action next time like a rabble."

Tony looked at him keenly. "You're all for the war now Uncle Joe's in it, aren't you?"

"Now don't come that stuff," growled Sullivan. "It's a different war now and you know it. Only a few days ago you were telling Dick Brett yourself how bloody near he came to be fighting for Hitler."

"Did I?"

"Yair. I suppose you were too bloody drunk to remember."

"Slim the war-winner!"

Sullivan scraped some more mud from his boots.

"We've got to win it, and you know that as well as I do," he replied calmly.

"Do I?"

He spoke softly, but all the hate, bitterness and corroding cynicism of Tony's career was in those two words.

"Yes," said Sullivan, looking up at him.

A few minutes later, Go Through stood outside Tony's tent, watching Sullivan's retreating figure.

"What's the old Sullivan organisin' now?"

"Come down to give me a lecture on the war effort," said Tony ironically.

"Fancies himself, the bloody Commo."

Tony answered him dryly.

"Don't make any mistake about him. He can buy and sell you and me . . . Fog him!" he added.

*   *   *

Beer for Christmas!

It had become a catch-cry throughout the battalion. It was a phrase of consolation as they eked out day after cold, dreary day; an assurance that gave some faint purpose to the nagging routine of the battalion. Almost desperate at times from the procession of duties and fatigues they sat in tents, watching primuses boil tea and told themselves:

"Beer for Christmas!"

It was common knowledge in every camp from Niuserrat to Qastina that on Christmas day every man was to get at least four bottles of beer. It seemed all that they had to look forward to.

Beer was something that exercised Baxter's mind constantly. When it came to beer, Baxter had his ear well to the ground.

The day before Christmas eve Baxter approached Peter Dimmock in the mess-line and drew him aside.

"Do you know there's a whole load of Australian beer come in?" he asked softly.

"What of it? Everyone knows it," replied Peter curtly.

"Do you know where most of it's going?"

"Where?"

"The officers' and the sergeants' messes."

"What are you trying to sell?" demanded Peter discouragingly.

"Nothing. I'm just giving you the tip—that's all."

"I suppose," remarked Peter cynically, "you're worried about us?"

"I don't want to be done out of my beer any more than you!" said Baxter indignantly.

"No!" Peter told him mercilessly. "You're more used to doing than being done."

"All right!" said Baxter. "Fog you! Sorry I told you. Should have kept it to myself."

"Too late now . . . Hey, you blokes!" Peter called over his shoulder. "Baxter reckons the officers and snakes are pinching our beer."

"Let 'em try!" said someone fiercely.

The news went back along the line, and murmurs, growls and oaths followed it along. Bob Hamilton, a cane-cutter from Queensland, a great, burnt, bull-voiced lump of a man, stepped out of the line, hitched his trousers and told the company with his eyes flashing:

"Let 'em touch our beer and there'll be a blue in this fogging camp that'll go down in history. Just let the bastards try—that's all!"

They shouted their agreement.

"What do you reckon, Slim?"

"Wait and see," said Sullivan. "You couldn't take Baxter's word."

Peter Dimmock took a handful of Baxter's shirt and snarled close to the cook's face:

"If you're just having us on I won't just throw a bit of stew over you, I'll stick you head first into it this time."

*   *   *

On Christmas eve the sun came out.

About midday the colonel stopped Sergeant-Major Varney on the verandah of Battalion Headquarters and remarked:

"Seems to be an unusual amount of noise in the lines today, Sar Major."

"Yes, sir. Christmas spirit, I expect, sir."

The colonel shrugged.

"I don't know what on. By the way, we're having some nursing sisters in the officers' mess as guests tomorrow. I want the lines clean and tidy."

"Yes, sir. Get some men on the job right away, sir!"

The R.S.M. performed an impressive salute and strode along to the Orderly Sergeant, one Bancroft, who was sunning himself on a form outside the Orderly Room.

"Orderly Sarnt! Round up some men for an emu parade and parties to tidy up slit trenches and fix guy ropes."

Varney swept past into the Orderly Room.

"Christ!" observed Bancroft. "Couldn't you find me a nice easy job like delousing a mine?"

He trudged off towards B Company lines. Here he met Dick. "Hey, Dick! Mick wants an emu parade and some jokers to level off the slit trenches and tighten guy ropes. Get some of your blokes together, will you?"

"You try getting them," Dick told him.

"What's biting you?" smiled Bancroft.

"Have you seen Battalion Routine Orders?"

"Haven't read 'em."

"Well, you should. There's three bottles of beer to every two men!"

"So that's what all the shouting was about?"

"Yes! And there'll be more than shouting soon. Take it from me!"

*   *   *

The moment Dick had seen their faces on parade that morning he knew something had happened. Crane had left him in charge of Six Platoon for half an hour's drill. As Dick faced them, he ran his eye along the ranks and saw that each man wore the same look: sullen and implacable. There was a barely discernible muttering among them. In the very movements of their bodies there was something hostile and defiant. He had been among them too long not to know the signs.

He marched them some distance away from the company lines to the fringe of an orange grove, then halted them and stood them easy.

"What's the matter with you fellers?" he asked.

"Kid you don't know!"

"No, I don't know. That's why I'm asking."

They did not reply. He looked from one to the other, seeking enlightenment. Their silence convinced him that there was indeed a gap between their minds and his own. He had a feeling of sharp regret. But their mood stirred a faint hostility in himself.

"Is no one going to tell me?" he snapped.

"You tell him, Slim," someone muttered. "I think he's fair dinkum."

"It's like this," explained Sullivan, "our beer's been pinched by the sergeants and officers."

"How do you know that?"

"By Routine Orders this morning. There's only three bottles to every two men. That's the beer ration for Christmas Day."

"Well, it's a lousy ration. But how do you know it's less than you should have?"

"Arch Temple told Go Through that there was to be a ration of four bottles for every man in Palestine. It was an Army Order. The Second Z and the Second Y are getting four bottles a man. Everyone is except us."

"If that's so," said Dick hotly, "I'll bring whatever I get and share it with you."

"That wouldn't go far among a platoon of us, Dick," replied Sullivan. "Besides, the sergeants wouldn't get such a lot, either. It's the officers that are copping it."

"There's gonna be a blue over this," said Bob Hamilton. "A bloody big blue."

There were growls of agreement.

"I'll get paraded about it for you," offered Dick.

"Don't make me laugh!" shouted Hamilton. "Parading never

194

did any good. The beer'll be drunk before you ever get to Groggy."

"Jack-up!"

"Yair, jack-up!"

"No beer, no duties!" Peter Dimmock told them. "No guards, no pickets, no mess orderlies, no fatigues, no runners—nothing!"

For a moment Dick felt his mind waver between concern for his rank and his instinct for being one of them. Then he was filled with sympathy, with exhilaration.

"Then I'm in it with you!"

"Good on you!"

He felt a glow shoot through him.

"Hang fire till lunch," he told them. "I'll see how much beer we've got in the sergeants' mess."

"Good on you!" they told him again.

In the sergeants' mess Dick approached Ted Olley:

"A decent stack of beer we have in, Ted."

Olley winked and agreed.

"Do you know that some of it rightfully belongs to the men?"

"No, I wouldn't know about that," replied Olley blandly.

"Well, someone better know about it! This seems to be the only unit where the men aren't getting four bottles apiece, and there's going to be trouble. They're talking of jacking-up."

"Let 'em!" said Olley shrugging. "No one except the cooks will do any duties on Christmas Day anyway, so who'll notice the difference?"

"There is the slight matter of their beer being filched!"

"Don't blame me—blame the colonel! He issues Routine Orders—not me."

"Any beer I drink in this mess on Christmas Day will stick in my throat," Dick told him.

"Why should it? It isn't your fault they're only getting a bottle and a half each."

"Put yourself in their place."

"Why? It's each man for himself in this bloody world."

"Look, Ted, I've only been a sergeant for a few days. These blokes are my mates."

"When it comes to beer, I've got no mates."

Angry and frustrated, Dick was silent for a few seconds.

"Anyhow, I'm going to have a word with Mum about it," he said.

"Do that if you like."

Ted Olley's composure made Dick feel vengeful and destructive.

"I ought to wait till the mess is all seated and tell them just what I've told you. It might shame a few of them."

"You'd get no change out of these blokes," Olley told him

cheerfully. "They're hard men. And you'd have Mick down on you like a ton of bricks."

"This is a lousy battalion!" Dick burst out violently.

"No worse than any other unit."

"An N.C.O.'s first thought is for his men," Dick quoted sardonically.

"An N.C.O.'s first thought is for himself if he wants to get on. You want to remember that, Dick. These blokes of yours won't think any the more of you for worrying about them. A commission's what you should be thinking of. A young bloke like you, good record, university education, good background, plenty of brains. You're luckier than me. I've got no education —I'll never be anything but a warrant-officer and to be that I've had to crawl—yes, crawl!—sink my pride, keep my tongue between my teeth." Olley tapped his chest and smiled knowingly. "The old Number One! I get on with the men but it's always old Ted, number one!"

It seemed futile to talk about it any more. The argument went out of Dick. If Chips were only here, he thought. What would Chips have done? He didn't have Chips's personality or Chips's power to shed laughter or glamour on his words. If only Chips—but no. What they wanted was not only someone who would help them regain a few bottles of beer, for this matter of beer was only a climax. It needed someone who could express the resentment, the exasperation, the steadily mounting bitterness of the past few weeks.

Dick sought out Henry Gilbertson in the B Company Orderly Room that same afternoon and told him some of what he had learnt from Six Platoon about the Christmas beer. He kept from Henry their threat of another jack-up, for it seemed that a sense of duty might compel Henry to take some action if he were warned of it. Henry himself had become a little less understandable to the men, a little indifferent to their everyday grievances. The course of the war itself had impressed these changes on Henry's temperament. Hitler's attack on the Soviet Union, the Japanese attack on Pearl Harbour, had turned the war into the great world crusade that he had dreamed of. Beyond this he saw little.

"I'll have a word to the C.O.," he promised. "You've left it a bit late."

"It didn't come out on Routine Orders till this morning, sir. The men believe that was deliberate, too."

"Very well. I'll see what I can do."

Beer! thought Henry. The Eighth Army had advanced to Benghazi; the Russians were fighting like tigers, men, women and children; the Japs were sweeping through the Pacific; and here his men were grumbling about beer!

He ached to communicate his sense of urgency, his vast scorn of the backwaters of the war. His thoughts were far away, hundreds of miles along the north coast of Africa. He imagined the cold nights of the desert, the exhausted forms huddled in greatcoats among the camel thorn; the silhouettes of tanks against the dawn as they rolled up to cover the infantry; the infantry itself, long bayonets upward at the port, stalking over the stony ridges behind the black wave of the barrage; the drone of bombers on their way to blast Tripoli. . . . The pitiless blazing days, the utter chill of the nights, the sand in everything, the daily mouthful of water, bully-beef, biscuits, the graves scattered along the path of the advance . . . the iron endurance and discipline of comrades in a cause . . . names that belonged to the distant deserts floated through his mind in stern grandeur: Siwa, Sidi Rezegh, Jarabub, Benghazi, Ajedabia, El Agheila . . .

Nevertheless, he did mention the matter to the colonel in the mess that night. He made the mistake of doing so in front of Barrett, Stamp and Pomfret.

The colonel bridled and tightened his lips.

"Dissatisfied, are they, Henry? After the trouble they've given since they got back here they're lucky I'm allowing them any beer at all!"

"This is our first Christmas away from home," Henry pointed out.

"It won't be our last," observed Pomfret.

"After all, sir!" said Henry restlessly. "A bottle and a half per man!"

The colonel smiled good-naturedly. Nothing could have destroyed his self-possession tonight. He was looking forward keenly to the next day and the visit of the nurses.

"Are you questioning my discretion, Henry?" he asked coldly.

"Oh no, sir!"

Barrett, who was at the bar ordering, called:

"What are you drinking, Henry?"

"Whisky, thank you."

Henry decided it was no use pursuing the matter.

Gloomily he drank the whisky Barrett gave him.

"Do you think we have any chance of getting sent back to the desert in the New Year?" he asked the colonel.

"I got a hint today," the colonel told the mess at large. "You can get used to the idea now of doing garrison duty in Syria in the New Year."

"Syria! Garrison duty!" muttered Henry. "Oh, suffering Christ!"

He downed his whisky with savage impatience.

*   *   *

The swy school that night quickly turned into a general gathering of the battalion's rank and file. Soon after the game began Tony Horne asked them what they were doing about their beer, his grey face alive with malice. Scornfully, he told them:

"You've been sitting round screaming about it all day, but what about doing something? They'd never have got away with this in the old A.I.F."

"Yair—what would you have done?"

"I'll tell you what we'd have done," Tony said harshly, turning on the questioner. "We'd have burnt the bloody officers' mess down!"

"Don't be sure that won't happen," a voice told him.

"Now you're talking!" exclaimed Tony.

"Pig's to that!" another voice cried. "A jack-up—that's the shot."

There was a loud murmur of agreement.

"A jack-up by the whole battalion," Go Through urged.

Happy's disconsolate tones now broke in upon the argument. "Yair, it sounds all right. But they won't stick. There's always some coot who'll scab on his mates."

"There were no scabs when B Company jacked-up," Hamilton told him.

"Well, you want to get it organised. Get all the blokes down here. Take a vote. See who'll stick and who won't."

"They'll all stick, don't you worry about that, sport!"

The crowd was swelling. Men sped off to their companies and summoned their mates. Go Through raised his voice every few minutes to cry:

"Jack-up till we get our beer!"

Tony Horne and Happy were each the centre of a hotly-arguing bunch of men. The voices grew to a steady roar and men lying in their tents heard it, rose, and came hurrying down to the clearing in the olive grove. Within ten minutes half the battalion was gathered there. They stood in small knots, while others amused themselves by going from group to group, spreading rumours or heckling those who were trying to put their points of view. It didn't last long, for dark was falling swiftly and men began to drift away in ones and twos, still arguing. When Sullivan came on the scene there were only about fifty of them left. Tony Horne had most of their attention:

"What good would that do?" his hard, bitter voice was saying. "Make a job of it—pay 'em out for everything in one go. Burn their bloody mess down!"

Sullivan stepped into the centre of the group. He faced Tony.

"Then you'd have a company of provosts down on you," he said calmly.

"We'd know how to fix the provosts," Tony snarled.

"We want beer," replied Sullivan. "Not a pitched battle."

"Who's this joker?" a voice asked.

"Reo from B Company," was the answer. "Bit of a Commo, they reckon."

Sullivan looked round at their faces growing dim in the dusk.

"The best thing to do now is sleep on it," he told them. "Get a meeting of the whole battalion down here in the morning——"

"Yair," said a man turning away. "What's the use of arguing here in the dark. Organise something in the morning."

"Tell your company," Sullivan called after him.

"What time?"

"Ten o'clock."

"Right-oh!"

"In the last war——" Tony began.

"The last war's over, Tony," said Sullivan. "This war's a different war."

"Well, the officers are no different. I can tell you that!"

Suddenly the flare of jollity came into Sullivan's eyes.

"You're always telling somebody something," he jeered. "How about that game of poker?"

"Ah, come on!" growled Tony.

*   *   *

At ten the next morning there were about one hundred and fifty men in the olive grove. Sullivan had been among the first to arrive, watching the men as they drifted in, his senses alert to their mood, arguing calmly and reasonably with whoever spoke to him. Some of them stood about glumly, taking no part in the discussions; others gathered around Tony Horne and Go Through, once again the centre of a noisy circle. Sullivan moved through the listening crowd on the outskirts, the silent, irresolute men waiting for some sort of guidance. When a few of them made sounds of disgust and turned to go, Sullivan knew the time had come.

"Hey, Tony! Go Through! Listen, you fellers. Let's make this one big meeting, and decide on something."

He spoke loudly, compellingly and they all stopped to look at him.

"Say a few words, Slim," mocked Go Through, and there was a ripple of laughter.

"Very well," replied Sullivan, unperturbed, "even if only to give them a rest from you."

There was louder laughter this time and Go Through acknowledged Sullivan's counter thrust with a grin and a wave.

"We need a chairman," went on Sullivan. "I nominate Bob Hamilton."

"Second that!"

"'Ow about someone to take the minutes?" asked Happy, malevolently.

There was more laughter and voices yelled:

"Up on your soap-box, Bob! You're elected!"

"All right!" said Hamilton. "I'll be the mug."

He swaggered out and straddled one of the lower limbs of a tree. Though his manner was playfully extravagant, it seemed to overlay a rather self-conscious resolve to be serious about his new role.

"Now," he told them decisively, "let's hear what anyone's got to say."

Now that the gathering had been formalised they were strangely reticent. Some of them were disposed to laugh, as much at themselves as at this new situation.

"Well, come on," growled Hamilton, drawing confidence and authority from their sheepishness.

"What's wrong, Slim?" jibed Go Through. "Here's yer chance. Tell us what Lenin would have done."

Sullivan hesitated. He had not wanted to speak first. He had planned to await the best moment, in order to destroy the influence of the wild men among them; and this was better done at the end, when they couldn't come back at him. Go Through's jibe had nearly stung him into anger. But now other voices were joining Go Through's in urging him to speak. To retain any confidence they had in him, he saw he must.

"All right," he said, coming forward and turning round to face them. "This is how I suggest we look at it. We're so mad about having our beer pinched that we've forgotten about all the other things that have been put over us. What about our messes? A couple of tents with not even the floor levelled off and only holding half of the men anyway. We're not given time to fix our own messes and yet every day there are fatigues to look after the officers' lines and make fancy paths around their tents. What about our amenities? There's a battalion comforts fund but what have we got? One tent with a few sheets of writing paper and a couple of checker boards. Captain Barrett's in charge of the battalion comforts fund but we're never given any sort of a financial statement. Meanwhile, they've got pretty curtains up in the officers' mess and mats on their floor——"

"And all the grog in the world!" someone interjected.

"Over at the Second Y," Sullivan continued, "the canteen's open every night. Here, it's open once in a blue moon."

"He's bloody well right, you know," someone else commented.

"This matter of the beer is the last straw——"

There was a great roar of agreement. They applauded him, yelled his name, encouraged him to tell them more. He saw he had captured them.

"Jack-up!" voices cried.

"The jack-up is our trump card!" shouted Sullivan. "We play that last."

"What else do we do?" they wanted to know.

"Dick Brett put the case to Gilbertson yesterday. He's gone to see him this morning to find out if anything's been done."

"Nothing'll be done! The only way to get that beer back is to take it off them."

"Well, where is Dick Brett? What's he up to?"

"I told you," Sullivan replied patiently. "He's gone to see Gilbertson. You see we're doing everything the right way first. If we fail to get our beer by these methods—then is the time to jack-up. By only jacking-up as a last resort we make out a good case for ourselves. . . ."

"Meanwhile they're drinking our beer!" Tony threw at him.

"Yair—why wait! Jack-up right away! Wreck the bloody joint! I'm fed up!"

Restlessness, cleavages, arguments ran through them once more. There was danger that they would again break up into disputing groups. He raised his hand for silence.

"Keep them quiet, Bob. You're chairman."

Hamilton responded with a fearsome roar:

"Shut up! Give him a go!"

The noise subsided.

"Who are you telling to shut up?" provoked Go Through.

Hamilton turned to him ominously:

"You!" he growled.

Go Through grinned:

"Thought yer were!"

Hamilton turned authoritatively back to Sullivan:

"Right-oh, Slim. Say your piece."

Sullivan resumed:

"I don't hold out much hope of Dick Brett coming back with any good news. But at least we've gone about it in the right way, and anything that follows is Groggy's fault."

There was a ripple of approval at these words. Confidence returned completely to Sullivan. When he continued he was relaxed, confiding and taking it for granted they would follow his advice.

"The next step is to organise a deputation to the officers' mess."

"Why not the whole bloody battalion?"

"All right—the whole battalion to converge in an orderly way on the officers' mess and a spokesman from each company to ask the colonel to give us our rightful beer ration. If that fails, a general jack-up!'"

At his last words a great roar of approbation went up.

"Do you know what you're doing?" protested a corporal from C Company, Norton by name. "We might call it a jack-up but the army calls it mutiny."

"Who's that mug?" asked Go Through.

"Splinter Norton from C Company. Got legs on his belly."

"There yer are," Happy pointed out with glum relish. "They're scabbin' already."

"If there are any who don't want to be in this they'd better declare themselves now," said Sullivan. "Let those who are against jacking-up if we have to, come to the front."

"Did yer hear that?" demanded Happy. "Scabs and dingoes to the front."

Arguing hotly with several of his company Norton came forward to the sound of hissing and booing. He faced Sullivan indignantly.

"I'm against all your proposals," he told him. "The best thing we can do is to break off and go back to our tents. You bloody Commos are all the same. Any excuse to start a blue."

"Don't you think we're in the right?" demanded Sullivan.

"I don't care who's in the right. I'm not taking part in a mutiny. I'm awake to your kind, Sullivan."

More jeers and cat-calls greeted him.

"If we get our extra beer I bet you hop in for your chop," accused Go Through.

"I don't drink," rebuked Norton, and any case he might have had was drowned in a torrent of mirth.

Dick sought out Henry Gilbertson at B Company Head-quarters.

"I'm sorry, Dick," Henry told him. "I couldn't do anything for you. The colonel sees no reason why the beer ration should be increased."

"The men won't like this," Dick began carefully.

Henry grinned faintly: "I don't suppose they will. But they'll get over it."

"This is the only unit that isn't getting a minimum of four bottles, sir. Does that sound fair?"

This seemed to disturb Henry, but there was resistance in the tone of his reply:

"Are you sure of that?"

Henry moved his shoulders evasively. He frowned, much as if he were being mildly pestered.

"Pretty sure, sir."

"Look!" he finally emphasised, half in appeal: "Does it really matter?"

"It does to the other ranks, sir."

Henry shook his head in mild distraction.

"Can't you and some other responsible fellows point out to them how fortunate they are to be back here for Christmas Day, aside from any beer? There are thousands of men up the desert there dining on bully-beef and biscuits. They're fighting! Dying! And here we are grizzling about beer!"

For a moment he had Dick ashamed, but it was smothered by a new resentment, a hostility to Henry and his attitude.

"This unit had nine months in the desert, sir," he told him.

His tone should have warned Henry, but Henry's mind had never been deeply in this matter and it was full of the urge to evade it still.

"I know," he said shortly. "I was there too. I wish to God I was back up there. Anyhow," he finished brusquely, "there's the position. They'll just have to battle along on what they've got and feel thankful."

"Very well, sir!" Dick spoke quietly and tersely, drawing himself to attention preparatory to leaving. His anger took on a half-ridiculous formality. "I'll tell them what you said, sir."

He made a perfect salute and walked away. He wondered whether he had made Henry smart, or merely amused him. Probably neither. Henry just didn't seem to care.

Dick got down to the olive grove in time to hear Tony Horne promising to murder anyone who scabbed. He pushed his way through the crowd towards Sullivan.

Beer! Curse the bloody beer! Curse their thirsty, indignant throats!

He reached Sullivan, who read Henry's answer in Dick's face.

"What did Mum say, Dick?"

"Wait and I'll tell you."

"How'd it go, Sarge?" someone asked.

"No good," Dick told him tersely.

"No good?"

Dick shook his head. His mind was still dulled by his anger. As Sullivan looked at him he saw for a moment all the precariousness of youth and emotions too disturbing for the occasion. It flashed into his thoughts that it was just as well Dick was not alone in charge of this business, with men like Tony ready to provoke almost anything. Hurriedly he summed up for Dick all that had gone on in his absence.

"I'm in with you on anything you decide," said Dick. "Gilbertson's ratted on us, with all his fine talk."

"You're wrong," Sullivan told him.

"Well, what do you call it?" Dick asked him, surprised once more into a sense of betrayal.

"He just doesn't understand what it means to these blokes.

He's been away from the battalion most of the time. He just can't see beyond the war."

"All he could say to me was: 'What about the fellows up in the desert?'—as if we'd never done any fighting at all. It sounded bloody self-righteous to me—fanatical!"

"Pity there aren't a few more like him!"

Sullivan was pleasantly reproachful.

"Anyhow," Dick told him, "I'm in it with you—and I don't care if I do my stripes!"

A sympathetic, half-amused flicker came into Sullivan's eyes; his reply was gently sane:

"Doing your stripes won't help us much. They might come in handy, so don't go making any heroic gestures."

He turned to tell the news to the battalion, most of whom already knew—or guessed—it. Nevertheless, it was greeted with turbulent chattering.

*   *   *

Sullivan sat in his tent, resting. For the time being, there was nothing more to be done. The whole rank and file of the battalion, with only three exceptions, was to assemble around the officers' mess at one o'clock. Sullivan and a spokesman from each of the other four companies were to ask to see the colonel and demand their beer; failing this the jack-up. Not a single order to be obeyed. The fact that a jack-up was very probable did not leave him with any clear feeling of satisfaction. His sharpest feeling was one of regret that they might have to resort to it at such a time. He was not without comfort knowing that, at any rate, it would be a disciplined sort of a jack-up, only resorted to after all else had failed.

Dick approached him along the tent-line, calmer now, but confident.

"A couple of other sergeants are coming in with us," he told Sullivan. "Ted Olley wished us good luck."

This seemed to amuse Sullivan. His eyes lit up with the suddenness that belonged to his humour. His skin came very tightly over his high cheekbones. It looked almost transparent in the sun.

"A couple of car-loads of nurses just arrived at the officers' mess," Dick added, squatting beside him.

Sullivan nodded.

"Where are all the boys?" he asked.

"Most of them are still down in the olives," said Dick. "There's a big swy game going."

Peter Dimmock appeared in the entrance of a tent opposite.

"How are they!" he complained. "They've got a mob of bloody nurses down there helping them to drink our grog."

"We know," Sullivan told him.

"I hope there's a bloody jack-up!" exclaimed Peter and disappeared behind the flap of his tent.

They sat without speaking for a while, enjoying the brief warmth of the winter sun. From the direction of the olive grove came a faint roar.

"Wonder what caused that?" mused Dick.

"I dunno. They're pretty worked up," Sullivan replied. "There was a lot of skylarking going on when I left." He paused and considered. "I wonder if it mightn't be a good idea to go down there!" He drew his long form to its feet. "Come on! I think we'd better."

Making their way through the maze of empty tents, they heard more faint shouts in the distance. Half-way to the olive grove they encountered the figure of Bob Hamilton hurrying towards them, his ruddy face working with excitement.

"They've beaten the gun!" he told them in a voice harsh with urgency. "The whole bloody lot of them are trooping over to the officers' mess. I was coming looking for you. I reckon there might be trouble."

Angrily, perfunctorily, Sullivan said:

"A man should have stayed down there with them!"

It was not said in his usual tones and was meant for himself only. Unwittingly they had redirected their steps towards the officers' mess. A few yards to their left Peter Dimmock bounded between the tents leaping into the air at every few paces and whooping:

"It's on! It's on for young and old!"

The shouts were now louder and they were near enough to catch odd words and recognise the thud-thud of running boots. There was something infectious about the huge confusion of noises; Dick was restraining himself from breaking into a run. Sullivan walked cleanly and hurriedly, head thrust forward, eyes grim.

"It might mean nothing!" he muttered. "It might mean they're ready to riot."

Damn him! Why doesn't he run, thought Dick, and saw the same nervousness in Hamilton's look.

As they emerged from the tent lines their ears were met by a tempest of men's voices: a roar that seemed to rise in a wave and carry shouts on its crest. The sight that greeted them was even more electrifying.

The officers' mess was the usual rectangular affair of coffee-coloured timber and around it, at a respectful distance, were the large tents housing the transport office, the blanket store and the regimental aid post. The mess was surrounded by a sea of khaki and bobbing slouch hats. The battalion was massed in a gigantic half-circle at a distance of twenty yards from the mess. Men stood or squatted, talked hilariously in disorganised groups, or sent derisive shouts towards the mess. It was a frightening sight. Men were everywhere; they even straddled the tops of the tents in tightly-packed rows. With a sense of alarm and wonder Dick was looking at the same seven hundred men who could march and drill as a single massive whole at the words of one man. These were the same men—this seething, leaderless, tumultuous crowd. Its anger was physical and overwhelming; its very mirth was a menace.

They were now on the edge of the throng.

"What will we do?" he asked Sullivan.

"Find the spokesmen we elected," he told Dick and Hamilton. "Get them out front. I'll move among them."

Dick began to push his way through the tight-packed mass of men.

"Spokesmen out front!" he repeated as he went. "Spokesmen out front!"

They made way for him and relayed his message so that it ran ahead of him.

"Good luck to you, Sarge!" someone called. "We won't forget you stuck to us!"

He encountered an excited Sergeant Bancroft who told him:

"I've sent two of the spokesmen out front."

"Thanks. That's all of them then. Could you and Allison move around and steady them up a bit?" He halted. Allison was the third sergeant who had thrown in his lot with the men. "Where is Allison?"

"He dingoed at the last minute."

"Oh! Well, do your best to keep them quiet."

"Right!"

Bancroft disappeared into the crowd, speaking urgently to them as he moved. Dick reached the front, where Sullivan and the four spokesmen stood. The roar of the assembled battalion had softened into a pervasive murmur. The officers' mess showed no signs of life. The door at its end was closed, the yellow curtains were still drawn across the windows.

"None of the officers appeared?" Dick asked.

"They're not game to!" one of the spokesmen laughed.

"Groggy will keep them in there and send for Billy Carr," said Sullivan.

Carr was the Regimental Provost Sergeant.

"Carr's paralytic drunk," Dick told him.

"He'll send someone along. That's when the trouble might start."

"They're under control at the moment," Dick said.

"I think so. But it only needs some fool to do his block for them to get out of control."

Sullivan gazed anxiously over at the officers' mess. Perhaps he, like Dick, felt something uncanny about the lifeless building.

At that moment Varney appeared round the far end of the mess. He marched. His face was crimson, his eyes started, his mouth was a tight pucker of outrage. As he appeared he began to shout, but his voice was drowned in the derisive roar that greeted him. He halted ten yards away from them, his face becoming more deeply suffused every second, his mouth working vigorously but soundlessly. In a lull in the laughter, his throaty roar asserted itself:

"Break off! Go back to your lines! Because it's Christmas Day do yer think you can go mad? I'll crime any man who's still here in five minutes' time!"

He bent his arm and looked down fiercely at his wrist watch. The response was another storm of hoots and jeers.

"Go home, yer mug!"

"Piss off, Mick—while you're still in one piece!"

Varney began to roar at them again. His eyes seemed about to fly out of his head; his face was contorted by the greatest vocal effort of his career. His body quivered.

"Break off, I said! GO BACK TO YOUR LINES!"

Another mountainous wave of laughter.

A clod of black mud sailed over and broke on Varney's shoulder. Contemptuously, he brushed off the dirt. There was sudden quiet, as if they were curious about his reaction.

"Is the man who threw that game to declare himself?" he asked, with an oddly formal air.

It was the voice of Happy that answered him:

"Are yer game to throw one back, yer silly old coot?"

For the moment, silence appeared necessary to Varney for the sake of self-control. He put his hands behind his back and glared searchingly at the mob in front of him. His eye at last came to rest on Dick.

"Sergeant Brett!" he snapped. "Have you ordered your platoon to break off?"

Dick walked out and stood in front of him.

"No, Sar Major, I haven't."

"Why?"

"In the first place they wouldn't take any notice of me. In the second place I'm in sympathy with them. You see, Sar Major, the men have been cheated out of their Christmas beer."

"Cheated! Nonsense! The C.O. decides their beer ration! You've been led astray."

"This is the only unit as far as I can gather that isn't issuing at least four bottles to each man."

"You've no right to be here with them! Break off!"

"You can feel thankful that Bancroft and I are here! There might have been violence if we hadn't kept order."

"That is no excuse for your behaviour."

"I'm not trying to excuse it! I'm telling you the facts."

"The only fact I'm interested in is that the adjutant phoned for me to come and disperse this rabble."

"This rabble is a battalion of men whose patience is worn pretty thin."

"I have an order for you, Sergeant. Break off and take your platoon with you."

"If I obeyed that order there would be trouble!"

"Do you want me to place you under open arrest?"

"Oh, for God's sake stop yabbering like a book of regulations!" Dick was talking violently now. Behind him he could hear increased restiveness. "Don't you realise they're in the mood to smash this mess and take the beer?"

This seemed to disconcert Varney and Dick pounced on his advantage:

"If you want to prevent a riot, go and tell the adjutant what it's all about. Tell him the men mean to get their beer."

"Don't tell me what I should say to the adjutant, Sergeant!" Varney was his old ferocious self. "I fully intend to report to him. Maintain order here!"

The sergeant major turned on his heel and went to the door of the officers' mess and knocked. It opened a foot and he stepped in. The door closed behind him.

As Dick went back to confer with Sullivan and the other spokesmen a confusion of noise arose once again. From the rear of the throng they heard Tony's voice:

"I still reckon we ought to burn the foggin' place down!"

Several voices shouted:

"We want our beer!"

It was taken up, and within a few seconds the whole battalion was chanting in a great, steady roar:

"We want our beer! We want our beer!"

Suddenly the door of the mess opened and the adjutant stepped out. He closed the door behind him and faced them, his lips drawn tight, his boyish features flushed. For a moment there was silence; then, once more, a confusion of shouts and jeers. The adjutant held up both hands. Gradually, the noise subsided.

"What is the meaning of this?" he snapped.

Happy's dry tones were the first to answer him:

"It means we want our beer."

A succession of voices confirmed this and the adjutant waited for silence once again.

"You men have your beer ration. That is all you're getting. Now go away and drink it!"

The adjutant had raised his voice to a shout, which was unfortunate for him, for it took on an adolescent ring. Amid the furious roar that answered him voices were to be heard calling him the Boy Bastard. Bob Hamilton stepped forward and shouted scornfully:

"We don't want to talk to you! Tell the colonel we want to see him."

The adjutant's eyes were now lively with rage.

"The colonel is busy——"

"Yair—busy drinking our beer!"

"He has no intention of coming out to you!" screamed the desperate adjutant. "But for it being Christmas Day——"

"Go in and get the colonel!" a hundred voices told him.

"Bring him out or we'll come in and get him!"

Sullivan threw an anxious glance at the crowd behind and called to the adjutant:

"I'd advise you to ask the colonel to come out, sir. The men are determined to have this matter out with him."

Fright was now plain on the adjutant's face. The crowd had surged noticeably nearer to the mess. Sullivan had grasped the arm of Bob Hamilton, who seemed to be poised for an attack on the adjutant.

"We're not arguing with you!" Hamilton yelled. "Go in and bring Fitzroy out or we'll come in and get him."

"Easy, Bob," Sullivan was saying.

"Burn the bloody joint down!" urged a voice.

The adjutant caught sight of Dick's stripes.

"There are ladies in that mess!"

"Well, get 'em out," Hamilton told him. "You can't hide behind their skirts."

The adjutant caught sight of Dick's stripes.

"Sergeant——"

Dick cut him short contemptuously:

"We can't hold these men back much longer. Get the colonel out here, for God's sake, and send those nurses away in case something does happen." Bewilderment seemed to have gripped the adjutant. "Hurry up, man!" Dick was shouting now, their ranks forgotten; Stamp was not the adjutant to him any longer, but a disconcerted young fool faced with something he had never believed possible. "Get the colonel! Get those women out!"

Behind him, Dick could hear Sullivan appealing loudly, desperately for order.

The adjutant suddenly turned and went back into the mess. Men at the back of the crowd were angrily demanding information; like a tide, the crowd closed around the mess, those at the front being pushed forward slowly but surely. Tony and Go Through had once again taken up the cry:

"Burn the foggin' place down!"

Within a minute, the door of the mess opened again and a dozen grey-costumed army nurses emerged, escorted by the adjutant. He seemed to have regained his aplomb, for he called out sharply and arrogantly:

"Make way, there!"

The crowd opened up a passage for the nurses. They were led by a stout, hard-featured woman of middle age, who swept her eyes angrily over the crowd and uttered the one word:

"Rabble!"

"Groundsheets!" retorted a voice bitterly.

Bob Hamilton turned swiftly and ominously:

"I'll drop the next bloke who makes a remark like that."

"Sorry to spoil your Christmas Day, Sister," Sullivan called cheerfully to a younger woman. "But that's our beer they're guzzling in there."

The woman threw him an embarrassed but friendly half-smile.

"Good luck, boys!" she said and hurried on, head down.

With the departure of the nurses the battalion seemed to scent victory. Once more, with one tremendous voice, they took up a chant:

"We want Groggy! We want Groggy!"

But it was Major Pomfret who was the next to step out of the officers' mess. He stood and looked at them without speaking. If he felt anger or alarm at the sight he saw, his features did not show any trace of them. It was the same moody, dispassionate look that he wore when they were drawn up before him in disciplined ranks. But he was missing nothing. Even when voices called him Animal and told him to get the colonel before they came and got him themselves his scrutiny did not change.

"What's he trying to do?" growled Hamilton uneasily. "Stare us out?" He raised his tremendous voice:

"Don't stand there gawking, Pomfret! Get Groggy out here!"

"Let him stare," muttered Sullivan. "The longer the better. He's summing up the situation."

Sullivan had barely finished these words before Major Pomfret turned about and re-entered the mess. His disappearance was the signal for a fresh howl of fury. Great clods of dried mud sailed over to land on the roof of the mess, where they shattered and rattled into the guttering. Several of them burst against the door, which shook noisily. At the same time the chant began once more, louder and more insistent than ever:

"We want Groggy! We want Groggy!"

Half a minute later, Pomfret re-emerged from the mess. This time he held the door open. Suddenly there was silence. A tremor of expectancy went through the battalion. The colonel appeared in the open doorway.

In the few soundless seconds that followed, the colonel advanced out of the shadow of the mess and stood in the sunlight, facing them.

Any who had imagined a scared or a guilty figure were disappointed. As the colonel came to a halt he stumbled almost imperceptibly. He held himself erect, his head thrown well back. The glitter of his eyes was a little watery, as though he were well in his cups. Pomfret stood behind him and a little to one side. Jerking his shoulders, throwing his head a littler farther back, the colonel uttered one word in a harsh, energetic voice:

"Now!"

A chaotic murmur ran through the battalion. The colonel held up his hand for silence with a motion that was elaborately contemptuous. When he continued, he smiled thinly and without mirth, relaxing his stance and speaking perfunctorily:

"I have very little of the Christmas spirit left in me at the moment——" Somewhere at the back a voice laughed briefly and bitterly—"my Christmas dinner has been spoilt, my guests frightened away. Against advice I have come out here to ascertain for myself the reason for this disgraceful exhibition——"

Then there was pandemonium. The spell was broken. For a minute he had disconcerted them, but these were the words of the Fitzroy they all knew. Hundreds of throats poured out abuse. The colonel re-established his rigid stance and looked straight ahead of him; for an instant his eyes fled sideways towards Pomfret but he did not turn his head. He had become slightly pale. Fiercely he controlled the quavering in the depths of his inside. He was dimly convinced that if he took his eyes off this mass of bodies poised on the edge of violence, to face them again might need an effort beyond his fuddled mind.

"You know what we're here for! We want our beer!" they told him.

Dick, Sullivan and Bancroft were facing the crowd, their arms flung upward in an appeal for order. The noise beat about their ears for a matter of minutes before they were finally heeded. The fringe of the crowd heaved a little nearer the mess; its body was alive with angry gestures. The colonel took the picture in as he covered his anxiety; he felt almost affectionate towards the dark-headed young sergeant who was managing to restore order just in front of him. Finally there was comparative quiet. The colonel summoned all his dignity:

"I think I've shown today that I'm a patient man. But I'm not going to stand here forever and bandy words with a mob of howling dingoes. If you have anything to ask of me you'd better appoint someone to put your case. Those are the only circumstances under which I'll consider your grievances at all. Come on now! Make up your minds! Who's going to tell me all about it?"

Gently, Sullivan pushed Dick's back and whispered:

"Here's your big moment, Dick."

Dick came forward. He halted in front of the colonel and saluted. The colonel returned the salute precisely.

211

"You are?" he enquired, chin thrown high, so that he looked down at Dick.

"Sergeant Brett, B Company, sir. I came here with these men because——"

The colonel gestured briefly and brutally; he tautened his lips and spoke from a slit whitened by his teeth:

"I'm not concerned with your personal reasons for associating yourself with this rabble. Are you the spokesman?"

Dick felt his temper flare dangerously. He turned his back on the colonel and barked:

"Spokesmen! Quick march!" The five elected shuffled quickly into a line and came forward, "Spokesmen, halt!"

Dick turned to the colonel again, saluted without looking at him, and said:

"These are the spokesmen elected by each company, sir."

"Does it take five of them to moan to me about a beer ration?"

"There are grievances other than beer, sir. More important ones," Dick told him.

"Indeed! And why have I not heard of these grievances through normal channels?"

"You have, sir. Repeatedly."

Dick had almost lost any desire to conceal his contempt of the colonel. In that moment that they had stared at each other and Dick had almost lost his temper he gained a sudden vision of a guilty and shaken man behind the arrogant front.

"Do you think," the colonel smiled, "that I'm going to stand here all day and listen to a long list of complaints?"

It was Sullivan who replied.

"We would like to be paraded about the other complaints later, sir. At the moment, it's the beer the men are incensed about."

"Your name?"

"Private Sullivan, sir. B Company."

"Sullivan! Well, let's hear your story."

"It's quite simple, sir," proceeded Sullivan, "the men want their proper beer ration."

"I decided what is a proper ration!"

"Not entirely, sir, I suggest. We believe there was a minimum of four bottles to be generally issued."

The colonel lost his detachment. He became hostile and brusque.

"What evidence have you of this?"

"We seem to be the only unit," Sullivan told him calmly, "not getting at least four bottles. Over at the Second Y they're getting six."

"I see!"

The other spokesmen nodded in vigorous agreement. The

men at the front of the crowd who could hear what was being said, passed it on to those behind. A loud murmur of assent came from the massed battalion. Once again the colonel became disturbingly aware of their common anger; he seemed to read contempt in the expressions of these five spokesmen. To save his face he knew he had to do something swift and startling.

Suddenly he laughed. He stepped back from the line of spokesmen and addressed the battalion in a loud voice:

"I'm told they're getting six bottles per man at the Second Y. I'm amazed to hear it! Those of you who have been up before me know that I like to talk a thing out man to man." He was almost grinning now. "Today, it seems, I'm talking it out man to men. Today, you've put me on a charge." There were laughs at this. "Well, here's my answer to your charge: you've given me a lot of trouble lately—I didn't think you'd earned your beer. But——" He held up his hand in the midst of the jeering that greeted this and raised his voice still higher—"But your neighbours are getting six bottles. Very well!" Confidence surged in him again. He began to feel light-hearted. "The Second Y has never outdone my lads in anything yet." There was more noise, less angry now, and his relief drove him on to a climax in keeping with it. "Very well—the Second Y are getting six bottles—six bottles!" He paused, looked at them challengingly. "Go back to your messes. Sit down, enjoy your Christmas dinner. The Second X will have eight bottles!"

They cheered tumultuously. Their delight was as thunderous as their anger had been now they had won. He turned to Pomfret and smirked victoriously; he felt himself revel in his sudden popularity, in a new sense of mastery. Their shouts elated him. With a reckless grandiloquent gesture he cried:

"Back to your messes! Eight bottles per man! Merry Christmas!"

They called back to him hilariously. Then he turned and walked into the officers' mess. Happily he told Pomfret:

"I think we need a drink after that, John!"

Outside an excited and victorious battalion was dispersing, chattering as it went, jeering and laughing at the colonel, already tasting its beer.

Among the men of the Second X, their doings on that Christmas Day became known as "The Revolution of Hill 57." Wild and colourful tales spread through the camps. When a soldier heard about it he added his own fancies, and passed the elaborated version on. A man from another unit, on meeting someone from the Second X, would stop him and demand to know if it was true that the Second X had burnt its officers' mess down, made a prisoner of the colonel and dispersed a company of provosts with rifle-fire. It was very often quite useless to deny these tales, for many a digger loved to spread sensation, regardless of truth.

A few days after the "revolution," the battalion quickly rid the colonel of any illusions he may have had over his handling of the matter. After his stupefying generosity with the beer he was less hated by them than he had ever been before, but they were cynical about it, putting it down to a combination of fear and too much whisky or one of his acts. Their tolerance was the tolerance of the victor. Nevertheless they remembered it with much laughter. It was the spokesmen, suddenly reminding their company commanders about their other grievances, that ended the colonel's exuberance. Sullivan had called the spokesmen together for this very purpose. As he spoke they listened gravely and alertly, for Sullivan was no longer just a reo, "a bit of a Commo," but a personality. Now that their anger was gone and the antics of the wild men had passed into legend, they knew Sullivan and a few others as the men who had won the day for them. But Sullivan had a cheerful disregard for praise and an equally strong determination not to let Fitzroy escape his obligations. So when he proposed that all the causes of discontent had to be pursued they went away convinced, and plagued their company commanders about the colonel's promise to hear their case. And the colonel had to keep his promise.

Sullivan met little resistance from Henry.

"I know all about it," Henry told him brusquely. "I shall certainly see the colonel hears the rest of your case."

"I'm glad you mean to, sir," was all Sullivan said.

From Henry's manner he sensed that Henry wanted to talk at length. Silently he waited as Henry frowned and pondered on where to begin.

"When a battalion riots, something's wrong," said Henry.

He stopped.

"Yes, sir," said Sullivan.

Henry used his pipe as though he were trying to prod at the heart of the matter.

"I mean wrong at both ends. I think I know these chaps pretty well. I've got a lot of time for them, and I know they don't lay siege to the officers' mess for nothing."

"No, sir. They don't."

"Don't go thinking I've got any sympathy for what they did, either. As far as I'm concerned it was bloody hooliganism."

"I don't——" began Sullivan.

"I know what you're going to say," Henry rattled on. "It would have been a lot worse if there hadn't been a few level-headed blokes at the head of affairs."

"We did things the right way to begin with," Sullivan told him dispassionately.

"I know that."

214

"Dick Brett came to you."

"But he didn't tell me they were prepared to come and take their beer!"

"If he had," said Sullivan, "they might never have got any beer."

Suddenly Henry grinned. He restored his pipe to his teeth.

"That's a shrewd one! Well—I admit I've been a bit out of touch with them lately. I didn't know things went as deep as they did. I've got a lot of discontent myself—of a different kind."

"Not so different, sir."

"Of course it's different! They still don't realise fully the sort of war we're involved in."

"They're beginning to, sir."

"From you, I believe it. About our discontent—I suppose you mean we're all bored and fed-up alike."

"They're bored, and know less than you."

"Whose fault's that?"

"Partly yours."

Half angrily, Henry stared at him. Sullivan's expression was calm and grave.

"The officers in general." Henry stated it as a fact.

"Yes, sir."

"Do you think they want to go into action again?"

"No man wants that. But they'll be there when the whips are cracking."

"H'm. How's young Brett? He was very distant and military this morning. Thinks I've let the men down, I suppose."

"He did for a time. Just now he's wondering where he is, exactly, after all this."

"He's a trier, that lad. Very sound ideals."

"He's thinking of reverting to the ranks, sir."

"What nonsense!"

"That's what I said. He's got some confused idea that being a sergeant often places him in a hostile camp to the men."

"Well, I can at least sympathise with that. He seems to do most things on some principle or other. I've spent a lot of my own life searching for principles. Now I think I've found the ones I needed."

"I think so too, sir," Sullivan said. "They just need to come a little closer to the earth."

Henry answered him swiftly, without resentment:

"This ought to be close enough for you. I'm going to suggest to the colonel that for as long as we're in camp he holds a weekly conference with representatives from the companies, where they can air their complaints and pass on ideas for keeping the men happy. How's that?"

"Very good idea, sir. One up to you!"

*   *   *

And so the colonel began his weekly "moan sessions," as they came to be called. The first one after the "revolution" was the most difficult. The spokesmen were respectful but determined. Sullivan talked for them mostly. The colonel's manner was in keeping with his new reputation for sensational gestures. He was the commander, the dare-devil, the soul of generosity. Underneath he was savage and humiliated. The spokesmen enjoyed themselves, and Sullivan was carefully grave throughout. The thing was to get what they had come for. The only time the colonel's dignity was imperilled was when Go Through, who happened to be on guard outside Battalion Headquarters, passed sedately by the open window of the colonel's office with his rifle at the slope and his eyes fixed sternly on his job, and called from the corner of his mouth as he came by:

"Bore it up 'em, Slim!"

BOOK FOUR

VICTORY

18

A SEEMINGLY endless convoy of army lorries, regularly spaced, thundered along the narrow road like a gigantic chain. On either side stretched desert which, in the moonlight, seemed eerie and frozen. The stars glittered remotely in a luminous sky, giving an illusion of peace, of unimaginable space; but the convoy was a thunderous, brutish intrusion. Ever since sunset it had been crossing this cold landscape.

The chain was slowing. Soon it moved at a crawl, finally it stopped. Shapeless figures in greatcoats descended from the lorries. Their boots clacked harshly on the roadway. Voices arose like whispers in the vast night. Even a shout sounded puny and forlorn.

Dick Brett emerged from the cabin of a vehicle and walked round to the back. Looking up at the dim figures behind the tailboard, he said:

"Stopping for fifteen minutes. No lights."

"Good-oh!"

The huge form of Bob Hamilton swung over the tailboard and dropped to the roadway. It was followed by others.

"Where the hell are we?" someone wanted to know.

"Somewhere in Egypt."

"You don't tell me!"

Dick passed on to give the same instructions to the two truckloads behind. Dooley swung a leg over the tailboard and mumbled:

"Good! I'm busting for a leak."

"How are you travelling?" Dick asked him.

"All right. Christ, I'm hungry."

"There's a case of bully in the front truck."

"I'm not that hungry."

Dick went back to look for Lieutenant Chips Prentice, commander of Six Platoon. The driver came round and said to Dooley:

"I'm going to risk lighting up."

"Look out," someone warned. "Here comes Captain Crane."

The new commander of C Company stopped when he saw his old platoon.

"Where's Lieutenant Prentice?" he demanded.

A couple of them turned their backs. The others stared rigidly in front of them. No one answered him.

"I said, 'Where's Lieutenant Prentice?'"

The meaning of the silent and unmoving figures made Crane

purse his lips and emit a tiny sound of impatience. Dooley's eyes were narrowed; they were sightless and unrelenting.

"Where's Lieutenant Prentice?" Crane repeated.

"Go and look for him," came a voice from the darkness.

Crane left them, calling "Lieutenant Prentice!"

Behind him someone mocked his call.

"That you, Dick?"

"Yessir!"

"Over here!"

Dick joined Chips in the shadow of a truck. "Crane was after you."

"He saw me. Reckons Six Platoon were yelling out at the Wogs a few miles back!"

"Why can't he mind his own business?"

Chips answered a little restively:

"Well, if we yell out, they'll pick us for Aussies. We are supposed to be incognito."

Dick chuckled. "Every Arab in the Middle East knows the Aussies are on their way to Alamein by this."

Sensing that Chips was tugged between his dislike of Crane and loyalty to a fellow officer, Dick decided to abandon the subject.

"Brennan's sick," he said.

"What's wrong?"

"Diarrhœa."

"Could be dysentery. Tell him to go and see the M.O."

"I did, but he won't go. You know how they are when they're going into action; much rather suffer than have their mates think they were looking for a way out."

"We won't be in action for a few days. If he's no better next time we stop, make him report sick."

"I will. Where do you think we are?"

"I could only guess, mate. Well south of Cairo, I'd say."

"You don't think we'll go straight into action?"

"No, I don't. But we'll be in soon enough—don't worry. Things are really crook."

"I hope to God they're not as bad as they look."

"They are. You can't get away from it. The Huns are seventy miles from Alex and the Poms have had it."

"They must have taken a horrible hiding. I can't see what's stopped the Germans at all."

"Geography's saved us. They've got to pass through a narrow neck between the Qattara Depression and the sea. They're a long way from home and they're probably taking a breather before they go for the break-through."

"I wonder if our blokes realise just how bad things are."

"They know!"

"They're not worrying."

"Nothing worries our blokes!"

Chips's chuckle was complacent. It identified him with the men he referred to. Away from the presence of other officers he was the same old Chips—another reason for them to idolise him.

Behind them was a swishing of sand and three figures emerged over a sandhill. One of them was Corporal Slim Sullivan. His companions greeted Chips:

"Ar yer, Chips!"

"Hello, mates. Happy in the service?"

They stopped and stood around him, prepared for talk.

"Brennan's crook," Sullivan told him.

"Dick told me."

"I'm bloody hungry," someone complained.

"There'll be a hot meal at daylight," said Chips.

"And a smoke," added Sullivan heartfully.

"When we stop at daylight," Dick told Sullivan, "send three men from your section to carry dixies and hot-boxes, will you?"

Sullivan nodded to his two companions:

"Us three will do."

"Trapped!" one of them mourned.

"You blokes been yelling to the Wogs?" asked Chips.

"Yair, why?"

Chips smiled. "Well, cut it out. I've had a visit from Captain foggin' Crane over it."

"O.K."

A series of prolonged whistles sounded along the convoy.

"There she goes!" cried Chips. "All aboard!"

In a few minutes the chain of vehicles was on the move again. Among their gear on the heaving floors, men slept fitfully.

The following night the convoy had found its destination at some spot in the desert, and there the Second X was left. There were no landmarks; just flat stretches of sand, and above them a cold, starry sky. Tents were erected for Company Headquarters, but the platoons huddled in the sand. Large malicious scorpions emerged from under the stones and bit them as they slept.

The battalion was ready for action. Their laden packs and kit-bags had gone to the rear. Every head wore a steel helmet now. Bren guns, Vickers guns, Boys rifles and mortars lay in their cases, oiled and ready for use. The battalion knew that not very far away from them the victorious Nazi armies lay gathering themselves for the final spring into Cairo and Alexandria.

There was no excitement. Those who had not seen action before took their bearing from the old hands, who rested, talked quietly, reminisced, joked and barely mentioned what lay ahead of them. But a huge unspoken thought lay over the mass of them like a cloud: before long many of us will be dead.

Dooley was waiting for Moffatt. Dooley had left gaol a little before Moffatt, but by the time they parted they had formed a close alliance. They had emerged bitterly and mistrustfully into the world. Each clung to the comradeship of the other as tenaciously as he clung to his hatred of screws and officers. So when Moffatt's turn came for release, they decided they would not be parted for long and Moffatt had agreed to apply for a transfer to the Second X. Men returning from military gaol were generally given a chance to go to another unit, and in some cases were forced to. Moffatt had travelled down from Syria with a batch of reinforcements, and was now due to be sent over to Six Platoon. Dooley sat with the rest of Six Platoon, but a little apart. He waited.

Little Peter Dimmock was holding forth:

"The old man's a wizard at it. As soon as he gets the good oil on the Cups double, he'll send it over. Then we'll make a bit of dough out of the Vulture."

"This is only June," said Sullivan. "The weights aren't even out yet."

"You can stick your doubles for mine," Hamilton told him. "I'll keep to the swy."

"You'll get cramped odds from the Vulture!"

Dick emerged from the darkness and stood looking down at their reclining figures. Peter greeted him:

"Hullo, here's trouble!"

"Everybody happy?" Dick asked them.

"You got a job for someone?" Hamilton enquired.

"Not at the moment."

"Then you can sit down."

Dick laughed and accepted the invitation. He glanced over at Dooley:

"How are you, Dooley?"

"All right."

"Where do you reckon we are, Dick?" someone asked.

"A few miles from Amiriya, I'd say."

"No. I reckon we're near Ikingi Mariut."

"I can tell you where we'll be tomorrow," announced Peter. "Alamein! Hey—what the hell!"

A jeep skidded past and showered them with sand. It stopped within a few yards and Go Through got out from behind the wheel.

"A man oughter drop you," said Hamilton, spitting sand.

"Don't tamper with death," Go Through advised him. "How are yers?"

"Where'd you get the jeep? Where's your Bren carrier?"

"Given the carrier away," Go Through informed them. "These jeeps'll do me."

"Gawd!" a voice broke in. "Look at the Vulture, will you. Actually doing some work!"

Sure enough it was the great hunched figure of Tony Horne, with a medical satchel under one arm and a folded canvas stretcher on his shoulder.

"And who," called Go Through, "might that fine upstanding specimen of a bronzed Anzac be? I can't quite make him out."

The specimen referred to turned and came towards them. Tony favoured them with a sour grin. He halted and dumped his burdens on the sand.

"Why," exclaimed Go Through, "it's Colonel Horne!"

"Yes," agreed Tony. "How are you, Brigadier!"

"Not bad, General."

"Glad to hear it—Field Marshal." Tony turned to Dooley and lowered his harsh tones. "How are you, Dooley?"

"Not bad. Waiting for me mate."

Tony nodded, as though he understood all that that meant.

"Don't let us keep you," Sullivan told Tony. "You look as though you were on your way to pick up a sick man."

To their surprise, Tony looked a little sheepish. He grinned and shook his head.

"No," he told them. "I've reached my destination."

"No!" cried Hamilton.

"Yes! I'm going in with Six Platoon as your stretcher-bearer. So please don't too many of you bastards get knocked."

"We'll keep it in mind," laughed Sullivan.

When the customary lurid insults had been dispensed with Peter asked Tony:

"You gonna run a book on the Cups?"

"Yer know," murmured Go Through, "I was thinkin' of going in for S.P.-ing meself when I get back to civvy street. Good easy life. . . ."

"It's a business same as anything else," Tony told him. "And it's a business you can go broke at. For instance, sometimes a stable doesn't want to spread money at the course and bring the starting price down, so they back the horse quietly with the S.P.s. It starts at a long price on the course and the S.P.s get caught for thousands. I've seen it happen. Then there's the coppers, always hanging around for a cut."

"Do you always have to sling to the coppers?" asked Peter.

"Course you've gotta sling!"

"What if they won't take a sling?"

"Every copper has his price," replied Tony serenely.

"There's a few honest coppers."

"They don't stay honest for long."

"My old man used to say," Dooley put in, "that there were two classes of criminals, and one wore uniforms."

"Who was the greatest Australian who ever lived?" suddenly demanded Hamilton.

"King Billy!"

"I mean fair dinkum. Who was it?"

"I dunno. You tell us."

"Ned Kelly, of course. And who caused his downfall? Who drove him and his mates into crime and hounded their women? Who sneaked up behind him and shot him in the leg? Dirty, sneaking, yellow-gutted coppers!"

And having said this in tones of stern finality, Hamilton became silent again, gazing grimly ahead of him.

In the darkness, Tony's teeth flashed for an instant.

"One time," he continued, "I was running a book in the lane behind a pub. Had all the coppers squared from the inspector down. I slung each week, regular. A quid for each copper on duty, ten bob for each one off duty. One of them used to come round dressed in his uniform on his day off to make out he was on duty and collect the full quid. I was awake to him, but I kept quiet because I was on a good thing. Then his mates woke up to what he was doing. Next thing I know, I've got a deputation from the local coppers protesting about this joker who's copping the full quid on his day off." Tony gave his brief, bitter laugh. "Reckoned it was highly unethical!"

He accepted their mirth without emotion, and concluded:

"See what I mean, though? The bastards can't even think straight."

"There's only two words cops understand," said Hamilton. "Bribe and bash."

Dooley looked at the ground and said in quiet, measured tones:

"There's a couple of coppers in Jerusalem who never want to go back to Australia. I know a few jokers who'll do for them dirty foggin' bastards."

"Including you?" asked Sullivan.

Dooley did not reply. He pinched his lips together and dealt Sullivan a brief glare.

"Shut up, Slim," said Go Through.

"Why make yourself miserable brooding about some lousy screw?" Sullivan asked Dooley amiably.

"You ever been bashed up by coppers?" Go Through enquired meaningly.

"Yes, he has," Dick broke in.

"Slim got a bashing and a month's jail in 1933," Tony told them.

"What for?" Dooley asked with a sudden change in his manner.

"Speaking to a meeting of unemployed."

"And a' course, yer wouldn't like to get the coppers that bashed you up a dark lane?" sneered Go Through.

"It doesn't help things much to spend your time looking for revenge," Sullivan replied dryly.

From out of the surrounding darkness a voice called:
"Dooley Franks!"

Dooley leapt to his feet exclaiming:
"It's me mate Moffatt!"

He sped off in the direction the voice had come from.

Peter Dimmock had a few words with his platoon commander before he sought his sleeping place.

"I'm not cut out to be a hero," said Peter. "How do you reckon a man will go? I'd rather get killed than turn and run, but they reckon you can do it without knowing it. That right?"

Chips chuckled deeply. "You won't run," he said. "If ya do, there'll be a few running with you."

"But I tell you I'm scared already," urged Peter.

Chips looked down affectionately at the simple, honest, disturbed little man before him.

"Everyone's scared," he told Peter. "You'll get used to it. Just keep your eye on Chips. If Chips goes to ground, you go too. Just follow Uncle Chips."

Peter nodded. "I'm an ignorant coot," he confided. "This is the first time in my life I've been farther than Brisbane." He waved his hand distractedly to indicate the desert landscape. His voice became resentful. "I feel a bit lost—thousands of miles from Aussie, foreigners everywhere, and these deserts . . . who wants to fight for a desert? The idea of thousands of blokes all busy trying to kill each other—well, as I said, I'm an ignorant coot, but to me it's——" he paused, gestured again—"It's unbelievable!"

Daylight revealed the spot to be drearier than ever. There was nothing in the waste to relieve the eye. Vision was restricted despite the flatness of the land, for only a mile away their surroundings dissolved into a tremulous haze. Awnings went up everywhere and the men lay listlessly in the shade. Throughout the day flights of bombers thundered to and fro above their heads. Their sound was never absent from the sky. Men paused and looked up to watch their passing. The planes were a grim reminder for them of what lay only a few miles ahead: a beaten British army hanging desperately to a narrow neck of land, and waiting for them. Sometimes they thought they could hear the distant sound of gun-fire. They would straighten up from digging slit trenches, and listen.

Dick was remembering the first time they had gone into

battle, over a year ago now. It was different this time. Nobody was light-hearted. Nobody seemed to think that war was an adventure. Had the men changed because the war had changed? They despised the Nazis—even those of them who had not yet seen action felt this way. Now, as they talked of the fighting to come they were graver, less cynical. They were anti-fascist—conscious and determined about it. Little as they knew about much of the war, they understood its nature.

Men had come and gone steadily during the Second X's garrison duty in Syria. Crane had become C Company's commander and Six Platoon had been overjoyed when the great Chips Prentice had returned from officers' training unit to become their new platoon commander. Lucas and Andy Cain had taken over command of the other two B Company platoons. Lucas's platoon had found him satirical but tolerant. Andy's platoon had declared him "a cranky bastard." This was the nearest they ever got to defining his loneliness and misery. In the officers' mess he was politely ignored by the colonel and his cronies. Closeness to them only increased his contempt. After several clashes, all due to Andy's surliness, Henry, Chips and Lucas were cheerful but wary with him. Once he had believed that as soon as he had won his commission he could rise quickly; but soon he struck the barriers of seniority and the colonel's whims. He found himself incapable of paying court to the colonel and contemptuous of the bickering cliques that existed among the officers. He found there was a difference between his own efficiency and the firm passion of Henry Gilbertson. It showed in the faces of the ranks.

Sometimes he was wrung with nostalgia for the days when he had had mates like Dick and Dooley. Now they passed him with a nod.

Walking through B Company's lines one night he heard the voices of Dick and Dooley. Unseen in the darkness, he stood and listened to the conversation of the group of men. He heard Tony tell them about the police and heard Sullivan explain fascism to them. He felt how much he would have liked to walk up to Sullivan and say: "I'm Andy Cain. I've been wanting to talk to you." He could imagine the constraint that would have fallen on the group had he done so.

Then he heard his own name spoken by Dooley: "Andy once reckoned Groggy was a fascist." How he would have liked to stroll straight into their midst and hear them hail him as the man who walked off the colonel's parade—the way they had hailed him long ago. Instead, he turned away and walked on.

Enveloped in his despondency, he must have wandered aimlessly around for an hour when he ran into Dick. The moon had begun to rise and they recognised each other. Andy had a wish for something more than the usual nod.

"Hullo, Andy."

"Hullo, Dick."

Andy stopped. Dick took a step onward, then stopped too. There was a silence.

"How's Six Platoon these days?" Andy asked.

"Much the same."

Humbly, awkwardly, Andy searched for something else to say:

"How's Dooley since he came out?"

"Pretty savage."

"Well——" Andy could find nothing more to say. The silence became hard to bear. It was Dick who broke it this time:

"Looks as though it'll be on any day for us."

"Yes—I'm afraid so."

"Well—good night."

Each turned away to walk on. Swiftly, Andy swung round and held out his hand:

"Good luck, mate!"

Dick strode up, his face alight, and grasped Andy's hand.

"Good luck—you old bastard," he said softly.

In the afternoon, several official photographers arrived. A platoon of men was ordered into battle dress to fix bayonets and charge while the photographers jumped around them. Said Happy:

"That photo'll come out in some paper back home as the A.I.F. shock troops charging the enemy!"

The photographers asked for the legendary Chips Prentice, and Chips was made to assume various poses while the photographers snapped him. Chips posed without embarrassment while his platoon stood by and offered advice to the photographers. Had the subject been anyone but Chips they would have mocked and jeered. Crane had the photographers take his picture simply by ordering them to do so. His company stood around and those who were not under his eye were lavish with their sneers.

C Company hated him as heartily as B Company had. His obsession over winning a decoration had become a byword and they gloomily told each other that in his pursuit of a medal he would probably get them all killed sooner or later. In his anticipation of the fighting he was like a schoolboy. Anyone, they said, who actually looked forward to bloodshed was a lunatic.

But they were not to see action as soon as they thought. Next day was the first of July and in the early evening they saw another brigade of Australian infantry go past them, bound for El Alamein. No order was given to the Second X to move. They fretted in this barren, nameless spot for nearly a week before they were piled into trucks and taken to the front.

Just on dusk the trucks began to lurch across the desert towards the road that led to El Alamein. As it made to turn on to the road the leading truck of Six Platoon stalled. The driver restarted it; it crawled on a few yards and stalled again. Cursing, the driver jammed his foot down on the starter. The provost corporal directing the traffic at the turn-off waved the truck impatiently forward and shouted:

"Get that truck moving!"

"Pull yer head in, copper!" yelled Dooley from the back of the truck.

From a ute parked at the far edge of the road a provost lieutenant emerged, demanding bumptiously:

"What's all this hold-up? Get those trucks moving."

The face was hidden beneath the brim of a slouch hat, but there was something a little familiar about that short, strutting figure. Dooley peered.

"Know who that reminds me of?"

Hamilton peered at it too. "By Christ, I do! No, it can't be. Wish I could see his face."

"Hey, short-arse!" Dooley yelled at the provost officer. "You with the pips. Show us yer face."

The officer threw up his head and, on recognising the outraged features that glared at them, the old hands of Six Platoon broke into a great roar of mirth and derision:

"Percy Gribble!"

The narrow, tarred road ran parallel to the coast. Once or twice they saw the sea, luminous in the moonlight. To their left lay the interminable stretches of the desert. Numbered signposts dotted the fringes of the road, pointing along wheel-eaten tracks. Each number meant an army unit: a dump, a vehicle park, a field ambulance; infantry, artillery, anti-tank, engineers, service corps, tanks or armoured cars; a divisional or brigade headquarters. Along these tracks they spread for miles, dug into the powdery dust or hidden beneath camouflage nets. They could be Australians, South Africans, New Zealanders, British, Indians, Greeks, French or Palestinians. Each was a small mindless piece of a single vast design, involving the movement of masses of bodies; the passage of endless loads of shells, bombs, bullets, weapons, food; the conveying of torn and disfigured bodies to the peace of the rear. A great, clumsy, pitiless, awesome machine along whose mysterious channels men were digested, then spewed up again across a strip of land, rent, torn and pitted with explosion and carrying a hundred forms of death. And in the brief lulls, by prearrangement of the civilised nations, other men wearing the red cross went out and brought in the corpses of the dead and planted them at the foot of neat wooden crosses with their names, units and army numbers painted thereon; or they gathered in sandbags the remnants of bodies and allotted the remnants a cross marked "Unknown;" and over both the chaplains said words, and called the dead blessed. Then they went to the living who were yet to do battle and told them that God was on their side.

And across the stony ridges, only a mile or two away, another and similar Thing functioned in much the same manner, that had made itself their enemy and the enemy of all mankind.

And that night, as the Second X Battalion moved up to be digested into this incredible organism they call war, few of them pondered on how they had arrived at this predicament, and not all of them even realised that there were human creatures who were guilty of it. They were subdued, casual and friendly. It was little use being any other way. Each one hoped that he would not die, or, if he were wounded, that he would not be turned into something helpless or repulsive to look upon.

19

THE Brigadier was a plump little man with fat, smooth cheeks and cold slits of eyes. He looked vaguely oriental. Before the war he had run an airline. He commanded the brigade by much the same methods as he had made the airline pay. Those under him quickly learnt to fear the results of their mistakes. His memory was infallible; his mind absorbed every detail of a manœuvre or a plan of battle, turning smoothly like an oiled machine. Human wastage was nothing to him personally. His considerations were military and nothing else. Nobody ever knew what his feelings were. About Nazi atrocities he was indifferent. He confessed to be far more concerned about the superiority of Rommel's armour. The Nazis he respected, because he considered them good soldiers, and, therefore, honourable foes. Anything else about them he disregarded.

That night, in a deep, well-lit dug-out, he outlined the situation to his three battalion commanders, one of whom was Colonel Fitzroy. They stood around a huge, celluloid-covered map of the battle area. The celluloid was criss-crossed with lines and dotted with hundreds of military symbols, marking strategic spots on the map. He had been talking for half an hour; now he summed up for them:

"Well, there it is. He's flushed with victory, but the last few

229

days we've managed to put him temporarily off balance. Get this deep into your minds. Desert warfare is changing. It's no longer fluid. The mine, the gun and the infantryman will decide this battle. In our sector we are to regain the initiative. The method is obvious: recapture the features. Our objective is Tel El Aisa. It's no use being over-optimistic at this stage. He still has a fair chance of breaking through and getting to Alexandria. Our task is to reach a position of equilibrium and gradually build up our strength. . . ."

Rapidly, tonelessly, he began to outline the task of each battalion. They discussed zero hour; the timing of their advance; the elements they must co-operate with; the strength of their support; the depth and nature of the enemy's defences; his probable strength. They were there well into the night. Some details the brigadier took them over again and again. He answered their questions instantly and precisely.

When the colonel emerged into the open again, the night was black. The adjutant awaited him in a jeep. At its wheel was Go Through.

The colonel got aboard and spoke briskly:

"Home, Potts!"

"Yes, sir," said Go Through, thankfully.

He started the jeep and it began to bump slowly along a track. The colonel leaned back, feeling weary but resolute. In the impending attack he was going to redeem himself with the brigadier; who had been coldly critical about the Christmas Day affair, and also show the Second X once and for all who its commander was. His thoughts were sanguine as he bumped along; pleasantly vengeful.

Suddenly, he sat up. He hit Go Through's shoulder with the flat of his hand.

"Where the devil do you think you're going?"

"Home!" Go Through told him laconically, without turning his head.

"Stop this bloody jeep!"

Obediently, Go Through stopped it. He turned and grinned tolerantly at the colonel.

"There's a fork a hundred yards past Brigade. You've taken the wrong fork," the colonel said.

Go Through shook his head patiently. "No, sir. This is the track. The other leads down to a dump. Just trust the old Go Through."

"Keep your humour to yourself. Bear right until you come on to the other track."

"Sir——" began Go Through, a little desperately now.

"Stop your confounded arguing! Swing right!"

"For the last time," appealed Go Through.

"Right!" The colonel gestured adamantly.

Go Through shrugged. "This is the last time I drive you," he muttered.

"Hold your tongue!"

"I tell yer you're getting us lost!" shouted Go Through.

"Potts!" broke in Captain Stamp. "Consider yourself under open arrest. I'll detail a new driver in the morning, sir," he told the colonel.

The colonel nodded. Still muttering, Go Through swung the jeep around and sent it bounding over loose stones.

"Steady!" snapped Stamp.

Go Through's muttering was lost in the noise of the engine. For fifteen minutes there was no other sound. The colonel became a little anxious. They should have struck the other track long before this. A vague doubt entered his thoughts: had this ignorant oaf of a driver been right after all? He had a moment of slight panic. Then he cursed to himself. His doubts only increased his annoyance at Go Through. He knew it was too late now to climb down and admit he may have made an error. Sooner or later, they had to come to a sign of some kind. He sat back, fuming and hoped for the best.

Their first warning of danger was an unfamiliar shout to their right flank.

"Huns!" yelled Go Through and swerved violently. A gun rattled and the jeep lurched. The colonel and the adjutant crouched as they felt the harsh impact of bullets along the side of the jeep. The engine spluttered and stopped. The next moment they were surrounded. Hands seized them and dragged them forth. There seemed to be about a dozen Nazis; probably a patrol.

It had all happened so swiftly and suddenly that they stood there, half held up by their captors, speechless and dazed.

Go Through was the first to find voice:

"You stupid, foggin' animal!" he shouted. He was berserk. He jerked in the arms of his captors. He looked at Fitzroy and his voice hissed with malignity:

"You dirty, bloody, mad bastard! One day I'll pay you out for this."

The colonel's stomach seemed to turn completely over. Stunned at first, he became numb with fear. Go Through was reviling him incoherently.

"For God's sake," stuttered Fitzroy.

A rifle butt across the side of his head suddenly silenced Go Through. He fell with a deep sound of pain to the ground, rose half upright and broke into a blind, staggering run. The Nazi next to Stamp took aim with his revolver at the semiconscious Go Through. There was a crack. Go Through fell and lay still. The Nazi walked over to Go Through and shot him once again through the head.

231

"You murdering bastard!" Stamp yelled shrilly.

The Nazi turned and waved his revolver at Stamp.

"Silence!" he said. "He tried to escape. This is war."

"I'm a colonel of the Australian army," said Fitzroy in a small, spiritless voice.

The Nazi, an officer, replaced his revolver and saluted Fitzroy. He gave an order in German and the two officers were hustled off into the darkness.

The colonel walked unsteadily, his eyes fixed and staring. Stamp stumbled frequently, and tears ran down his cheeks—tears of rage and horror.

20

THE following afternoon Henry Gilbertson called the hundred odd men of B Company around him to address them. They came out of their trenches, to sit around the base of a small sandhill on which their company commander stood. They knew what this meant. Henry had spent the morning going over maps with his three platoon commanders and sergeants. The platoons had been warned to be ready to move at a minute's notice. But the warning that they would be going into action within the next few hours had taken second place to the news that the colonel, Captain Stamp and Go Through were missing, and Major Pomfret had taken command of the battalion. Fitzroy and Stamp they declared well lost, but the absence of Go Through left them glum and depressed, for the battalion had lost an institution. The Second X without Go Through seemed no longer the old Second X, and his disappearance was the first note of tragedy and change. None would tolerate the thought that he might be dead; they told each other he had been taken prisoner. Chips remarked that he had "gone through" for the duration, and a little grimly they consoled themselves with this joke. They were thankful that Pomfret was to lead them. Much as they hated him, they told each other: "The Animal's at least a good soldier."

Ted Olley silenced them and Henry began to speak:

"This is it, chaps. We go in tonight. Your platoon commanders will give you the full dope later. I just want to sketch the show that we'll be doing. This will be a brigade attack. The Second Z will go in first, the Second X will pass through, and the Second Y is in reserve. Our advance will be on a two-company front, B and C forward, Don company rear, and A Company in reserve. Our objective is a bit of high ground called Tel El Aisa. Remember it. This is a very important job we've

232

been given. I think you know the position. Rommel has driven the Eighth Army all the way back to El Alamein."

"Bloody Pommies . . ." someone murmured.

"Never mind the Pommies," Henry told him. "They've put up a hard fight. They still haven't been given a tank that can stand up to the German Mark IV. It's the British who've been mainly responsible for stopping the break-through. Now it's our turn."

"She'll be right, Mum," someone else drawled, and there was laughter.

Henry held up a hand and surveyed them keenly:

"I'm glad you feel so cheerful about it. It's nine months since we've seen any action, and a lot of you have yet to see action at all. Steadiness is what we need. Your officers and N.C.O.s are all experienced men—they won't let you down. This is not going to be easy, but I think we're going into this with our eyes open wider than they were before. This is a fight that's worth fighting. We're helping to rid the earth of something foul and rotten. I mean fascism—German fascism, Italian and Jap fascism—and we're not alone. The Russians are fighting it, the Americans are fighting it. Everywhere, we're holding our own. That's a good thought to go into the fight with."

The battalion moved up to the attack at eight o'clock that night. Somewhere ahead of them in the darkness was the Second Z. They went to the start-line in silence, except for the faint clink of their weapons and the swishing of boots in the sand. Their start-line was marked by a long strip of "four-be-two" stretched over the ground. On their way, B Company passed several twenty-five pounders, their camouflage hauled back and their snouts pointing up at a sharp angle, ready to fire.

"Which arty are yous?" Dooley asked them.

"British," came a voice from inside the net. "Give 'em fook, mates."

The Australians chuckled and went on. Darkness swallowed the guns behind. Somehow, the sight of those blunt snouts had cheered and heartened them. They had not gone much farther before the barrage opened up.

A tattoo of convulsive bangs assailed their ears and one or two of the inexperienced crouched and went to earth.

"It's all right," the old hands told them. "They're ours!"

Behind them, a chain of huge flickerings revealed the rim of the earth and a misty sky. At odd moments, their ears detected the shrill passage of shells above them.

Chips looked at his watch and shouted to Dick through the din:

"We're a hundred yards from the start-line. The Second Z move off in seven minutes."

The barrage seemed to mount in fury. Silent figures came out of the darkness and guided the forward companies to their positions on the start-line. Henry halted his company along the strip of narrow, white cloth and ordered them to lie down. He walked along, checking on his platoons.

"That you, Chips. All correct?"

"All correct, Gilby!"

A Very light burst, bathing the desert in nightmarish radiance. It revealed Henry's pale, audacious features and Chips's calm grin. It revealed the prone forms of men and a desolate landscape. Then it was dark again.

The men lay close to the ground without speaking. Waiting. For each of them at this moment all thoughts were private. Peter Dimmock was telling himself over and over again that, whatever happened, he wouldn't turn and run. He had already taken on the rigid, glistening, wax-like appearance of a man who was submerging his terror. Dooley told himself he was a fool to be there at all. Tommy had been right. What had their country done for them? The Nazis couldn't be any worse than Groggy and Crane, or those rotten screws. He hoped for what Tommy had hoped for—a nice, convenient wound. Poor little Tommy! Sullivan, who had spent his life among ordinary men, had never liked or admired them more than at this moment. He had never been more moved by their patience and dignity. In the past he had sometimes thought about a place like Stalingrad, where there were no doubts among the anti-fascists; no half-measures, no Fitzroys or Cranes; but all fiery and splendid resistance. At this moment he would not have been anywhere but where he was. Now the Cranes and Fitzroys did not matter. Despite them El Alamein would become as mighty a name as Stalingrad. He and his mates would make it so.

Dick lay next to Chips. When you had been afraid often enough, fear became your friend. You carried it inside you and it no longer made any difference to what you did. A new dose of action was a plunge into a bad old dream. A man's worst fear came of not knowing the meaning of things. One by one, the brightest moments of his past ran through his mind. He felt as though he laughed, cried, sang, sorrowed and rejoiced all at once, like a man living those few exquisite moments of life before he drowned. He had an illusion of rushing onwards into something new, shedding the past as a tree sheds its dead leaves. The character of death itself had changed.

Henry Gilbertson watched the luminous hands of his watch. A minute to go . . . more Very lights—red, green, red—the Second Z had reached its objective . . . thirty seconds to go . . . If I come out of this, I'll write Jane a magnificent letter—if I don't—good-bye, my darling . . . ten seconds to go . . . five . . . four . . . three . . . two . . . one——

234

"Forward, B Company!"

They advanced at half-pace in a steady line. For a few moments the barrage had lifted and in the lull they could hear ahead of them the rattle of rifle and machine-gun fire. Tracers cut brilliant curved lines in the darkness. Then the barrage began again. Bayonets fixed, the riflemen stalked along with their rifles held at the port. The tommy-gunners carried their guns cocked under their armpits; the Bren gunners held their guns with muzzles upward across their chests. Slowly the ground began to rise; sand gave way to rock-strewn ground. Suddenly, ahead of them loomed wire. A horde of men in dull green uniforms stood on emplacements behind the wire with their hands raised. Among them stood Australians. Dead and wounded were strewn over the ground here. Next to each inert figure a rifle was struck by the bayonet in the sand. Where the figure was obviously dead, the steel helmet was hung on the rifle butt.

The Second X came through the great gaps that had been torn in the wire. They leaped across trenches and skirted weapon-pits and as they passed the men of the Second Z greeted them from drawn and blackened faces.

"You've got the job ahead of you, mate," a man called to Dick. "These are nearly all Ities—only a handful of Huns."

Now they were through and into open ground again, which became steeper and steeper. Ahead of them the darkness began to flash and scream. It was their own barrage. They went to earth until it lifted, then rose, and came on again. Smoke drifted about them and pricked their nostrils.

The earth about them flashed and cracked; an incredible screeching cut their ears. In the ghastly, split-second proddings of light men were to be seen falling or writhing on the ground. Now the machine-guns puttered ahead of them and tracer bullets zipped among them. More of them fell. But above the consuming din the voices of Henry and his platoon commanders screamed: "Charge! Charge!"

"Into the bastards!" roared Chips.

The Bren gunners on the flanks poured fire into the strong-posts ahead of them. Men rushed up to hurl grenades at the figures that crouched over guns; Nazis emerged from the ground to shoot it out with the tommy-gunners. Riflemen leaped into the trenches, bayonets thrust downward. Peter Dimmock threw himself into a trench. A Nazi loomed beside him and something hard hit Peter's chest. Peter staggered, hit the side of the trench, suddenly tensed his arms and lunging forward, pierced the Nazi's throat with his bayonet. The Nazi gurgled and went down. Peter fell on top of him. They were both dead. Dick sprayed a trench with his tommy-gun and shot a Nazi a second after he had thrown a stick-bomb. He threw himself flat and felt the explosion pluck and tear his clothes. Behind him someone howled. Dooley came forward with his Bren and calmly shot the wounded Nazi machine-gunner. Chips, with a grenade, had accounted for three Nazis in a dug-out. In ten minutes it was all over. They had reached their objective on Tel El Aisa.

Ted Olley was dead. He lay with a shattered head in front of the captured position. Andy Cain lay in a pool of blood, but alive. A stretcher-bearer was applying a field-dressing to a wound in his side. Hamilton, badly hit, was being looked after by Tony Horne. Sullivan was missing.

Swiftly, Dick began to check the casualties. Tony told him that he had bound up a wounded Sullivan when the enemy counter-barrage first hit them.

"He was out to it," said Tony. "Got it in the head. Brennan copped a bit in the leg. Moffatt's done for."

Dooley was searching the trenches calling: "Moff! Are you there, Moff?"

"Dooley," Tony called to him.

Dooley came over, eyes staring whitely in a grimy face.

"Moffatt's had it, mate," said Tony gently.

Dooley turned away. He threw his Bren down and commenced to walk back the way they had advanced.

"He's had it, mate," Tony cried. "There's nothing to be done."

"Dooley!" shouted Dick. "Come back!"

Dooley kept walking.

"Let him go," said Chips. "Moffatt's just back there with his brains all over the ground."

"Might have been for the best," said Tony bitterly. "He was half mad, you know."

They began to clear the post they had captured. More stretcher-bearers arrived to take away the dead and the wounded. Henry ordered his company to dig itself in farther along the slope from the captured position, which the enemy began to shell as they were leaving it. They dug in feverishly, for they knew the Nazis would probably counter-attack at dawn.

They attacked at first light, a regiment of them, but Vickers guns had come up during the night and dug in among the Second X. They mowed the Nazis down pitilessly. When the sun came up, silent heaps of Nazis covered the stony ground.

21

FOR days, the Second X held on to its newly-won positions. They were shelled, dive-bombed and machine-gunned. German tanks penetrated their posts, shattered the lighter British tanks and called upon the Second X to surrender. In answer, they leaped from their pits and broke sticky-bombs on the tracks of the Nazi tanks, and Chips even climbed on to one, lifted the hatch and dropped a grenade down with his time-honoured cry of: "Split this up among you!" Happy engaged one from his carrier with a Vickers gun in the hope that he would find the vision-slit with a bullet. The bullets whizzed harmlessly off the armour, and Happy immortalised another saying when he gloomily described it as "like spitting on a hot stove." Several of them caught above ground were crushed beneath the tracks of the Nazi tanks.

* * *

On the second night the Second Z, on their left, made a new advance. They passed safely through the minefields, but as it went through the gap an anti-tank truck was hit and blazed fiercely. By its illumination the Nazis made the gap impassable and blanketed the rear of the Second Z with shell-fire. Unable to withdraw, the Second Z fought onward. All that night the Second X heard the fighting rage ahead of them. Tracers and shell flashes plagued the darkness in the distance. By daylight all was silent again, and none of the Second Z returned. So, in a few hours, passed a battalion.

* * *

On the morning of the third day, the Nazi infantry reached the wire that B Company had thrown up, and only the Vickers guns halted them. Nazis overran the positions on their left and engaged B Company in a duel of machine-guns. The Nazis brought up mortars and the air was full of their harsh whispering. The dead and wounded in B Company mounted. Over the telephone, Pomfret instructed Henry to withdraw. Henry asked for artillery to cover his withdrawal and more stretcher-bearers to take out the wounded. He had barely set down the phone when he was conscious of a sudden silence. He came up from the company dug-out to discover its cause.

"They're waving the white flag," the company runner told him.

From the German trenches, three Nazis emerged, one of whom carried a white flag. When they were fifty yards away, Henry cried out: "Halt!"

The Germans halted. One of them cried:

"We want to surrender to you!"

Henry's heart bounded. No withdrawal now! He called back:
"Tell your men to come out with their hands up!"

One of them turned and shouted something in German.
About twenty Nazis rose above ground with their hands aloft.

"Lucas!" cried Henry. "Round them up! Be careful!"

He came above ground himself and Lucas led his platoon
across the open ground. Henry headed for the Nazi officer who
had called to him.

The next moment, the Nazis had thrown themselves flat on
the ground; machine-guns suddenly appeared behind them and
cut a swathe in the ranks of the exposed Australians. Half of
them fell, the others ran back towards their trenches. Henry
fell riddled. He rolled over and tried to call to Lucas, but no
sound came. His eyes took in the sky for a brief second and then
death flooded them.

As the Nazis tried to regain their trenches, Lucas leaped to
his feet and sprayed them from a tommy-gun. Howling
frenziedly, Chips led Six Platoon out in a wild charge, tossing
grenades. They were upon the Nazis before they could recover
from their confusion; and the rest of B Company followed
them.

Mindless with hate, they killed and killed. They spared not
one Nazi.

That night they withdrew with their dead. They walked
slowly and they did not speak. As they came to safety they
passed Pomfret, who said gravely: "Well done, B Company."
But they did not heed him.

The company commander was buried beside the men who
had perished with him. Padre Hobbs recited a burial service in
his sensuous, melancholy voice and just for this once it had a
kind of meaning for them:

*". . . Thou carriest the children of men away as with a flood.
They are as a sleep; in the morning they are like grass which
groweth up. In the morning it flourisheth and groweth up;
in the evening it is cut down and withereth. . . . For all our
days are passed away in thy wrath; we spend our years as a
tale that is told. . . ."*

And so another tale came to be told about the battalion called
the Second X.

22

IT was now September. Like two bloodied beasts, the armies had retired beyond the ridges to lick their wounds. Only occasionally a fang flashed out in the shape of a patrol or a sortie by the tanks. From their hidden lairs the artillery rained smoke and singing steel on several spots as part of their daily programme. Eighteen British bombers sailed each morning above the German defences and pattern-bombed. The silvery bombs were visible, falling in a precise design, as if they were sequins on a transparent curtain being lowered down the sky. Then came the racket of the German flak and the eighteen would glide sedately through a forest of tiny white pom-poms that seemingly came from nowhere. Sometimes one of the eighteen would begin to trail smoke and would detach itself from the design, to be lost behind the distant ridges.

The ridges! How many lost bodies lay out on the littered stones to blacken in the sun, swell fantastically and spill their putrescence with a horrible noise—as if they had made their final protest of all. How many a pile of derelict steel; how many torn helmets, bloody pouches and strips of shattered men.

Day after day the sun struck a shimmering haze from the stony rises and the scorched sands. A tank or a truck crawling across the waste sent a great plume of dust rolling out behind, that crept backwards and then skywards, thinning as the sun hived it—looking like a golden miasma, an effusion of the disease of war.

Early in September the Second X came out of the line to a spot that was only a mile from the sea. They dug in along the edge of a ridge and, as the days went by, gradually deepened and enlarged their dwelling places in a search for shade and coolness. Trucks brought paper and envelopes, cigarettes, socks and odd tins of delicacies. Three times a day they came to their company cook-houses under the ragged canvas awnings and collected bully-beef and tinned vegetables in their dixies. As they ate, their hands waved ceaselessly over the food, discouraging the fat, black flies already glutted on corpses.

Once again their boots were worn white and their khaki clothes grown stiff and yellow with dust. Their webbing was bleached and their skins darkened.

Someone suggested to Lieutenant-Colonel Pomfret, D.S.O., that the troops might like to swim in the sea and, as efficiently as he did anything else, he organised a system whereby two companies at a time spent three days on the beach and Captain Chips Prentice, M.C., D.C.M., led B Company on a march to the beach feeling like a boy let out of school, for, among other things, he was famous back home as a swimmer, and his youngest platoon commander, Sergeant Dick Brett, though not famous, was just as ardent a swimmer.

The beach was so white that it was hurtful to the eyes. In a perpetually delighting contrast it joined the deep rich blue of the Mediterranean. The troops erected rough awnings among the sandhills and there, throughout the day, they lazed between swims and slept at night.

The battles of July and August had left Dick with an exhausted, old man's body and a curiously numb mind. Now, on the warm comforting sands in the drowsy shade, he felt power and youth creeping back into his body. Strangely, his mind felt at rest. The last two months were like a remote, impossible dream, only the fringes of which his mind dared touch. Sometimes, though, in the depths of sleep, some horror would probe like a flash into his memory, and he would wake disturbed and puzzled, asking himself whether such things had really happened to him.

Mostly, he thought of Naomi and their last few days together in Syria, when he had been given seven days' leave and she had come up from Palestine to be with him. They had spent their first day under the Cedars of Lebanon, walking silently in the cushioning snow, and gazing up every now and then into the ageless gloom of the great trees. They had stayed at an old stone hotel high in the mountains. Their bedroom window gave them a view straight down a green-clad precipice the bottom of which was lost in a haze. The open-air café was built on tall stone pylons right over a rushing stream, its water the loveliest of lucent green, breaking into creamy turbulence around the rocks. In its centre it tore along loudly, but at the shallow edges it loafed past with a sound like a bell. They ate wonderful ice-creams, apricots, baked quail and drank arak and pale Syrian beer. The proprietor, a bearded old Jew with a skull cap, had welcomed them with a gentle, delighted smile and sought them out constantly for the sake of conferring shy favours—always with a conspiring twinkle as though he had known that sooner or later he was due to be host to a fine woman and her soldier lover. Dick did not want to think very deeply about Naomi or to remind himself that the future would demand a choice of them. Such decisions were at the whim of war. And the war was now something he believed in, something in which he had to play a part—and something which might destroy him.

Sullivan's head wound had been slight and he had been back within a month. For hours on end they would lie together in the sand and talk. They talked about anything and everything.

"Slim, what are you going to do after the war?"

"Same as before the war. Do a job of work somewhere—organise my mates. Union activity. Meetings, classes."

"Classes! I never imagined you as a teacher."

"There's a few things I know," said Sullivan dryly, "that I can pass on."

"How much education did you have, Slim?"

"You mean at school? Left when I was twelve."

"And you've worked ever since?"

"Yes—ever since. Down the mines—on the canefields—on the wharves; out of work for two years . . ."

Suddenly Sullivan was silent, held by a vision of gaunt, hungry faces marching in ranks; policemen wielding batons; a miner crushed in a fall turning up the whites of his eyes; rough banners in the wind, grim, angry, desperate faces. Work, work, organise, explain . . . Ever since . . .

On behalf of the company, Dick wrote a letter to Henry's widow. It was not a long letter. As simply as he could, he tried to tell her of the affection they had had for him. As he wrote it he was strangely moved; and suddenly words came more easily for he had begun to recall the simple honesty, the courage and the humanity of the man who had believed in a new world, but had not lived to see it.

A new tale was told about Happy. The Germans had begun to use air-bursts, the most terrifying of all shell-fire, bursting twenty feet in the air and raining shrapnel downwards so that slit trenches were almost useless. On one occasion, when a company was moving up to occupy a new position, the air above them had become overcast with the wicked black clouds of air-bursts. Men were falling, and in the middle of it, a demented man on his knees implored: "Oh, God, come down and get me!" Moving past in his carrier, Happy leaned out and pointing upwards, asked: " 'Ow the 'ell could 'E get down through a barrage like that?"

*　　　*　　　*

In a hospital near Alexandria, Crane sat up in bed. He had won his medal. Men still spoke with wonder of the mad courage with which he had led his company to the attack on Tel El Aisa. In their admiration they forgave him the past—but it was too late now: he would never see the battalion again. His right eye was gone, and half of the right side of his face.

The surgeon had done all he could. Crane was going to be horribly disfigured. He sat propped up on the pillows, his head swathed in bandages, his remaining eye staring before him, distant and terrible.

At first he had not been able to believe that his face was half destroyed. Then when the fact became inescapable he had lain sleepless for days and nights, his mind racked with a wild protest. From this he had passed to an agony of self-pity. He sat there heedless of the life about him. He roused himself to revile the fate that had thrust this horror upon him. His very insides wrenched and cried out at the injustice of it. No longer would he feel splendid in his own eyes. Never again was he to be a leader of men. Pity and revulsion were the only emotions he would ever arouse. Now he remembered who it was he had heard utter the words that had haunted his mind . . . the Italian consular agent he had met in Sydney: a smiling, smooth little man with shining teeth and glinting black hair—an ardent fascist. "Bloodshed resolves everything, Mr. Crane. It is the supreme decision. It is eternal. It is life. We worship it like a goddess. We learn it, we take it to our bosoms. To us fascists it is a cult. Ah, the dark beauty of violence!"

*   *   *

The war seemed incredibly remote during those days at the beach. Even the fact that they were in the army was half forgotten for there were few reminders of it. Colonel Pomfret appeared from nowhere in a jeep one day, stonily enquired why slit trenches had not been dug and ordered them to be dug immediately.

They cursed him privately, dug till he was out of sight, then went back to the water. As a grim reminder of Pomfret's apparent infallibility, the same afternoon a stray Messerschmitt strafed them on its way past and, chastened, they completed the slit trenches. Padre Hobbs visited them once or twice, his head held high and that remote spiritual look in his eye, to enquire meekly whether the Protestants would care to come to a church parade.

The Protestants politely told him no. His soft manner confused them and behind his back they referred to him as "Creeping Jesus."

Father Bourke appeared over the sandhills several times in search of Dooley, who, as a man recently released from military gaol, must sooner or later find the need to unburden his soul —or so the priest believed. In a harsh voice Dooley told him about the screw they called the Shark who had beaten him up and starved him—a Catholic.

"Sure, Dooley, but the man had his duty to do, did he not? And you can't say you didn't deserve a little rough handling. It's a sore trouble you've been. There must have been many a sin to pay for. And if he was a good son of the Church, then what he did was all for your own good."

Dooley swallowed his anger and the profanity that was on the tip of his tongue.

242

"Just you leave me alone," he said sullenly. "I'm a renegade and I always will be."

"I'm staying here until I've had a long talk with you, Dooley," Father Bourke insisted.

"Please yourself," shrugged Dooley, and dashed into the sea.

Angrily, the priest went as far as the water's edge and waving his arms, called:

"You can swim to Crete, Dooley Franks, but I'll be waiting for you when you come back!"

Dooley swam round and floated by turns for nearly half an hour and finally the priest gave it up and disappeared back over the sandhills.

One morning in the early dawn. Dick woke suddenly. What seemed to have aroused him was the carolling of magpies. The world was grey and still. The only sound was the faint lapping of the ocean. Perhaps that had roused him and on the moment of waking his memory had caught the echoes of other dawns. Distant dawns. Then it came to him. Their camp back in Australia. Huts shaded by towering white gums. Often he had wakened in the first cool greyness of the new day and from near at hand would come the liquid music of the magpies. When they sang it seemed that the joyful trilling made the whole world pause. The memory of those far-away dawns suddenly came back to him with a strange poignancy. He was filled with a longing to wake to them once again.

It had been by far their best camp. It lay on the fringe of the bushland a mile from the town. The life they had lived there seemed incredibly remote now: Lucas, grinning cruelly, putting them through their first clumsy movements of rifle drill. . . . The newly-formed platoon in shapeless fatigue clothes marching along the bright red soil of the road, with Crane at their head. A Crane they were still feeling their way with, talking down his nose at them one moment, trying to talk in what he imagined was their language the next. . . . Always intent on being their commander, wrapped in a cloud of lonely pride, despising them and yet conscious of their necessity; sometimes, when he found something in common with them, being humorous or affable . . . afterwards, he had just given up trying to know them and getting to like them. They didn't seem to fit in with some selfish vision . . . Tommy and Dooley coming back drunk from town in the early hours, arousing the whole hut with their shouts and pretended quarrels . . . their days a riotous succession of trips to town in pursuit of beer or a woman. The war might never have existed for these two. Dooley grinning at an angry Crane and calling him "mate" . . . Tommy being brought back to camp by the provosts . . . Andy Cain, reticent and bitter, coming into the army with a ready-made contempt for the like of Crane and Fitzroy . . . Henry Gilbertson, calling them "chaps" and being determinedly familiar and often looking disappointed when his assumption of comradeship met with sly derision. . . . Chips, huge, brown and magnificent, winning the heavyweight boxing championship, laughing richly in the pub over a pot of beer and sending them into mirth by the sheer force of his good humour . . . the bivouacs in the silent bush among the ghost gums . . . the first battalion parades and the inhuman bawl of Varney . . . the neat, handsome figure of Fitzroy with the small black moustache and arrogant chin telling his battalion he intended to make it the finest in the army . . . the birth of identities: Go Through, Happy, the Vulture, Groggy, the Boy Bastard, the Animal, Mad Mick.

Only two years ago, yet already like a dream! So many of them dead, so many of them wounded and shipped home. None of them could ever be quite the same again, least of all himself.

*   *   *

On the coast road that ran past El Alamein, a great signboard had been erected at which all Australians who passed looked proudly and with mirth. Once again Haw Haw the traitor had given them a name. Those who survived from Tobruk days no longer were Rats and those who had come after Tobruk were glad to share with the old hands a new name. Though none of the infantry had heard him, within a few days they all knew of the traitor whose voice from Europe over the radio had resentfully announced their return to the Western Desert.

Although their new name was once more given them in contempt, they seized on it as before and made it a thing to be proud of.

And so the sign which told all comers:

THE TWENTY THOUSAND THIEVES

23

THEN came October.

Something, they said, was looming. One by one they noted the signs. A new tank appeared, as big as the German and with a cannon just as powerful. It was brought up at night on the back of a huge tank-carrier, covered with a tarpaulin and somewhere hidden away. But the one or two who saw it told the others and soon they all knew that the days when the flimsy little Crusader tanks should scurry and shatter before the Mark

244

IV were gone. Strange new British bombers flew across the sky. A two-engined fighter plane with a round short nose and strangely hushed engines was seen sweeping westwards at nightfall. Its name was Whispering Death. Everything was in some way transformed. They were marched away from the sea and, there on a marshy flat ten miles behind the ridges, they were trained with rifle, bayonet, mortar and grenade; as hard and mercilessly as though they had never seen them before. And the anti-tank one day were deprived of their little two-pounder guns and the next day given a big new gun called the six-pounder. And then came British soldiers, pink-skinned and fresh from their homeland. To each company of Australian infantry a handful of them was attached, and night after night they went with the Australians in penetrating patrols, to become wise in the ways of desert war. By day the harsh sun crimsoned the skin of their legs and by night the skin was grazed and stripped on the stones as grinning Australians urged them over the spaces of No Man's Land. And they ground their teeth and stayed side by side with the Australians, for they knew what was soon to come. The Second X were taken out several nights in a row, in full battalion strength and practised advancing on a two-company front at a hundred and twenty paces to the minute—A and B forward, C and D on passing through. They practised till they were weary to desperation. Engineers came among them and showed how to delouse the Nazi mines: the S-mine and the Tellermine. From the very highest downward, old generals went and new generals took their place. They heard stories of drones and desk-soldiers being herded out of the Cairo hotels because of the new general, Montgomery, who neither drank nor smoked and was devoted to physical jerks. So they added the signs up, one by one, and knew that something tremendous impended.

The night of their final battle rehearsal was a wild one. Thunder and lightning, wind and rain transformed the desert. Inside their doovers in the white sandhills they sat dejectedly and watched the rainwater coursing over the sandbags. They sat there in wonderment. They cursed.

"It rained once before," said Dooley. "In Tobruk."

"Surely," mused Hamilton, "they'll call this stunt off now."

"It's a brigade show," growled Dooley. "They won't call it off."

"It's a farce," sighed Brennan. "We know it by heart." He began to recite: "Two thousand yards at a hundred and twenty to the minute. Dig in. Wait for the Very light—red over green over white. Swing half right. Go another two thousand. Dig in again. Make contact on your flanks. Patrol five hundred yards forward. Keep behind the ridge."

245

Dick, water dripping from his body, poked himself half-way into the dug-out. He looked at his watch.

"It's eighteen forty-nine. Assemble at nineteen hundred."

"Do you mean to say it's still on?"

"I do."

"Well, it's foggin' well crazy!"

"I'll pass your remarks on to the brigadier." Dick disappeared into the streaming darkness.

"I'm not going," said Dooley suddenly. "I'm jackin'-up."

They considered his decision silently.

"Want to be in it?" he asked them, looking sharply wicked.

Hamilton waved his great hand. "I'll be in it!" he said.

Dooley looked at the others. "How about yous?"

"Yair, we'll be in it."

Dooley rose and spoke to Hamilton.

"Let's tell the whole company there's a jack-up on."

Hamilton rose too, and together they ran off into the tumultuous night.

At seven o'clock Sergeant-Major Bancroft stood outside on the sand and cried above the storm:

"All out, B Company!"

The wind carried the last three words of an answering cry to him:

". . . not coming out!"

"All out, B Company!" he cried again.

Chips appeared at his side. "Hurry 'em up, Tom."

"All out!" yelled Bancroft again.

A faint cry came back to them but no men appeared.

Bancroft's features looked disturbed. "I smell jack-up, Chips."

"Balls! They wouldn't jack-up on Uncle Chips." He lifted his head and conquered the storm with his great rich voice:

"All out, you blokes!"

The sandhills stood deserted. Then a voice spoke behind them. Sullivan's.

"It's a jack-up," he told them.

Stern and angry, Chips turned to face him. He was all officer now.

"Is this your doing?"

"Might be or it mightn't. I'm just telling you."

"I'm obliged to you," said Chips bitterly. And there was anguish in his voice.

Sullivan spoke to him without anger:

"I think a jack-up at a time like this is a coot of an idea. I'm going back to my doover."

"Stay here," said Chips. There was pleading in his tone. "Fall in. They'll follow you."

For a moment Sullivan wavered. His eyes held both pain and anger. Then he shook his head:

"I'm too old to scab," he said.

He walked away.

Dick approached them. "I can't make them budge," he said. "What will I do?"

"Go back to your doover," said Chips dejectedly. He turned to Bancroft. "You, too, Tom. Ask Lieutenant Lucas to ring battalion and tell them the storm's delayed us."

They left him alone.

Silent in their dug-out, B Company heard his voice at intervals above the howl of the storm. Torn between shame and the common decision, one or two of them thrust out their heads and peered across. The lightning revealed a deathly-white floor of sand and standing there, quite still, a tommy-gun under his arm, rain pouring from his helmet, their commander. His face was raised. It was stern and implacable. He did not move. He waited.

They avoided each other's eyes.

Hamilton could bear it no longer. He rose, took up his rifle.

"Call me a scab," he said, and left the dug-out.

"Me too," said Sullivan, and also rose.

"Let's all be scabs," growled Dooley.

In ones and twos, his company assembled before Captain Chips Prentice. He did not even look at them. He turned and they followed him.

Wet through and numb with cold, they reached the assembly point. A company of the Second Y passed them, and Dooley's head swung round to stare at them.

"I'm seeing things," he muttered.

Another flash of lightning confirmed the reality of the vision: Father Bourke, marching with a platoon, and on his shoulder carrying somebody's Bren gun.

Dooley swore softly and beside him Sullivan chuckled.

When they reached the end of their mock advance the storm cleared. Darkness, unlit by lightning, enveloped the desert. They dug trenches. Their limbs were painful with cold. For warmth, they sat in the trenches and pulled the sand in over them. After an hour's wait they were ordered back. The last rehearsal was over.

Tramping back to their positions, they were still silent and depressed. Suddenly Sullivan stepped from the ranks, crying: "Company, halt!"

Confused, they came to a halt. Chips and Bancroft turned to stare at him angrily.

"Sir," he said before they could speak, "we're sorry about that."

There was a low growl of agreement.

247

Chips looked at them for the first time in many hours. Joy came back into his eyes.

"Forget it," he said.

Now the might of the gathering battle infected and sobered all their thoughts. Tanks, guns, trucks and men weaved forward and assembled. Like a wave the attack was collecting itself, ready to raise a crest of maddened and frightened men—a wave the enormity of which was beyond the human mind.

In the few days before the battle they rested. A quietness, a common mood of contemplation was on all of them. Quietly they went about their ways. All anger was lost. They wrote their letters home. They sat and thought of those to whom they had written—thoughts that none would share. They remembered their lives and thought of their death. And the young men whom past battles had made old shrank from believing that this time they would not escape. Sometimes, inside, they wept at the resignation of their minds to the slaughter that impended. But those who had not yet seen battle had no resignation and no certainties. Visions invaded them like a plague.

A boy sat in a dug-out alone one afternoon. He knew that he could not face it. He had never been anything but gentle. He was pale and full of terror. He cocked his rifle and shot off his toes. The sound of the shot brought several running to him, and in the dug-out they found him, apparently indifferent to his shattered foot—all the wildness gone from his eyes and tranquillity on his young boy's face. "I did it because I had to," he told them. They hushed him and carried him out. Tony bound up the foot and someone sent for Chips. The boy looked around at them and saw in their faces, not the hate or the scorn he had prepared for, but sorrow and compassion. In a frenzy of shame, he wept. And when Chips came he protested: "I had to do it. I did it on purpose. I can't explain."

"We understand, son," said Chips gently. And then they bore him away on a stretcher, Tony and Dooley.

"It was an accident, Tony," said Chips.

"Of course," said Tony, "I saw it."

Then came the full moon and it all began.

The Supreme Commander called his generals together and they their colonels and brigadiers. In a matter of days the plan of battle passed from the highest headquarters to the section's dug-out. And Chips called his company around him.

"This is it," he said. "We go in the day after tomorrow." He told them of the tens of thousands that had massed for the attack. He told them of the uncountable hordes of tanks and guns and planes. He spoke like one who could already see victory.

248

"The battalion is at half strength," he said. "But our task is still one of the hardest. Most of those we will strike are Nazis. If they surrender and show any signs of treachery, shoot them. Our numbers are too few to waste men escorting prisoners back."

A plan of the battlefield was made out of wet sand and he showed them their starting-point and their objectives. Then, when all their questions were answered, all their tasks clear, he spoke his final words:

"I'm not as good at this sort of thing as Gilby was, but I'd like to say it. I don't know much about politics but I know we believe in things like freedom. Well, in this attack we're going to roll back the Nazi. No one has any doubts now what this war's about and we realise we're doing a good job."

He dropped his head—that fine, sleek head—for a moment, as though deciding what to say next. Then he looked up smiling all over and cried:

"Good luck, mates!"

*   *   *

On the night of October the twenty-second, in the year 1942, Lieutenant-Colonel Pomfret, D.S.O., led his battalion, four hundred and twenty strong, into prepared positions a mile or two west of the railway station called El Alamein.

All the next day they lay below ground in shallow pits; when evening came they emerged, stretched their limbs and took the cool air into their bodies.

They filled their pouches with bullet-clips, tommy-gun magazines and grenades and they cleaned and oiled their weapons. Then they were met by trucks with dixies of stew and hot tea that tasted of tinned milk and chlorine.

Soon the light was all gone from the earth. The darkness about them became alive with engines and voices issuing commands. And the land hummed and trembled beneath the massing of something gigantic and irresistible.

In that darkness, as far as an eye might have seen, the armies swarmed over the face of the land.

Company after company of infantry filed behind their commanders towards the start-line. Chips and B Company weaved their way between the long lines of trucks, between the tanks and the armoured cars and the silent groups of men who waited. Then they came to a maze of great humps and these were the guns—their nets drawn back to reveal the blunt, raised snouts—one every twenty yards. Deadly those upraised snouts, and eager, as though they could already scent death on the wind.

"That the Second X?"

"Yes."

249

"We're supporting you. Good luck. Keep your heads down."

Forward of the guns and farther into the darkness ahead—nearer to the enemy. There at a point where all his companies must pass him stood Pomfret; and as each went by he called: "Good luck!"

Soon after, they reached their start-line. They lay down flat and spoke to each other softly.

There was no fear left in Dick. No doubts. He was calm and his mind was clear. For a few seconds he had a huge vision of tens of thousands of men who lay waiting as he did. How many were there like himself?—angry at life no longer, unafraid of death, yet knowing the meaning of what was soon to happen. Seeing this battle as the end of a crime and themselves as its victims. This tragic, this just, this terrible battle. The victims—and yet the victors. The betrayed, the lost, the unhappy, and the deceived. The fearing, the noble, the mean, the loved, and the detested. This night they would have in common fear and agony. These made them brothers. And many must die. This was war. *Curse and damn to the ends of the world all those who had made it necessary.*

And now to more killing and perhaps the end of my life.

Then the moon began to rise.

Dick looked at his watch. Zero minus sixty. Zero minus forty-five . . . thirty . . . "Ready, Six Platoon . . ." fifteen . . . ten, five . . .

"Forward, B Company!"

As they rose, the rim of all the earth behind them flashed. The world shuddered. They looked back in wonder. It seemed as though the firmament was aflame below the earth's rim and that half a hemisphere was lit by the flickering. It rose, fell, flared and pulsed. It never ceased. And the most stupendous sounds of their lives fell upon them. They were like all the thunders of the universe.

So they advanced over the moonlit sands. A wildness, a scorn of all danger took hold of them. They stalked forward like machines, their eyes always ahead, their faces like stones. And under their feet the earth seemed about to burst.

Above them at times they heard the moaning and shrieking of shells. Soon, across the milky face of the desert, a mist of sand and smoke crept back to them. Ahead now, they saw the myriad flashing and heard the endless crashing of their shells. They lay down while the barrage lifted and crept onwards. As it did, the mist drifted away and they saw earthworks and wire entanglements.

Enemy mortars began to fall among them. They flung themselves flat again, like lizards on the sand. They felt the explosions pluck at their grovelling bodies. They rose and passed through the screen of explosions, but some remained on the ground, struggling or quite still.

With a great wild cry they swarmed through the shattered wire, over the earthworks, across the parapets, and down into the trenches, shooting without thought or mercy. Dazed and stumbling, the Nazis died like rats in their holes, or scurried above ground, hands groping upwards, sobbing to be spared. Men dropped away from their sections to drive the prisoners back to collecting-points.

A change in direction and they went forward again. The barrage was now far ahead of them. On each side they could hear the clatter of machine-guns. Tracers drew shining lines across the seething air. Chips saw the Very light from the company on their flank and led B Company towards it.

By the time they reached their final objective they had obliter-ated two more gun-posts. By dawn they had dug in; and as the first sad light came over the desert, the great clanging tanks rolled among them and disappeared into the tumult ahead.

A little after daylight Chips led them onward to a position just behind a shallow ridge. Here they dug in thoroughly, and in this place they remained for three days and nights while the ground above them was scythed and seared by enemy shells. Deep in their pits they huddled while their minds went numb or mad with the never-ending crash and whine of the shells. The dive-bombers fell upon them and tore up the surface of the earth once more. The dead and the wounded went back in a steady procession. Nazi infantry advanced close to the posts until shell-fire cut them down and left them strewn on the desert like blades of severed grass. And in the sky above them the bombers flew to and fro endlessly; and in the clearness of the morning, high up in the shining sky the fighters twisted around each other and fell to the earth. Sharing Dick's pit with him, his runner reached the end of his endurance. He uttered a shriek and began to sob and retch. Like a driven thing he rose, eyes all whites, to clamber out of the pit. But Dick held him to the ground, beating him calmly and cruelly until he fell whim-pering to the bottom of the pit. After a while, the runner gave a childish sob and lapsed into unconsciousness. Dick sat and looked at him, and then a low sob rose in him. He had to lie down, to close his eyes. He wondered a little if he too were about to crack.

On the afternoon of the third day the enemy shells became fewer and farther between. The ammunition truck came up two hundred yards behind, and Dick took Sullivan out with him to meet it. Fifty yards away from it a shell plucked them up and flung them apart. Noise and darkness.

Dick opened his eyes to the dazzle of sunlight only a few

seconds later. He crawled across to where Sullivan lay. Sullivan's chest was shattered. He lay looking straight up at the sky. Blood flowed out of his lips. His eyes were alive and still intelligent. Dick took the head in his arms and Sullivan looked at him. They gazed at each other hungrily, silently. A soft and deathly sound came out of Sullivan's chest. He raised his head a little and looked at Dick harder. For a moment his eyes were piercing and splendid. Then he turned them away, and died.

That night the Second X made its final advance. They swung northward, towards the sea. It was before the moon had risen.

B Company was forward. As they crossed a sand ridge an enemy Very light revealed them starkly. Shells poured down on them. From the Nazi positions ahead tracers leaped out and pierced their line. Cut off from the rest of the battalion, Chips led them forward.

They reached the Nazi strong-post, where Dooley's Number Two was hit, and as he fell the sight released all the ravenous hate in Dooley. He stalked the Nazi, wounding him. The Nazi rose and tried to surrender. Dooley fired again and the Nazi fell. Dooley stood above him, his Bren at the Nazi's head.

"This is for Moffatt," he said. And he fired until all that was left of the Nazi's head was a smear on the sand and splashes on Dooley's boots.

The shell-fire found the rear of the Second X, killing Pomfret and Varney. By dawn C Company had also fought through and dug in beside B Company.

At first light the Nazis counter-attacked and part of C Company was overrun. Swift and terrible, Chips led B Company out in a charge to retake the position.

Beside him Hamilton fell. But still his company saw Chips on his feet. They did not know he was riddled. He tried to throw a grenade. The life was leaving him but he found new strength to hurl the grenade. The blood gushed down him. Fearsome and splendid, he leaped among the Nazis. His great voice rose above the clamour of gun-fire; feet apart, he wielded a rifle like a club and the Nazis fell about him. He went to his knees with a roar of rage and another Nazi shot him through the head. He turned his bloody face round and cried to his company. Then he sank to the ground.

They fell on the Nazis like maddened beasts.

And so Chips died—Chips who was like the laughter and strength of all his people: who had never feared or spoken a word in anger to even the meanest of them. He in whom had flowered all the splendour and richness of life, lay dead. What had he not had? Strength and beauty—so much more than I. Joy and wisdom and compassion—far, far more than I. Why